An Anthology

Edited by

Karen Dales

Dreaming the Goddess

Copyright © 2021

Trade Paperback ISBN: 978-1-928104-17-9
eISBN: 978-1-928104-18-6

Cover Art © by Mary Ancilla Martinez
www.maryancilla.com

Cover Design © by Evan Dales
WAV Design Studios
www.wavstudios.ca

Dark Dragon Publishing
88 Charleswood Drive
Toronto, Ontario
M3H 1X6
CANADA
www.darkdragonpublishing.com

Printed in the United States of America.

An Anthology

Edited by

Karen Dales

Dark Dragon Publishing
Toronto, Ontario, Canada

Contents

For all the Hidden Children of the Goddess.

Introduction

I NEVER EXPECTED TO DEVELOP and edit an anthology. I knew from the time I was single digits old that I wanted to be a writer. How long ago was that? Probably when I discovered the magic of putting pencil to paper. I have vague memories of being in grade school writing short stories and having my teachers praise them.

I was a very imaginative child, always coming up with strange and fun scenarios in which my friends and I would take on character roles to play. This was about the same time when *Dungeons and Dragons* first came on the scene, but my child-self didn't learn about DnD until High School. Winter was my favourite time for this as the cold and the snow lent itself to an otherworldly feel. Even when I was on my own, walking home from school, my imagination would churn and bubble with strange stories. Few were eventually written down, but most stayed happily in my head, where they became best friends to keep me company.

It wasn't until I entered high school that the bug to write really bit, and hard. Being an avid read of science fiction and fantasy, I joined the school's Sci-Fi and Fantasy Club. There, for the first time, I met others who were like me—imaginative! In a society that tends to frown on creative people, I believed I had found my tribe. We even went as a group to my very first literary convention: Ad Astra. There, I was even further exposed to creative writing and the culture that surrounded it. It inspired me to take a Grade 12 class for fiction writing. It was by far my most favourite class, with Ms. Hartley cheering me on and believing she would one day see my stories in print.

I progressed to university where, in my second year, I was permitted to audition for a placement in the brand new creative writing program. Out of the thousands of applicants, I was one of the one hundred and fifty students to be accepted for the first year. I loved the course! So, I auditioned for the next year. Again, out of one hundred and fifty applicants, I was one of the fifty that placed. Spurred on by my successes in those courses, I applied in my last year for the coveted final course where only fifteen could be chosen. I was over the moon. I got in! I learned so much about writing in those three years.

During my exploration of creative writing in high school and university, I became more involved and delved deeper into Wicca and Paganism. Did my creative writing influence my discovery of Wicca, or did my journey into Wicca influence my creative writing? I would have to say they walked hand-in-hand and continue to be connected within me.

Once I married and had my son, I was blessed again: my first two novels were published into a limited edition by Dark Dragon Publishing, a then new Indy publisher. They eventually published two other novels in my series, *The Chosen Chronicles*, and even hired me to edit other authors' works until Dark Dragon Publishing made me their Managing Editor.

I honestly never expected to edit an anthology, but it happened. I was asked to do so by my publisher, after the success of *Canadian Dreadful*—Dark Dragon Publishing's first anthology edited by David Tocher. I foolishly agreed.

I wanted to do something different, something I haven't seen or read before. But what?

The idea of combining my experience and knowledge of Paganism into the world of creative writing illuminated my light bulb. In fact, I realised that there really hasn't been any fiction written geared towards Pagans. Sure, there are LOTS of Pagan/Wiccan/Heathen authors who have published their stories, often having them placed in such genres as paranormal and horror, but nothing specifically created for Pagans/Wiccans/Heathens.

The light bulb grew brighter.

The stories need to be new, different. They also had to teach something about those specific Goddesses to an audience who, not only is new to Paganism but to those who have been Pagan for decades. Something fun and entertaining.

I glanced up at my bookcase filled with Pagan related non-fiction and the answer smacked me in the face.

I'll create an anthology that will exhibit the Goddess in Her myriad of manifestations!

The concept of Dreaming The Goddess was born.

In these pages, you will read about many different Goddess, all of them fiction, but one thing is certain, in every story Her myriad of mysteries will be revealed in new ways, through modern eyes and experiences.

I and all the authors hope you are entertained by each story, but more than that, we hope that you learn something new about the Goddess and how She is perceived and experienced around the world.

Karen Dales
Toronto, Ontario, Canada
Samhain 2021.

iii

Raven's Wrath

By Moira H. Scott

I SAT ON THE FLOOR in the attic, going through family stuff that had been stored there for years and years. I never liked decluttering, just the act of picking up something that at one time had served a purpose but was now considered useless didn't sit well with me. The memories here were numerous and varied, and now they were being reduced to nothingness. Perhaps it was the history student in me that shuddered at the thought of tossing such things away without another thought, and this definitely wasn't the way I wanted to spend my Reading Week.

Behind me, my mother wordlessly rummaged through some dusty boxes adorned with labels from grandiose stores that no longer existed. The sight of their names brought back a flood of recollections. My mother loved to leisurely wander through those stores before heading straight for the cosmetics counters. There she'd buy just the right amount of perfume so that she'd get the free makeup palette, umbrella or matching duffle bag which she'd give as gifts at Christmas. She loved things and their subsequent acquisition. It puzzled me why she chose to divest herself of her dragon's hoard now.

I stopped to watch her for a moment and sighed as she was throwing a lot of things—without even looking at them—onto a dusty pile of rubbish. I felt my palms begin to sweat, as I listened to the thud, thud, thud of unwanted items landing in the heap. With each strike, small tornadoes of dust would swirl up and then disappear into nothingness. It felt surreal watching her resign the items to the bin in such a banal fashion. How odd it must be not to care about one's own past. I turned away.

The thuds stopped.

Looking over my shoulder, I saw her standing, her body turned away from me, staring at something in her hand. Instinctively, she cradled her chin in her other hand, and I thought I saw her heaving a heavy sigh. I decided to take my chances and ask her. I edged closer. I noticed she held a damaged brown photograph of a woman I did not recognise. I braved the question trying to sound as small as I could. "Mummy, who is that?"

She flinched and spun on her heel. The picture fell from her hand and landed to the floor. Her eyes bore into me as she monotoned, "No one you need to worry about".

With that, my mother strode purposefully to the attic's ladder, descended, and disappeared into the relative normalcy of our suburban home.

I strode over to where the photograph had fell to the floor. The evening sun streaming its fading light through the small round window near the roof cast some strange shadows. The crossbars bracing its glass within a large circular frame cast an otherworldly Celtic cross along the floor and walls. A single light bulb, hanging on an old cord hung from one of the ceiling's broad beams, dangled. I thought perhaps I should grab a three-legged stool, sit beneath it, and let the ghosts that lurked among the forgotten treasure begin their interrogation. What did I know, and how did I come to know their seemingly obliterated past? Or better yet, what did *they* know and what were they not telling me? A lot, I should imagine. Mother's obsessive secrecy about her family's history propelled my naïve imagination into overdrive, running wild with all sorts of bizarre or often completely non-sensical explanations—maybe she was a spy or some sort of royalty in exile. All I knew for certain was that I would never know, and I should just leave it at that.

I wandered back to the photograph lying face down in the dust. There was something written on the back. I remember my Mum's family's penchant for adding dates and names to the insides of books, photographs, you name it. It was the art of possession, an indelible stamp of the self on inanimate objects. While she wanted us to know from whence the books, photographs and diaries came, to be able to trace their existence within our family to her, she was just as careful not to reveal her own origins. The scrawl on back of this photograph, however, only read "Vimy, 1917".

I caught my breath.

Flipping it over, I examined the photograph again. A woman's face smiled back at me. A flicker of recognition, sputtered, then died, yet the familiarity lingered like smoke in a dimly lit room. Tall, slender, and statuesque, her delicate hands brandished a burdensome Lee Enfield rifle. Blinking, I tore my eyes away for an instant. Drawing a deep breath, I stared at it again. Why in the nine Hells was she wearing a soldier's uniform and looking so damned smug about it to boot?

My eyes slowly scanned the shot yet again. Behind her a trench yawned. Men struggled as they carried provisions loaded on their backs were climbing back into it. On one of the trench's support beams sat a large black bird in profile. It appeared to be transfixed upon something out of frame and the men seemed to take no notice.

I put the photograph down on one of the piles of dusty boxes for a moment and flopped down onto the floor sending the miniature dust storms swirling skyward yet again. Burying my face in my hands, my mind reeled. I needed to focus and breathe. Scanning my surroundings, a glimpse of an ornately carved oaken box bedecked with a tarnished brass closure sitting a few feet away beckoned me. Hesitating for a split second, I crawled toward it.

Snatching it into my hands like a greedy thief, my fingers trembled as I tried to pry it open. The clasp would not budge.

Sighing, I gritted my teeth and pushed again on the catch. A quick snap and the lid opened just enough to tease my curiosity. Its velvet interior, black as pitch, revealed nothing for the moment. Small wisps of grey smoke, coiled themselves around my fingers, and then vanished. Hesitating, I slipped my hand inside. Its black velvet interior gave the illusion of a vast depth that hid its contents. I reached in, not knowing what I would find and pulled out three long black feathers bound with red ribbon affixed to a silver raven's head charm.

In one of its eyes a deep red jewel shone. The other eye socket was empty, as if it had become blinded by time itself. Holding my breath and using my fingers to feel for any other objects, the soft, warmth of the velvet gave way to a cold sting. Yanking my hand out of the box, dark rivulets of blood began to cascade down my wrist. Wiping my arms on my jeans and applying pressure to my sliced fingers, I carried the box closer to the dangling light bulb to get a better look and turned the box on its side. A gleaming silver dagger with a triple skull adornment beneath the guard fell into my hand, my blood, still fresh on its blade.

My heart stopped.

A faint rustling broke my focus, the room's temperature plummeted ten degrees. Rubbing my arms, my teeth chattered as I glanced around the attic looking for the source of the slight breeze. Finding none, I watched, transfixed as it rose a couple of inches above the pile of dusty boxes, lingered for a few seconds then landed on the floor. The breeze subsided. The warm air returned as quickly as it had vanished.

I grabbed the photograph again. The great bird's position had moved. I could have sworn it was in profile before. Now, it was almost turned toward me. Muffling a scream, I threw it to the ground as if something bit me. I stared at the photograph for a moment. Everything fell to slow motion for what seemed like an eternity.

Throwing the blade back into its box, and slamming it shut, I tossed it upon the pile of dusty boxes. Scrambling down the ladder and storming into the kitchen, I stopped dead upon seeing Mother, oblivious to all else but creating her signature dry martini, pretending not to notice.

"Mum!"

No response.

"Muuuummm!"

My mother took her time to stop what she was doing, raised her eyes as if she was glancing out the window and turned to me. Her pale face revealed a mouth crinkled into a half-smirk.

She raised her chin to look down at me beneath half-hooded eyes. "What is it, *dear?*"

Dear?

DEAR?

She'd never referred to me like that before in all my life.

Taking a deep breath, I squared my shoulders and tried to speak, but my cracking voice sounded worse than a pubescent boy. I watched as she raised the martini glass aloft and stared at it was as one would admire a work of art.

Breathe.

"M-m-mum?" My voice shook, "I-I need to know who…"

"Who *that woman* is?"

"Y-yes. Who is she?"

Her lips drew tight into a snarl. "I already told you, you do *not* need to know."

Simple Q&A was not working. It was now or never. I cleared my throat and lobbed the first grenade.

"I found the dagger."

I watched as the martini glass slipped in slow motion from her fingers exploding into a million shards upon impact with the slate floor.

"What? Dagger?"

"You know damned well what I'm talking about. You were going through the box that it was in. You *know* which one. I'm surprised you didn't hide *that* from me too!"

Her eyes narrowed to mere slits as she took a step toward me then stopped. Throwing her face skyward with a silent scream, she winced as she trod on the glass fragments. "Jesus CHRIST!" A small trickle of blood began to pool around her bare feet. "Damn it! Well, don't just stand there! Go get the mini-vac and bring some bandages. NOW!"

I did as I was told. But I was not going to let this go.

I returned with some bandages and antiseptic spray. Without

warning, she snatched them from my hands and sat heavily on to the kitchen chair in a deluded heap. With a heavy, dramatic sigh she began cleaning and bandaging the wound, her eyes would not meet mine.

"Why won't you tell me who she is?"

She raised her head in my direction but seemed to look beyond me. Her dark brown eyes sank back into the shadows of her deep-set sockets. Drawing in a great breath, she tried to straighten herself and groaned. "She's my mother. We do not speak of her in our family."

"I'm aware of this, but I'd like to know why. I know absolutely nothing about my heritage and that's just wrong! At least tell me her name."

The cold stare returned. "I chose not to tell you about Alice Meredith because—"

"Because *why?*"

"She brought dishonour—"

I tilted my head and cocked an eyebrow. "How so?"

I felt a curious calm begin to envelop my being. My panic had transferred itself to her. Dr. Freud would've been proud. Her shoulders tightened. She blinked and shook her head as if as someone had grabbed her by the throat.

"She was a Witch."

"A Witch?" My gaze skyward before landing on her again. "Mother, plenty of people call themselves Witches. What's the big—"

"You saw the photograph. You saw what was written on the back. 'Vimy Ridge, 1917'.

"I did. And?"

She sighed again. "Canadian women weren't permitted to fight. I don't know where she got that uniform, but she completely faked her way to get there."

"Go on."

I had stoked the fire. Remaining calm and clinical had broadsided her. She expected me to kowtow to her arrogance, but not this time. Narcissists really hate it when you go off script. They don't know what to do with themselves. I had her on the ropes. I surprised myself with the sheer pleasure I took in watching her squirm. It felt good, but there was more to come.

She squared her shoulders. Tossing her head, her cold, shark -like eyes met mine. "Tell you what. Why don't you go back up there? Dig around in the box for all I care."

I found myself laughing despite this break-through moment. Her eyes flashed anger again.

"Oh, come now, mother. She's long dead, what possible harm could—"

Her voice sank to a low rumble. "We are done with this conversation. You've already found some of her things. "

Some?

"Fine. Since you do not wish to discuss this, I will keep digging."

Silence.

Rising to her feet, she turned her back to me and began the methodical creation of yet another martini. A distinct rhythmic clinking of glass filled the air as she stirred the remaining gin and vermouth. She'd found her coping mechanism. I'd not yet found mine.

With quiet resolve, I returned to the attic.

Twilight filled the space. The shadows on the wall had faded into the woodwork. Beneath the harsh yellow cast of the dangling light bulb, I dug into the mysterious box to retrieve the dagger. Subtle electric shocks pricked my fingertips as they ran over the side of blade. With its energy erupting, curiosity mixed with fear which danced with the idea of holding it in my hands yet again or shoving it back in its box again forever.

I held my breath as I reached for the blade. The light bulb blinked twice before it began to swing like a pendulum. Over-head, the rhythmic creaking of its wire swaying from the rafter beat like a drum.

I grabbed the photograph from the pile of boxes. The large bird now faced me, its beak wide open in a scream. The hairs on the nape of my neck stiffened. Goose pimples burst through my skin. My hands felt like ice. I tried to scream, but my parched mouth would permit no sound. Small wisps of silver-grey smoke began swirling around the photograph.

The great bird's head almost filled the picture's frame. Its beak agape and its wings spread wide. Closer, the beak gaped wider, the light began to disappear. Consumed and thrust into darkness, I clutched my throat, gasping for air. My shoulders pulled as if I was being sucked down... down... as I began tumbling through a blackened tunnel.

Somersaulting through air, my arms and legs flailing, my body's weight picked up speed as I twisted and turned. I tried to scream, but no sound came. Muffled noises in the distance began to grow louder. A cacophony of shrieks melded with drumbeats and ear-piercing blasts.

Gunfire?

I threw my hands to my ears, but nothing could quell the horrendous noise laying siege to my senses. Small dots of light, like exploding stars filled my vision. Falling faster now, they merely blurred into each other forming pale streaks like claw marks rending the blackness with light. My head swam as I spun head over heels, twisting, turning as if being drawn and quartered.

Within what felt like an eternity, my body hit something hard enough for me to see stars. I tried to open my eyes, but the agony that sang through my head wouldn't let me focus right away. Blinking stupidly, I finally willed them to stay open.

My eyes focused upon a long, black beak mere inches from my face. Dark eyes looked down upon me as I lay flat on my back. A ruffling of feathers. A throaty croak.

"Badb! Enough!"

The great bird screeched in response, then fell silent.

Footsteps crunched over the gravel, heading in my direction. My neck screamed in pain. It must've been the first part of my body that hit the dirt before I came to. I couldn't lift my head far enough to be able to see who approached. Jamming my eyes shut, the sounds of explosions, machinegun fire, and men wailing piteously as they lay dying in the mud filled my ears. The footsteps stopped. I opened my eyes to see the great bird lifting off as it flew away from my sight.

A woman's voice rang out, "Get t' yer feet and face meh."

I flinched as the butt of a spear was thrust to the ground with a thunderous thud, mere inches from my face.

I closed my eyes and began to drag myself to my knees. Every muscle in my body cried out in protest as I pulled myself up. My thoughts swam in a sea of confusion. I still didn't know where the Hell I was.

"Look at meh."

I blinked and rubbed my eyes.

"I say t' ye again, get t' yer feet and face meh!"

Before me, stood a tall woman dressed in a black leather jerkin, leather breeches and boots that laced to her knee. In her hand was an ornate wooden spear topped with a bronze, teardrop shaped blade. Her thick, red wavy hair cascaded down her back.

Her eyes were deep set dark. Her lips, blood-red, were slightly parted showing her teeth. At her hip was a dagger that resembled the one I—Oh, dear God! Where was it? I felt a wave of panic begin to rise as my eyes frantically searched the ground around me.

She did not blink once as she looked me up and down and sighed. "Ye'll need new vestments. Come."

Overhead, a loud flapping of wings, the raven circled overhead and landed on her shoulder as she walked toward the one of the snake-like trenches, striding between the soldiers taking their positions and snipers buried within their observation posts. I gagged at the stench. Small rivulets of blood coagulating with mud and rotting dead flesh flowed into the flooding trenches. Stumbling as I tried to avoid them, the woman in black grew impatient as I fell behind. Yet, no one seemed to notice her nor I as I followed her behind the trench line.

I tried in vain to keep up with her, but she always remained about two strides in front.

"I—I don't think we've been introduced," I blurted.

Without turning to face me, she replied, "Indeed. *We* have not." Her voice trailed off.

I followed her down a ladder into a small, dilapidated structure at the end of the trench, partially covered in a threadbare and mouldy tarp. I shivered as a light snow began to fall. Delicate snowflakes spun in slow, dizzying circles around me. I hesitated as she pushed aside the tarp's flap and disappeared into the darkness below.

"Come. We're waitin'."

We?

Wordlessly, I made my way down the ladder and gazed into the darkness. I felt the subtle warmth caress my face. My gloveless hands began to regain their movement as I opened and closed them in a vague attempt to get the blood flowing again. My eyes began to adjust to the shadows when the tell-tale snap and hiss of a match struck against flint startled me. A pale white hand lit one of lanterns. I startled when I saw her sitting before me. She turned her face to meet my gaze smiling the same smile as the woman in the photograph. She reached into her rucksack leaning against the muddied tarp wall. She turned to the woman in black, "I see you've met my Grand-daughter."

"Grandmother?" I stammered. "Grandmother Meredith?" Instinctively, I tried to run my hands over my dishevelled clothing in a vague attempt to smooth any wrinkles and show some sort of decorum but failed.

Rising, she moved toward me and held out the dagger I thought I'd lost.

The woman in black declared, "It's yers now. It knows ye and ye will ne'er lose it again. Take it. Now sit."

The tall, red-haired woman leaned up against a whisky-tierce. "If ye are tae break bread wi' yer granny 'n me, ye must share a drink as well."

I nodded, still unsure as to what to make of either of them. The red-haired woman poured a generous portion of whisky into a battered tin mug and handed it to me in silence.

I watched as Grandmother Meredith sliced a bit of crusty bread and finally spoke. "My name is Alice. No need to be so formal." Taking her cap off and shaking out her bobbed blond hair, she smiled. "Here, though, I'm known simply as Alfred."

I cocked an eyebrow as my eyes darted back and forth between the two women. I drew a deep breath and turned my gaze to the tall redhead clad in black. "I do not believe we have been formally introduced."

Eyeing me as she were a cat and I but a mere field mouse, she pushed away from the tierce.Pulling herself to her true height, she hooded her eyes as she laid her bronze spear against the wall. "I am known by many names. By the time we are done, ye will know them all."

The hairs on the back of my neck bristled. I didn't know whether to nod, bow or flee.

She continued. Her resonant voice commanding yet somehow hypnotic, I could not help but listen as she intoned her proposal. "If we are t' work together, I must know that ye will swear fealty. The choice is yours. Swear to me and ye will be under ma protection or depart this place and ye be on yer own. Choose wisely."

My eyes darted from her face to Alice's searching for a reaction. Alice remained pokerfaced save for a slight curl of her lips. I turned to face the lady in black. A slight tilt of her head and cocking of an eyebrow told me that the woman was not yet done. Outside the dugout, the shots rang out. Men's cries amid the cacophony of machinegun fire exploded like a choir singing from the gates of Hell. And yet, these two appeared quite calm.

Raising my chin, I responded. "Before, I swear this oath, I must ask to whom I am addressing?"

Towering over me, the woman in black took one ominous step toward me as she spoke. Her voice lowered to a croaking whisper, "Ye ha'e always known me in yer dreams. Ma deeds ha'e shaped my names. Ma battles and wars embody and ensure ma sovereignty o'er the land. But to ye, child, I am known as the Morrígan."

I averted my eyes. I didn't want her to see that I was in disbelief. This wasn't happening. I just wanted to wake up at home, in my own bed.

"Ye doubt me, child?"

"N - no. It's just that… I don't understand. Why am I here? Wh… why here, why now?"

Alice rose to her feet. Her steely eyes met mine. I noted the details of her uniform and the insignia of her regiment. All of it fit nicely, but I did not understand why *she* was here. "The world—*our* world—is at war, and we are in the thick of it as I am certain you have noticed. We answered the call, and as you can see, there is need of my assistance, but this was not always so. I had offered my services in 1914 but was rebuffed because of my sex. It mattered not that I was a fully trained medical doctor. It only mattered to *them* that I was not wearing pants and should never be seen doing so.

"Not to be dismissed so easily, I fought my way all the way to the powers that be in recruitment. By the time, I had pushed my way to meet with the Commanding Officer. We fought passionately over my demand that I serve my country, against his desire to demonstrate decorum. He permitted me to join and assist on one condition."

Alice paused. Her eyes bored into me with a ferocity I'd never seen. The edges of her thin lips curled into a snarl. "I was never to reveal my true identity, and should I be found out, I could face numerous charges for impersonation. The most likely? Firing Squad."

I drew in a deep breath and replied that I understood when I clearly did not. I tried to pull my thoughts together, but the chaos and horror that engulfed the small dugout—our tiny refuge—kept me from running.

I gave in and straightened my shoulders. I needed answers. Clearing my throat, I looked the Morrígan in the eyes. A flicker of understanding sparked within her gaze. "Why have you called me here?"

A moment of heart-stopping silence intervened. Alice studied me. "Because you doubt yourself."

I clenched my jaw. "Yes, this is true." My throat began to tighten. I was never very good at receiving criticism.

The Morrígan grabbed her spear and pounded the earth. "I challenge ye! You must emerge from the shadows. Come out from beneath the aprons and skirts of the women around you. Especially, your mother's."

Gut-punch.

Alice stepped forward. "Indeed, she is your biggest adversary, and it is up to you to rise to the challenge or fade into nothingness on the battlefield. Should you continue to reside in your head, to live in the past, your goals will always be mere inches from your grasp—taunting you. A war rages in your world, but it is not one fought with weapons. It is one that requires compassion, eloquence yet firmness of action."

I let that sink in.

Alice turned her back as the Morrígan pushed forward. "In this place, with all here gathered, *yer* place is not of one carved in stone! Listen to the cries of the men outside and know that they are pushing—sacrificing fer change—to make the world a better place. Before ye, stands your Grandmother, who risked her identity, station and very life so that she may save others. What have *you* given?"

Without turning to face me, Alice chimed in. "Blood of my blood. Blood of the Lady, state now your will. Will you choose to divest yourself of your responsibility or will you choose to stand and fight. Not only for yourself but for others who are less fortunate?"

I rotated my shoulders to release the paralysing tensions. I knew what I had to do. In my mind's eye, I saw the shadows of doubt and reticence begin to part the veil that had enshrouded me for so long. Stepping away from the known and into the breach, I made the assay. "Grandmother, I see your challenge. My Lady, I hear your words."

A faint smile cracked as the Morrígan reached for the battered tin cup, "Then drink and make it so".

I hesitated and deeply inhaled.

Trembling, I stepped forward and slowly drew it to my lips. Never had something tasted so good, yet so unfamiliar.

"It's WHISKEY, child! Ye don't sip it! Down it now!"

A faint, mocking titter emanated from behind the Lady. Grandmother Meredith was not going to let this one go without a comment. All the more power to her!

Without hesitation I knocked it back, coughed, shook my head, and met her gaze again. Her eyes bore into me. Her voice sunk to a deep croak. "Take up your dagger and hold it aloft."

I gasped at the electricity of its vibration in my hands.

"Un-sheath it."

Fearing I would drop the blade, I held my breath as I pulled it from its scabbard. A small glint of light caught its edge, blinding me for a second. I blinked, exhaled and held its tip to the sky.

Unblinking, she commanded, "Now, make your mark."

I hesitated, not comprehending the command.

The Lady grabbed my left arm and steadied it, twisting my palm skyward. I flinched as the pressure of her strong hands almost crushed my wrist. "Yer oath shall be sealed with blood. Draw yer blade's edge across yer palm."

Grinding my teeth, I slowly drew the sharp, silver edge along the heartline. Small blood bubbles oozed forth.

Refilling it in silence, the Lady thrust the battered cup toward me without words. I held my bleeding palm over the cup and let three drops fall. Her deep green eyes met mine. A glimmer of understanding sparked.

Nodding to me she commanded, "Drink."

My eyes fell to the cup I held within my cold hands. The blood had mixed with the whisky, swirling widdershins.

"Drink!"

I took a sip, drew the back of my hand across my mouth, and handed it to the Lady. Without a sound, she drew it to her lips then passed it to Alice, who averted her eyes from my gaze.

"Doctor, ye may bandage the wounds. And ye, meh child, must libate yer offerin' upon the wounded earth."

Alice approached and bound my hand with linen, taking it between her two hands. Her gaze met mine. She smiled, but it was not out of warmth. An air of concern tinged with under-standing illuminated her face. Releasing my hand, she mouthed 'go'.

As I climbed up the dugout's steps and parted the tarp that had concealed us from the madness, I raised the cup to the sky and whispered my appreciation and my wish before emptying it upon the bloodstained mud. The chaos of the battlefield and trenches faded, as the last drops of the bloodied whisky fall to the ground.

Darkness…

Not a glimmer of light.

Silence…

Not the faintest of sound for a moment.

Overhead, the tell-tale squeak of the light bulb swinging from its cord affixed to the ceiling as the wind began to rise filled my ears. As my eyes adjusted to the rising light, the tiny tornadoes of dust began to settle. The shadows cast by the trees at dusk, crawled bony fingers across the attic's walls.

Exhaling, I collapsed to the floor in a heap. Out of the corner of my eye, I detected something fluttering and spiralling to the floor. Without looking, my hands reached for it.

She was there in the photograph. I blinked hard and looked

again, waiting for my eyes to focus amid the dying light. The great Raven flew away over our heads.

Our.

Alice stood with one hand on her Lee-Enfield and the other encircled my shoulder. I thought I looked rather dashing in my olive drab.

Moira H. Scott is a Gardnerian Witch living in Toronto, Canada and has been interested in Canadian Military History for many years. Active in the local Speculative and Science Fiction fandom community since the early 1990s, she has presented panels on Wicca, Witchcraft, folklore as well as popular culture.

Moira lives in Toronto and is currently working on a novella about Spiritualism and Technology at the turn of the twentieth century in Canada. When not hard at work doing research, Moira also reads Tarot professionally and continues with her studies in Heraldic history.

Goddess Given Advice

A Triptych

By Ira Nayman

1.

WHY DO THE FACES IN trees always look like they are in agony?
Julie-Anna wondered as she confidently strode through the
forest in the direction of the Earth Tree. *Could it be that they are
imbued with all of the suffering that they have witnessed in the decades that
they have lived? Or, perhaps, the burden of time weighs heavily on their…
branches. Or, maybe, I'm over thinking things. Dabnabbery! Yeah, I'm
probably over thinking things. I do that sometimes.*

When she was a child, Julie-Anna's mother and some of her
woman friends would march to the heart of the forest and
commune with the Earth Tree. Julie-Anna loved those times, so
much so that when she came of age, she happily joined the
group. She had been to the Earth Tree so many times, she knew
the forest like… well, not the back of her hand, which, even
being only seventeen, she realized she didn't know all that well.
She knew the forest like something she did know really well, like
the lore of the Goddess, or the plot to every episode of *Gilmore*

Girls.

Julie-Anna climbed the rise and entered the clearing that was home to the Earth Tree. She greeted the pained face with a warm smile (just because you considered yourself spiritual didn't mean you couldn't be contrary). She laid her PETA backpack on the ground and spread her arms to bask in the glorious summer sun.

After making herself all warm and toasty, Julie-Anna removed a red and white checkered tablecloth on which she had drawn a complex mandala and laid it on the ground in front of the Earth Tree, facing north. She pulled out a plastic container holding devilled eggs she had prepared the night before and laid five on the tablecloth at the points of a star within the mandala—the offering. She set a tan lavender-scented candle she had made on a tray next to the mandala, and lit it. Finally, chanting a summoning incantation, she put her arms around the Earth Tree and closed her eyes.

After a while, Julie-Anna's head began to pound. Had she been out in the sun too long and suffered a stroke? She opened her eyes to discover that she knelt on the floor of a dance club, her arms wrapped around the seat of a bar stool. Eww! Undignified! Julie-Anna freed her arms and stood up.

The club was loud and hot with the press of bodies, but, despite the bright neon lights, Julie-Anna could only see people's shadows. The one exception was a stunning young woman, tall, long blond hair, perfect moon-face, wearing a designer ball gown. Julie-Anna suspected that even if she hadn't been the only fully visible person in the room, her attention would still have been drawn to the woman. So, Julie-Anna made her way to the bar. The shades in the room whispered breathy complaints about being rudely shoved aside, forcing Julie-Anna to apologize for knocking into them more than once.

"Jimmy Zeus and the Zeus-tones," the woman informed her shady companions. "Talk about a power trio!" The pair of shadows in front of her bobbed their heads in appreciative laughter.

"Umm, excuse me," Julie-Anna politely interjected.

"Yes?" the woman off-handedly responded.

"Are you a… a Goddess? I… I have a problem I don't know what to do about…"

The woman turned to look at her. "Oh, no, no, no, no, no," she muttered. "This will never do!" She waved her hand in front of Julie-Anna. Her baggy *Save the Whales* t-shirt and jeans were replaced by a sleek black dress that accentuated the curves of her small breasts and her long, slender legs. "If you want to crash my party," the woman explained, "you should at least *try* to look like you belong!"

"I'm sorry… umm…" Julie-Anna replied, a mixture of awe and embarrassment in her voice.

"I am the Maiden. I have gone by many names: Rhiannon, Persephone, Blodeuwedd, Ostara, Geshtinanna—I'm very popular. You may call me Artemis."

Julie-Anna shivered in delight. Artemis! The youngest aspect of the tri-partite Goddess represented such things as enchantment, inception, expansion, the promise of new beginnings and youthful enthusiasm. If anybody could understand her predicament and give her solid advice, it would be Artemis.

"I am truly sorry, Artemis," Julie-Anna contritely said.

"Anyway, Goddess is such a sexist term. I am not a diminutive version of a male deity! I prefer to think of myself as a female God."

"Ooh, female god! I like that!"

The enthusiasm must have pleased the Godde—female God, because Artemis smiled brilliantly and, patting the stool next to her, beckoned, "You've come a long way to be here. Come sit by me and tell me all your troubles."

Julie-Anna must have looked askance or two at the shadowy figure on the stool, because Artemis added: "Oh, don't mind Rhys. He's very comfortable once you get to know how to sit in him."

The figure waved an insubstantial arm at Julie-Anna, beckoning her. She was not at all comforted by the gesture.

Ever so reluctantly, Julie-Anna sat on the stool. The shadow enveloped her like a warm, dry mist. Otherwise, she didn't feel anything. Artemis focused her full attention on the young woman, making Julie-Anna feel like she was the only human being in the universe (which, not knowing exactly where the club existed, might have been true).

"Well," Julie-Anna started, "there was this boy—"

"Isn't there always a boy?" Artemis interrupted. "It's an age-old story."

Nearby shadows convulsed with laughter. *It wasn't that funny*, Julie-Anna thought. Out loud, she tried to continue: "Mark. We—"

"Mark is such a boy's name, isn't it? There's a reason boys in these stories are so often named Mark."

Julie-Anna took a moment to compose herself before persisting: "We had been drinking at a party, and—"

"Drinking? A Party? Julie-Anna, if this story were any more typical it would be positively archetypal! Honestly, when are young women going to learn to stay away from alcohol?" With no apparent sense of irony, Artemis waved a hand at the shadow behind the bar, which filled a glass and set it down on the counter in front of her.

If she wondered how Artemis had known her name, Julie-Anna didn't show it. Instead, she soldiered on. "Mark dared me to kiss my best friend, Emily. I had never kissed a girl before, and, like I said, we were drinking and maybe had one or two too many. So, I did it. I kissed a girl."

"And did you like it?" Artemis balled her fists and rested her chin on them, enrapt.

Did I like it? Julie-Anna thought. *Emily had the softest lips I have ever felt. So round. So sensuous. And she was so playful, teasing, but in a good way. Mmm...and when it finally happened, it was so firm, but tender at the same time. It made me feel warm all over. No boy has ever kissed me like that. Uggh! It's like they want to grind your lips to dust! And their tongues! Double uggh!*

"No," Julie-Anna answered with a shudder.

"Really?" Artemis responded. Female Gods come equipped with advanced bullshit detectors.

"Really."

"Really really?" Artemis insisted.

No, not really. Sure, I liked it. I liked it fine. But the high school—it's a jungle! They get even the slightest hint that I liked kissing a girl and they'll chop my ego up into little pieces and feed it to sharks! Dammit, why did I have to go on that class trip to Ripley's Aquarium? Not important. The important thing is that I like kissing boys, too, and that's "normal." So, to stay popular, I'm going to stay normal.

"All the reallies you've got," Julie-Anna assured her.

"Oh." Artemis moued in disappointment. "You know, there's nothing wrong with kissing a girl and liking it."

"No, no, absolutely not," Julie-Anna hurriedly agreed. "It's good for people who are okay with it. It... it's just not for me." *Not at this point in my life.*

Robbed of a love triangle she could resolve, Artemis brusquely asked, "So, what's the problem?"

"Mark won't shut up about it!" Julie-Anna blurted. "I mean, I told him I wasn't into it. But he argued with me—said maybe the problem was Emily wasn't my type. So, he suggested I try kissing Georgina Dimpflemeyer. I mean, really, Georgina Dimpflemeyer!"

"What's wrong with Georgina Dimpflemeyer?" Artemis asked.

"She's dumber than a warthog!"

"Oh, I don't know," a soft voice whispered all around her. "Warthogs are actually smarter than most people give them credit for."

Julie-Anna jumped out of her seat. "Eww!" she ewwed, swiping at her clothing as if she could get misty Rhys-essence out of it. "Eww! Eww! Eww! Eww! Eww!"

"Oh, Rhys, do behave!" Artemis playfully scolded.

Julie-Anna thought she could hear a laughing breeze, but now that she was no longer sitting... in Rhys, she couldn't be sure.

Artemis put her drink down and rose from her chair. She was a head and some taller than Julie-Anna, but the young woman didn't get the feeling the female God looked down on her, even though she physically looked down on her.

"Okay," Artemis said. "You have some options. My first suggestion would be: dump his sorry ass. You can do better. There are lots of fish in the sea." To emphasize the point, she waved her arm at all of the people in the club. The fact that they were insubstantial grey mists did not reassure Julie-Anna.

"Yeah, but, Mark..." she responded.

Artemis pursed her lips. Then, she rolled her eyes into the back of her head until only the whites showed. On most people, this would be kind of gross, but it made her look powerful.

After a couple of seconds, her pupils returned. "I see what you mean," Artemis remarked. "Mark is dreamy. Still, you can't let him boss you around. You need to do something to teach him that you are a strong, independent young woman. But what?"

"I—"

"Hush, dear. Big sister is thinking." As if to emphasize the point, Artemis put a perfectly manicured finger to Julie-Anna's lips for a moment. Eventually, her face brightened and she enthused. "Got it! I know what you have to do!"

"What's that?" Julie-Anna found the female God's enthusiasm catching. She didn't know how she knew it, but she felt all of the shades in the club holding their breath, waiting for the solution to her problem.

"Punch him in the nards!" Artemis shouted. "That will teach him not to mess with you! Punch him hard! Right in the nards!"

"Ah," Julie-Anna said as the club began to breath.

A faint, "Punch him hard! In the nards! Punch him hard! In the nards!" chant could be heard under the music.

She ignored it. "I don't think—I mean, I'm grateful for your advice—don't get me wrong, but... I—it's just not... me. I don't think I could...do that."

The chant petered out.

Disappointed, Artemis blew a stray strand of blonde hair off her face. "No nard punching for you?"

"Sorry." Later, Julie-Anna would wonder why she apologized for not taking advice she didn't agree with. In the moment, though, it felt right.

"Well, then, I've got nothin'."

It was Julie-Anna's turn to be disappointed. "Oh."

"Except, maybe, one... rule? You know, to guide you to the right action?"

Julie-Anna perked up. "Yes?"

"You are who you are. Don't ever allow a man—a boy, really—to make you feel bad about being you. Now, bring it in."

Artemis spread her arms, inviting a hug. Julie-Anna spread her own arms and prepared for the embrace... and found herself back in the forest, hugging the World Tree.

Julie-Anna considered what Artemis had said as she packed up the tablecloth and candle (the offering, half of which had already been consumed, stayed—first rule of interacting with the spirit world is you don't take back an offering). She thought about it throughout the journey back home. By the next time she saw Mark, it had become an integral part of her thinking.

*

If there are two words in the English language that send a dark chill through a parent's soul, they are: par and tay! Despite this, you will always find some sort of festivities going on over the weekend. Somewhere.

This weekend, the par-tay took place at Dana Jackaronda's house. You know, the four bedroom, five bathroom dream house with the pool out back that her mom got outright in the divorce from her dad, the creator of a new dental amalgam who had been convicted of abusing his patients while they were under anaesthesia. Mom was a nurse who had to go out of town three times a year for conventions to "keep up her knowledge base of cutting edge medical theory and practice." This weekend, the convention took place in Moosejaw. Mom's loss was Dana's gain. And the gain of all of her friends. And the gain of the strangers who, inevitably, caught wind of the par-tay and kee-rashed it.

On the main floor, the stereo blared a steady stream of Whitesnake, Scorpions, Iron Maiden, Metallica and other bands that reminded Julie-Anna that nostalgia for the 1980s was over-rated. The metal was occasionally replaced by a Madonna song; either somebody hijacked the sound system, or Dana had a cruel sense of humour.

Julie-Anna and Emily were talking in the kitchen. Shouting, really, but the kitchen was as far away from the music as one could get and still be in the house. (You didn't want to be by the pool because clothes had a habit of disappearing out there, and you didn't want to be in any of the bedrooms on the upper floors...for much the same reason.) They were holding plastic cups of beer that they had been nursing for over an hour.

"...ell, of course the books were better," Julie-Anna shalked. "But we may never get the last book in the series—at least the TV show gave us some kind of closure on the story."

"Hey! The TV series was different from the books, but that doesn't make it bad!" Emily countered. "The acting was great, and it looked lovely. And… and… and—dragons!"

Julie-Anna smiled. "Dragons," she sighed in agreement.

They considered dragons for a moment. Then, Emily started, "Do you think—"

"There you are!" Mark's voice, which easily conquered the noisy environment thanks to the way it rolled around in that gorgeously sculpted chest of his, overrode her. His body followed his voice into the kitchen a moment later. "I've been looking all over for you two!"

Emily rolled her eyes and, mumbling an excuse, left the room.

"What's with her?" Mark asked, watching Emily weave her way through bodies and out the door, where she became lost to sight among the bodies in the den.

Julie-Anna used the two words guaranteed to stop a guy from inquiring further: "Women's problems."

"O…kay." Although he tried to hide it, those two syllables contained a world of disgust. "Do you think she'll be back soon to—"

Not wanting to have this conversation, Julie-Anna blurted: "Mark, we're through." This was *not* what she had planned on saying, and she had no idea where it came from.

"Through?" Mark asked as if she had sworn in some alien language.

"We're done." Now that she had started down this path, Julie-Anna felt curious to see where it would lead.

Mark blinked. "Done?" He still wasn't getting it.

"It's over."

"Ov—"

"Our relationship, Mark. It's finished. Over. Done."

Mark blinked a couple more times, and then said with authority, "No."

"No?" It's amazing how much incredulity Julie-Anna can pack into two little letters.

"I'm not the breakupee," Mark explained. "I'm the breakuper. Always. No relationship I'm in ends until I say it's over."

GODDESS GIVEN ADVICE

POP QUIZ, QUESTION 1: At this point in the conversation, Julie-Anna's first impulse was to throw the remainder of her drink in Mark's face. But she didn't do it. Does this make her a good girlfriend or a bad girlfriend?

Instead, she told him: "A relationship can only continue with the ongoing consent of both participants. If *either* person withdraws their consent, the relationship is over."

POP QUIZ, QUESTION 2: At this point in the conversation, Mark thought, *Where did you learn that feminist bullshit?* But he didn't say it out loud. Does this make him a good boyfriend or a bad boyfriend?

Instead, he set his chin, steeled his voice and told her, "Fine. Be that way. But you owe me an explanation, at least. What did I do wrong? What did I do that made you so miserable that you would even consider breaking up with me?"

"You keep pushing me to kiss Emily. The first time was... okay, but I don't want to do it anymore."

Mark digested this for a few seconds. Then, he grinned. "Is that all? Really? Oh, baby, I thought we were all just having a bit of fun. It's not that important to me. If it makes you uncomfortable, don't do it."

"Really?" Julie-Anna melted like a snowflake in a dryer.

Mark put an arm around her shoulder. "Of course. But honestly, why all the drama? 'I wanna break up with you!' Why didn't you just tell me how you felt?"

POP QUIZ, QUESTION 3: In her head, Julie-Anna played all of the times she did tell him how she felt. She remembered every time he dismissed her concerns, or changed the subject, or stared at her uncomprehendingly until, embarrassed, she changed the subject. But she didn't share that with him. Was she following Artemis's advice and being good to herself, or was she ignoring Artemis's advice and being bad to herself?

Instead, she said, "I tried. I guess I just never found the right words."

"Well, next time you have a problem, find the right words," Mark playfully admonished her. "The most important element of any relationship is communication."

The kiss they then shared made everything better.

And Julie-Anna and Mark lived happily ever after.

Meanwhile, three universes down and two to the left...

Why do faces in trees always look like they're sneering at you? Julianna wondered as she picked her way through the forest in what she hoped was the direction of the Earth Tree. *They say it's hundreds of years old. It must have seen a lot in that time. Yeah, sure, I'm not nearly that old, and there's lots of stuff in the world that makes me wanna sneer. But permanently? Hmm... would I have a perma-sneer if I had lived for hundreds of years?* Julianna shuddered. *I hope I never get that old!*

When she was a child, Julianna's mother and some of her woman friends would march to the heart of the forest to commune with the Earth Tree. She had been there so many times, she assumed that she would have no trouble finding it. But she had been young and not really paying attention and, three and a half hours after she had set out, she realized that although autumn had just started, she should have dressed warmer.

Julianna blew into her hands and considered giving up for the day and trying again tomorrow. It would be Sunday, she could start earlier—humbler and undoubtedly grumblier—and have the whole day to—

Wait! This rise felt very... familiar. Julianna eagerly climbed it. There the Earth Tree stood, its trunk so thick she could fit her whole room inside it, its branches longer than Julianna's long legs. The face, larger than the front of her mom's Subaru, scowled down at her. At seventeen, Julianna still felt like sticking her tongue out at it in defiance. *Not the best way to get help*, she reminded herself. *It would be satisfying, but no.*

Julianna put her Wonder Woman backpack down on the forest floor and started taking objects out of it. She put a plate of chocolate chip cookies she had made the night before in front of the Earth Tree—the offering. She lit a candle and placed it on a plate behind the offering, being careful not to place it between the offering and the tree. It was a no-drip candle. Julianna didn't want to be responsible for burning down the part of the forest that contained the Earth Tree. Nobody survives that kind of karma! Finally, she took her cell phone out of her pocket. She had found a chant to summon the spirit of the Earth Tree on YouTube (you could find anything on the internet!). She played it as loud as the phone would allow, which, in the stillness of the forest, was plenty loud, let me tell you!

Had it been an ideal summoning? No. Julianna was aware of that. She had always been told, though, that spirits rewarded effort. She was about to discover if that was true.

Placing the phone down next to the plate of cookies, Julianna walked up to the Earth Tree and threw her arms around it. They barely got a quarter of the way around the trunk. Unlike with people, gaining girth as you aged was a point of pride for trees, a sign of good health. Julianna closed her eyes and listened to the chanting that she barely remembered and didn't understand.

Minutes passed. The tree appeared to grow warmer, but Julianna didn't look for fear of breaking the spell. She kept her eyes closed even when she smelled... dough?

Eventually, a rich, warm voice said, "Girl, if you don't get offen me, I'll never get aaaaany cookin' done!"

Julianna opened one eye, then the other. She was hugging a large, middle-aged woman. The woman held a mixing bowl in one hand and a large wooden spoon in the other; they were out to either side of her, allowing Julianna to squeeze her. Although there was annoyance in her voice, she gave Julianna a warm smile.

They stood in a kitchen. It contained all of the ingredients of a standard kitchen: drawers, cupboards, a sink, a stove. Only, better. The white tiles of the floor gleamed. The silver knobs on the drawers and cupboards sparkled. The window over the sink let in sunlight so bright that it hurt Julianna's eyes to look at it. This was no mere kitchen, it was the Platonic ideal of a kitchen.

"Ahem," the woman ahemmed, bringing Julianna back to

the moment.

She released the woman and took a step back. The woman began stirring the contents in the bowl with the spoon. "Hello, Julianna," she said. "Long time, no see."

"Umm, yeah, well, been busy. You know how it is…" Julianna uncertainly stammered, shyly looping a strand of black hair around one finger.

"Yessss…the world turns quickly. There never seems to be enough time for *all* of the important things we need to do."

Julianna felt pretty sure there was a whiff of merriment in the woman's observation, but it was overpowered in her imagination by the smell of the cookie dough in the bowl. "Exactly," she felt it best to agree.

The woman looked at Julianna with a critical eye. "You're too skinny," she said. "If you stay long enough, you can have a cookie. I'm making them for Artemis and Hecate, but neither of them has much of an appetite, so I end up eating them myself or feeding them to the birds. And we're gettin' some awfully fat birds 'round here. I am the Mother, by the way. I go by many names: Danu, Arianrhod, Frigga, Demeter, Hera, Isis, Inanna— mortals are endlessly inventive. You may call me Selene."

Julianna frowned. The Mother aspect of THE tri-partite Goddess was not whom she was hoping to encounter. Combing through her memory, she found that Selene was the Goddess of fertility… sexuality—okay, that seemed relevant. Stability was in the mix, too, as was power and life. All good, but Julianna didn't get much support from her own mother, so she didn't know if she could trust this older woman Goddess.

"Julianna,". she responded shortly.

"Oh, I know who you are, child. I never forget a spirit. What I don't know is: why you here?"

As she watched Selene spoon out the dough onto a tray and shape it into roundish blobs, Julianna explained that three months earlier, her boyfriend, Mark, had dared her to kiss a girl at a party. They had been drinking, but that was really no excuse, Julianna had always been curious about what it would be like. So, she kissed her best friend, Emily. And she liked it.

"I don't hear no problem, here," Selene grinned as she carefully placed the tray of cookie dough into the pre-heated oven.

GODDESS GIVEN ADVICE

The problem, Julianna continued, was that Mark had been urging her and Emily to go further. Kissing was fun and all, but they had talked about it and kissing was all that she and Emily were comfortable doing. Every time Mark had suggested something... more suggestive, she had explained this to him. It had been like talking to a brick wall—a buff brick wall with wavy light brown hair, deep blue eyes and a smile that could melt steel, but a brick wall nonetheless. It had been frustrating. And his buff brick-wallness made it all the more frustrating.

"Boys," Selene enigmatically nodded as she reached into a drawer and pulled out a plain brown oven mitt. (Although Julianna had to admit that it was the most perfect plain brown oven mitt that she had ever seen.)

Seeing the Goddess—since there is no objection forthcoming, let's stick with that word, shall we? Seeing the Goddess turn and bend over to open the oven, Julianna objected, "Are you, uhh, sure the cookies are done?"

Selene haughtily turned back to her, seemingly growing as she glared. "You gonna tell me how ta cook in my own kitchen?" she challenged.

Julianna suddenly felt very small. "Oh, ah, well, it's just that... the, uhh, cookies have—you know—only been in the oven for, maybe, five minutes?"

Without a word, Selene turned, opened the oven, and retrieved the baking tray. Plonking it down on the counter next to the oven, she said, "My oven runs hot, child. Very hot."

Before she could respond, Julianna realized that her mouth was watering. It took her overwhelmed senses a moment to tell her why: the cookies smelled heavenly. "Oh! You really know your kitchen well, don't you?"

The anger which had swelled Selene's body immediately turned to pride. "You should always respect your elders, child. We have more experience than you do!"

"Yes, ma'am." Julianna reached for a cookie, but was rewarded with a swatted hand. "Wanna burn your tongue? Hot oven means hot food! Tch tch, spare me!"

Chagrined, Julianna considered how best to ask about her problem. Before she had the chance, she heard the pit-a-pat of little feet. Two small figures ran into the room, from where she couldn't tell, as neither of the doors to the room was open, and each hugged one of Selene's legs. Smokey shadows in the general shape of children chittered in a language that Julianna did not know, yet appeared to be highly expressive.

Selene clapped her hands, delighted. "There's somethin' about the smell of baked goods that youngsters cannot resist!" Using the glove, she brought the pan down to the child-wraiths' level. "Just one! You gotta learn to share with others!" Each of the children took a cookie.

"Hey!" Julianna objected. "What dabnabbery!" She was stung that the mother could be playing favourites.

"Oh, hush, you," Selene gently admonished as she returned the tray to the counter. "The heat doesn't affect the youngsters."

Julianna watched with fascination as the child-wraiths took bites out of their cookies, the pieces immediately turning to smoke. "So, umm," she pulled her attention away, "About my problem…"

"Children," Selene commanded, "close your ears. Adults talkin', now."

"Can they… do that?" Julianna hesitantly asked. For all she knew, child-wraiths had ear-lids.

Selene laughed. Throaty and warm. "It's just a figure o' speech. So. You wanna know what I think?"

"Yes, please."

"You are who you are. Don't ever allow a man—a boy, really—to make you feel bad about bein' you."

Before she could ask anything else, Julianna found herself back in the forest, hugging the Earth Tree. Her first thought was disappointment: *My cookie!* Her second thought was gratitude: *Thanks for the affirmation!* Her third thought was regret: *But my cookie!*

Shivering in the cold autumn late afternoon, Julianna turned to start packing up. She noticed that her plate of chocolate chip cookies had been reduced to a single sample. It was plumper than she had remembered making her cookies. The brown was a deeper gold, the chips were more plentiful. It was, in short, the Platonic ideal of a chocolate chip cookie.

Julianna smiled. Selene had her back.

*

When God created the torture chamber that is the modern high school, He believed he had perfected it. Because, God. Everything He does is perfect. Then, the Devil went Him one better and invented gym class. If high school gyms had existed in Darwin's time, he wouldn't have had to travel to the Galapagos Islands to see survival of the fittest in action.

The purpose of gym class is to recreate the conditions of primitive humanity, which involves a lot of running around and grunting. The point is to make bodies softened by years of a modern diet and too much time sitting in front of screens run the way they evolved, except the terror of starving to death or being eaten had been replaced by the terror of looking weak to your peers.

Hard to tell which was more motivating.

Given the time of year, gym class was actually held in the gym, taking away the fig leaf of being overlooked in the vastness of the field in the back of the school.

The boys in Julianna's class, including Mark, practiced wrestling on a dozen mats clustered around the far half of the gym. Many of the pairs of wrestlers were more or less inert, either unaware of the moves they should be trying or afraid that where they put their hands on the bodies of their opponents might reveal something about their sexuality that they weren't ready to acknowledge. Others, including Mark, wriggled and groped and grunted in their best approximation of Olympic athletes.

"Ellison!" Coach Frangipani bellowed. "Stop flopping around on Scalzi like a dying fish! Remember the holds I taught you!"

Coach Frangipani was a short man with a moustache that might have been described as "dapper" if the twenty-first century hadn't waged a war on quaintness. He could be described as a bulldog of a man, not only because he barked commands to his students the way a leashed puppy would greet a squirrel, but because most of his students suspected that he carried more muscle on his small frame than it could reasonably hold, which would make his bite much worse than his bark.

In the other half of the room, the girls in Julianna's class took turns jumping on a pommel horse. Most did simple vaults.

Only a couple dared to somersault over it (Millicent Duvalier should completely recover from her concussion in four to six weeks). One of them was Julianna, who had accomplished far more daring moves on the dance floors of clubs all over the city.

Ms. Tremblant, the elegant young French teacher, kept a watchful eye on them. Her PhD in the rhetoric of 19th century Parisian literature had not prepared her to help young women discover and strengthen their bodies (except, perhaps, for Marie -Anne de Bovet), but when Mrs. Greyson was forced to take a leave of absence to "settle her nerves," somebody had to take her place. Ms. Tremblant agreed (the extra money, which went into the fund that would eventually pay for her campaign to run for Parliament, may have been the deciding factor).

"Good. Good. Good," she absently enthused. In truth, her mind was more on her campaign slogan than her immediate task.

Julianna had thrice executed a perfect somersault, sticking the landing like her feet had hit flypaper. She asked if she could be excused and run some laps on the track along the outside of the gymnasium. Ms. Tremblant hesitated. Julianna was one of the few students for which her enthusiastic support hadn't been feigned. In the end, she reluctantly agreed.

Emily, who had been given a pass from the pommel horse because of her vertigo, jogged alongside Julianna as they made their way around the track.

"... at's the thing," Julianna said, barely breaking a pant. "Just because we're not as racist as the United States doesn't mean that we're perfect. Black people in our society are still marginalized and we still wage a genocidal war against our Indigenous people. If we don't see it, it's just because we're so *polite* about it... "

"It's not... " Emily panted, "not... not the... the...the..."

"The same?"

Emily was going to say "a fair comparison," but she gratefully agreed to Julianna's version instead.

"You see?" Julianna decisively concluded. "The fact that you can say that with a straight face is exactly the problem I'm—"

Mark, excused from wrestling for showing up the other students, jogged up behind them. "Hello, ladies," he greeted them.

"I'm going...going to... to... to the..." Emily panted.

"Showers?" Mark suggested, matching his gait to theirs.

Emily glared at him for a moment, and then made her way to the door leading to the showers.

"Smooth," Julianna commented. She tried to run past Mark, but he easily matched her pace.

"What?" Mark feigned ignorance (although with boys, you never could be one hundred per cent sure). "I just finished her sentence for her."

"We need to talk," Julianna informed him

"Oooh. Ominous."

"Emily and I have talked, and we're not comfortable making out like you're trying to get us to do."

"Why? You seem to enjoy kissing each other."

"Yeah. Sure. *Kissing*. But what you want us to do goes far beyond that."

"But you're my girlfriend," Mark pouted. "Don't you want to make me happy?"

"Emily's not your girlfriend. You don't get to demand things from her." Then, remembering what the Goddess had told her, Julianna added, "And anyway, what about *my* happiness? Isn't it important?"

"Of course your happiness is important!" Mark placated. "It's just that I think that making out more with Emily will make you happy."

Why do boys think they know you better than you know yourself? Julianna wondered.

They passed the next two and a half orbits around the gym in silence. Finally, Mark asked, "So, what are you gonna do?"

"I... I gotta do what I gotta do," Julianna told him.

"Fair. But I gotta do what I gotta do, too."

"Fair. So, where does that leave us?"

Mark grinned. "Doin' our do." Then, he turned and ran back to where Coach Frangipani, fed up with their pathetic half-efforts, had all the wrestlers doing jumping jacks.

Julianna admired Mark's tush the whole way.

And Mark and Julianna lived happily ever after.

Probably.

Maybe.

It could happen.

3.

Meanwhile, five universes down and eight to the right…

Why do faces in trees always look like they're smiling at you? Jules wondered as she wandered through the forest in the hope that she was going in a direction that would take her to the Earth Tree. *I mean, shit, by the time you've got a face in you, you have to be hundreds of years old. I'm only seventeen, and I'm already pissed off at everything. If I lived to be hundreds of years old, I would have exploded before I reached my first century!*

When she was a child, Jules' mother and some of her woman friends would march to the heart of the forest to commune with the Earth Tree. They had taken her with them when she was six years old. She had cried and stomped her feet and generally made herself unpleasant. Her mother took her once a year in the hope that Jules would gain an appreciation for the experience, but all that happened was that the young woman's negative behaviour grew more sophisticated. Despite only being there a handful of times, Jules was confident that she would have no trouble finding the tree. Pulling her winter coat tighter to stave off the cold after over four hours of searching, she had not been disabused of this notion, even if doubts had started creeping in around its edges.

Despite her worst efforts, Jules walked over a rise and discovered the Earth Tree. She sneered at the look of glee on the huge face in front of her.

Jules put her *Rage Against the Machine* backpack down on the forest floor and started taking objects out of it. She put a half-eaten granola bar she had bought a couple of weeks earlier and didn't enjoy enough to finish in front of the Earth Tree—the offering. She took out a flashlight (she had put new batteries in the night before—she wasn't totally unprepared!) and laid it on the forest floor so that the beam hit the tree square in the face.

Finally, she started chanting, "Tree Goddess, don't be a bitch/ Give me my fondest wish" (interspersed with the occasional, "I can't believe I'm doing this!" and "Freezing my ass off to get a Goddess' advice? Oh, that's rich!"). She couldn't remember the chant, so she made one up. Spirits appreciated when you made the effort, right?

Whatever.

Jules stood, hands on her hips, and watched the tree as nothing happened. Desperate that her time in the forest not be in vain, she went up to the tree and put her arms around it, barely getting a quarter of the way. Closing her eyes, she continued chanting. After a few minutes, she could feel a chill in her bones.

She was about to give up when a voice from behind her cackled, "You gonna stand there all day like a damn fool, or you gonna talk ta me and get what you come here for?"

Jules opened her eyes and discovered that she stood in a forest. The face in the tree grinned at her like it was in on a joke she would never get. "Well, that was…anti-climactic," she commented. Immobile as a car on blocks, the face looked like it wanted to nod in agreement.

She turned to face an old woman, with long, scraggly strands of white hair and a face that looked like it had spent its life sucking lemons. She carelessly held a knitted shawl around her shoulders with one hand, seemingly indifferent to the cold. Her other hand helped her lean on a gnarled piece of wood that supported her bent over frame. Jules, fascinated by the twisted piece of wood, could have sworn that, in a couple of places, it resembled an intimate part of the female anatomy.

"It's just your imagination," the old woman seemed to read her thoughts. "Sometimes, a twisted piece of wood is just a twisted piece of wood!"

"How—"

The old woman snorted. It was a snort born out of experience, and, truth be told, a basically ornery nature. "You think I been waiting all my life for you to show up? Girl, I was advising people like your mother since before you were born! If I had to create a Frequently Unasked Questions file for queries I've heard a million times before, I'd die with my quill stylus in my hand! I'm not going to waste what time I have left on this plane doing that, and if you think I should, FUQ you!"

"Do you have to be so—" Jules shivered from the cold. "So—so—so hostile?"

The old woman considered this question. "Do I have to be so hostile?" she asked herself. She pursed her lips and nodded her head. Eventually, she responded, "No, I don't haaaave to be so hostile. It just makes the time pass more quickly. For me, anyway." Seeing Jules wrap her arms around her chest to keep herself warm, the old lady melted a little. "So, you wanna tell me what I can do for you before you turn into a human popsicle?"

Like a wind-up novelty toy, Jules told her story through heavily chattering teeth. Six months ago, she had been at a party with her boyfriend, Mark. They had been drinking a little, and Mark had dared her to kiss her best friend, Emily. Jules had never kissed a girl before, so she hesitated. Eventually, curious, she did. She found it pleasant enough, but not enough to want to do again.

Except...

Except, Mark thought it looked "hot" and insisted that they kiss again. Jules was head over heels for Mark, and, although she didn't find out until much later, Emily was head over heels for her, so, eventually, they kissed again. And again. And again. Over a period of a few months, Jules found herself enjoying kissing Emily more and more. Their kissing became increasingly passionate, until, within the last couple of weeks, it had been accompanied by rudimentary fondling. You would think Mark would have been happy.

As if!

Before Jules could continue, the old woman said, "The noise of your teeth clacking is making it hard for me to follow what you're saying. If I treat it like Morse Code, it tells a very different story! Take this..."

The old woman nodded towards the Earth Tree. One of its thicker branches held out a steaming cup of liquid. Jules walked over to the tree and took the cup, warming her hands with it. Then, she took a sip. Oh... Cocoa. If she had one weakness, it was for Brad Pitt. If she had a second weakness, it would be for eighties club music. If she had a third—okay, one of her weaknesses was cocoa. She sipped it appreciatively, letting its warmth spread through her.

Last month, Jules continued when she had warmed up and had completely drained the cup, Mark started making snarky remarkys about "a couple of dumb lesbos." Sometimes, he would pull Jules out of an embrace with Emily to kiss her hard on the lips, something she had never enjoyed. Mark's lips were too thin to be a soft cushion. They were more like a throbbing clothes line.

Last week, he made a scene in the cafeteria of their high school, insisting that Jules and Emily end their relationship. They weren't making out or anything, they were just laughing about a frog joke that Jimmy Emtshwiller had made in biology class. No matter how much they tried to explain that they weren't laughing at him, Mark insisted they stop laughing at him.

"It's so unfair!" Jules summed up. "I mean, he encouraged my relationship with Emily, who, by the way, I've known since third grade, and now he's pulling this dabnabbery? WTF?"

"Boys!" the old woman snorted, a world of contempt in that one short sound.

She seemed satisfied that this explained everything. Not quite. So, Jules asked, "Umm...could you, maybe...elaborate?"

"Their egos are like accordions," the old woman obliged. "Sometimes, they inflate so big there's no space left in a room for anybody else. Sometimes, they're thinner than onionskin!"

"Onionskin. Got it." The frown on her face said otherwise.

"When your boyfriend, whom I will not dignify by saying his name—honestly, I am not pleased by having to refer to him as your boyfriend—cajoled you into kissing your friend Emily, he must have been so full of himself, thinking that he could get a cheap thrill out of it," the old woman explained. "But the more room you made in your life for Emily, the less room you seemed to have for him. He became jealous of what he had started. Stupid? You bet! But that's a boy for you!"

"Oh. I understand." This time, the nodding of her head supported her words. "So, what am I going to do?"

"Well," the old woman sagely advised, "the next time you want to ask for my advice, you will learn the chant and bring a proper offering. Hecate is willing to indulge the children of ardent followers, but only so much!"

"Your name is Hecate?" Jules inquired.

The old woman rolled her eyes. "Hecate...Cailleach... Morrigan... Skadi... Cerridwen... Ereskigal... more I've probably forgotten—I'm an old crone, don'tcha know? Call me whatever will end this conversation the quickest!"

"You're so old!" Jules blurted.

Hekate turned her gaze on the young woman, who didn't flinch under it. Much. "I got wisdom," Hekate hectored her. "You don't get wisdom when you're young. You get it from experience. I got repose, calm, acceptance, all things that come with knowing that you've done almost everything in life you're gonna do." Hekate softened a little. You had to look very carefully around the edges of her eyes, but the signs of softening were definitely there. "Yeah, I also represent death. But you can't have rebirth and renewal without clearin' away old life first. Think you'd be here if none o' your ancestors had died?"

Jules took a moment to digest this, then continued, "I meant about Mark. What am I going to do about Mark?"

The old woman glared at Jules, making her feel small, quite a feat considering that Jules was the one who loomed over the hunched older woman.

"Learn the chant. Bring a proper offering. Got it."

The old woman smiled. She only had three teeth, which seemed to be placed in her mouth to maximize their eeriness, but Jules was surprised to find herself warmed by the expression.

"You are who you are," the woman gently advised. "Don't ever allow a man—a boy, really—to make you feel bad about being you."

"Thank y—" Jules started.

She was alone in the forest, no longer holding the cup that had once held cocoa, her teeth shivering like castanets played by a speed addict. The flashlight sputtered, the batteries in it must have liked the cold even less than she did, so she turned it off and threw it in her backpack. She left the granola bar for what-ever animals were not hibernating. Pulling out her phone, she called up Google Maps. The forest would be a blank space, of course, but as long as she could find the nearest road, she would get out of there before the sun went down.

*

Adults tend to romanticize their youth, probably because they need to believe that there was a point in their lives when they could feel happy and free, where they didn't have to snatch moments of happiness or freedom out of a seemingly unending flow of responsibilities and regrets.

Or, so I've heard.

High school is *Lord of the Flies* with designer clothing and cell phones. But by the time adult memory has cut off the social traumas and sanded down the unnecessary drama, what's left is *The Brady Bunch*. With designer clothing. And cell phones.

Jules wore enough black clothing and mascara that the *zeitgeist* at Pollyanna High considered her a Goth, but she wore the occasional flower print dress and red lipstick to show anybody who paid attention (she wished!) that she wasn't beholden to received ideas about her identity. Honestly, she just liked to go to clubs on the weekend and lose herself in the sights and sounds. The 80sier the music, the better, as far as she was concerned. All music after the 80s was just a commentary on Depeche Mode.

This attitude put Jules at odds with the cool, hot girls. They couldn't understand why somebody with her height and cheekbones, her obvious stellar-model potential, wouldn't naturally be begging to join them. The fact that she "stole" one of their boyfriends was a perverse sign to the group that she belonged. Not to the member who lost her boyfriend, obviously, but to everybody else. She was also shunned by the nerds. They couldn't understand why somebody so undeniably smart wasn't interested in arguing endlessly about eternal questions like which was a better representation of its series: *Star Trek Discovery* or *The Mandelorian*. The good Catholic girls hated her, warning that she would go to Hell if she didn't find God, like, immediately. Although Jules didn't care about the insults any of the cliques directed towards her, she cared even less about the insults from the good Catholic girls, since they said pretty much the same thing to anybody who wasn't one of them, including the teachers. The good Catholic boys kept their own counsel. The jocks were disdainful of all girls on general principle. Not that they could articulate that principle... or any principle, truth be told, that didn't involve "giving 173 per cent" or "breaking past our limitations" or "wanting it more than the other guys" or other words of wisdom instilled in them by their phys-ed teachers. Although they made an exemption for that special category of human female known as "the girlfriend." In public, in any case.

It was the principle of the thing.

Jules had met Emily at a Cure reunion concert, and they had been besties ever since. Sitting at their own table in the cafeteria, Emily ate salads because she identified with the brachiosaurus. (I give that youthful passion another two and three quarters, three and a third years tops. Woe to the meat packing industry if she next identifies with the T-Rex!) Jules was a meat-eater because, well, you don't really need an excuse to be a meat-eater, do you? Not that the "meat" served in the cafeteria was likely to satisfy her. she had brought a sandwich made from leftover roast beef to avoid the uncertainty.

"He's calculating the value of pi to as many digits as he can," Emily commented.

"Sixty-three," Jules responded.

"Sixty-three?"

"He gets distracted at sixty-three and loses count."

"Always?"

"Every time. He—oh! Did you see that grimace? Like he just ate something bad?"

"Yeah?"

"Sixty-three."

"Couldn't he have just eaten something bad?"

"Eating something bad *can cause sixty-three.*"

"Oooooooohhh..."

One of the ways Jules and Emily entertained themselves in the unstructured time known as "lunch" was to imagine what went on in the minds of the students around them. The unwitting subject of their amusement this day was Larry Morgenstern—acne-pocked, pocket protector wearing, chess club member for life Larry Morgenstern. He was unenthusiastically eating "stew" while staring into the middle distance. who knew what thoughts lay behind that blank expression?

"Do you think calculating pi turns him on?" Emily wondered.

"Totally," Jules informed her. "But it ultimately frustrates him."

"Frustrates him?"

"Of course."

"Why?"

"Because of the sixty-three barrier."

Emily frowned. "That's what he calls it?"

Jules shrugged. "What else would you call it?"

"Fair point."

"That damn sixty-three barrier! It makes all of his calculations foreplay with no climax!"

"Ouch!" Emily squinched up her face in what she hoped was an expression of pained solidarity.

"Ouch to sixty-three decimal places!" Jules grinned.

"But after giving himself a brain shower, he tries again. Do you think…?"

"Horny bastard!"

Jules and Emily laughed.

"Do you think all the math nerds know about the sixty-three barrier?" Emily wondered.

"Of course." Jules unhesitatingly responded. "Why do you think they look so frustrated all of the—"

"Emily," Mark interrupted. While the attention of the young women was focused on Larry Morgenstern, Mark had manfully swaggered up to the table. He had walked with a manly swagger since the age of seven. In most situations, the manly swagger had served him well, so why change it now?

Jules was not one of those situations.

"Jules, can we talk?" Mark asked, although it was more of a command. Commasked.

Jules sullenly looked up at him looming over her. "So, talk."

"In private."

Jules sighed dramatically. It was a Tony-worthy sound. "No," she answered. "Anything you have to say to me, you can say to Emily."

Mark suppressed a sneer. He didn't always agree with the girlfriend exception, but he knew better than to go against it in such a public place. He glared for a couple of seconds, instead. (For some men, knowing how to communicate with women was a life-long learning process.) "Okay. Maybe that's for the best. You—look, are you my girl or not?"

"I'm my own woman."

"You know what I mean."

"Oh, I know what you mean. Do you know what I mean?"

Mark groaned. Simple, declarative sentences—was that so hard? Why did girls have to make things so complicated? Okay, if he was honest, he would admit that he didn't actually care what Jules meant, but he knew it was important to show her that he did. For some reason. "Sure I do, baby. Of course, I do. It's just that you seem to be spending more time with Emily than you do with me."

"What? I'm not allowed to have friends, now?"

Emily was listening to this exchange with interest.

"Sure, but—"

"Anyway, what are you complaining about? You were always pushing me to get more physical with her." To emphasize the point, Jules put her hand over Emily's, entwining their fingers.

Did Mark notice? "Yeah, but I didn't expect her to turn you into a dike!" Oh, yeah, he noticed.

Jules looked into Mark's eyes as the cafeteria held its mac and cheesy breath. She didn't find the faintest glimmer of understanding in them. Nobody can "make" you gay. you're born that way. And anyway, Jules still liked boys. if she had to be labelled (and, hey, labels are for clothes!), she would more properly be called bisexual. And dikes? Really? She had heard the term used with Pride, but this was the opposite of that. How could she communicate all of these complicated ideas to her boyfriend?

Jules punched Mark in the nards.

He immediately doubled over, cupping his private parts with his hands. His teeth clenched and his eyes screwed shut. He hadn't been in this much pain since he started lifting weights at the age of five.

GODDESS GIVEN ADVICE

Jules grabbed the collar of his crisp white shirt and pulled his face close to hers. As loud as she could without appearing to shout, she intoned, "Considah dis a divohce!" and pushed him away from her.

Hunched over, Mark crab-walked away from the table.

Emily wanted to applaud. Instead, she just said: "Wow."

"You can't let boys define you," Jules advised, pulling Emily close and kissing her on the lips. Hard.

And Jules and Mark lived happily ever after.

Just not with each other.

)O( )O( )O(

Ira Nayman is a humour writer who stumbled into speculative fiction over a decade ago and decided to hang around. His latest novel, *Bad Actors*, was recently released by Elsewhen Press; it is the seventh in his Transdimensional Authority series, the second in the Multiverse Refugees Trilogy. He was the editor of *Amazing Stories* magazine for two and a half years. In the first week of September, 2022, he will celebrate the 20th anniversary of *Les Pages aux Folles*, the website that features weekly updates of political and social satire.

Mother of Stars

By Robin Rowland

"I'D LOVE TO SAVE THE Milky Way," Gabriel Pennington said. "But politically my hands are tied. I can't be seen stalling a seventy million dollar project that will bring the College of Astronomy and Astrophysics into the 21st century in a new building with the very latest technology."

You old fogey, Aileen thought. No guts.

Pennington was the head of the department, in his seventies, white hair and beard, jeans, a white dress shirt and a blue hoodie, a man whose CV ran to ten pages and his publication list, going back to when he was a precocious teenager, was fifty pages. Pennington's usual and elegant office in the old wing of the College of Astronomy was closed due to ongoing renovations. He had commandeered one of the smaller conference rooms in the more modern Northwest Wing; a room that featured wall size photographs of starscapes and galaxies taken by the Hubble Space Telescope. He held court from a high-end ergonomic leather chair at the head of a boardroom table piled high with books and file folders. Aileen sat about halfway down the table in one of conference chairs that had seen better days.

The chair creaked.

Pennington leaned forward on the table and grinned. "Of course, the university is always worried about student activism, especially these days. A student campaign to save the Milky Way Mosaic would have some traction. It must be more than a few Tweets, a Facebook page and a couple of signs. Aileen Casasaya, if you want to save the Milky Way, you have to come up with an argument to persuade the university president, the administrators, and the university Senate, not to mention the government providing millions of dollars of the budget, that it's worth preserving."

Aileen nodded but didn't answer. Seventy million dollars. The old prof was right. It would take more than a couple of posts on Facebook to save the Milky Way mosaic.

"So how are you going to do it?" Pennington asked.

Aileen thought for a moment before she brightened up and smiled. "This mosaic is something that doesn't fit. Not only is the mosaic block something out of the ordinary for all those years ago, the stars are definitely not right for that era. It's an anomaly," she replied.

"I'll have to agree there," Pennington nodded. "At least out of the ordinary to us. Not, apparently to the College a century ago."

She sat up straight in her chair. It screeched. "I'll do the same as an astronomer would look for an exoplanet or even a comet. We look for anomalies, incongruities, like the barest shadow of a distant planet passing in front of a star light-years away. That's how I'll do it."

"Ms. Casasaya, you're one of our top undergrads in fourth year. Most of your work in my astrophysics lab has been top notch, that's why I agreed to meet you. You're mathematically inclined, although you do have a reputation as a bit of rebel. You're very sure of yourself, at least that's the impression. I know you can wrangle equations, but historical research, can you do that?"

"I don't see why not, Professor Pennington," Aileen's voice was firm. She sat up more in the squeaky chair. "My mother manages the science section at the Metropolitan Reference Library. I worked as a page at my local library when I was in high school."

"Shelving books after school is different than doing original historical research." Pennington pulled a file from the pile on the desk and opened it

"This is something we might hire a grad student in the history department to undertake," Pennington said, fiddling with some papers. He picked up one sheet. "You've got thirty days to do it."

"What?" Aileen asked, bewildered.

"Thirty days. There are contractual obligations to the companies involved. The project has a strict deadline.

"I'll tell you what Ms. Casasaya, there's almost nothing known about the Milky Way Mosaic. The files in the university archives amount to some old plans and little else. Find out who created it, how and when. Come up with a way to save it. Do that in the next thirty days, and no matter what the outcome with the administration, I'll give you a full semester credit for independent graduate-level study."

"Thank you, sir," Aileen said, getting up from the chair. It groaned. "I'll need a pass to get through security."

"Already filled out," Pennington smiled, handing her a plastic card that had been waiting in the file folder. "I knew you could do this. You can report to the site office in the morning." He chuckled. "I just had to make sure you were serious about taking this on."

"Thank you," Aileen said, taking the card.

As she walked down the hall toward the exit, Aileen pondered her future. She wanted to study the origin of the universe and grew more intrigued by the ever growing number of exoplanets. In the coming weeks, Aileen had to figure out which grad schools she wanted to apply to. Graduating students needed to leave to widen their horizons (go to a galaxy far, far away was the in-joke). A recommendation from Pennington would certainly help her future.

*

Aileen exited the Northwest Wing and walked the half block to what was now called the "Old Wing". Surrounded by a wall of bare plywood construction boarding, plenty of windows allowed students, professors and passers-by to see the work on the site.

The elegant neo-Gothic College of Astronomy, solidly built of granite blocks, had been completed in 1897—the Victorian age—when North American universities attempted to duplicate Oxford or Cambridge. The granite had survived more than a century with some weathering from wind, rain, snow and blackening from decades of air pollution. The fine pink sandstone trim, carved with stylized stars, had eroded with few features that were recognizable.

Work was wrapping up for the day. Aileen could see a couple of figures in high viz vests and hard hats. The mosaic was in the Great Hall, inside the building, and out of sight from the street.

The College of Astronomy was renovated in the 1930s as a Depression make work project. In the early 1960s, as the space race aimed at the moon and the boomer cohort crowded into the once sedate campus, it was expanded with the "Northwest Wing," a brutalist concrete addition. For the next sixty years, budgets were limited. The money had to go to the necessities. The electrical wiring had been upgraded—somewhat. An old storage room had been converted for the computer servers. The roof leaked in places. The heating system dated from the 1960s. In what was now called the "Old Wing," the Victorian fireplaces had roared every day in the winter until municipal clean air regulations put a stop to fires. Hallowe'en, Christmas, New Years, and faculty dinners were the exception. There was no air conditioning. With climate change and soaring summer temperatures, it was unbearably hot.

After years of lobbying and then begging, the university decided that the upgrade could no longer be put off. The Old Wing was closed. The senior faculty moved their offices into the 1960s addition while junior faculty and grad students had to relocate to temporary portables. The Old Wing was to be replaced with an ultramodern, glass and steel nine story tower, topped with a decorative glass onion-style dome that resembled the Royal Observatory in Greenwich, England. The design preserved the original stone as a facade.

The demolition crew working in the Great Hall had removed a lathe and plaster wall that ran the length of the

Victorian building, creating a cloud of dust and debris. As the dust settled, the astonished crew beheld a black basalt pylon embedded with shining stars and the Milky Way. The workers all grabbed their phones and captured wide shots and close-ups, posting the images on Facebook, Twitter and Instagram. The photos of what was quickly called the *Milky Way Mosaic* went viral, making television news.

Aileen Casasaya's status was even lower than a grad student. She was a month into her fourth year undergrad. As Aileen saw the images on her phone, in that second, seemingly out of nowhere, she had a feeling the artwork was in danger of demolition. Something at the core of her very being told her to save it. Impulsively, she created a Save the Milky Way Facebook group.

The pylon was where the elevator shaft and much of the wiring infrastructure was going to go. The architect was unimpressed with the find and didn't want to change the plan.

Most of the faculty and the students had signed on to the Facebook group. Aileen worried for a moment if she had done the right thing. Had she had bitten off more than she could chew? Aileen suspected that some of the grad students, who, she thought, would have taken the lead, did not want to rock the boat.

Many at the university asked how the mosaic and pylon had ended up in the building in the first place. A couple of the senior astronomy faculty declared "the stars are in the wrong place". It was folk art, so why bother? Most of the art and architecture faculty also thought the mosaic was unimportant folk art. A couple of art scholars disagreed in a raging Facebook debate, arguing it was not even a mosaic, but a unique form of inlay, resembling Renaissance Italian *pieta dura*.

The local historical societies demanded the mosaic be saved, even threatening to go to court under the Heritage Act.

On the boarding, Aileen saw the usual sign: "Personal Protective Equipment required on this site."

"At least that's no problem," she thought. "I'll also have to bring my camera."

Aileen already had full PPE; hard hat, safety boots, safety glasses, gloves, high-vis vest. After she had turned eighteen, thanks to her older brother, a journeyman electrician, she had been hired for summer jobs as a flagger on work sites. The money was a lot better than serving coffee or slinging square burgers.

*

About half of the Old Wing appeared demolished. The grey granite walls, exterior and some interior that were to be part of the new tower, were braced by steel beams. Excavators dug the new foundation, dumping glacial rock and soil that underpinned much of the city into waiting dump trucks. Dust filled the hot early fall air. As Aileen walked to the site office, she heard the constant beep beep of equipment and trucks backing up.

At the trailer that acted as the site office, the manager merely glanced at her pass and then handed Aileen over to a beefy white haired man with "Tony" on his shirt.

Tony led her across the site to where sheets of plywood had replaced the front doors of the Old Wing. Beside the plywood sat the faded sandstone cornerstone inscribed "1897" .

"What's your job?" Aileen shouted above the din.

"Speciality demolition and restoration," Tony said. "We're a subcontractor on this job. So, we know what we're doing."

Tony opened a padlock on the temporary doors and waved Aileen into the old building. "I wouldn't want to see it end up in one of those dump trucks," Tony yelled over the beeping.

Inside, it was quieter and cooler.

In the previous three years, Aileen and other students had walked down The Great Hall to attend lectures or meet with professors. The walls, plaster with faded white paint, had disappeared. Now, everything was stripped back to the original granite.

"Look up. Look at those beams," Tony said, pointing.

Aileen stretched her neck to see the roof supported by heavy wooden beams.

"Old Oak," Tony said. "You won't find those anymore. Of course, like the Milky Way, the plans don't call for preserving them.

"Our contract allows us to salvage anything the university

doesn't want so that we can repurpose or resell." Tony explained. "That increases our profit. We don't waste anything." He pointed toward the beams, as if counting them, something he must have done at least a dozen times. "We've sent a memo urging that the beams be preserved. If they aren't, we'll find the oak a new home, either in restoring some heritage building or perhaps in someone's new monster home.

"Why the hell did they put in a ceiling over those gorgeous beams?" Tony grunted. "Same with the false wall hiding the mosaic. We know it was built in the summer of 1937, old newspapers were stuffed into some cracks.

"Over here." Tony shook his head as they walked down the empty hall. "Given the era when they built that false wall, they could have at least done some Art Deco rather plain plaster. What were they thinking? Here's the mosaic."

"Wow," Aileen exclaimed as she saw the polished black monolith up close for the first time. A horizontal block, about two metres high and three and half metres long, it stood on a foundation of grey granite setting the galactic starscape at eye level.

"We wanted to see what the mosaic really looks like, so we've done basic, careful cleaning," Tony said. "Mostly ninety years of dust, a little mould. Nothing that would damage it. It looks even better than we uncovered it.

"Good as new," Tony beamed with pride. "The night sky is polished black basalt. Most of the stars are tiny chips or even grains of clear quartz. Others are fragments, chips and grains of semi-precious stones."

Tony pulled his phone from his belt and thumbed an app. "We had one of our consultants take a quick look. The stones are orange or green agate, garnet, and amethyst, yellow, orange and green quartz, red or yellow jasper, and maybe jade. Possibly some coloured glass as well."

The sparkling inlays showed the arc of the Milky Way over the distant hills to the southeast of the campus, hills now obscured by office towers and apartments. Aileen recognized the constellation Cassiopeia at the centre of the image, with the top of the Southern Cross just rising above the horizon.

"Hardly a piece of bad folk art," Tony sniffed. "I know

good stuff when I see it. So, you're going to be the one to save it?"

"I hope so," Aileen said.

"I hope you can too," Tony said. "Damn it. I want it preserved. Look how heavy it is. Moving the pylon will blow the budget out of the water. Not to mention, the job would hold everything up by at least a month, if not more. Demolishing it to make way for an elevator shaft will be a crime. You've got your work cut out for you, young lady."

"First I have to photograph it." She used a good DSLR camera, taking shot after shot of the mosaic. "Then I can study it more closely."

*

Thanks to her construction job, Aileen could afford her own cramped bachelor in another Victorian-era building recently renovated into ultra-modern student furnished apartments. Aileen sat at a flimsy, desk, barely wide enough for her high resolution 27-inch screen desktop computer. One of the apartment's advantages was a top of the line, ultra high speed fibre optic Wi-Fi.

Aileen used photo software to stitch together a high resolution image of the mosaic. The profs were right, she thought, the stars were wrong—at least they wrong for 2018 and for 1897 when the Old Wing was dedicated.

Aileen had access to the world's best astronomical software. All she had to do was figure out how the stars aligned and when.

She knew the artist would have been looking southeast from the longitude and latitude of the College of Astronomy. On three different programs, Aileen ran the figures five more times. The result always came up the same. The artist had, for some reason, chosen to show the moment just before sunrise on the winter solstice about six thousand, five hundred years ago, around 4,500 BCE.

Aileen took a coffee break. "Why would anyone in 1897 choose to create an inlay, mosaic, or whatever, for what was then one of the most sophisticated astronomy departments in the world, portraying the winter solstice six thousand years before ground was broken for the building? There has to be a clue somewhere. Where's the anomaly?"

Aileen kept looking at the computer screen until she was too tired to go on. Sleep and dreams brought no new ideas.

In the morning, Aileen microwaved a frozen breakfast before returning to her computer to go over the photo image again, this time almost pixel by pixel.

Finally, barely noticeable in the bottom right corner, she found a clue. There appeared to be a small name made of fine silver wire that possibly read "Brigid".

So, the artist was a woman.

Aileen metaphorically kicked herself. Give the mosaic dated to 1897, she had easily assumed the artist was a man. Was that the anomaly she was searching for? There was something else. Yet a question about the mosaic nagged her. Something she couldn't put her finger on.

*

The original university library and archives, built in a Romanesque revival style, was now the entrance way to a ten story concrete tower. The archive reading room was off the main entrance, a space completely modern with no trace of its nineteenth century origins. Aileen had put in a request to the university archives for any documents relating to the planning and construction of the original astronomy building, and to cover all possibilities, any other information from the years 1896 to 1906.

The duty archivist, a short sandy haired woman probably in her late forties, pointed Aileen to a table. "Your first request is waiting for you—the old plans we pulled when the mosaic was first uncovered. The documents are fragile, so we'll go through them together."

Aileen followed the archivist who wore an ankle length denim skirt and green cotton shirt, across the room to the table. Old blueprints, some of the diagrams barely visible on the yellowed and cracked paper were spread out on the mahogany table. The archivist took a pair of cotton gloves from her skirt pocket.

"Use the gloves," archivist directed, pointing to a pair of white cotton gloves in a plastic bag beside the blueprints.

"There's not much," the archivist said. "We already looked up the blueprints for the building after the discovery of the mosaic. Obviously something was part of the original planning, but the blueprints don't give any indication it was to actually be a mosaic."

With her gloved hand, the archivist carefully pointed to one section of the blueprints without actually touching the fragile paper. Aileen leaned as close as she could.

"As you can see, there's a blank wall with the notation 'stars'. Not much help for any research I'm afraid," the archivist said. "Any financial records, contracts or minutes of meetings, unfortunately, disappeared long ago."

"How about records of staff, faculty and students?" Aileen asked.

"We have them waiting for you," the archivist said. "You can photograph the plans if you wish. No flash. Then they go back into safe storage."

Aileen took a couple of shots of the blueprints with her camera.

The archivist carefully replaced the blueprints in a large folder. "I'll be right back," she said, taking the folder with her. "We've got a list from convocations. As well there are some old photographs you will be interested in."

The archivist brought a library cart with grey acid-free archival boxes filled with documents and photographs, before leaving to help other researchers.

Aileen first went through the convocation lists from 1896 to 1906, listing men and only men. "Sexist pigs," Aileen muttered.

"No information on staff or if the artist was a contractor," Aileen grumbled.

Aileen turned to the boxes with the photographs. Still wearing the white cotton gloves, she carefully took the photographs out one by one and put them on the table. The first ten were portraits, head shots of white Victorian men with beards or mutton chop moustaches in tweed suits—the senior faculty. The eleventh photograph was different. It had a small brass plaque on the frame that read "1897". The photograph was a group shot in front of the university's old observatory at the top of the hill to the southeast; long shut down for active astronomy and now a tourist attraction. Some of the faces appeared familiar from the portraits. In the back row stood the patriarchs of the faculty, men with white hair and beards. Standing beside one of the men was a woman in a white dress. The second row was made up of the younger faculty, men in their thirties and forties, some clean-shaven, others with dark beards. The front row filled with kneeling fresh faced young men, the undergraduate students. There were no names.

"Are you Brigid?" Aileen asked.

The last photograph from the first box had a plaque that read "1901". A couple of the white bearded men were missing. One of the dark bearded men had obviously been promoted, and beside him, once again, stood the woman in the white dress. The second row was the junior faculty and the front row, kneeling, was a new crop of undergrads.

"Why didn't you record the names?" Aileen wondered.

She used her DSLR to take photographs of the group shots, focusing on a close up of the woman. She turned to the other boxes. Much of the images were similar, portraits and group shots as time went on, even shots of young men in army and navy uniforms.

She opened the last box and pulled out a framed coloured photograph—a group of people sitting in some bleachers. Men in white shirts, dark pants, narrow ties, and sunglasses, and one woman, in a white dress, long hair and strangely pointed sunglasses. Aileen turned the photo over. There was a typewritten note. "Faculty and staff delegation, Cape Kennedy, launch of Apollo 11 to the Moon, July 16, 1969, 6:32 a.m." and a list of names. The woman was one Diana Watling.

One last framed photo was from 1969, also in colour, Aileen recognised immediately—she had been there once herself—the observation deck of the Empire State Building in New York. Three men and one woman posed smiling for the camera, with skyscrapers in the background and in the far distance, a tiny green Statue of Liberty. A list on the back again identified the woman as Diana Watling.

Aileen looked at the image display on her camera. She compared the close-ups from 1897 with the photos from 1969. The faces of the mystery woman from the turn of the last century and Diana Watling appeared almost identical.

Aileen retrieved the photos from 1898 and 1901 and put them beside the two 1969 photos. It didn't seem possible. The women looked like identical twins. Each was short compared to the men. Both wore white dresses. The only difference was marked by the fashion of the day. The 1898 and 1901 photos had the kind of feathered hat a woman of the era was expected to wear. In the 1969 Apollo shot, she wore a headscarf. At the Empire State Building the same year she was bareheaded. Both women had wavy, black hair reaching just down to the chin line. What were pale grey eyes in the black and white images were bluish-green eyes in the colour photos. Those eyes, in the colour image, were framed in a face with a brownish complexion, although it was hard to tell due to the lighting. The bright Florida sun made the woman look as if she had a good suntan, while in the New York photo she appeared to perhaps be of North African descent.

"If this was astronomy," Aileen said, "this might be a pixel of light in the wrong place." She walked over to the desk and asked the archivist if there were any files on anyone named Watling.

The archivist entered the name into the computer catalogue and looked up. "There are two files. One is the personnel file on Diana Watling. That is restricted because she is still alive and as a former employee, receiving a pension. If you want to reach her you have to go through human resources, unless the Astronomy department has her contact information. There's a second file labelled 'Watling papers' with no date and open for research. I can retrieve them for you."

It took more than a half hour for the archive's clerk to deliver the thin grey "Watling papers" archival box, probably, Aileen mused, because it was buried in the farthest reaches of the basement, never consulted.

Aileen examined the meagre contents one by one. There was a folder with a few brown, crumbling, acid ravaged newspaper clippings, a tattered academic journal, a flimsy carbon copy of a letter and what appeared to be galley proofs of astronomical art, mostly galaxies.

Aileen picked up the musty journal. It had the mundane title "The Year's Work in English Studies Vol IV, 1923." She opened the cover and saw an elegantly inscribed note on the title page. "Dear Miss Rumilia Waeclingas. Thank you for the valuable information you provided to me…" Rumilia Waeclingas, another name to figure out? Aileen read the rest of the note. "I hope you will find my contribution to the history contained in this volume enlightening. Most sincerely, J. R. R. Tolkien."

"What?" Aileen looked around, realizing she had spoken aloud, but apparently no one had noticed. *Oh wow!* "This is almost like finding a new planet. Almost."

Aileen opened the journal. The paper with the unimaginative title "Philology General Works" was indeed by J. R. R. Tolkien. A Google check on her phone showed that in 1923 Tolkien was a young, barely known scholar—not yet at Oxford—but at the University of Leeds. The paper was a spin off on Tolkien's work on the Oxford English Dictionary.

In the paper, Aileen read how, in what later would become England, for thousands of years, the original hunter gatherers, and later bronze age and iron age Celts, used a track through the forests and moors that ran from the southeast coast to the northwest coast. The Roman legions paved the track into a road that still existed in the 21st century, now known as "Watling Street."

When Saxons invaded, the Celtic and Latin names were long forgotten.

Tolkien suggested the Saxons observed the road seemed to mirror the Milky Way in the night sky. They had named the road "the street of heavens"—"Waeclingas" which also meant the Milky way. Over the centuries, as language evolved, the Saxon word became Watling.

What was the connection between a woman named "Rumilia Waeclingas", the mystery woman "Diana Watling" and an ancient road in England?

Aileen opened the file with the clippings. One caught her eye immediately. *"ANOTHER UNIVERSE SEEN BY ASTRONOMER. Dr. Hubble Describes Mass of Celestial Bodies*

700,000 Light Years Away." Pencilled at the top of the clipping was *New York Times*, January 22, 1926. Aileen knew on that January day the universe had changed. Edwin Hubble, an astronomer at the Mt. Wilson Observatory in Pasadena had proved the faint concentrations of light, then called "spiral nebulae", were, in fact, distant galaxies. The *Times* story was the first report informing the public that the Earth, the Solar System and the Milky Way were no longer the centre of the universe.

The other clippings, in the years between 1926 and 1933, had nothing to do with astronomy. All were local and all about how good the river fishing was at place called Silver Heron Landing.

The final item was a carbon copy of a letter, dated December 1, 1937, to Rumilia Waeclingas, addressed not at the university but, for some reason, to a shop on Thorney Street in London, England.

The letter began, "Thank you for your must valued work as our computer for the Department of Astronomy."

What did that mean? Aileen wondered. Computer? A Goggle check showed at that time a "computer" was not a machine but highly skilled individual, usually a woman, who did complex mathematical calculations in fields like astronomy and physics, usually on behalf of male scholars.

The letter continued: "We fully understand your unfortunate resignation is due to the necessity of returning to the vital work you carried out during the latter half of the Great War and you are once again directly needed in view of the likelihood of a coming conflict."

Who was Rumilia Waeclingas? Aileen checked Google on her phone. The name did not register.

*

Aileen carefully made sure everything, but the journal, was put back in the proper boxes and returned the cart to the archivist at the reference desk. "You should see this," Aileen grinned, casually handing the open English Studies journal to the archivist.

Aileen chuckled as the archivist's eyes widened at the signature whispered, "Oh my god. Thank you, Aileen." The archivist quickly began to leaf through the old journal.

As Aileen walked out of the archives into the sunshine, she chuckled. "I bet that old box just got an upgrade."

*

Aileen spotted Rebekah Manent smoking a cigarette outside one of the portables used by the College of Astronomy. In her late fifties, with blond hair turning grey, Manent was the astronomy professor who had taught Aileen and other freshman the mathematics required in introductory courses.

Manent waved to Aileen, who waved back. Manent motioned Aileen to come over.

Manent had a double reputation. Among faculty, Rebekah Manent was a brilliant loner, always burying herself in her equations. For undergrads having trouble grappling with the maths, she would often patiently take them though an assignment until they grasped it.

"How's the campaign to save the Milky Way?" Manent asked. "I noticed you haven't updated the Facebook page in a couple of days."

"Been busy," Aileen replied. "Trying to figure out who actually created the mosaic. Any ideas?"

"Not a clue, " Manent replied. "Way before my time. I saw your Facebook posting on the date of the star field. Six thousand years ago. Is that right?"

"There were comments from a couple of the grad students that confirmed my figures," Aileen said. "It really is a big mystery."

"Have you tried looking into astroarchaeology?" Manent mused. "There might be a clue or two there. Ancient sites lined up with stars and all that sort of thing. Trouble is we don't have anyone interested in the subject in the faculty here. Pennington is promoting our astrophysics work, more likely to bring in grants than having someone trying to figure out if some old stone is aligned with Mars."

"Mars. Wait. I thought this was about stars?" Aileen said.

"That's a joke," Manent chuckled. "It comes from an old song. Before your time Aileen. Back even before I was in university. I have an old friend from grad school I can check with if you like."

"Yes, please." Aileen thought for a moment. "Did you know a Diana Watling?'

"Watling?" Manent replied. "Yes, Watling was the department's staff artist and administrative assistant starting sometime in the 50s."

"What was she like?" Aileen asked.

"I didn't have much contact with her since what I do is mathematics."

Manent blew smoke into the air, away from Aileen. "The one thing I remember about Diana was her eyes. She had the most amazing green eyes. Eyes that would look right through you. Does this have anything to do with the mosaic? Thought it was nineteenth century."

"I am still trying to figure out who did the mosaic," Aileen replied. "I don't know if this Diana Watling had anything to do with it, but she might. That's part of the mystery."

"Astroarchaeology will be a better bet," Manent smiled, "than a staff artist from the nineties."

"So, what happened to Diana Watling?" Aileen asked.

Manent shrugged. "I joined the faculty in 1995 and Watling was retired in 2000. In those days, the support staff serfs all had to take mandatory retirement when they turned 65. Unlike faculty, of course, who, if they want to, can stay on until they either drop dead or their brains no longer function properly."

Manent took a drag on her cigarette. "I'm taking early retirement the day I turn 60. This place is no longer a community of scholars. It's a bean counting corporation."

Aileen replied. "Any idea where Diana Watling is now?"

"My memory is hazy, but I think she said something about going fishing."

*

Back in her apartment, Aileen did a computer search on Diana Watling. Images appeared, mostly artistic concepts of galaxies and nebulae in astronomical publications, both public and scholarly, before 1990 when the Hubble Space Telescope was launched to capture actual images. Diana's stellar art was heavily featured, often pirated by online astro art fans. Aileen found a brief biography on a fan website. It said Diana Watling was born in 1935 and joined the university first as an admissions clerk in 1956. By 1958, Watling was on the staff of the astronomy department as a combination secretary and artist and became a full time artist beginning in 1967. She retired in 2000 at 65. The fans asked where Diana Watling was now and if she was still working on her art.

Aileen's renewed search on both the internet and academic databases on Rumilia Waeclingas again came up with nothing. And who was the mysterious Brigid? How was she related to Diana Watling? How did this Rumilia fit into the picture?

Aileen ordered pizza and kept working. She came up with the idea of searching the names of the faculty in 1897 and "Brigid." Nothing. Knowing the uncertainty of computer searches, she tried an alternate spelling—"Brigit." Aileen got a hit, then another and another. The references came from the acknowledgements in long forgotten but recently scanned astronomy textbooks. All thanked "Brigit Nuada, the typewriter."

Another strange usage, Aileen thought. Google revealed that at the turn of the last century, a typewriter was not the instrument but a person during the brief time being a typist was a specialized technical profession before the rise of the secretarial pool.

Aileen knew, from her freshman course on ancient mythology, that Brigit, or Brigid, was a Celtic goddess mostly revered in Ireland. Nuada was an Irish god. Diana was the goddess of the hunt in ancient Rome. Aileen searched Rumilia and found according to Plutarch, she was the Roman goddess who protected and suckled babies. The Romans would pour milk into the River Tiber as a sacrifice.

There must be some connection with mythological goddesses and gods. *What did it mean?* Aileen wondered.

"I am a scientist," she said out loud. "Not a humanities major."

Before Aileen went to bed, she dashed off an email inquiry

to the archives, copied to Gabriel Pennington and asked for any information on Brigit or Brigid Nuada. She also asked Pennington to ask Human Resources for contact information for Diana Watling.

Aileen dreamt of stars, nebulae, galaxies, and the Milky Way, not at all unusual for an astronomy student. Something still bothered her. She wasn't sure what.

The emails were waiting when she got up. The archives had no records of a Brigit Nuada. Pennington had nothing to add on Nuada and waited for a response from HR.

Aileen checked Wikipedia for Thorney Street, the last address for Rumilia Waeclingas on the old letter in the archives.

"Yeah. Now I'm getting somewhere. Watling Street is also Thorney Street," Aileen shouted to the screen as she fist pumped toward the ceiling.

The online references revealed the ancient track, later called Watling Street, had reached the River Thames at a small mid-river eyot. The tiny island, little more than an bramble-covered overgrown sandbar, created a ford where travelers could cross the Thames long before the Romans built the first bridges in the city they called Londinium. A few hundred years later, Londoners would call it Thorney Island.

As London grew and the banks of the Thames expanded, the island became part of the mainland. The old ford became Thorney Street; a road that followed the ancient route of Watling Street.

Aileen pulled up a Google satellite map and the Google street view of London. Thorney Street was at the rear of a large neoclassical office called Thames House. More online research showed how in 1937, Thames House was known as the head office for a big industrial corporation. The building had a secret. The upper floors of Thames House were the headquarters for the Security Service as Great Britain prepared for war with Germany. Aileen found an online spy blog that said a news-agent and tobacco shop, also on Thorney Street, was a spy's mail drop for personal letters that did not say the more obvious Thames House.

"Curious and curiouser," Aileen muttered. "Rumilia leaves the university in 1937 to do vital work with a spy agency that was located on what in ancient time was Watling Street, which was also the Milky Way. Does this have anything to do with the mosaic? Again, why are the women named for goddesses?"

Aileen kept checking Wikipedia. Thames House had been renovated in the 1990s, and now was once again the headquarters of the security service now known as MI5. The back entrance for the spy agency was still on Thorney Street.

*

An answer came with a beep of a text on her phone.

No phone/email Diana Watling. Pension direct deposited account. Mail address is Box M31, Silver Heron Landing. Hope this helps with the mosaic. GP.

*

After all, M31 was the original catalogue designation for the Andromeda galaxy.

"Of course, Pennington's wondering about the Milky Way. So am I," Aileen said aloud. "Now where is Silver Heron Landing?"

Silver Heron Landing wasn't on Google Earth—-almost everything in the world could be found on Google Earth. She kept searching and eventually found a passing mention to the landing on a fishing blog. "One of the best kept secrets," the blog said. "Which is why we're not going to tell you where it is."

"You're a big help," Aileen said, then she thought, *If not fishing, what about bird watching? My brother's a bird watcher.*

With a name like Silver Heron bird watchers have to be interested and they chart locations around the world.

Silver Heron Landing did appear in a 2003 entry in an almost dormant bird watching blog. The link to an enhanced Google Map showed a crossroads along a riverbank about 200 kilometres from the campus. It was just a couple of streets on the outskirts of a small township called New Dorchester—the reason why Silver Heron Landing didn't come up on standard searches.

Aileen zoomed in on the satellite image. Silver Heron

Landing had a couple of dozen houses. There appeared to be boats anchored along the riverbank. Icons on the map revealed the crossroads hamlet had two bed and breakfasts, a coffee shop, a posh sea food restaurant and a hardware/tackle shop/gas station. Aileen clicked the links for the websites of the B&Bs, found a reasonable price for a tiny third floor room, made a reservation for the coming weekend and called her brother and asked to borrow his car.

*

The early morning sun was bright and warm, becoming hot, as it streamed through the small window in her apartment. It was probably the last good weekend of the fall and a great day for a drive into the country.

As Aileen finished breakfast, her phone beeped. "Now that's interesting," she said as she read the email.

> *From: Rebekah Manent*
> *To: Aileen Casasaya*
> *Subject: Ancient stars and Neolithic gods 3.0*
>
> *After our chat, I checked with an old friend of mine from grad school days. The new field of computer assisted astroarchaeology is upsetting a lot of old ideas. Anyone, just like you did, can use software to see how the skies looked thousands of years ago. When I was a young lecturer you had to book expensive off time in a planetarium to even try to do what you can now do in minutes. Old academic silos are breaking down, with the archaeologists collaborating with linguists of Proto-Indo-European (they call it PIE) and even what he called Pre-Proto-Indo European languages. There's currently a raging debate over an old idea that went out of fashion for a while that the primeval gods in most Eurasian cultures are folk memory of the deities of the mid to late Neolithic, adapted and changed through the centuries to fit the local culture. One idea the PIE scholars keep repeating is the various forms of the Iron Age words or names for gods, goddesses and even rivers, Don, Dee, Dhainu, Dagdae or Dānu, even Diana, could all have a root in the forgotten name of an*

original Neolithic goddess. It's all quite esoteric about the evolution of linguistics, which I know nothing about. Hope this helps. Good luck in your quest.
RM

*

As Aileen left the city, the traffic bunched up on the freeway, probably heading out to enjoy the last warm weekend. At one point, she was boxed in a parade of rumbling tractor trailers, and she breathed in the distinct whiff of diesel fumes. *How long before I get to the turnoff for Silver Heron Landing*, she thought as the car crawled behind a big semi.

After a quarter hour, the traffic eased. The last high rise apartments of the city gave way to lines of trees starting to turn to scarlet, orange and gold. "Now can I relax," Aileen sighed.

It was a smooth drive until Aileen reached the exit and turned off onto a two lane regional road. She drove though a countryside of farmers' fields, old houses and roads lined with oak and maples.

After an hour, the car's GPS told Aileen to turn off on to a narrow road. She stopped at the side of the intersection to check her real world bearings and saw a small directional sign "Silver Heron Landing 21 KM."

The road was paved, how long ago was anyone's guess. The faded grey "blacktop" was cracked every hundred metres and there were the occasional potholes. "They really don't want a lot of visitors," Aileen said out loud.

Aileen passed herds of cows in green fields with large round yellow ochre hay bales scattered about. Eventually, the road curved left along a riverbank with stretches of green reeds. The river sparkled in the noon sun. Mallard ducks floated leisurely along with the current.

The road turned away from the river into a grove of oak trees which soon opened up, to the village ahead. The river was on her right, and across the road from a dock she saw the shops that made up the "main street". A century old brick building featured a slick hardware chain franchise LED logo sign. The store had a modern extension, with gas pumps and a mechanic's shop. Beside it was the River Raft Cafe, older style houses and the white Art Deco style Silver Heron's Catch Seafood restaurant.

The bed and breakfast was up a hilly side street, another Victorian style house, red brick with off white gingerbread trim. At the front door, there was an envelope with her name containing a set of keys and a friendly invitation to settle into the third floor room she had rented.

Aileen left her computer and roller bag on the queen size, duvet-covered bed, which took up about three quarters of the room. Hungry, Aileen decided to walk down to the River Raft Café for lunch and ask if anyone knew Diana Watling. She took her small blue backpack holding her camera, phone, a notebook and the printout of the Google satellite map.

*

There did not seem to be anyone around the village as she walked back down to the cafe. *Diana Watling*, Aileen thought, *retired at 65 in 2000, so in 2019, it shouldn't be too hard to spot an eighty-four-year-old white-haired lady.*

If the River Raft Cafe was Victorian on the outside, inside it was modern cafe chic with sandblasted brick, sofas and easy chairs. A blackboard menu, a couple of dozen jars of various coffees, more for teas, an expensive espresso machine and a 1950s diner style glass front fridge for soft drinks lined the serving area.

The server behind the glass counter was a cute, sandy haired teenage boy, perhaps eighteen, happy to finally see a customer. He suggested Aileen might like the salmon wrap. "Nice and fresh. Not canned," the boy said.

"I'll have a salmon wrap as well," a woman's voice came from behind Aileen.

Aileen turned around and found herself looking into a dark face that framed fierce blue-green eyes. The woman stood a bit shorter than Aileen's under-average height. She appeared to be in her late twenties, wore white jeans, a white shirt and a white hoodie.

"Are you a Watling?" Aileen blurted. *The woman couldn't be*

Diana. She looked identical to the women in the photographs of Diana Watling in 1969 and Brigit Nuada in 1898.

The boy ignored his customers, focusing on building two fresh salmon wraps.

The woman's eyes widened for a millisecond then she smiled and nodded. "I knew that someone would come here once they found the Milky Way Mosaic."

"Are you a Watling?" Aileen asked again. "Are you a relative of Diana Watling?"

"Perhaps," she smiled.

"Perhaps?" *Strange,* Aileen thought. In the next breath, impatient, Aileen asked. "Do you know about the Milky Way Mosaic?"

"I saw the mosaic on the news," the woman said. "Then I found there's a Facebook page that's trying to save it from the wrecking ball. We should talk, but wait until Darren has our wraps ready.'

"That's me," Aileen said smiled. "I created the Facebook page."

"Patience child. It's a rather long story. We're not far from my house, just a five minute walk.'

Darren handed the two wraps over the counter.

"We can chat over lunch in my kitchen. Let me get this for you," the woman said. She paid for the wraps. "To thank you for creating the Facebook page and for your efforts. If you'd please put the wraps in your backpack. Then, if you like, we can go back to my house and talk privately."

Why is someone who is probably about five years older than me calling me "child"? Aileen wondered. *What does she mean by "perhaps"? She's either the relative of Diana Watling or not. Unless this is one of those weird families that you see on the DNA genealogy shows.*

The woman in white guided Aileen along the road as it followed the river. Aileen wanted to ask her more. Then she heard the word "patience" in her head. She decided to stay silent.

They turned onto a path that snaked through a grove of oak trees. Leaves turning red, orange and brown, flanked with long green and yellow tufted grass. A warm breeze rustled the leaves. Far off, Aileen heard the distant quacking of the ducks in the river.

"We haven't even introduced ourselves," Aileen said, walking beside the woman. "I am Aileen Casasaya, and you are?"

"You can all me Diana," she replied with a motherly smile that encouraged Aileen to relax. "Yes, I know the young are always impatient. It's easier to understand things over a cup of tea. Welcome to my home, Aileen Casasaya."

Through a gap in the trees, Aileen glimpsed a peaked roof with dark wooden shingles. Diana led Aileen into a clearing. The house was two stories, a perfect circle built of polished wood.

"Wow. That's…" Aileen said. "I don't know what it is. In some ways it looks like a Mongolian Yurt," adding to herself, *and something from the imagination of a set designer for a fantasy movie.*

Diana turned and smiled. "I designed it myself," she said,. "from a time when I was much younger."

The property was surrounded by a stone wall, covered in generations of grey or brown fungi and bright green moss. The wall on the river side behind the house stood much higher, probably as a flood barrier.

At the wall, Diana waved her hand. The wooden gate opened.

It took Aileen a second to realize what she had just seen.

"No one comes in without my leave," Diana said. "Anyone who tries can never pass the wall nor open the gate. You are welcome, child."

"How did you do that?" Aileen asked softly. "Why me?"

"Why you?" Diana chuckled. "Have you ever read Sherlock Holmes?"

"No. I've seen the TV shows," Aileen replied, looking back as the gate closed by itself.

They walked down a moss covered dark grey shale flagstone path toward the strange house.

"You should read the Holmes stories. 'You see, but you do not observe.' *Sherlock Holmes: A Scandal in Bohemia.* I thought astronomers were observers. You're wearing the College of Astronomy sweatshirt. I knew someone would come about the Milky Way. You have great talent, child, otherwise you would not have found me in Silver Heron Landing. You also have much to learn."

"This can't… but you did it." Aileen stammered. "How can you keep people out?" A stray thought came into Aileen's head, from the times she'd heard people say something on the evening news, usually about some startling event: "I thought it was a movie?" Aileen's right brain replied, "I'm a scientist, there has to be a logical explanation."

"Come into the house," the woman replied. "Then we can talk."

Diana led Aileen through a side door opening into a kitchen where a wooden table and four chairs carved with intricate spiral designs sat. One polished wooden cabinet was filled with fine china. Aileen thought would be a hit on an Antiques Roadshow. A shiny stainless steel stove, microwave and fridge looked as if they had just come from a showroom.

"Let me put the kettle on," the woman said. "Have a seat."

The kettle was sparkling clear glass and shiny metal, with a row of LED lights at its base. Aileen kept standing, looking around the kitchen.

"To know all," Diana said as she filled the kettle and plugged it in. "We must do some astronomical observation."

Observation on a sunny afternoon? Aileen wondered.

Diana opened a drawer at the bottom of the cabinet and took out a black wooden tray. She then opened the door and picked out a teapot, sugar bowl and a small jug. The service was clearly exceptionally fine and probably incredibly old, made with translucent greyish-green porcelain. Aileen guessed it was Chinese.

Diana looked back over her shoulder toward Aileen as she arranged the china on the tray. "Do sit down child, you must be tired after that long drive."

Aileen sat down at the kitchenette.

Diana added two teacups to the tray. "Aileen, I did check out your Facebook profile as the admin of the Save the Milky Way group," Diana said softly, as she arranged the tea service on the tray. "I am somewhat remiss on social media, too much idiocy, nonsense. Too new…"

"New," Aileen frowned. "You can't be more than four or

five years older than I am. We all grew up with it."

"Facebook, Twitter and the rest think they're new." Diana shook her head. "No different than nasty village gossip, drunken arguments in taverns and lies from the politicians or the courts of kings, emperors, popes and caliphs."

The kettle whistled. "Don't forget to take the wraps out your backpack," Diana said as she unplugged the kettle. She poured the hot water into the teapot.

Aileen took off her backpack, put it on the table and took out the two wraps. Part of her subconscious recognized an anomaly. "That's not an old style whistling kettle like my grand-mother had," Aileen pointed to the kettle. "It's got a LED indicator and so the sound must be digital. Yet you say you're new to social media. We all grew up with computers and mobile phones."

Diana brought the tray over to the table and sat down opposite to Aileen.

"I am an old, old hand at computers. It's just that I am way too old to TikTok." Diana grinned. "I will tell you my story. Then I will help you save the Milky Way Mosaic.

"You have many questions, child. I will answer them." Diana took a sip of the tea. "I can tell it from your face, something you already suspect. I *am* Diana Watling and Rumilia Waeclingas and Brigit Nuada and many, many more."

Aileen stared at her teacup, silent for a moment. "How can this be?" She shook her head. "It doesn't make sense."

"It does make sense, Aileen, if you ask yourself one question," Diana replied. "As a scientist, ask yourself how the Milky Way mosaic was created a century ago, without the aid of modern computers?"

Think, Aileen said to herself.

"Ask yourself why it was created that way in 1897?" Diana pressed.

The afternoon sun streamed through the window. Aileen heard the far off quacking of ducks on the river. Almost outside the window came the distinctive high pitched "ok-a-lee" call of a red wing blackbird.

Aileen sighed. "The only explanation that I can think of is the person who created the mosaic was either a mad genius or the person who actually saw the constellation Cassiopeia on the arc of the galaxy over the horizon six thousand years ago, but that's impossible."

Aileen looked into Diana's greenish eyes and for the first time, Aileen wondered if she was dealing with someone who was either nuts or a con-woman. *Was I too eager to follow that clue from the file?* she wondered. She shook her head. "I am not convinced. As for why you or anyone could or would do it. I have no idea."

It was if Diana could read Aileen's thoughts.

"You are a scientist, Aileen. I have known some of the world's greatest scientists. That means you require proof. Ease your scepticism for a moment and consider a hypothesis that is not popular in this secular age. That I am a goddess."

"A goddess?"

"As I said, have patience. And courage," Diana replied. "In the next few minutes, you may be frightened, but I assure you there is nothing to fear. I wanted to wait until after lunch, but it seems we must do this now. Ready? Please stand up."

"Ready for what?" Aileen asked as she stood.

"Take my hand," Diana said.

Aileen grasped Diana's hand.

In an instant, everything went dark. Aileen felt a breeze across her face. She looked up. It was a black night. Stars sparkled.

For a second she was terrified. A moment later, she was fascinated. She had never seen the stars as she saw now.

She let go of Diana's hand and walked a few steps ahead, staring at the gorgeous, brilliant shining heavens.

The Milky Way arched with hundreds of thousands of white, blue and yellowish lights. Aileen and Diana stood in waist high plants and scrub bushes. Aileen could see the silhouettes of a handful of trees scattered here and there blocking out the stars. A black horizon that also cut off the stars was distant hills. The air smelt clean and clear, with hints of fragrant flowers.

There was just enough reflected star light for Aileen to see Diana, who still wore her twenty-first century white jeans, white shirt and white hoodie. In the darkness, she appeared a grey ghostly figure. A cool breeze stirred the bushes. Aileen felt a chill go up and down her spine. She was torn. Half of her felt this was an opportunity no other twenty first century astronomer could have experienced. The other half of her was worried, even frightened.

"Where are we?" Aileen asked.

"The question is, 'when are we?' Do you have any ideas? Without using a computer to help?" Diana asked.

"I'm not sure," Aileen said. Her mind raced. She tried to figure out the alignment of the stars. "The sky is so clear. I've never seen it like this."

"No light pollution," Diana replied. "In your time, except in the middle of the ocean or a deep desert, wherever you are, there is always residual light pollution."

"How did we get here?" Aileen wondered aloud.

"We came here because, as I told you, I am a goddess. I want to show you where and when I was first worshipped." Diana's voice sounded a little bitter. "Aileen, what do you see?"

"The arc of the Milky Way is closer to the horizon than it is in the twenty-first century," Aileen replied. "So that is a case of the precision of the equinoxes over thousands of years."

"When are we?" Diana asked.

"That would also depend on where are we?" Aileen replied. Her scientific training overcame her bewilderment. "The constellations rise at different times in different places," she stammered.

"We are in what today is called Anatolia, a valley in Turkey."

"What do you mean?" Aileen asked, looking up at the sky. Aileen braced her legs, unconsciously making sure she had a solid footing on the soft soil in that strange, unexpected land-scape.

"What is that constellation?'

Aileen's right brain was both frightened and fascinated. Her left brain was back in class—although this was like no class she had ever attended, trying to figure out Diana's question.

"Cassiopeia, of course," Aileen said declared. "Oh, now I get it. Oh wow," she muttered."Oh shit. Is this what I saw in the mosaic?"

"It wasn't called Cassiopeia then," Diana said. "Do you have any idea what year it is?"

Aileen gasped. "Must be a few thousand years ago." She looked up the stars, tried to figure out a clue. Her mind wasn't working properly.

"It is nine thousand five hundred years from your time," Diana replied.

Aileen wondered were there astronomers in this time? *Wow*, she thought, *of course, not even astrologers—too early for that—but probably wise women and shamans who tracked the path of the stars.*

The breeze sprang up again. Aileen thought she heard voices. She wasn't sure.

Her number crunching brain cells kicked in. She looked at the horizon again, which prompted a question. "It's earlier than the mosaic. Am I right?"

The voices sounded like a chant, to Aileen's mind, very faint and distant, as if she were listening to music on a phone with a drained battery.

"You are right, Aileen." Diana replied. Her voice was soft but firm. "Do you know why?" The wind still carried the faint chanting.

"Of course. Precision of the equinoxes, the twenty-six thousand year cycle of Earth's rotation around the sun," Aileen replied as if she was in a seminar. Startled, Aileen grabbed her shoulder. "I just realized… my backpack! It's on a chair back in your kitchen. It's got my phone and my camera."

"Why do you need your camera? Is something wrong?" Diana asked quizzed.

"I am not sure this is real," Aileen said. "If I had my camera, I could prove to myself and others what I am seeing."

"It is real. I have brought you back in time," Diana replied.

"How do I prove it?" Aileen asked demanded.

Diana reached out and put her hands on Aileen's shoulders. As Diana's hands touched, Aileen's anxiety began to fade.

"There is nothing to fear," Diana whispered. "You are under my protection. No harm will come to you. As for proof, my child, this adventure is for you and me alone. This is the beginning time of the worship of the goddess of the Milky Way. In a few minutes, I will take you to the time of the mosaic.

"The lessons you learn in our journey will be the foundation of your future."

"Future? I'm a scientist," Aileen shook her head. "Gods and goddesses are just fairy tales. I'm still not sure this real. You could have drugged my tea. Oh shit. What am I saying? I just don't know what's happening."

"I am not a fairy tale," Diana snapped. "I am not going to turn into a golden cloud or become a giant to prove to you I am a goddess. Believe me or not, by the end of this journey, you will know who I really am."

Out of the corner of Aileen's eye, dark shadows moved a few metres from where they stood. She turned, remembering to keep a tight hold of Diana's hand. The breeze carried a faint lowing sound. Aileen then could make out a herd of cows. She gave a sigh of relief. The herd turned toward them.

"Do not fear, Aileen," Diana said. "We are but shadows here. We have no substance. The cattle cannot see us."

Aileen thought the cows were there and not there, one moment solid, the next moment as Diana had said "shadows."

The herd must have sensed something. It parted, passing some distance either side from where Diana and Aileen stood. Many of the bovines were dark against dark, but some must have been white for they appeared as ghostly pale shadows. Aileen felt a twinge in her stomach. She grasped Diana's hand harder. The feeling of anxiety faded.

"Now child, listen and learn. This is a rich land with flowing rivers. Those you hear follow the herds. The herds follow the rivers. Times are changing. The chanting comes from the bank of a river not far from here, where the people greet the dawn.

"The people of this land have domesticated the wild goats and sheep that feast on this land. They have learned from those goats and sheep that their milk gives sustenance to children. The cows we see are still somewhat wild but are on the cusp of true domestication. The people have captured a few of the more docile cows for milk. Keep holding my hand. Shall we gather at the river? "

"What?" Aileen asked.

"You don't get the reference?" Diana led Aileen through the grass, as they followed the herd. In the crisp, clear air, the lowing mixed with the chanting, now closer.

"Some sort of song? I must have heard it somewhere,

perhaps in a movie?" Aileen asked.

"It's a Christian hymn, from your time, written back in 1864," Diana whispered. "At the time I built Milky Way Mosaic, 1897, I sang in a church choir in the university chapel. The composer and the choir never guessed, but gathering by a river to worship is ancient, more ancient than even this time. Here at this river, it was I, the goddess of the river, the goddess of cow's milk, and the goddess of the Milky Way who was worshipped."

Diana sang softly, "On the margin of the river/washing up its silver spray/we will talk and worship ever/all the happy golden day."

Dark figures appeared before them, a crowd standing along the edge of a river.

"Remember," Diana whispered. "We are but shadows. These people cannot see, hear or feel us. To us, they too are shadows, an echo in time. Now, look to the east."

The band of the Milky Way sparkled in the sky as it rose between two distant hills. Cassiopeia's bright stars formed the two well known triangles.

"Look at the horizon," Diana said. "What do you see?"

Aileen thought for a moment. "That's the Southern Cross, also known as Crux, just rising above the horizon."

The sky along the horizon was tinted with by a light grey.

"Why are we here? What are we seeing?" she asked Diana.

"This is the morning of Midwinter, the solstice, the shortest day in the northern hemisphere," Diana replied. "The world is reborn. The year begins again. Now, look carefully and see why we are here."

The sky between the two hills was now faint bright blue-grey.

"I am not sure," Aileen said. "What am I supposed to see?"

"The rebirth of the sun, of course," Diana sounded a bit exasperated. "In this time, in this place, this where I, a goddess, gives birth to the sun, also a goddess, my daughter.

"It is perhaps, not your fault," Diana's voice became softer. "The idea of the Southern Cross has created a bias in your mind. What else can that constellation be?"

"I'm not sure," Aileen was hesitant.

"For these people, and other ancients, it wasn't a cross, but a diamond, or lozenge." Again, there was a hint of regret in Diana's voice.

"That's possible," Aileen said.

"Look now." Diana's voice was an irresistible command.

A bright, almost blinding moment illuminated the brilliant white yellow rim of the sun edging above the horizon between the two hills. The people at the riverbank bowed toward the horizon.

"At this moment," Diana said. "I am giving birth to the sun goddess from my womb. As the newborn sun travels in the heavens, she drinks the milk of the Milky Way from the two breasts of what in your time is called Cassiopeia."

From the crowd, a woman walked toward the river. Aileen guessed she was the priestess. There was just enough light for Aileen to see that the priestess was pouring milk into the sparkling river water.

In moments, the sun was above the horizon.

"What do you notice about those hills?" Diana asked.

"I'm not sure," Aileen replied. "They appear to be rather steep."

"Look closely and you will see the shape of the hills resemble the horns of the cow. You see my triple aspect, goddess of cow and milk, of rivers and the Milky Way."

The people on the riverbank began to sing.

"Come with me, Aileen." Diana said, pulling Aileen's hand.

The herd was not far off, some munching on grass, other cows looking toward the humans at the river. "What was it she said?" Aileen thought to herself. "Oh yes, almost domesticated."

The morning sun ascended higher. Aileen could see the two white cows at the front of the herd. She glanced back. Diana was right. The crescent of the hills matched the curve of the horns.

"Before we go, watch," Diana commanded. "Remember we are shadows." She led Aileen up beside the two white cows then raised her free hand in a blessing.

"These sisters are the foundation of many to come," Diana said. "I blessed this herd in this time in another year. But to show you my power over the centuries, I tell you now that thanks to my blessing, these cows will be tamer than the others, will produce more milk and better calves."

They turned and Diana led Aileen away from the herd and the river. "Of course," she said. "These are not the only cows that I—to use your modern word—enhanced over the centuries. I am, as you know now, a goddess.

"We must leave this place and go to the time and place when I was at the height of honour," Diana said. "We travel forward in time and to another place. Keep holding my hand."

The morning light faded. Once again, the sky was dark.

*

"We are now in the midst of the Great Sea of Grass. The steppe that stretches across Europe and Asia to what will be, thousands of years from now, the Great Wall of China," Diana said. "The time is now about 5,000 BCE in what will, in your day, be Crimea.

"What do you notice about the Milky Way?" Diana asked.

"That's amazing." Aileen said. The curve of the galaxy, the arc of the Milky Way, was even closer to the horizon than it had been in Anatolia. The tall grass swayed in a breeze, grey, in the starlight. The grass appeared to caress the Milky Way.

"In the twinkling stars and the curvature of the galaxy, it is I dancing the erotic seduction of the Earth God. Yes, to these people the Earth was male. Here, the sky goddess lies with the Earth God."

Women's voices carried on the wind.

"Not far from here is what in your time is called the Don River. The people here named the river in my honour. Dhainu, in what your scholars call Proto Indo European. It means the giver of milk, milk from a woman's breasts, milk from a cow, and from the Milky Way. As those nomads, the ones you call Indo European traveled, they named other rivers for me: the Dnieper, the Danube and more. Later as language changed, and there were great migrations, in old Ireland there was river called Bóand, the white cow. In your time it is the Boyne. The Milky Way, the river of stars, is their principle goddess in this time.

"Here they called me 'Daunarnayht,' a name that is

unpronounceable to you.

"One more place to visit."

"Wait a minute," Aileen said. She tightened her grip on Diana's hand. "Is this what we see in the mosaic?"

"Not quite," Diana replied. "The mosaic portrays how the sky would have looked in the location of your university at a time I chose when it looked its best. Now we must go."

*

The warmth of the steppes changed abruptly to the chill of winter. Aileen shivered. They were now in the centre of a ring of standing stones on the shore of an ocean. The night was crystal clear. Icy white snow crunched under their feet and sparkled on the sharp peaks of the upright stones. Reflections of the brightest stars danced on the ocean waves.

"The ancient Welsh name for Cassiopeia was 'Llys Dôn' later called the 'Court of Dôn or Danu', meaning 'she who gives milk' that breast-shaped constellation in the Milky Way," Diana whispered. "This is the last time I was worshipped as a goddess, here on the coast of Britain, four thousand years ago, 2,000 BCE as the galaxy rises between those two stones."

Diana whispered, "The people who came after, the Celts remembered me when the ancient Welsh name for Cassiopeia was 'Llys Dôn' later called the 'Court of Dôn or Danu', meaning 'she who gives milk' that breast-shaped constellation in the Milky Way,"

A chilly sea breeze blew off the ocean.

Diana sounded sad, wistful. "You see the galaxy is now reaching higher into the sky. Keep holding my hand. Now, let's go home."

*

In an instant, bright light made Aileen blink. The chill melted to warmth of a sunny autumn afternoon. Back in the kitchen at Silver Heron Landing, Aileen looked around and, exhausted, sank into one of the chairs. She wondered what came next. She stared at the tea pot and the unopened wraps lying on the table.

"In this time, it is as if we never left the house. The time we spent in the past, are but microseconds here." Diana sat down, moved her chair closer so as to put her hand on Aileen's. Calming warmth flowed from Diana to Aileen.

"The tea is warm. It will refresh you," Diana said softly. Suddenly Diana looked up over the edge of her teacup. "And then... On I should have asked. You're drinking your tea black. Do you want milk? I forgot to fill the jug."

"Oh yes please," Aileen replied.

Diana walked over to the fridge. "You want proof of my story?" Diana took out a carton of milk.

"The proof of my story is in milk," Diana said. She walked back to the table. "The mutated gene for adult lactose tolerance probably began someplace in Africa as long ago as 20,000 years ago. For thousands of years, it was rare."

Diana stood at the edge of the table and poured the milk, a shiny white crescent flowing into the jug.

"How did you do that?" Aileen asked.

"I am a goddess," Diana chuckled. "In Anatolia, at the time as the sun rose from my womb, the gene that allowed adults to digest milk slowly began to spread in the population."

Diana sat back down. "About seven thousand years ago—at the time when I was worshipped on the Great Sea of Grass from the Don to the Danube and beyond, the lactose tolerant gene that you and many of the people of the planet have became dominant in the population."

"That is your proof, Aileen," Diana said firmly, as she raised the fine china cup, then sipped her tea.

Aileen poured the milk into her teacup and stared as the dark brown tea dissolved to a light tan colour.

"Drink your tea, child, and eat your wrap. You're still jumpy. Relax. I will tell you my story. And know this; I will help you save the Milky Way mosaic that—yes—I created.

"If I remember my mythology course," Aileen mused. "Are you a goddess or the Great Goddess?"

"As social media says, or at least one of the few things I noticed on social media, it's complicated," Diana chuckled. "First, know you humans always create gods and goddesses in their own images. At one time I was one great goddess, the goddess of the heavens spanning the continents.

"Times changed. Beliefs changed." Diana shrugged. "I am a goddess. You have seen my powers. I am and always have been one of many. You know how many goddesses are listed on Wikipedia? I looked it up. There are hundreds."

Aileen's stomach growled. She realized whipping back and forth in time had made her hungry. She took a bite of the salmon wrap. "What happened?" she asked between mouthfuls.

"Patience." Diana took a bite of her wrap and then a sip of tea. 'If we were talking in twenty-first century terms, it was a case of the goddess and mandatory retirement." She chuckled. Then the blue green eyes became sad. "Time changed. The stars aligned differently as you should know."

"The precision of the equinoxes. Not just ecliptic but other constellations,' Aileen nodded.

"The sun no longer rose in the womb of the galaxy the way it had in Anatolia or on the Great Sea of Grass or in the last years the British Isles." Diana replied. "Think, Aileen, the foragers of the savannah and the nomads of the steppes followed the herds, whether wild, semi-wild, or domestic, always traveling. They followed the stars. They searched for rivers. The guide was the Milky Way, the river of the heavens. The road of heavens came later once there were roads."

"Like Watling Street, named by the Saxons after the Milky Way?" Aileen said.

"Yes, like Watling Street." Diana nodded sagely. "When people domesticated sheep and goats, milk flowed from their teats, just as it appeared that starry milk flowed from the breasts of what became Llys Dôn or Cassiopeia. The goddess led them—via the stars—to sweet river water. She blessed and protected the herds and provided the nourishment of milk."

Diana sipped her tea. "Do you remember what Homer called Hector?"

Aileen thought for a moment. "'The tamer of horses.'"

"On the steppes, archaeological evidence has shown both women and men tamed horses. That is the origin of the legend of the Amazons.

"In other lands, taming of horses became a man's job. Why? The ewe, the she-goat and later the cow were more valuable than the bull, kept for milk as well as meat and hides. Most bull calves were slaughtered for meat and hide and bones." Diana said.

"Horse herds are different. The stallion leads, not the matriarch like many other species. Men saw that when they tamed horses for herding or traveling. From India to Ireland, the great legends of cattle raids survive to this day. Men cannot conduct a cattle raid without taming the horse.

"Later, farmers came to dominate over the herders. It is legend as old as time, like Cain and Abel in the monotheistic holy books." Diana said. "That has now been confirmed not just with the changes in language, but in the evidence of DNA haplogroups that track human migration. Earth provided. The beliefs of the hunters and herders faded. With the rise of farming and civilizations, an already existing belief that Earth was the Mother became dominant. The sky became the Father. The stars aligned against me.

"I faced what today is mandatory retirement. I was not totally forgotten in my so-called retirement. My legend can be found in the tales of primal goddesses, gods and titans. The dance of the sky and the earth legend can be found in the lost memories of creation tales. The first religious texts from Sumer written on clay tablets, 3,500 BCE. That is four thousand years after the moment we stood on the riverbank. Your archaeologists have recently found, in what is today Russia, the first evidence of bit wear in the skulls of horses, 4,500 BCE, a thousand years before the Sumer tablets.

"Think about this," Diana said. "There are four thousand years, between the time I showed you in Anatolia, the birth of the sun in the womb of the galaxy and the first tablets of Sumer. Four thousand years is the same time between today in the 21st century and the building of Stonehenge. That is how languages, beliefs, and goddesses and gods change over time.

"I was a mysterious goddess. My name became one of the pantheons, like Nut the night sky of Egypt. In ancient Egypt, Nut is always portrayed as a starry arc of night sky. There was the night goddess Nyx in Greece. More tea?"

"Yes, thanks," Aileen replied

Diana got up, brought the teapot over, and poured the tea into Aileen's cup. She put the teapot on the table. For the first time Aileen could look at it closely. The teapot had an engraved intricate abstract pattern, possibly a dragon. Like the teapot, the cups were a translucent grey green glaze that reflected the sun light streaming through the kitchen window.

"How old is that teapot? How long have you had it?" Aileen asked.

Diana sat back down and moved her chair closer to Aileen.

"Haven't thought of that in years," she replied. "It's Tang dynasty, Yue ware. I bought the set probably about fourteen hundred years ago, and no I didn't get it in China. It's a trade set for export. I bought it in the market in Baghdad."

Diana smiled. "In one way, I am the stereotypical little old lady, a house filled with memories, souvenirs and bric-a-brac. Only for me the collection is from a thousand lifetimes and more. I'll show you around a little later."

"So, when you were in the College of Astronomy in 1897..." Aileen interrupted, wanting to get back to her quest.

"You're always impatient, aren't you, child?" Diana sighed. "No matter, I should get on with my story. What was I to do? I am an immortal," she shrugged. "What do unemployed goddesses do? They can slowly fade away to nothingness. They can retreat to the Otherworld and let time pass unnoticed. They can become minor goddesses or saints for some new religion. Some become devils, like Lilith. Some are reduced to fairies and friendly spirits or sometimes to dangerous demons. They can appear to be human." She chuckled, "These days many gods and goddesses are being reborn as comic book superheroes."

"Oh my." Aileen said. "I just figured out what was bothering me."

"Yes?" Diana smiled.

Aileen said. "The galaxies. In 1897, apart from Andromeda, the galaxies were mysterious, distant, indistinct blobs of scattered light, called nebulae. As for Andromeda, that galaxy is close in the night sky to Cassiopeia. In the mosaic, you've got the visible galaxies exactly right. They are tiny bits of glass and stone, but your mosaic, inlay or whatever, has the galaxies in place and the right shape, spiral, barred, elliptical or irregular."

"Of course, I did." Diana leaned forward and grasped Aileen's hand. "Consider, Aileen, child, perhaps it is the galaxies that are the Great Mothers of all the planets. I know people will eventually once more worship the Mother of Stars.

"You see me today as I was first worshipped by an ancient wandering people, ancient hunter gatherers who came out of Africa into Eurasia, people who had dark skin and blue eyes. Not many see me this way."

"And?" Aileen asked.

"Simply put, as I said, I am a goddess. I chose to be human. People see me—as with all deities—as they want to see me. A distinct advantage as I have lived in the human world for so long, especially during the past five hundred years.

"Everyone saw what they wanted to see. Reflections of themselves. A few, a handful, like you, child, throughout time, can see me as I as I really am. They weren't sure who I was, or they didn't care, or they sensed my powers and my place in the universe and through that the love of a mother goddess."

The room grew quiet for a moment. Aileen could hear the faint lapping of the river, the breeze through the branches of the oak trees and the occasional call of a duck.

"You are my child, you know," Diana said wistfully. "Not directly, of course. I chose to be human. That meant I took lovers now and then over the centuries. When I chose to have a man as a lover and then if I chose to carry a child, most often it was a daughter. I did have a few sons, perhaps half dozen or so in nine thousand years. The daughters carried my line."

"So, we both would carry mitochondrial DNA?"

"Probably. You're ever the scientist, Aileen. Well, I haven't bothered to do a test. Why should I? I know where I come from," Diana sniffed.

"I tracked the rising and movement of the stars in Babylon. I advised sailors, the Phoenicians, the Greeks, the Arabs, the Vikings and Irish on the wisdom of the stars. I was priestess of a dozen religions, a nun, a seer and healer, a scholar, a scientist, a wife and mother, a milk maid, a dairy farmer, a fisher and river guide and an artist. I have always worked to restore the dignity and majesty of the Milky Way.

"I was often an astrologer, casting horoscopes and using my powers to know the client's real fears and hopes. That is until the Christian church considered me a witch—although, as a goddess, I could never be harmed and those who accused me would regret it when I got my revenge.

"I worked behind the scenes, inspiring, suggesting, nudging, for until recently it was men, men who needed to be pushed in the right direction. I used everything from naive suggestions to actual seduction. Centuries after I stood on the peak of the ziggurats of Babylon, I returned to Baghdad, a servant in Bay al-Hikmah, the House of Wisdom at the time of the Golden Age of Islamic astronomy.

"My foresight told me to travel to England at the time of Gloriana, the first Queen Elizabeth, knowing I would meet someone who would help on my quest to restore the awe of the stars. I came to be in the employ of Her Majesty's spymaster, Sir Francis Walsingham. I met another of his spies, who called himself Sir Henry Fagot, but who, in reality, was Giordano Bruno."

"Bruno, who envisioned there were many worlds in the universe," Aileen interrupted.

"Yes," Diana said. "He was a young man who I did not have to push, nudge or seduce. A brilliant mind."

"He was burned at the stake in Rome by the Inquisition," Aileen stated.

"By an ignorant, arrogant, power hungry and frightened church," Diana's face flushed red with anger. "As I said, he had a brilliant mind." She shook her head. "When we had the chance, we had such astounding conversations about our infinite universe. I warned him not leave England, but the political situation became precarious and so he chose to flee. I could not protect him."

"Is that the first time you became a spy?" Aileen asked.

"Patience. Let me finish my cosmological journey. I stayed in England. Later, from the 1780 to 1820, I became a house-keeper in the household of William Herschel, the King's Astronomer, and his talented sister Caroline as they studied the sky and catalogued nebulae without knowing they really were galaxies."

"Caroline Herschel created the New General Catalogue of nebula in 1828," Aileen said. "Still used today."

Diana smiled. "Yes. Two thousand star clusters and

nebulae. Many of them my sister galaxies.

"What about Edwin Hubble?" Aileen asked.

"I met—that is Rumilia Waeclingas—met with Edwin Hubble when he came to the university for a conference," Diana shrugged. "He was already on the right track. Others I had to push, for Hubble I just had to give few hints."

"And Tolkien?" Aileen asked.

"For years," Diana continued, "the Oxford English Dictionary asked for suggestions from the public. So, in the 1920s —I was Rumilia then—I corresponded with a junior lecturer named Tolkien who was working on the back end of the alphabet."

"Oh yes," Aileen asked slowly. "Rumilia had a career in the twentieth century intelligence services. So how many times were you a spy?"

"Oh, you figured that out. You are definitely one of my descendants." Diana's smiled wickedly before settling to ironic. "When you have thousands of years of human experience, sexual or otherwise," she whispered. "There are a million ways to seduce a man—or a woman—whether it is for love, for lust or as I something I had to restore the worship of the skies and the stars.

"I was a spy. Not just recently, many times in fact. Otherwise, immortal life can be boring. Even if you aren't a goddess, you could find out a lot if you were doing the laundry for a Roman legate or an English knight; writing proclamations on parchment for a bishop or sheikh for distribution to the faithful; serving dinner in the harem of a caliph or cooking meals for the merchants of Venice or Amsterdam; sewing or mending the kilts, robes or trousers for the armies of Alexander, Babur or Napoleon. For centuries, changing jobs and locations meant I could change identities.

"As for my recent adventures, in the First Great War, as Brigit Nuada, I got a job as a clerk typist in Navy Intelligence. I used my experience as a spy to slowly advance up the ranks. After the Great War, Rumilia Waeclingas took her place.

"When I joined the Security Service in the Second War, I got a job creating 'legends'—the cover identities—for secret agents. It wasn't all selfishness on my part, Hitler and the fascists had to be defeated if the world were to continue.

"With assignments and secondments, I worked with them all, Operative M31 at MI5, MI6, MI9, SOE, OSS, CIA. I actually stayed on until 1956. In an age where there are more and more records, I had to create my own legend.

"Rumilia Waeclingas left the Security Services, with confidential thanks of a grateful 'free world'. The next day Rumilia disappeared. A few weeks later, with the help of my friends in the CIA, Diana Watling became a secretary at the College of Astronomy."

"Who are you now?"

"Still Diana Watling. No one cares about a forgotten pensioner living in a riverside village few people know about. If anyone shows up here, as I said, unlike you, daughter, they will see what they want to see. That usually will be a tiny white haired old lady who walks carefully with a carved wooden cane.

"I am building up a new legend for the future, but these days it takes time. Even if a goddess wants to hack into records, she has to know how to get into a dozen different systems before she can use her power to change the data to her advantage.

"This time, if I am to promote the worship of the stars, I am thinking of becoming a screenwriter of space epics. Hollywood does not know it, but tinsel town has featured two movie stars who, like me, are authentic redundant immortal goddesses who chose to be human. Their old names are almost forgotten. I'll leave you to guess who those screen goddesses might be. These days, a goddess in the writing room would make things interesting."

Diana finished her salmon wrap and poured the last of the tea into her cup. "Now we will figure out how to save my inlay mosaic. Then I will help chart your future, Aileen Casasaya. Come into my office."

The office was as strange as the rest of the house. The furniture could have come from a museum or an ancient history movie. Diana led Aileen to an elaborately carved desk that Aileen thought belonged in a nineteenth century English mansion. On the desk was the latest version of a powerful desktop computer. Beside the desk was another ultramodern feature, an expensive, black leather backed ergonomic office chair.

"Pull up that chair, Aileen, and we can chat."

Not far from the desk was a chair with four curved and carved dark brown polished legs. It was upholstered on the seat and back with emerald green velvet,

"It is more comfortable than it looks," Diana said. "The chair is a Greek design, the *thronos* of the gods, a seat of honour. I have very few guests and all of them are special in one way or another." She smiled. "Unlike the tea service, which is original, this is a replica I commissioned. It's not if I could carry a chair like that with me everywhere I go."

The chair looked heavy, but as Aileen pulled it up beside Diana at the desk, it was surprisingly light.

"Let me tell you the story of the Milky Way wall," Diana said she sat at her desk. "As part of my work as a typewriter, I saw the plans for the new Hall of Astronomy. I wanted to bring my Milky Way back to the world. How was I to do it?

"To the men of the College of Astronomy I was just the typewriter. I prepared a sketch of what I wanted to do. I am the Goddess of the Milky Way. It was simple to open closed minds and convince the committee I was one for the job.

"I let them use the men doing the construction to place the polished basalt slabs forming the background. I waited for a time when the university was closed--not too long, just a few days. I planned for the appropriate time. It should have been the spring equinox, but the university was open. So, I chose Easter weekend 1897—the first full moon following the equinox—to do the work, which would have taken a human a year.

"I did it in three days and three nights. Every star, every nebula, every galaxy is in its proper place. In Neolithic temples, quartz was used to recreate the Milky Way on the ground. I used chips of quartz; a clear stone appears to be white for the main sequence stars. Betelgeuse is a fragment of red jasper. Blue Rigel is lapis lazuli. The Orion Nebula inlay is tiny, but look closely. The Orion Nebula is accurately represented by dust particles of green jade, rose, orange and white quartz and amethyst. Yes, they knew about the Orion Nebula at the time, it was photographed in 1880 and 1883 but in black and white. I added the colours. You'd have to use a magnifying glass to see the accuracy of the detail.

"After Easter, the faculty returned and marvelled at the art, never wondering how it was done over a long weekend," Diana chuckled. "With a little subtle persuasion, I became part of their astronomy team. Not a full member, being a woman. I did do some observing, made many sketches, and, of course, helped with the making of the lunches for the hilltop observatory. Nothing surprises me."

"I have to save the mosaic," Aileen said. "How do I do that?"

"You shall."

Diana waved her hand. A file folder appeared on the desk. Diana handed it to Aileen.

Aileen shook her head. "I still don't believe this. Like they say on TV, it's right out of a movie."

"This is real. Very real," Diana replied handing her the folder. "All you need is this file. It is all authentic. I have created nothing. I have simply resurrected files and letters and photographs that actually existed and were lost over time. You can tell your professors you got the file from the descendent family of Brigit Nuada. The idea is simple. I am cynical after ten thousand years of all kinds of politics. These photographs will show my true self." She laughed. "Not as some saw me back then. Present Brigit Nuada as—what are the words—'the hidden figure' of the Hall of Astronomy. They will fall over themselves to preserve the Milky Way."

Diana had a wry smile on her face. She passed her hand over the desk. It wasn't really a wave, just a gesture. Another file folder appeared out of nowhere. "These plans will tell the contractors how to move it safely. The international firm I consulted has a couple of thousand years' experience. All very up-to-date, of course."

Aileen looked at the plans and a detailed instruction set with the letterhead. "Vishvarman, Shen, Vulcan & Daedalus. Consulting Engineers."

"Don't worry," Diana said. "The plans are sound. The very names will convince the architect and contractors to accept the plan although they won't know exactly why.

"Now, child, onto your future." Diana sat forward in her

chair and reached out, taking Aileen's hand. You are a child of one of my children. I shall guide you, but only when you ask. I know you seek the true origin of the universe. Your path is the river in the sky, the road of heaven, the Milky Way. I am sure the best place for your graduate studies is the University of Cambridge. I have long ties going back to Isaac." Diana chuckled. "Confirmed bachelor Isaac Newton had a nosy and often immensely helpful next door neighbour. Follow the standard application procedure, but rest assured Cambridge is where you will study. You will find what you seek through me, the Goddess of this Galaxy. I do not ask you to become a priestess in a new cult. The cult will come eventually on its own after your lifetime. In the meantime, I will have to accelerate the creation of my new identity."

*

"Today we will see for the first time, in the Hall of Stars in the new Astronomy and Astrophysics Research Centre, the beautifully resurrected and restored Milky Way Mosaic," Gabriel Pennington said from the podium in front of the shrouded mosaic. It was covered with a black cloth with constellations embroidered in a shining silver thread.

Aileen sat in the front row of chairs reserved for the VIPs, the university president, the dean of science, the mayor and the federal minister of science and innovation. Sitting beside Aileen was a woman who now called herself Hathor Niall, who had once been Diana Watling, Brigit Nuada and Rumilia Waeclingas. Television cameras were set up to one side of podium, photographers crouched near the front, and the rest of the seats were filled with guests: Aileen's parents, her brother and his girlfriend, faculty and students from the College of Astronomy, Rebekah with her old grad school friend the astro archaeologist, Tony and his restoration crew, reporters and anyone else who had cadged an invitation.

After the fall weekend at Silver Heron Landing, Aileen returned to the university. Aileen scanned the two folders— "Make sure you don't lose them," Diana had said—and kept the original files.

MOTHER OF STARS

Aileen sent one copy to Gabriel Pennington and a second to the student newspaper. She posted a third on her Save the Milky Way Facebook page. As Diana had predicted, the story (or perhaps the spirit) of Brigit Nuada was the tipping point. The architect was now eager to move the elevator shaft so the new Hall of Stars could incorporate the mosaic. That meant the plan to create a new ceiling had been scrapped. As Tony had wanted, the old oak beams were restored. Although it wasn't part of the nineteenth century original, the university had accepted an idea from a faculty committee to make the restored roof into another mosaic, black tiles with silver and gold stars; a modern version of an ancient temple.

"Today marks the anniversary of the spring day that saw the unveiling of the original Milky Way Mosaic," Pennington's voice boomed from the speakers. "I call upon Hathor Niall, the great-great-granddaughter of its creator, Brigit Nuada, and our brilliant student Aileen Casasaya, soon to leave us for Cambridge, who in just a few days, found the family and with it the story of this beautiful work of art to come up and unveil this masterpiece."

Robin Rowland is a Canadian author and visual journalist based in Kitimat, British Columbia. His recent fiction works include short stories for the Darkover Anthologies and the Canadian Dreadful anthology. He is the author of five non-fiction books, including three historical investigations, two on Prohibition gangsters and one on Japanese war crimes during the Second World War. He co-wrote Researching on the Internet, published in 1995 one of the first books on how to search the internet, as well as radio plays for the Canadian Broadcasting Corporation in the 1980s. He worked as a news producer and videographer for the Canadian TV networks for three decades and continues to work as an independent visual journalist, shooting both still photographs and video.

The Osun

By Steph Minns

SOMETIMES SHE WOULD WEAVE BASKETS on the riverbank, enjoying the kiss of the sun on her face, bronzing her skin to perfection. Parrots from the forest would join her, perching on her shoulders to chatter, and she would delight in the gifts of jewelled feathers they would leave as they flew back to the tree canopy. At other times she would wade into the river, letting the cool water dance sensually around her legs, swirling her bright skirts in the rippling current, while the wild creatures curiously watch her from the deep green shadows. When the children came to play at the river, she was always there, not intruding but keeping a watchful eye, lest one fall into danger. When the children crawled safely from the sparkling water to shake themselves off, laughing, Osun would smile in that motherly, affectionate way of hers and listen to their voices fade away among the trees as they rushed back to the village for the evening meal.

Nigeria, they called this land now, but she preferred to call it by its old Yoruba name. After all, she was old and this land had not been 'Nigeria' when she had come into being. She prided herself that, after all these ages, she still remained supple and lithe as a girl as she thrust through the clear water, forging with delight against the current. Fishes darted affectionately at her face and rode on her black braids as she swam. After a while, Osun would climb onto the bank to dry off and watch the sunset slide behind the iroko trees and the twisted lianas, content to let go of the day and to sink into the vibrations and sounds of the forest at night.

Yes, this was a good place to be, she thought, dancing for joy on the banks of her river, a river that wove through forests, villages and the city, mile after mile. Sometimes, she would return at night to her husband, Shango, but only if it suited her. No one dared tell Osun what she should do.

*

Adeola had found the city daunting at first. Her upbringing on a small family farm had not prepared her for the frenzy of the streets of Osogbo, the thunder of buses and cars, and the thrusting crowd. The busiest place she'd ever seen before had been the local market, but that faded in comparison. Now, she was into her second year at the University as a medical student, and she relished the bustle, the traffic, and the noise of so many TVs chattering out of open windows onto the sun-baked streets. All of it was a wondrous adventure, and she felt confident she'd arrived at last, was touching her dream. After all the hard work she'd put in at her village school, Adeola was determined to make something of herself, make her family proud.

Day dreaming over her lunch at the kitchen table about all of these future prospects, she glanced up when her flatmate, Ibeke, came in with her two male cousins.

"New jeans?"Ibeke asked as she stepped through the door into the cool, air-conditioned apartment.

"Yes, in a sale," Adeola replied defensively.

American jeans did not come cheap, and she sensed a judgemental tone to her flatmate's voice.

"You're looking the real American dream girl these days,"

Ibeke remarked.

Adeola picked up the tart of sarcasm and refused to respond, just busied herself clearing her lunch plate away. Adeola had formed a growing dislike for this girl since she'd moved in, though she tried not to show it. The flat-share had been arranged by the University so she'd had no say in the matter.

"Perhaps your time would be better spent in attending to matters of the spirit instead of the flesh," Ibeke continued spitefully.

Adeola caught her breath to steel herself from replying, preparing for the cousins to chime in next, as they usually did when her flatmate started on one of her religious lectures. Alem (the ugly one, as Adeola thought of him) sat down at the table and fixed her with a cold, reproachful glare.

"Yes, you know you're always welcome at our study meetings at the Mosque, provided you dress appropriately of course," he added.

"I have no need of superstitious, fantasy beings of any sort to dictate my life, as we have discussed before," Adeola replied stiffly, wishing he'd just shut up and leave her alone. Why were they so relentless in their hounding, picking at her skin like irritating insects.

"So you always tell us," Alem sneered. "But look at the life you lead. How can your parents be proud of the way you dress, and of your visiting drinking places with men?"

She spun angrily from the sink to face him.

"My parents are very proud of me, and my life and how I dress are none of your business! I believe in what I see. Religions are fiction to control people's minds and keep them in their place."

"There is only one true God," Alem began, sermon-like, but she cut him short.

"Don't all religions claim the same, that their God is the only true God? How can that be?" Adeola snapped. "I don't see holy men, just irrational men squabbling and creating petty 'holy wars'—deluded fools and hypocrites. All the holy books of the world are written by men, not the hand of any imaginary God."

A tense silence fell and Adeola grabbed her bag, feeling their eyes boring into her back as she marched down the hall and slammed out of the apartment. Her one pleasure was that the 'ugly one' had not managed any smart come-back. The younger man, Gbayi, who she felt was the softer one, had glanced quickly away from her triumphant glare as she'd spun past. Of the two, he seemed the more likable of the brothers.

Adeola had been raised by liberal parents that loosely considered themselves Christian, but worked and socialised happily with Muslim neighbours as well as those who still adhered to the old traditional multi-deity Yoruba beliefs in her village. Tolerance and acceptance had been the watch-words she'd been raised with.

"We all depend on each other," her father had lectured her once after she'd squabbled with another girl in the village. "So don't fall out about nothing. Imagine if something bad happened here, like a flood, and no one here had food or a home to go back to? What would we all do if we couldn't pull together as a community and help each other out? There's no room for intolerance and bigotry in this short life."

Adeola's tolerance had certainly been tested to the limit lately by the self-righteous, arrogant Alem and Ibeke, looking down their noses as though she were dirt on their shoes. *How can one argue logically with the illogical and irrational?*, she thought, as she strode down the cracked pavement towards the market square.

Supping on iced lemonade at her regular street café, she calmed down. The place was buzzing with fellow students, but no-one she recognised. It was too early yet for her meeting so she had some time to kill, determined to stay away from the flat. Bright, cheerful and sociable, Adeola had carved herself a niche among her fellow students and was an established activist in the human rights society at the University. Confident this afternoon's talk on the changing role of women, which she'd helped to set up, would draw a large crowd, she looked forward to a lively debate.

*

Adeola returned late to the apartment after the meeting. She'd stayed at the bar to talk politics with two visiting lecturers until well past midnight. Tired and exuberant, knowing her flatmate would be visiting her parents until Sunday evening, she relaxed in the knowledge she had the place to herself for the rest of the weekend. No sniping remarks or religious ranting, she thought, as she turned the key in the door.

After a cup of hibiscus tea, she changed for bed and heard someone fumbling at the front door. Suspicious, she pulled on her dressing gown and switched on the hall lamp to investigate, but realised whoever was at the door had a key. Assuming it was Ibeke, back for some reason, she felt disappointed that she'd no longer have the place to herself. Why had she come back?

The front door opened. and Alem and Gbayi, her flatmate's cousins, came stumbling into the hallway.

"What are you doing here? How dare you let yourselves into my home?" Adeola shouted out in alarm.

Neither of them spoke, but Alem grabbed her arms roughly and started to haul her towards the front room. Outraged, Adeola screamed and kicked out, but her bare feet became entangled in the dressing gown. Gbayi turned on the main light and she saw his tense face in the harsh electric glare, watching them both warily.

"You filthy, atheist bitch!"Alem shouted viciously in her face. "You will be treated as you deserve to be."

Adeole struggled, but his weight pinned her firmly down on the sofa.

"Help me! Hold her arms!." Alem barked at his brother.

Gbayi stood frozen like a lizard caught on a path by lamp-light, staring as his brother wrestled with the pretty young woman. It seemed he was about to challenge his older brother, but then Gbayi silently obeyed. Alem began fumbling with the zipper on his trousers, his hands shaking. Twisting her head, Adeola tried to scream, but Alem thrust a dirty handkerchief from his pocket into her mouth. She spat it out and tried to jab her knee up into his ribs as he leaned over her, pinning her into the cushions, but she could not fight the two of them.

"Hold her, I said!" Alem demanded.

Unable to complete what he'd started, Alem hastily fastened his trousers again. He hoisted Adeola to her feet and set about punching her, shouting, "Witch! See what you done, you sister of evil!"

Reeling backwards, Adeole attempted to run for the door, but they caught her again between them. She managed to get a hefty kick into Alem's thigh, but this enraged him further and made him hit her more. Her lungs near tore with bellowing for help, but the awful reality dawned on her that no-one would hear. Their apartment was at the end of a long corridor, the neighbouring room a laundry room, and the nearest inhabited flat was two thick concrete block walls away from hers. She realised the danger she was in and knew that she could not afford useless expenditure of energy. She decided to play passive, see if an opportunity came to make another break for it.

After the failed rape, they tied her with tape around her wrists and ankles, Alem holding her down on the floor, his knees pinning her back, while a nervous but compliant Gbayi secured her. She could feel his hands trembling, could smell his nervous sweat. Hands secured behind her back and ankles hobbled, she realised she'd lost what little chance at self-defence she'd had.

"Why are you hesitant? Always weak and womanish," the older brother mocked his sibling. "No backbone for anything."

"Can we let her go now?" Gbayi offered.

"No! She'll be going nowhere!" Alem countered.

Steeling herself to think calmly, to work out her best action, Adeola turned her face to Gbayi, reasoning that she may be able to appeal to his better nature. Sure he held a glimmer of attraction for her, maybe she could play on this. He had come to visit Ibeke once and Adeola had let him come in to wait for her, even sat at the table to drink coffee with him and chat about their favourite films. He'd thanked her politely for the coffee, smiled at her. But now he was capable of this?

"Gbayi, please. Why are you hurting me? What have I done to you?"

Adeola tried to speak quietly, keeping any panic, fear or accusation from her voice. Gbayi opened his mouth to answer, but Alem butted in first, hissing. "Don't speak to her. Shut up, whore!"

Adeola could see the fear imprinted on the younger

brother's face, could sense how wary he was of his bullying sibling, so she tried pleaded again, more boldly this time.

"You call yourself a religious man, Gbayi. Please. You are not the animal he is. How will you face Allah if you do this? Perhaps Allah will forgive you if you stop now before you go too far."

She could see something else, perhaps shame, in the young man's face now and her spirit leapt, sure she was winning.

But as Gbayi tried to speak, Alem suddenly slapped his brother's face, hard, shouting. "You are righteous and you will shine in Allah's eyes for teaching this wrong-doer a lesson."

Alem snatched the duct tape from Gbayi's hand and roughly secured Adeola's mouth. She tried to resist as they carried her between them down the rickety wooden backstairs to Alem's van, parked in the dark lot below. The van stank of putrefying meat from his butchery business, a contrast to the soft scents of summer blossom that filled the night air. As they bundled her into the back, slamming the doors, she hoped desperately that someone would look out of a window and see her. But the flimsy curtains in the only two lit windows above remained closed, and no one walked the streets at this time of night.

"She needs to be silenced," Alem was muttering to his hesitant brother. "Go where she can't spout any more of her nonsense about women's rights and other blasphemies. You promised to help me. Don't let me down."

Adeola heard them walking around the sides of the van, the driver and passenger doors slamming. As the van bumped forward, she squirmed around in order to sit upright and strained her neck to try and catch glimpses of the darkened buildings streaming past the van's rear window. Clutching at any detail, anything familiar she could make out, could be useful if she survived, she thought. When they drew up at the deserted docks near the edge of the city her panic began to rise again, choking her as much as the tape that jammed her bruised lips together. Remembering Alem's comment of silencing her, it dawned now that they intended to kill her here.

The two men argued in hushed, tense voices at the front of the van. When the back doors opened and Alem dragged her out, the twisted loathing on his face chilled her soul.

THE OSUN

"Help me, idiot." He barked at Gbayi.

The younger man's expression under the moonlight appeared stiff, fearful. Gbayi shot uneasy glances first at his brother and then at Adeola, as though torn as to what to do. *If I could only speak, I'm sure I'd be able to stop him*, Adeola thought frantically, grinding her lips against the tape.

Alem slammed her head against the side of the van. Sparks of vivid light distorted her vision as she crumpled to her knees. He pulled her roughly to her feet again. *This is it then, this is how I die*, she thought bitterly, fighting to stay focussed through the throbbing pain and the buzzing in her ears.

The handful of lights in the apartments across the river swam in front of her eyes like flies around a dead calf, and she could hear the waters of the mighty Osun River swirling through the pillars of the wooden quayside they stood on. Alem still had a firm grip on her arms, bound painfully behind her back, and she wished desperately she could believe in God now, any God at all if it could guarantee she would at least pass to some afterlife and be able to see her family again someday. Instead, she would be just another anonymous statistic; a woman found dead in the river whose obituary would a brief two-line mention in the daily newspaper. *That will be the sum of my life now*, she thought angrily, not a doctor saving lives but just another abused woman murdered at the hands of vile, bigoted men.

Alem shuffle-marched and part carried her across to the edge of the jetty and then came the push at her back. She hit the dark water hard. Desperately, she held her breath as she descended down into its cold depths, her sodden dressing gown an unwitting accomplice. Her lungs struggled to hold what little air she'd managed to snort up, but the precious bubbles finally slid out, running up towards the surface like desperate last words encased in balloons, to pop quietly around the quayside.

Above, her murderers strained their eyes against the darkness to watch her sink.

The last gasp gone, the blackness flooded in with the water that ran up her nose, bursting blood vessels and flooding her lungs. Adeola faded, unable to scream her defiance.

Consciousness lost, she was not aware of the swift, deft

fingers that ripped the tape from her face, wrists and ankles.

*

Adeola came around to find she was floating on the surface of the river. She could see stars and the moon above her in the velvet sky.

I'm still alive, she thought groggily. *How?*

Her first instinct was to gasp the blessed air, realising her mouth was now free of tape, gagging and spluttering. As full consciousness came back to her, she also realised that a strong hand gently cupped her chin, keeping her face above the water.

"Child, relax." Her saviour's voice sounded strident but kindly. "Lie back and let me tow you. Trust me. I will take you to safety."

A woman's voice, close to her left ear.

Adeola felt movement of the water pushing against her sodden pyjamas and gown as her rescuer's strong legs pumped beneath her, propelling them both forward. She sought to get a grip on what was happening as the woman continued pulling her silently along on her back, cradling her to her side as a mother does a distressed child after a fright. Adeola surrendered to being towed, realising she was safe.

She gasped and instinctively thrashed out as a boat swept past at speed, a river monster storming out of the night to swamp them both with a wave of dirty water tasting and stinking of engine oil. As she choked again, the woman beside her stayed calm and kept swimming against the boat's wake, continuing to hold Adeola's head above the water.

She's so strong, the student thought, *like an athlete. Who is she? Did she see me thrown in and jumped in to save me?*

A voice whispering out of the darkness inches from her face held a confidence and authority. "I am The Osun, and I believe you already know me."

"How do I know you? Did you see me thrown in?" Adeola twisted her stiff neck as best she could, straining to make out the woman's face, but it was too dark to make out much detail. Her questions were met with silence.

They continued for some time down the river, drifting in the current until the sun rose and started to paint the sky with soft golds and pinks.

Adeola tried kicking now life had come back to her legs. The water felt freezing when she'd gone in, but now it felt warm, soft, like a bath. It was about five o'clock she guessed by the position of the rising sun in the sky and the waking noises of birds and creatures along the bank. As the sun climbed higher, details sharpened and Adeola was able, for the first time, to see the face of her wondrous rescuer.

Her rescuer appeared as stunning Yoruba woman in her prime. Her beautiful teeth shone moon-white, as she smiled back at the girl. Tiny mirrors and pieces of copper and gold sparkled and flashed in her long, wet braids, catching and spinning the early sunrays into a crown around her head. Her broad, bronze face with its sparkling, mischievous eyes seemed to tease Adeola, daring her to remember.

"Osun," Adeola managed. "That's the name of this river and of the nature Goddess that people say guards it."

"Ah." Osun laughed gently. "You do remember me after all, and I thank you for your gift. It made me sing. Such wonderful blossoms."

"Gift?" Adeola, engrossed in the moment, had put away her recent terror. Curiosity bloomed by this entrancing woman.

"Don't you recall your little boat of leaves that you sent me, filled with hibiscus flowers? Of course, you were just a child then."

Fragments of memory came floating back to Adeola, of the day she'd gone to the Osun-Osogbu festival as a little girl. She, mother and oldest aunty had taken a bus and then walked to the shrine. They'd walked miles through the forest, for hours it had seemed to her at the time. As they'd got close to the riverside shrine to the Goddess, the festival celebrations had swept them all up with the dancing and music. Even aunty had creaked her old bones and supped some brew as they'd followed the procession to the sacred spot, where they'd spread their flowers and fruit on the riverbank as offerings.

Adeola remembered. The shrine's priestesses had been throwing themselves around in a wild dance, invoking the Goddess to speak through them. Mamma had dragged her eagerly to the front of the surging crowd, hushing her when she'd cried in fright.

Wide-eyed, she'd watched those possessed women shaking and dancing as though a storm-wind buffeted them, eyes rolling and shrieking invocations in an ancient tongue she couldn't understand. Their costumes had boiled like a sea of patterns around their shimmying hips, and bangles on their wrists and ankles jangled and rang with the wild gyrations. She'd been very afraid.

Her mother had leaned close, explaining. "Osun is the mother of all of us, humans, animals, birds. She is the bountiful Lady of Precious Water, and we all need water, so Osun is always inside each of us when we drink. Don't fear the priestesses. They are her assistants so She can offer advice to us through their voices."

The following day, still awestruck and a little afraid of the power of the Orisa, she'd gone down to the river where the village children usually played. She'd gone alone, not even telling her best friend what she had planned.

That small girl she'd been back then had folded up three large leaves to form a tiny boat, filled it with hibiscus flowers from a bush, and pushed it out onto the river as an offering, as she'd seen the festival goers do the day before on this same river. Her heart had been beating manically with anticipation. Would Osun appear like some rotting river monster, dripping weed and stinking of dead fish and decayed human bones? Would she drag Adeola into the river to drown and then chew her up, scrunching her face with powerful claw-hands and sucking her eyes from her head like oysters from a shell?

"Please don't hate me. I'm sorry I cried and I didn't mean to offend you or your priestesses," Adeola had whispered.

The little boat had bobbed down the river, spinning in the current and spilling its flowers when it hit a rock at the bend. Taking courage that no monster had risen from the depths to devour her yet, little Adeola had crept down the bank to watch it finally disintegrate, peeling apart.

Nothing terrible had happened. The sparkling water had continued chuckling over the riverbed, as it always did, and some monkeys had chattered teasingly in the lianas overhead.

THE OSUN

"How small you were then, and so sweet and naive." Osun chuckled, letting go of Adeola now she was able to swim for herself. The river had widened and slowed at this point.

"But," the student began, dumbfounded. "I believed you were real then, as a child. Now I'm an adult, I don't. I can't."

As Adeola struggled with her thoughts, Osun's face seemed to shimmer and change a little as she gazed on her companion. Were the copper ornaments and mirrors in her hair not just fish scales after all, glimmering in the sun? Were her braids perhaps river weed, just giving the appearance of hair?

"Some things are indeed beyond the brick and concrete of mundane daily life and not easily explained," Osun mused. "You believe in the power of a rational science. But science can't measure all things in the human experience."

Osun grinned, a warm, teasing smile, and continued as she swam beside Adeola. "Perhaps I exist simply because so many human minds have formed me over many, many years, believed in me, made me like hands that mould the bread dough into a loaf. Maybe it's the same for all the deities of the world that were ever conceived by human imaginations. What power all those human minds, all that emotion, working together can have. What could it do in the future for your world if honed to its finest, highest point and all humans were capable of singing together in harmony? Just for one moment in time, just one song."

Osun had stopped swimming and was treading water in the middle of the river.

"You will not, of course, remember this little encounter very well. It will fade from your mind, but you will retain the essence of it to draw upon as your life goes by. Go. Up the bank, now. The people in that little lodge under the afara tree are good souls who will help you. They have a little shrine to me behind their house, and I always ensure the husband has a good catch of fish to share with his neighbours."

Osun's strong brown hands pushed Adeola from behind, shoving her towards the muddy slope of the bank. She managed to scramble up and stagger to her feet. She turned to look back at the river, to thank Osun for her help, but all she could make out was a woman swimming way away out in the main stream, an elegant woman that suddenly dived and was gone in a shimmer of green and blue skirts. No matter how long Adeola stood and stared at the moving water, the woman did not resurface.

Slathered in mud, she walked, dripping, up the wooden walkway to the lodge.

Oddly, when recounting her tale later to the police, she could not recall how Osun had swum her down-river to safety. Try as she might, the images would not come, only a half-real glimpse of a woman's smiling face, glimmering with fish scales, and a bizarre notion of a tiny boat made of leaves, floating down the river.

Steph has been a keen story writer and artist since childhood. Originally from the suburbs of London but now living in Bristol, UK, she works part-time as an administrator and spends her spare time writing. Her dark fiction stories range from urban and folk horror to paranormal crime thrillers

Steph's professional publishing history includes several short stories and a novella, published by Grinning Skull, Dark Alley Press and Zombie Pirate Publishing, among others. She also has a paranormal crime thriller novel, *Death Wears A Top Hat*, published by J. Ellington Ashton Press. She has two collections of short horror stories, *The Obsidian Path* and *The Old Chalk Path*, you can find more details on her website
https://authorstephminns.weebly.com/

Blessed

By Rose Dimond

MY SISTER KAMALI STOPPED BEING the Goddess when she turned eighteen. As soon as the palace sent word, Mother started cooking. Any time she spotted one of us children, she sent us to the market for more food, while Father grumbled about the expense.

The evening of Kamali's return arrived before we became beggars, and the whole family clustered together at our house's blue double-door entrance. Father and Mother, trembling, hovered behind us while Ram, Devance, Parvati, and I shoved in a constant war for the best front-row view, with Mother continually interrupting to send one of us to stir something or remove it from the fire. We squinted through the pouring rain for a first glimpse of the sister we'd seen only in public. I was the only one born, just nine months old, when three-year-old Kamali became Goddess, so I don't remember her either, though I might have implied otherwise to my friends and the tourists at the hotel where I work after school. They tip the Goddess' sister better than the market vendor's daughter.

The palace sent her home in the grocer's cart. Our house wasn't too far from the market. Just up the mountain a bit, hardly out of his way at all. The grocer panted for show, though his skinny hump-backed bullock did all the work.

I gulped as the only passenger, a thin girl in plain dusty-gray robes, climbed out of the cart. The last time I saw her, she rode in a golden chariot and wore red and gold silk, hard to see under heaps of flowers and gleaming jewels. The noise hurt my ears: bells, drums, chants, cheers, and nearby shouts of "That's my sister!"

Today, I heard only pattering rain. Kamali just stood by the cart, like she was too good to come inside.

Not on the highest step up the mountainside, but high enough never to have flooded, our house had three stories, if you count the attic. Grandfather and Father built the sturdy walls with more brick pieces than mud. In our neighborhood of rainbow houses, they painted the outer walls a unique cheery shade of salmon and used our village's beloved bright blue on the trim. The roof doesn't have shingles, but you won't find a thicker thatch anywhere. Kamali should have been glad to return to such a fine house.

The grocer snarled, "You get to take all you can carry from the palace, not all I can carry."

Though chosen for her beauty, today Kamali looked like nothing special, her figure straight as a stick, as she pulled on a burlap bag, almost as big as she. It shot over the side of the cart and tumbled to the ground with a splash and a thud.

"Everything she can carry from the palace? She must have brought all the treasure!" Pushing aside our youngest brother Devance and smallest sister Parvati, my brother Ram ran to help Kamali. Mother called Ram the Goddess's Blessing because she conceived him, her first son, after her daughter became the Goddess. That's not what the rest of us call him.

I glanced to see if the neighbors were watching. Mother's friend Najju ducked back from her window. Her daughter Rashmilla was Goddess before Kamali. Najju's warnings still rang in our ears like the temple bells on top of the Goddess's palace.

She'd cackled, "Kamali has been the goddess longer than

anybody ever, right? Fifteen years of doing what she pleased, being carried everywhere, no one teaching her anything except what she wanted to learn. You think a child ever wants to learn anything? Manners, for instance? Who tells the Goddess how to behave? And you're stuck with her the rest of her useless life, for it's terrible bad luck to marry a girl who's been the Goddess. Who'd marry someone who knows nothing, even without the curse? Me, I was clever. When my husband's mother fell ill, I sent Rashmilla to care for her. Rid myself of two scourges at once, I did. When the old woman dies, I don't know what I'll do with Rashmilla."

My grandparents died long ago, so we didn't have that option. Now we just stared as Ram led the sister we'd seen only on the balcony of her palace or during her festival trips through the village.

When he made it onto the porch, he dropped the sack, heavy even for him, with disgust. "Books! She could bring any-thing from the palace, and she brought books." Ram swears he'll never read once he's out of school.

Mother and Father looked hopeful. A goddess daughter who could read was more than they'd counted on. As she climbed the steps to the porch and came to stand between the blue columns, Kamali half-smiled, as though still waiting for the adoration of the crowds.

"We have a bookcase in our bedroom," said Parvati. The eight-year-old danced in place. "It's upstairs. I'll show you."

No one offered to help this time, even though Kamali's sack made ruts in the floor when she dragged it to the stairs. Sure, the ground floor is dirt, but we have some nice rugs. I followed to make sure Parvati didn't take my things off the shelves, the things the tourists gave me, magazines about TV, and cosmetics that I can still use if I pour water in them.

The foreigners stay in the hotel before and after they climb the mountains. I like to watch TV while I make the beds. Next year, when I'm out of school, I want to work more and save enough money to go to college, maybe in America, where the tourists come from. I'll shorten my name to Sara so it sounds American.

We count our village fortunate to attract so many wealthy

tourists. It stands in the middle of the country, between high and low, hot and cold, rural and metropolitan. The Goddess blesses us in the balance. To the south our capitol city wallows in its excesses. To the north are the highest mountains in the world, blanketed in snow. The mountain people graze their even hardier shaggy yaks and goats up to the tree lines. On the bare peaks nothing lives except the gods. That's why tourists climb our mountains. I suppose they have no gods of their own.

Our climate is temperate; the soil, rich. We cut terraces into the mountain side to have level ground both for our crops and our houses. The land looks like a giant temple, with steps to the homes of the gods. The river generously overflows each summer to water the rice, which most villages cannot grow, but the Goddess favors our land because of our great devotion to Her. She provides for us and watches over us. During my sister's reign, we never had a flood, as often happens in other towns. But they don't have a Kumari. The Royal Kumari lives in the city of the king, but he commends his son, the prince, to us. The prince celebrates every festival with us, and our Kumari blesses him, standing in for all of us, by tracing a holy symbol on his forehead with her special spices.

But all women must bleed, and now my sister has become mortal. We must search for a new Kumari, a girl five years or younger with thirty-two bodily perfections who can pass the tests the Goddess decrees.

"I wish you'd stopped being the Goddess sooner. Then I might have been the Goddess too," complained Parvati as we took our places around the wooden table, faded to gray after so many years since my grandfather made it for his bride, but still sturdy enough for our family and probably Ram's too.

For her eldest daughter's return, Mother prepared a wealth of dishes, more than for the festivals even, some even with chicken and more vegetables than I could name. You'd think the prince was dining with us. Smoke still poured from the kitchen coals, and the open fireplace made the whole first floor uncomfortably warm.

"Saraswati couldn't have been the Goddess," Parvati continued. "Her teeth are crooked."

I swatted at her. "Only one tooth, you little beast, and it

hardly shows at all."

"Both Parvati and Saraswati would have been great Goddesses," said Father as he helped himself to the steaming dishes. "And it is a special mark of favor that Kamali continued at the palace for fifteen years, the longest anyone can remember. No doubt our adherence to traditions in the face of temptations pleased the Goddess."

I looked at my plate and scowled. Father hates my working at the hotel, where he thinks I'm exposed to evil, but he's glad enough for the money I bring in. And where would he be without tourists in the market?

Parvati inhaled the sharp spicy aromas as we passed the dishes. "Mmm. I can't wait."

With a quivering smile, Mother told Kamali, "Daughter, today we have the special red rice. Also chicken, especially for your homecoming."

"Chicken!" said Ram. "I'll take some."

"Too bad the Goddess doesn't come home every day," said Devance. He yanked the bowl from Ram. "Hey, leave some for other people."

When the dishes finally rested in front of her, Kamali looked around as though she didn't know what to do. Mother nodded her encouragement. "Hurry," whispered Parvati as she wiggled in her seat. "I'm hungry." Then this great, blessed goddess who ruled for fifteen years picked up the serving spoon with her left hand.

"Gross!" shouted Ram. "I'm not ever touching that spoon again.

Mother gasped and hid her face as Father stood up and knocked the spoon from my sister's hand. "The lowest of the low know better than that!"

Parvati leaned over and whispered, "Use your other hand. Like this." Her smug smile told me she enjoyed being superior to someone. Little rat.

Kamali imitated her and heaped her plate high. Her lower lip trembled once. You'd think they starved her at the palace, but I've seen what the temple sets out for the poor on the Goddess's Table.

The greedy pig took a second big helping. Halfway through

that, she chewed slower and pushed the food around on her plate. My poor mother bowed her head in shame.

I said, sharper than proper, "Goddess forbid we insult our mother's cooking by not eating everything we take."

Kamali looked up from the pink hills on her plate. She studied each face around the table, everyone confirming what I'd hinted. She scooped a spoonful and chewed it twice as long as necessary before swallowing it like it was a stone. On the third mouthful she stopped chewing, as her cheeks faded to a sickly yellow. She jumped to her feet, clasped both—both!—hands over her mouth, and ran into the street.

Over the splattering rain, we heard her retching. Mother covered her face. Parvati skipped to the window. "You won't believe what she's—"

"Parvati, be quiet." Father drew his brows together—a bushy black caterpillar crossing a raging red sea.

We didn't dare look at each other. Parvati and I went to bed as soon as we finished washing the dishes. The boys had already fled to their room.

Kamali crept back into the house later that night. She crawled onto her sleeping mat without speaking, except to mumble an answer to Parvati's "Good night, sister." Later she woke me with her crying.

"Mama, mama, mama," she sobbed with barely a breath.

I could still hear her over the rain. A new person made our bedroom seem mean and tiny. I used to be proud of its size. I shoved Kamali with my foot—Ouch! Her leg felt like a board—and hissed, "Mama's room's in the back of the house, if you dare to wake her."

"She probably won't beat you, since it's your first night," said Parvati. "But Father will call you a big baby."

"I should hope so! She's eighteen. And what are you doing still awake, Parvati?"

"Same as you."

Kamali turned to the wall and made no further noise.

In the morning, she asked to go to the temple with Mother, who declined in haste. Mother likes to be alone in her worship. Instead, I had to drag Kamali along to fetch water. We had to go by the market, and you'd have thought the girl never saw it before.

"I haven't, except for festival parades," she said, craning her neck to see through the scooters, pedestrians, shoppers, and stalls. A far-away car beeped its horn in despair. It had no chance of getting through the crowds, even if the stall owners allowed enough room for a car to pass. "It wasn't allowed. Everything is new and wonderful." She smiled at a man selling roosters.

"Come on." I hurried her away with a firm grip on her arm. She winced and stumbled, lurching toward a scooter, whose rider had to swerve, scattering the people on his other side. "And don't smile at everyone, particularly not with your teeth showing."

"Special deal for two!" The rooster man shouted over the curses. "Best find anywhere."

I almost ran, not even slowing by Tashi's father's jewelry shop. I didn't want Tashi to see my clown of a sister. I did cast a wistful look backwards, weighing the possibility of the match, as we rounded the corner to our alley. His father works silver; my father works gold. But his father has a shop with five smiths, making gewgaws for the tourists, and my father sells his wares at a stall in the market with no one to help him but my brothers.

I can't bring much to a marriage, but Mother always says, "You yourself can be your dowry." That's why she encourages us to get as much education as possible, long after the five required years. She never complains about the extra work she has to do with Parvati and me in school. We study hard to show our gratitude, to make the most of chances Mother says she never had.

But now we have this helpless sister, who'll have to be cared for the rest of her life, who'll swallow up the money that might have sent me to university.

Later that day, I took her to school so the principal could decide where to place her. Most girls her age have finished their education, unless they go to university, but after our neighbor's warning, Mother and Father wanted their eldest to catch up, at least to the same level as other girls her age.

I think Kamali's books gave Mother too much hope.

As we prepared dinner in the evening, I raised my voice over the sizzling vegetables. "She can barely write her name. I had to remind her which hand to write with."

"But the books," pleaded Mother, her face forlorn.

"Oh, she can read, but what use is that when she can't sit for exams or do her sums? The principal says she should start first grade at the new term."

Silent and still, Kamali looked at the floor, getting in everyone's way as we tried to get the dishes to the table. Mother struggled to contain her feelings, but when we sat down to dinner, and Kamali took only one spoonful of rice, tears streamed down Mother's face like the rain falling outside. I thought neither she nor it would ever stop. She cried more in two days than in my whole life. I could only glare at my sister.

Kamali carefully spooned one more scoop of rice to her plate. Then she sat there with a silly look on her face, head cocked to one side, one eyebrow down, the other raised high. When we finished eating, she went to the door.

"Where are you going?" demanded Father, his expression foreboding, as though his daughter caused enough trouble for one day. I agreed.

"I must go to the palace. The Goddess has need of me," she replied, her hand raised to her forehead.

"You'll go nowhere by yourself. You're not the Goddess anymore."

She hesitated, furrowing her brow harder than ever.

As his face reddened, he growled, "Go help your mother."

As useless in the kitchen as everywhere else, she broke three glasses. I was almost glad when a peon from the palace came to the door. "The Goddess has need of the Lady Kamali," he said.

Father couldn't repel the Goddess's servant, but he did declare, "Saraswati will accompany her."

My heart skipped a beat with the thought of walking slowly past Tashi's house of fine white stone, but Kamali gave me no time. She moved faster than I'd ever seen her, most unseemly. I suppose I should be glad she didn't gawk this time.

She strode ahead of the servant and moved through the twisting streets with ease, seeming to avoid pedestrians and scooters instinctively.

As we approached the imposing red brick palace, she exclaimed, "I am late."

To be sure, two older women marched between the two twelve-foot white lion sculptures and headed for the main entrance, the arch with twice as much ornate carving as the other arches, most of them windows. The women's shabby dresses sadly contrasted with their surroundings. Surely Kamali didn't mean she was meeting them!

After we passed between the lions, decorated in happy red stripes and cheerful gold collars and through the carved door, Kamali had a brief word with the guard just inside. I took over gawking duties. I'd never been inside the palace, which looked so solid from the outside. Instead, four narrower buildings surrounded a large inner courtyard. We entered a long gallery with tall, arched windows on the street side and handsome arches facing the courtyard. To be sure, the gallery spread wide as our house and tall as two floors, with great fat pillars painted in that beloved sky blue, just like the walls and ceilings. And so much gold trim! The Goddess' circles danced among myriad golden swirls. I couldn't distinguish between surface paint and carvings. I don't remember any furniture, not with the decorations leading my gaze in dizzying circles. I hadn't taken it all in when from behind a pillar appeared a huge feline head.

Cats have their uses, but they associate with witches, and I'd rather they kept their distance, especially this one, whose head came up to my waist.

The monster threw its enormous speckled body at Kamali. I screamed and ducked to roll out of its way. When I raised my head, I saw my sister rolling too, tangled up in the beast's huge paws. "Help her!" I choked off my scream as something odd struck me. Kamali giggled.

Flat on her back, she ruffled the silver mane above her. I moaned as the beast opened its mouth. It licked her face and made her laugh all the more. She threw her arms around its neck. "Chita, Chita, I've missed you so. Do they take good care of you? Do you like the new Goddess?"

"Now, Chita," said the guard, a tremor in his voice. "Let the Lady Kamali stand."

The great snow leopard put a paw on Kamali's chest. It

110

raised its lip to show excellent fangs. The guard took a step back.

"Be nice, Chita," Kamali chided as she slid from underneath the cat. Soon she was on her knees, hugging Chita's neck.

Embarrassed at my undignified position, I scrambled upright. I brushed off my robes and adjusted them with a few twitches. I inched toward my sister but stayed out of the big cat's reach.

"That's your pet?" I asked Kamali.

Her eyes closed in bliss, she explained, "Chita belongs to the Goddess."

Snow leopards live in the mountains. They avoid humans, though they happily plunder grazing flocks. The government forbids hunting them because of their rarity, but I never heard of one living in a palace. Wouldn't a wild creature with teeth and claws be dangerous indoors, especially to the Kumari? Any blood flow makes the Goddess mortal.

"On my sixth birthday, a traveler brought a baby leopard to show me." Kamali rubbed her cheek in the silver mane as sadness flitted across her face. "A yak herder had killed her mother. The traveler planned to sell her for her coat, but I cried and demanded to keep her." Her smile returning, she hugged her pet. "Of course, he could not disobey the Goddess. I named her Chita, 'leopard' in his language. Mama told me he wanted to sell the poor kitten because he had no money, so I gave him a large present."

Before I could ask how Mother had anything to do with it, Chita lashed her thick, spotted tail, as long as her body. Kamali laughed as the meter-long tail wrapped around her, but I stepped back.

Kamali scratched Chita's forehead. "They cut her claws every month and made me wear thick gloves until she learned not to bite. Not that there was any danger. I explained matters to her."

"Why didn't they let her go when you left?" I asked. I hoped my face didn't show my fear despite Chita's friendliness to my sister.

"Oh, that would be cruel. She's not prepared to live outside." Kamali looked deep into her pet's eyes. "Besides, she belongs to the Goddess."

"Lady Kamali, the gathering in the Goddess' courtyard is nearly complete," the guard hinted. He turned to me. "You will enjoy a cup of tea here."

I looked askance at Chita, but she padded after Kamali. While the guard gave orders for my refreshment, I edged behind a courtyard column, wider than I could reach across. Determined to unravel Kamali's mysteries, I kept my shoulders hunched and my eyes lowered so the guards would ignore me, just a submissive, dutiful woman. I pretended to examine the decorative painting—Does gold paint have real gold in it?—but I also kept an eye on the courtyard, hard to do while lowering your eyes, but I've practiced my whole life. I called it self-defense until the tourists told me that was something different.

The older women who entered before us had joined two others, one of them our neighbor's daughter Rashmilla and another near her age, teetering off the precipice of youth. They stood at four points around an elderly, bent woman, her skin dry and thin as paper. She hunched down on a plain wooden stool that wouldn't be out of place at our house. Kamali lay on the ground with her arm around the old woman's knees.

"Mama, mama, mama," sobbed my sister, just like she did her first night at home. Chita pressed against her and rubbed her head on Kamali's thin back.

A little girl dressed all in red skipped over to Kamali and Chita. She used both hands to pet Chita's back over and over. "Kitty. Nice kitty."

As she ran her hands down Chita's massive tail, I saw the third eye painted on her forehead. I realized with a thrill that I might be the first person outside the palace to see the new Kumari. Her name, we were told, was Roshoweri. No one else would see her until the festival next month.

Kamali still sobbed, but silently. The old woman cradled her closer and then jerked her head at the other women. Three of them stepped in closer, while Rashmilla sat beside the new Goddess and talked to her in quiet tones. Rashmilla seemed to be showing her how to stroke the snow leopard—a ticklish business, for who can tell the Goddess what to do? If they could, my sister wouldn't be so stupid.

The crone spoke in a wavering voice. "Are you not the most beloved, our longest-serving Kumari?"

Kamali cried through sobs, "I *used* to be!"

"You remain so. You studied hard and served the Goddess faithfully, unlike some, like this lazy, greedy Rashmilla here, hardly worth training. Only eight years she gave us!"

Plump Rashmilla smiled as she stroked the silver cat.

"And me, Honored Mother. Only four years I gave." A woman near Rashmilla's age bowed her head. Her thin nose fluttered in a delicate sniffle.

The hag shook her head. "Ah, Anuja, who can know the mind of the Goddess? No blame attaches to you for that accident and the cut that ended your reign. Some might call it part of Her plan. And you continued your studies and still serve the Goddess. But Kamali here, who can doubt that she is beloved?"

Kamali wailed louder, easily finding doubt. "Nobody even likes me! And at dinner I—"

"You gobbled everything in sight," said the Honored Mother. "They all did, even though warned. It is no shame."

The other women murmured agreement.

"Out in street acting like an animal—" wailed Kamali.

Rashmilla transferred her petting hand to my sister's shoulder.

A middle-aged woman, tall, her brown skin still stretched tight, said in a voice vibrating like a long flute, "We know. I remember like yesterday. And Honored Mother said the same thing to me."

Next to her, Anuja nodded.

I wondered where these former goddesses lived now. They dressed like poor women, in plain, faded clothes. One looked like a kitchen maid. I wondered what her employers thought when the palace summoned her.

The old crone spoke again. "Can you doubt the Goddess's wisdom in showing you the extremes of life, that you may be more useful to Her?"

I gave thanks that Mother, her heart broken already, couldn't hear all these women, including her own daughter, calling this old witch "Mother." I felt miffed with Kamali too, carrying on like we sent her out with a begging bowl instead of doing our best to educate her where this grand palace failed.

A servant woman appeared at my elbow with a cup of steaming tea, with strong aromas from the herbs and fresh butter. But the Goddess would have the best of everything, wouldn't she?

The servant woman herded me away from my post. It's harder to fool a woman. "It is a delight to welcome you, and we urge you to refresh yourself adequately before allowing us the honor of escorting you home."

The Americans at the hotel would have said, "Get lost," but our ways are different.

"Your kindness does you honor," I replied. "My concern for my sister forces me to presume on your hospitality."

"Your sister—may she continue to be blessed—may be detained for some time, feeding her snow leopard." The woman looked over her shoulder, back into the courtyard where Chita lounged. "We give thanks for the privilege of escorting her home."

She guided me closer to the entrance and hovered in false solicitude while I drank my tea, the most delicious ever, but it would have been rude to ask for more. Then the man who had escorted us earlier accompanied me home, and I had nothing to say to my parents besides, "She had to feed her cat."

*

The Goddess summoned my sister several times each week. Kamali always knew when, but Father never let her go out until a palace servant arrived. Strange things happen after dark, people say, though our teachers don't allow us to believe in ghosts. I could tell my father wanted to forbid these excursions, but even if he would risk the Goddess's wrath, I think he enjoyed the house returning to normal for a few hours. Mother's worry lines smoothed out, with her goddess daughter off doing goddessy things, like she had for fifteen years, and we all sank back into our accustomed places, with no new sister to reprimand or trip over.

With a frown, Father asked her once, "Does the Goddess

ever mention a salary for all this attendance?"

"Serving the Goddess is its own reward," answered Kamali, her face serene and confident.

"I'm sure it is, but it doesn't go very far in the market, and you are likely to remain in my house many years," he said, his eyebrows drawing together as he warmed up to one of his money lectures.

Mother put her head in her hands, preparing for a good cry. No one marries a former goddess. You can see why. The Goddess probably turned away from Kamali for life after she started bleeding. Who would risk marrying such a cursed one?

"Going to school," said Father in haste, glancing at Mother. "You have much school left."

That at least averted another weeping fit.

Kamali said, "At the festival, the prince will give me a gold coin."

Father groaned.

Growing up with everyone anxious to give her everything, Kamali hadn't yet grasped the concept of money, nor the smallest social conventions. I often found Parvati explaining things any child should know, like the afternoon I arrived home from my work at the hotel to find them preparing to go to market.

"We're going to buy a present for the Goddess," explained Parvati, dancing around like she always does. She's really old enough to learn how to keep still.

"With what?" I asked, clutching the pocket that held my day's earnings.

She opened her hand in answer. I gasped at the sparkling diamond.

Kamali, her expression studious, said, "Parvati has explained. I will give this gem to my father, and he will give me money in return. Is this correct?"

A cunning idea stole its way into my mind. "He's more likely to ask you where you stole it and claim it for your room and board. I've got a better idea."

Kamali's brow wrinkled in confusion. "The palace allowed me to bring whatever I could carry. Honored Mother helped me pack. My father, will he not—"

I said in the same tones I use with the younger children, "Kamali, listen to me: I will take you to another jeweler who won't feel like he owes you anything but a fair price. But let me do the talking."

I led them to Tashi's father's shop. My heart fluttered as Tashi greeted us. He really did smile more at me, when he excused himself to fetch his father. I held my head high, proud to be a customer with valuable goods to sell. It could only help my case with the Chand family.

I had trouble maintaining my dignity when Mr. Chand recalled all of us as babies. Fortunately, for my burning cheeks, he focused on Kamali. "And you, my dear, how many years have I watched you at the festivals! And now you are come back to live as one of us mortals."

I held my breath, but Kamali just said, "Yes, sir."

"And you wish to buy some pretty baubles like you used to have, I suppose." He held the stone to the light and eyed it through his glass.

"No, sir," said my sister in soft tones. "The new Kumari Roshoweri will soon be six, and I wish to give her something to mark the occasion."

"Six already?" Mr. Chand shook his head. "Not even introduced? Of course, our Kumari are particularly long lived. Fifteen years you reigned, a blessed time for us. Well, we must find something suitable for our new Goddess, that she may be pleased with us. Perhaps you see something? For the Goddess, I could give you a special price."

Parvati pointed to an elaborate headdress covered in rubies. "She'd like that. I'm nearest her age, so I'd know best."

"You couldn't wear that until you're fifteen," I told her. I looked around, doubtful. Jewelry stores don't have much for six -year-olds.

Kamali said with the same deference she spoke to everyone, "Thank you, sir, but the Goddess doesn't want jewelry. I will buy her some flowers and a small box for these gifts." She opened a drawstring purse and showed us two tubes. Mr. Chand scurried away to find the perfect box.

I stared at my sister. "Lipstick? Where did you get lipstick?"

"Max Factor Hypo Allergenic," said Kamali reverently.

"And Clearasil Stick."

"But from where?" They looked barely used, unlike the gifts I receive at the hotel.

Kamali smiled at a delightful memory. "Two years ago, holy women from all over the world came to meet the goddesses in the mountains. One of my sister goddesses brought word, and all our town's kumaris welcomed them."

"I thought you couldn't leave the palace except for festivals," said Parvati, proving that children hear everything, even when dancing around a shop and seeming to pay you no mind.

"I am the Goddess."

"Were," I said through clenched teeth.

Kamali's eyelids flickered. "One woman noticed the blemishes on my forehead from so many years of painting the third eye there. After she returned home, she sent me several tubes of red paint and healing paint. I did not use them all before I left." She rubbed her forehead. She did that a lot, as though it ached.

I swallowed hard. "Many women might like lipstick, not just the Goddess."

"Sister Goddesses, eh?" Mr. Chand's shoulders shook with amusement as he held out several boxes.

I cringed, embarrassed. "She meant former Goddesses, of course."

I would have picked the silver box with blue stones glinting in its lid, but Kamali indicated the wooden one with a delicate inlay of silver swirls. She said, "These are small tokens, but what truly pleases the Goddess is when we care for Her people."

"You mean the rich people?" Parvati darted around the shop like a fly, darting whenever she spotted something sparkly.

"The Goddess's people are those who need Her," replied Kamali.

"Like that old beggar woman across the street?" asked Parvati, pointing out the door.

Kamali stood with the same silly expression she gets before the palace servant comes, her head cocked to one side, her brow wrinkled. Then she ran, almost knocking down three people before she reached the beggar.

My cheeks flaming, I completed the purchase and scooped up the silver box and the rest of the money. Trust Kamali to ruin my chances with my future father-in-law. Taking Parvati by the hand, I crossed the street with no other thought but to shield my crazy sister from his eyes.

I gripped Parvati's shoulders to provide more of a shield. "What are you doing?" I snapped at Kamali, kneeling in front of the hag. The dirt covering her had to be older than my mother.

"She is the Goddess," said Kamali.

I wanted to slap her. "Kamali, she is not the Goddess. You are not the Goddess. The only living Goddess is a six-year-old girl at the palace. Get up and let's go." I looked over my shoulder at Mr. Chand's shop, but I saw no one at the window.

Despite the stink, Kamali leaned in close, as though listening, though the old woman did not speak. "She lived at the palace at one time, did you not, sister?"

The woman cracked her lips in a smile. I shuddered at the sight of the one brown, chipped tooth.

"Give her some money and come away." I remembered that I had all the money. I pulled off a bill: too much, in my desperation.

Claw-like ancient hands grabbed the money, but still Kamali lingered. "Sister, do you not have a place to live? Come with me. I will care for you."

Mr. Chand's door opened.

"Bring her, then," I snapped. "She can't stay with us, but we can't stay here. Parvati, don't touch her!"

I yanked Parvati's hand and walked ahead of them. Kamali supported the filthy crone's halting steps. Parvati kept twisting around to describe their progress.

Once in our alley, I waited for Kamali and her burden to catch up. "You can't do this! Father and Mother will never allow it."

"She is the Goddess."

"Stop saying that!" I wailed. "It doesn't matter if she was the Kumari a hundred years ago."

The old woman grinned at me, and I stepped back, covering my mouth and nose with a handkerchief. "Come on! People are coming out to look at us."

Mother didn't like it any better than I did. Father liked it less. Kamali led her protégée away. Later they reappeared with newer clothes and fewer layers of dirt on the old woman, I assume the same one.

"Now she is clean," said my stupid sister. "And her name is Du-to."

"She still eats," said Father. He gave Kamali a lecture on economics, wasted on a girl who wanted to sell a diamond to buy flowers.

But she gave him a wide-eyed stare that passed for attention. When he finished foretelling our probable dismal fate, she said, "I will ask the Kumari what's to be done."

As she prepared to go out, I looked at my family. Each face, even Devance's and Parvati's, expressed doubt that a six-year-old would have any useful advice.

"Saraswati, go with her." Mother sounded exhausted.

"Be careful of the ghosts," said Ram. "People say they come out at night." He waved his arms over his head like ghosts flitting through the air.

"Yeah," said Devance, raising his hands in claws. "A big tiger ghost that sneaks up behind you and pounces! My friend's cousin saw it."

"So come protect us," I snapped.

They ran to their room.

*

The palace guards turned me away, but I stayed nearby, determined to find out more. Kamali had too many secrets.

I went to the temple, on the east side of the palace, where the servants set out food on the Goddess's Table twice a day for the poor. It looked delicious, fit for the Goddess herself, and I helped myself to rice pudding. Then there was nothing to do but pray. I made a small offering of flowers and begged for Tashi to be my husband.

You can say that only so many ways and only for so long, no matter how much you want it. Fortunately, I looked away in time to see the ex-goddesses emerge from the building. Though wrapped in tattered cloaks, their forms gave them away: Short Rashmilla and four tall and lean others, Jambayang's shoulders rounded with age, and my sister, thin as a year-old sapling.

They headed into the center of the town, the square with the dancing fountains by the hotel, where the busy crowds scurried all night. There they split up. I hesitated, not knowing which to follow, and in the next instant, I could identify none of them. I waited, thinking they would come back the same way, but the crowd, like a river, carried me forward toward a dark alley. I shoved back, but I may as well have tried to reroute the river.

"What's a pretty lady doing all alone?" said a voice from my nightmares. A tall man, lean and full of hungers, towered over me, far too close.

I pasted on my best outraged expression. My heart sank at the sight of his friends, grinning in anticipation.

Time stopped. My heart pounded and my mouth went dry as I stiffened in fear.

Surprisingly, the evil man sailed into the alley wall. His head smacked the bricks and sounded like an egg cracking. A young woman in a scruffy cloak hissed over him, "The Goddess is very angry."

His friends ran, but a silver missile flew through the air and pinned one of them to the ground. He screamed as his friends deserted him. I backed into a wall of jagged bricks that scraped my arms bloody.

"No, Chita! Don't bite!" said my sister in a voice more like her own, after she glanced at the man moaning by the wall. To Chita's prey she said, "Um, the Goddess is very angry with you, too."

More footsteps pounded toward us: Shefalta, thin and middle-aged, and the round Rashmilla. As Kamali pulled Chita off the first man's friend, Shefalta told him in sterner accents, "Take your friend and go home. May your care for him mitigate the Goddess' anger. She expects you to attend the temple every day and contribute to the unfortunate. And it will go ill with you if you ever threaten Her people again."

My would-be attackers scurried away like the rats in the alley. Chita bounced after them too.

"What are you doing?" I asked as I wiped off blood off my arms.

"Answering prayers," said Rashmilla.

Anuja, she with the thin, pinched nose, joined us. "Kamali, you dropped your basket."

Kamali took the covered basket, where something yipped. "A puppy belonging to Pima Soyang, missing for four days," she explained to me. "I'm starting with small prayers."

"You've got to make that cat stay home," said Anuja. "The police can't ignore a snow leopard on the loose."

From the square, we heard the elderly Jambayang's voice, exasperated with repetition. "I said: Help! This thief has robbed a helpless old woman."

As the crowd fell away, we saw that she had the thief by the arm. I didn't see any other woman around. Smooth-skinned Shefalta started to go to her aid, but Jambayang, tired of waiting, picked up the man and tossed him into the fountains.

She herded us away, saying we'd attracted enough attention for the night, though she did send Shefalta into a house where a woman screamed in pain during a man's drunken tirade. She dispatched Kamali to the palace to feed Chita, and Rashmilla and Anuja to walk home with me.

I found the old kumari on Kamali's sleeping mat. That was the very last straw. I burned for Kamali to come home, to tell her a thing or two about answering prayers. But I fell asleep just as the sky brightened.

I awoke to the sounds of Kamali going to fetch water, as Father and the boys departed for the market and Mother made her daily pilgrimage to the temple. I had to attend the hag myself, which made me mad. She kept asking for water.

When Kamali returned, she put the water on to boil. She'd learned that much anyway.

"Where have you been?" I snapped. "And not just now. What is this answering-prayers business?"

"I do the Goddess's work. It's why She chose me, what I trained for." Kamali picked up a pan to make breakfast.

I sniffed. "You're not the Goddess anymore. Everyone knows that but you."

Kamali slammed the pan on the burner with a clang. I

winced, reminded of the man's head splattering against the wall last night. "What does everybody know? When everybody spends the night in a room full of severed goat heads, then I'll pay some attention to what everybody knows." She reached her hands deep into the rice and flung a shower of grain at me. "When everybody starves at banquets so that the rest of the world can eat, then I'll listen to them."

I squealed as the pellets needled into my skin. "You're wasting food!" I tried to catch some in the folds of my robes.

"The Goddess will give you more, won't she? Some other child is learning to starve for the good of her homeland."

"Wa—" creaked the crone.

For the first time, Kamali ignored her. "And let me tell you: After the maze of bloody goat heads, they put us girls who remained in the temple with the Goddess' statue and said, "Don't leave until the Goddess tells you to. And the other two wandered off, but I stayed because She never told me to leave. And She never has!" If Kamali had had a bosom, it would have heaved. As it was, her ribs blew in and out like the blacksmith's fierce bellows.

"Wa-ta," the old woman gasped.

"Oh, here!" I snapped as I filled her cup again.

"What?" exclaimed Kamali. She cocked her head to one side and made that funny face with one eye squinting and the other wide open, almost to her eyebrow.

"She's been asking for water all morning," I said.

Kamali dropped to her knees and took the woman's scabby hand in hers. She sat there with her eyes closed for a second and then jumped up. "Get everyone to high ground!" she shouted as she ran out the door.

I ran after her. For someone who'd been carried most of her life, she ran fast. I could barely keep her in sight, no mean feat as she twisted through the morning traffic, crowds of people trudging through just one more day. The scooters grumbled with impatience; nobody moved for them at this hour.

I reached the guardian lions just as she persuaded the guards to let her in. "Escort!" I gasped as I grabbed her arm.

The guards looked inclined to argue, but Chita bounded to the doorway and put her paws on Kamali's shoulders. The guards melted back, and Kamali led Chita and me to an inner room.

"Daughter," said the one they called Honored Mother She did not look from her meditation pose, one leg lifted, arms reaching for the sky. Many younger people would like to be so sturdy while standing on one foot, or even one. The little Kumari stood in front of her, trying to balance like her guide.

"Mama," said Kamali, not even winded, as she sketched a bow. She spoke before she raised her head. "Does the Goddess see the river rising?"

The old woman put both feet on the floor and looked down at the little girl, now turning somersaults. "Goddess, do you see the river?"

The Kumari nodded and rubbed her forehead, smearing the third eye painted there. "See, sister? I'm using your paint."

"The river, Goddess," reminded the Honored Mother.

The little Goddess spun around in circles, like Parvati. "Water, water. Lots of water. Can I play in it?"

I turned to the sound of running steps: Jambayang and Shefalta, faster than many people my age. "The river!" they exclaimed together.

I'd never lived through a flood, and neither had Kamali. But she knew what to do. The Honored Mother gave commands, and her Goddess army carried them out before she finished speaking. Jambayang set the palace's monstrous gold bells clanging. Soon the whole town crawled like a hive: people saving their goods, throwing sandbags, mattresses, anything and everything to use as levees. Others moved the very young and elderly to higher ground. "Bring them to the palace," commanded the Honored Mother. "It is the Will of the Kumari."

"Uh huh," said the Goddess, rubbing Chita's fur backwards.

The former goddesses ran towards the river. Frightened, I clutched Kamali to keep her with me, but when we reached the market's edge, she told me to help our family and old Du-to escape. "And tell Parvati to get my treasure."

"We can't take all your books!"

"Not the books. The ivory inlaid box buried in the mud up in the attic. She knows." She removed my hand and ran after the other kumaris.

I passed Father and the boys, already running to the river. In the house, Mother tried to save everything, dragging sacks she couldn't pick up. The old woman, still muttering, sat where I left her. I redistributed the sacks' contents and gave two light ones to Parvati, who cried as she clutched her doll. She showed me Kamali's box, buried behind so many other boxes and plastered into the mud walls. I had to chip it out with a chisel.

Mother wanted to watch for her sons and husband, so we climbed the hillside steps of rice fields, as far up as the old granny could go with Parvati's and my help. Du-to muttered and stared into the beyond. I could hardly hear the bells over the river's roar.

Father and the boys worked right beside the prince. Father kept Ram and Devance well behind him as they passed sandbags to build a levee. I shouted encouragement to Devance, struggling to lift the same things the men did, but I couldn't hear my own voice.

Parvati screamed and pointed. Kamali stood on top of the levee, building it higher with the heavy bags passed to her. Mother turned pale and swayed. I spotted the former kumaris all along the river, as they built the levee alongside the men. For the first time since last year's festival, I felt proud of my sister.

Now we could see the river as well as hear it. The levee builders retreated, running up the hillside like a cracked whip when they saw the waves cresting. Kamali turned to run, but the boy beside her, barely Ram's age, slipped. She lifted him up, and he sprinted over the bags to safety. But his momentum pushed Kamali backwards, and the river grabbed her.

We shrieked.

"We have to save Sister!" shouted Parvati, stumbling on the steps and tangling in the rice.

I stooped to gather her against me. I paused my own screaming to sob, "She's gone. No one can save her."

Parvati howled and hugged my neck so hard that it cracked.

Mother shrieked, "She's swimming! She can swim!"

I stood up, Parvati still clinging. Sure enough, a black dot surfaced.

"Why doesn't she swim to shore then?" asked Parvati, still

sniveling.

"The current. She can't swim against it." Mother bit her lip.

Kamali might be strong—I still remembered kicking those powerful legs on her first night home—but not stronger than the river.

Another wave snatched her. We screamed again, but this wave threw her into the topmost branches of a tree, almost submerged.

"She's safe!" Mother bowed her head and clasped her hands in prayer.

I turned away, knowing the river would grab her again in seconds.

Then I noticed the old kumari Du-to. Back straight for the first time, she faced the sun, eyes closed, arms lifted to heaven. She looked like she could remain so forever, if need be.

"Father's going to save her!" Parvati jumped around like a flea. No one told her to stop stomping the rice.

Mother prayed louder and louder in competition with the river.

We saw Father talking to, maybe arguing with—though both seemed impossible—the prince. Anuja and Shefalta inched down the terraced slope with a monstrous coil of rope. They dropped it by the men, who continued their strong-opinioned discussion. Other men gathered around, offering their advice.

Rashmilla tied the rope around her waist and jumped in the rushing water, while Shefalta braced herself and held the rope's other end. Shocked, the men shouted and then grabbed the rope to help Shefalta. Rashmilla flowed easily with the current to Kamali's tree. When both women had the rope secured around them, Shefalta, Anuja, and the other people on the bank towed them in. People urged the prince to safety, but he ignored them and continued to pull, just as strong as anybody, even the Goddesses. He even lifted the two soaking kumaris out of the water: a tactful solution, because young women should not be touched by men. Princes enjoy many exceptions, though. Old Jambayang directed that the Goddesses be laid on the stretchers she acquired from somewhere. We ran after them, splashing heedless through the water pooling around us. A cold knot in my stomach told me we could have been following their corpses.

Because Kamali's arm broke when she hit the tree, the Honored Mother decreed she should be cared for at the palace. At the last minute, she asked Mother to come nurse her daughter. Mother wept.

The festival took place anyway a short time later. The lion statues looked especially brilliant in their red and orange floral necklaces. Hardly any of the rice crop survived, but no one died in the flood. The prince said, and the priests and the Kumari agreed, that we should give thanks. He asked his father to send rice from other towns.

The new Kumari received the prince on the golden balcony of her palace, on the third floor above the now-familiar entrance. When she stood on a box, we could easily see her. Her red silk robes sagged with gold trim. Her gold headdress had the third eye worked in rubies. The Honored Mother stood beside her new charge, and beside her stood all our kumaris, dressed once again in royal red: Old Du-to, now returned to her rightful home, Jambayang, Anuja, Shefalta, Rashmilla, and my sister Kamali.

The prince leaned down to let the little Goddess trace the holy symbol for faith on his forehead. She smeared the red rice powder a bit, only to be expected her first time. Then he turned to us in the square and announced in a loud voice. "This town is particularly blessed in its Kumari, and we have much to be thankful for."

We cheered.

"Furthermore, it seems to me, in light of recent events, that the Goddess never lifts her hand from those She has chosen. I would like to ask our Goddess if this is so."

The young Kumari stopped waving to her family and looked up at the prince. The Honored Mother leaned down to receive her answer.

"The Kumari says this is true," said the old woman in a voice just as powerful.

"Then it seems to me that we must never lose our respect for those chosen, particularly in light of their dedication to our community. If it is pleasing to the Goddess, I would like to provide a larger pension to our previous kumaris than the yearly gold coin given to them in the past."

The Honored Mother leaned down and brought back the answer. "The Goddess agrees."

"And if it is pleasing to the Goddess, I would like to bring all the kumaris back to the palace, to continue their service to the Goddess, if they have no family obligations." He looked at Kamali, standing closest to him.

The Honored Mother leaned down again. "It pleases the Goddess that the two eldest should dwell in the palace, and that the others visit on a rotational basis."

I marveled at the young Kumari's vocabulary while Jambayang and Du-to bowed their gray heads in gratitude.

The prince never turned his eyes from my sister. She appeared unconscious of his gaze as she looked straight ahead into the crowd, the way I always remembered her, a slight smile curving her perfect lips. Her robes carefully hung over her cast, the cast applied by the prince's own doctor.

The prince made one last announcement. "It further seems to me that we must do all we can to abolish unfortunate superstitions about our kumaris and set an example by embracing the future."

"The Goddess says to take things slowly," said the Honored Mother, without consulting her charge.

After that, the Kumari Roshoweri traveled through the streets in her golden chariot to bless us all. My sister did it better. The older kumaris rode behind in their own chariots, not as glamorous, but festooned with flowers, like the lions. It made a fine procession.

Later that night, Parvati and I met Mother at the palace entrance. She brought us to Kamali's room. Statues and paintings, carved in swirling patterns more intricate than a peacock's tail, covered the walls. So much beauty hurt my eyes; I was afraid to go in the room.

Mother took her place in a comfortable, cushioned chair by Kamali's bed—a real bed, like in the hotel. Parvati ran to her and crawled in her lap.

"How could you?" I exclaimed. "How could you stand to come live in a—a *hut* of broken bricks and mud?"

Kamali smiled, tired. "The Goddess ordained it. Besides,

where else would I go?" She fingered the embroidered blanket with her healthy hand. The threads gleamed like real gold. "I wanted to see my family, Sara, closer than from three stories up on the balcony."

"We wanted to see you too!" Parvati piped from Mother's lap.

Overwhelmed, I thrust Kamali's ivory box into her good hand.

"At least I'll use the correct hand until my arm is healed," Kamali said in a painful attempt at a joke.

Mother scolded, "Why can't you remember, Kamali? You're not stupid. But really, to be using your left hand…"

"The Americans call it being left-handed," she said with a wry smile. "Maybe I should go there and shorten my name to Kim."

I returned her smile but couldn't meet her eyes. "I didn't open the box."

"I know."

I gasped. "Are you still that much of the Goddess?"

"No. It's a puzzle box." With only one hand she had trouble pushing the ivory panels. "How is the house?"

I sighed. "Not livable, but I dried your books."

Parvati bounced on the bed. "Kamali, does the Goddess talk to you, like they said about the flood? That's how you knew?"

Kamali smiled and rubbed her third eye. "The Goddess always talks to everyone, but we don't always listen. Even the kumaris."

Parvati's eyes grew even bigger. "Could you teach me to listen?"

"Me too," I said, hanging my head. "I haven't listened very well."

Kamali's expression turned somber. "Are you sure you love the Goddess that much?"

"Of course I do!" I exclaimed. "She saved our village!"

"Would you still love Her if She hadn't?" asked Kamali.

The shock took my breath away.

Kamali smiled, but sadly. "It's easy to love the Goddess when you live in a palace, when life is good. What merit is that?"

"You get to do whatever you want and eat anything you want and be carried everywhere!" said Parvati.

"You didn't, though, did you?" I asked, studying her through narrowed eyes. "Eat anything, do anything you wanted."

"The Honored Mother taught me to eat one thing from the banquets prepared for me and to send the rest to the Goddess's table. She said if I didn't eat much, it would delay my bleeding, and so it did, for all of us, except Rashmilla, who didn't absorb that teaching well, though she is skilled in other ways. You should see her kick through a wall!" Kamali fell silent. "The Honored Mother helps us remember who we are."

"Who *is* this Honored Mother?" I demanded.

"She came to serve the Goddess as a young woman," said Kamali. "The Goddess chose her younger sister as Kumari after Du-to. Her sister came home at age thirteen and threw herself in the river not even a season later. The Honored Mother made a vow and has served the Kumari ever since."

Mother patted Kamali's good shoulder. "I would not have worried so much had I known she was caring for you." She kissed Kamali's forehead, just to the right of the third eye, and Kamali looked more transcendent than she ever had in her divine duties.

"Mama—" It was the first time she'd said that to our shared mother. She shifted the last ivory tile on her box and slid the top off. She put something into Mother's hand. "Could you use this for a shop for my father? To fix the house? And education for my sisters and brothers education? And dowries? I am sorry I cannot give you all of it, but the Honored Mother says I should save some for myself, and not to put my trust in princes."

Mother clutched her hand closed. Two perfect pearls slipped through her fingers and bounced on the floor. Parvati skittered after them. Mother looked bewildered as she examined the jewels remaining in her hand. "Kamali, why didn't you show us these treasures right away? They could have been lost. Your father has a safe place for valuables."

Kamali leaned back and closed her eyes. "I wanted you to love me just for myself."

BLESSED

*

The Kumari Roshoweri is twelve now, and she has grown gracious in her duties. The Honored Mother passed on three years ago. Jambayang is Honored Mother now. Some say we'll be finding a new Kumari soon, but I hope not. Tashi would like to see our daughter Kamali as the Goddess, but her aunt, who lives with her friend Rashmilla, when she's not staying at the palace and attending university, smiles silently with me. We would rather see young Kamali serving her people with her education, maybe as a doctor or a teacher. The Goddess is merciful, but Her way is hard.

As well as she can remember, Rose Dimond (she/her) was born reading, possibly also writing. A fascination with all things spiritual led her to this anthology. She's also worked as a fabric artist, musician, florist, technical writer, editor, book designer, and cat rescuer. She has several stories published and hopes a novel will soon join them.

Follow her on her website, dimond.me
Instagram: mrdimond18,
Facebook as Madeleine Dimond (Rose Dimond).

A Walk With Inanna

A Meditation

By Mary Malinski

THE MEDITATION BELOW IS ONE of the first meditations I wrote when I started leading rituals. It guides the reader or listener through their own Descent to the Underworld to face their shadows. Be warned, if you decide to connect with Inanna, She is a demanding mistress! Connecting with Inanna inevitably leads to a connection with Ereshkigal, also an exacting ruler, who will hold you accountable in all areas of your life. Together, they strike a beautiful, if challenging, balance.

No one returns from the Underworld unscathed.

)O( )O( )O(

Note to readers and guides: If you are recording this meditation or guiding a group, pause at the end of each paragraph for approximately 15-20 seconds, or the length of time it takes to inhale and exhale very slowly and deeply three times. Where I have indicated a long pause in the text, pause for one and a half to two minutes, to give those meditating plenty of time to experience and envision the thoughts presented.

)O( )O( )O(

Take a deep breath in and let it out. Take another deep breath in, and as you let it out, release all the events of the past day, week, month. Take a few moments to focus on your breath. As you inhale, gather in all the positive energy, the happiness you have spread during the day. As you exhale, let go of any unnecessary energy you might have picked up today. Send it back to the Universe to be recycled.

Go to your safe place. This sacred space can be anywhere, real or imagined, in the past, present or future. Wherever your sacred space is, it is somewhere that you feel completely safe, calm and comfortable. Reach out with all your senses. Where are you? Are you indoors, or outside? What do you smell? What is the light like? What sounds do you hear? Can you taste the air? What can you feel? What is the temperature like? Fill in as many details as you can.

Your safe place is yours and yours alone. Nothing can harm you here, or on any journey you take that begins here. Feel the comfort of this familiar, protected place. If at any time you feel uncomfortable going on, you may return to this safe place.

Relax and feel all your muscles release a little more deeply. Continue breathing slowly and deeply. Within the comfort of your safe place, take a walk around, exploring until you find yourself strolling along a gravel path. Feel the crunch of the stones under your feet as you follow where the path leads.

It is late afternoon and the path leads you through a changing landscape, through open fields and dense forests. Eventually, you find yourself in a lush river valley, the sun hanging low in the west. The river quietly follows its course between palm trees and fields of grain. In the distance, you can see foothills of mountains that reach up to the heavens. The sun sets behind the peaks, revealing the thin sliver of a waning moon in the sky above you, and the night is cool. You come to a branch in the river. As you approach, you can tell that this tributary is manmade. It is straight and narrow—an irrigation ditch. You decide to follow the track along the ditch, which leads towards the foothills.

You walk for a time along the irrigation ditch between the fields, until they end. The path continues, sloping gently upwards as you climb into the foothills. The path curves around a steeper slope, and you see that it leads to the opening of a cave. You know quite certainly that this is the entrance to Ereshkigal's realm, the Underworld, and as you approach the entrance, an imposing figure steps out of the shadows. He holds himself with an air of power. Moonlight washes his robes and gaunt features in monochrome.

He speaks to you, "You have come to the entrance of Kur, the Underworld. Are you ready to journey below and face the darkness within? This is the first of seven gates through which you must pass to reach your goal. At each gate you will be asked for an offering before you may go beyond. I ask for the purple silk scarf around your head."

You hesitate a moment, because you don't remember putting it on. Then you realize the scarf represents the protective energy around your crown chakra. You think it is a strange offering, but you take it off and hand it to the guardian. The figure moves aside, and you enter the cave.

The cave is warmer than outside. The sand-colored stone holds the memory of the hot days of summer. It is spacious as well, more than tall enough for you to stand upright, and just wide enough for you to touch each side when you stretch your arms out. Your fingers brush what feels like fine grain sandpaper, neither rough nor smooth. The ground is even and uniform, worn by the passage of many footsteps over the ages, yet it still has that sandpaper grip.

There are no torches, but after your eyes adjust, you have no trouble seeing your way. The cave seems to emit a magical glow that allows you to see just enough to make your way with confidence, though the darkness looms a few steps ahead of you, as well as behind when you turn to look back in the direction from which you've come. The path slopes gently downward as you walk. Soon you come to an elaborate gate shaped like a large eye. A figure in a dark hooded robe steps out of the shadows near the gate, and speaks to you, "Welcome to the second gate. Before you may pass, you must give up the indigo scarf around your forehead."

Again, you don't remember having put the scarf on, but it is there. You take it off and feel your third eye chakra open and unshielded. The guardian accepts the scarf, steps back into the shadows, and the gate opens. You step through the eye and resume your journey deeper into the cave.

You continue on the path, gently sloping further down into the earth. It curves gradually to the left, and as you round the turn, you see the next gate. It is shaped like a musical staff with notes on it. A hooded form steps out of the shadows next to the barrier. It looks very much like the creature at the last gate you passed through. Is it the same one? It is difficult to tell in the dim light.

"Welcome to the third gate. To pass, you must give up the blue scarf at your neck."

By now, you've become used to the surprise of the scarves you didn't remember wearing, and the offerings have been easy so far. You take off the scarf at your neck and hand it to the guardian. You sense the protective shield leave your throat chakra. You feel open, light, and somehow slightly less yourself. As the guard steps back into the shadows, the gate opens and you pass through, continuing on to the Underworld. Your curiosity has been piqued, and since you've come this far, you may as well continue.

The path still curves to the left, a bit tighter now. You no longer need to stretch your arms to reach both walls. Once you are out of sight of the third gate, you see the fourth gate before you, in the shape of a heart. The guardian of the gate emerges from the shadows as you approach, its face hidden beneath the hood of the dark robes that allows it to blend so well into the recesses of the cavern.

"Welcome to the fourth gate to the Underworld. If you wish to continue, I ask for the green scarf at your breast."

You look down without surprise and remove the green scarf. Your heart chakra is now open and unguarded. The sentry takes the scarf and seems to melt into the walls of the cave as the heart-shaped gate splits down the middle. You feel light as you pass through.

The passage curves more sharply to the left, and angles distinctly downward. It is not long before you come to the next gate. This one is shaped like the sun. You see the guardian of the gate waiting for you.

"Welcome to the fifth gate. Please remove the yellow scarf around your ribs to advance."

Without pause, you remove the yellow scarf and hand it to the guardian. Long sleeves on its dark robe hide the hand that takes the scarf, and the figure vanishes as the gateway opens. Your solar plexus chakra instantly feels open and unshielded. You feel lighter than ever, and you begin to feel exposed. You set your doubts aside, however, and continue through the gate. The path curves ever more sharply to the left and ever more steeply downward. It seems like no time at all before you come to the sixth gate, shaped like a giant vulva.

The guardian of the gate steps forward. "Welcome to the sixth gate. Your journey is almost complete, but before you can go on, you must remove the orange scarf around your waist."

You hesitate a moment before removing the scarf, remembering the feeling of exposure as you took off the last scarf. You have come a long way though, and it would be a shame to turn back now. You remove the scarf around your waist and give it to the guardian. Your sacral chakra is now open and unguarded. You sense the first twinges of uneasiness at being so open, but you hurry through the gate.

Your pace is quicker now, and you are eager to get to the last gate. There it is before you, a simple round gate. The guardian stands between you and the final portal. "Welcome to the seventh gate. You have done well to make it this far. Are you prepared to continue? Then remove the red scarf from your hips, and go to meet yourself."

You take off the scarf around your hips and hand it to the guardian. Your root chakra is now open and unguarded. All of your chakras are open and unshielded. You feel very vulnerable and a little afraid. You turn to look at the guardian for encouragement, but there is no one there. You gather your courage and pass through the gate.

A few steps beyond the gate, the narrow passage opens up into an enormous throne room. The sandstone gives way to polished marble spires and arches. In the center of the room, is an obsidian throne, delicately carved and decorated with lapis lazuli and gold leaf. Ereshkigal stands in front of the throne, waiting for you. She is terrifyingly beautiful, tall and voluptuous with honey colored skin and dark brown eyes that see into your soul. Her long legs end in feet that look like the talons of a large bird of prey.

"Are you ready to meet yourself?" She crosses the floor and takes your arm, guiding you to stand in front of a mirror on the wall to the left of her throne. The mirror is large enough to see your entire reflection, naked, with your chakras glowing brightly. As you gaze, they darken. Your body shrivels and turns gray. Ereshkigal laughs as she reaches above your head and pulls a chain from the ceiling. At the end is a large hook. She takes your withered body and hangs it on the hook so that you can still see your reflection.

"This isn't quite what you were expecting, is it?" Ereshkigal leaves you to stare at your dark self. Images of things you have done, or said, or thought—and didn't like after—appear in the mirror. Each image stays until you accept it and forgive yourself.

(long pause)

Inanna and Dumuzi enter from a doorway behind Ereshkigal's throne and come to stand near you, one on either side of the mirror. Inanna speaks to you. "It is a difficult thing to face the darkness within yourself, but you cannot be whole without it. However, you can let the light shine from within you as much as possible in spite of the darkness."

They gently remove your body from the hook, laying you tenderly on the ground, and Inanna blows the breath of life into your mouth. You feel your body begin to expand. Dumuzi pulls two small vials from his vibrant green robes, and sprinkles the food and drink of life into your mouth. At first it tastes like ash. Then, as your body begins to regain its former shape, you taste the most delicious food you have ever tasted. The drink of life refreshes you more than the purest cold water. Energy returns to all of your chakras and sends pleasant tingles throughout your entire body. As you glance in the mirror, you notice that your chakras and your aura are glowing brighter than before.

Inanna speaks with gentleness, "At your most vulnerable, you faced your darkness and accepted it. You have taken another step towards the Light of your chosen path. Keep this lesson with you as you continue your journey. Our gift to you is to go refreshed back into the world. Don't worry. We will take your place so you may safely leave the Underworld. Now go!"

Inanna gives you a gentle push towards the gateway. As you pass through the root gate, it closes behind you, and the red scarf reappears around your hips. You hear a roar from the other side of the round gate, and you start to run up the path, around to the right. You pass through the sacral gate. It closes behind you and the orange scarf reappears around your waist. You run up and around, through the solar plexus gate. It slams shut behind you and the yellow scarf is there at your ribs. You hurry on up the path, and the slope becomes less steep. You pass through the heart gate. It locks behind you and the green scarf rematerializes around your breast. The path curves less sharply to the right now. As you hurry through the throat gate, it closes behind you and the blue scarf reappears at your neck. You speed up the path and through the third eye gate, which closes and returns your indigo scarf to your forehead. Your breath comes easy. You do not feel tired at all as you run unhindered through the crown gateway, the entrance to the cave, and your purple scarf returns.

You slow to a walk now that you are out of the cave. You know that nothing pursues you. It is still night, but it seems brighter. The moon is no longer a waning crescent, but a waxing one. There are buds on the trees. It is spring, and you can feel the energy of the divine blessing you have received coursing through you, just like the sap running in the trees. As Inanna and Dumuzi promised, you feel refreshed and ready for a new season of your life to begin.

Take a deep breath in, smell the scents of spring and growth and enjoy the energy. The feeling of lightness remains with you, even with your shields back in place.

Gently become aware of your physical body. Wiggle your fingers and toes, and slowly move and stretch in your space. Take another deep breath in, and when you are ready, open your eyes and return to the room.

Take your time as you return from your meditation journey. Move slowly, with intention. Have a drink of water, and something to eat, to ground you back into the present time and the present place. Write your experience and any insights you receive down in your journal so you can remember them.

Reverend Mary Malinski is the Archpriestess of the Aquarian Tabernacle Church of Canada, and the founder of the Circle of the Sacred Muse, the public ritual group for ATC - Canada. She has been leading rituals for more than twenty years, and writing guided meditations for almost as long. Mary also teaches at the Woolston-Steen Theological Seminary, and holds a Bachelor in Wiccan Ministry from the same school. You can read more of Mary's writings and find her other guided meditations at www.WalksWithin.com.

By Rosemary Edghill

Is it not passing brave to be a King,
And ride in triumph through Persepolis?
- Christopher Marlowe
Tamburlaine, Part 1 (c.1587)

The torch is passed from hand to hand but never really falls
They say that Art is all that lasts
And I suppose it is
A pleasant thing to have been a king
Who rode in triumph through Persepolis
-John M. Ford
(20th century poet)

Dedication: To Fenris Encampment. Absent Friends.

HORSEMEN IN BABYLON

MY NAME IS KAREN HIGHTOWER, and I used to be a witch.

It's some forty years now since that was first true. After the turn of the century, I ran as far away from Manhattan as I could. In the process, I rage-quit the Craft several times, not that anybody noticed. Despite myself, I kept coming back to Her, but I am (She is) Crone now. If, as Yeats would have it, there's a country that isn't for old men (and, presumably, old women), there's also one that does not admit the young. I am a citizen of that country now.

Oregonians think of Portland as a city, which is cute. They worship coffee and books there, which makes it habitable. And I found a job there, after being encouraged out of my then-current job for being insufficiently nubile.

There hadn't really been a job opening at The Baffled Spaniel—I'd gone in by mistake. I'd been making the rounds of the various local printing shops to try to drum up enough freelance design work to keep me solvent. By the time I realized that The Baffled Spaniel had no use for my skills with InDesign, I'd been hired.

I was depressingly grateful to discover someone who thought I wasn't over. Tamar, owner and operator of The Baffled Spaniel, was ecstatic to find someone who knew that "books" didn't just mean eBooks and whatever you could get with Print on Demand. After Tamar hired me (dogsbody, general factotum, designer, and occasional book binder) I built another life for myself (more boho, less suit), got a decent(ish) apartment, and settled in to wait. Your guess is as good as mine as to what I was waiting for.

The phone call came just before The Plague really hit, which would make it early in 2020. The Goddess and I were on another time-out that year, and I knew I had to get past the wall of *resentment* that was cutting me off from participating (as nobody says) in Life's rich banquet. I probably jumped at Alex's invitation because I thought it might settle things between me and The Lady, but I still wonder—looking back at that weekend from the other side of insurrection, anarchy, riots, Federal invasion, the threat of permanent fatal death, and the renewed threat of nuclear war—whether it might have been the way I perceived what I discovered that made it real. That caused it, in fact, to have happened that lifetime ago. Love may laugh at locksmiths, but Magick cuddles right up to quantum physics: the linear relationship of cause and effect are suggestions, not rules, in the magician's world.

Later, I told Tamar some of it. She said it sounded like an overcomplicated way of taking the blame for everything. You can decide for yourself.

It started when Alex called, although in all fairness, it started long before that, even though it started *with* Alex. Kind of.

So let's go back to the beginning. *Once Upon A Time...*

*

Once upon a time there was John and Feral and Jon-not-John, and Katie-the-Lark, and Kate (aka Mistress Boom), and Saskia, and me. The Lambs.

I was the latecomer to our sacred band. Most of us frequented an occult bookstore called The Serpent's Truth, so we knew one another by sight and even by name, but the six of them became the seven of us at a bar called The Slaughter.

I think Katie was the one who first made the joke about "Lambs to The Slaughter", and none of us could resist a good in-joke, so the name stuck. Feral was a stage actor in waiting, Katie-the-Lark did photography. Mistress Boom was a dancer and a future fashion designer, John painted, Jon-not-John wrote (essays and philippics, and the last ones were gathered up and published as a book but I could never bear to buy a copy), and Alex...

Alex called herself Saskia in those days, and Saskia was a performance artist.

Really, she could have said she was Queen of Rumania for all anyone cared. We were generous with our credulity, scattering it like alms, as befit kings and queens in Babylon. The world was highly entertaining when Saskia was around, and we all loved her, even those of us who saw her clearly, none of whom was me.

Our lives in those days, retold by us, were tales of myths and quests and adventures, everything holding a Campbellian numinousness. One of the adventures that bound us together was Katie-the-Lark's art project. Like me, she was Pagan. Like me, in love with Manhattan. She wanted to fuse her two loves together in the strongest way she knew: by creating a Tarot in photographs. The city would be her backdrop. *("And all her friends and enemies featured players,"* quoth Feral.)

It takes a long time to set up a shoot like that if you're scrounging all the props and models plus trespassing to reach your venues. In most of a year, Katie-the-Lark had only gotten the Major Arcana done—except for one card: The World.

And then she was murdered. Shot six times with a small caliber handgun: four times to the stomach, once to the chest, once to the throat.

And four decades passed.

*

It was late January, and so it was raining, and I was tucked up in my second floor cubical generating workflow documents. Next door, in an even smaller cubbyhole, Jason, our Master Penman, was laboring on through his current task. Neither of us had any idea of why the client wanted a handmade copy of an obscure novel from the 1970s—handmade, in this case, meaning hand-written on actual parchment, then bound in stamped and jeweled doeskin with gilded edges and unique endpapers and a slipcase cover. But if she only took on logical projects, as Tamar was fond of saying, she would have gone broke decades ago.

At this exciting workaday juncture, my phone rang. I fumbled it out of the desk drawer and looked at the screen. An unknown caller from Washington State. I took it anyway.

"Is this Kasey?" an unfamiliar voice asked. "Kace? Hello?"

I disliked my given name long before it became an Internet meme, but I'd *really* hated my middle name. Few people I'd met since 1985 knew I even had one, but for a few years back in the day, I'd gone by my initials, which were K.C.

Kasey.

"Who is this?" Tamar is always on me about my New York manners. The locals seem to think they're confrontational.

"This is Alex. *Alexandria.*" The voice sounded faintly miffed by my lack of immediate recognition. "Is this Kasey Hightower?"

"I don't know any Alexan..." I said slowly. The voice started to sound familiar. More than that, it held the assumption of rights that is very hard for even an experienced liar to fake—and using a version of my name that almost nobody knew. *"Saskia?"* I asked.

"Yes!" Saskia/Alexandria sounded relieved—and more like herself by the moment. "It's taken me ages to find you! If William hadn't remembered your last name I don't know what I would have done! Not that he was much help, because I've PM'd half the Hightowers on Facebook. Can you come up this weekend?"

"Hi, nice to hear from you, I never knew your name was Alexandria, who's William, what's this about, and that depends on where you live," I said. (Tamar may be right about my manners.)

"Feral, Kase." Alex said. "You don't think it ever said *'Feral'* on his driver's license, do you? I found John and Will so much easier than you, and they're coming. But wait till you hear!"

"Hear what?" I asked, trying not to sound either paranoid or disgruntled as I totted up facts in an invisible ledger. "William" was Feral, and John had always been John, and that left me and Alex—or Alexandria—who had used to be someone named Saskia, and who had collected—or at least located—all the surviving Lambs.

Fine so far, but when someone calls you up after forty years and acts as if you've just seen each other yesterday, one's first thought (or at least mine) is criminous intent—except for the fact I had nothing that anybody would bother setting up a cinematic-quality sting for.

I hadn't seen Saskia since—what? The mid-80's? She'd been as much a Ceremonial as anything, back then, so we travelled in different circles. So to speak. I was preparing the "too busy to leave work" excuse, which had worked excellently at severing all the other ties I'd wanted to sever, when she produced the irresistible lure.

"We've found Katie's Tarot."

After I'd inexplicably promised to come to Seattle on Friday, and ended the call, I realized that Alex-now-Saskia had lied to me.

She'd said she'd found me on Facebook. Only I don't list my phone number on my account, and she hadn't DM'd me to get it. Okay, so maybe she used one of those "we can find anybody" lookup services, and didn't want to come across as some kind of creepy stalker. And then I realized she could easily have found Lark, or Tony, or half a dozen other people who could have pointed her at me. She could even have led off her call with finding Katie's Tarot, and not bothered with how she'd found me.

But she'd lied to me.

And so when I went home that night, I dug through several boxes that have travelled with me through at least a dozen moves, until I found the one containing the leather jacket I'd worn when Saskia knew me. I thought it would be the perfect thing to wear this coming weekend, all things considered.

The box also contained some ancient t-shirts, including one for The Slaughter and one for Left Rite's "New York Is The World Tour", some clutter that had been important to me at the time I packed it, and my embarrassingly naive and earnest pre-Initiate Book of Shadows.

I flipped through it, wincing. It was filled with bad poetry (mine and others), earnest and passionate essays about The Real Truth, and outlines for rituals that would have taken six hours and the resources of most of Broadway to enact.

For She is Themis, Lady of Truth, and She is Ma'at, Goddess of the Balances, and She is Æquitas, Spirit of Fairness, and in Her measures She metes out fate.'

I wanted to dismiss the writer, my younger self. To call her callow and idiotic and far too credulous. To point out to her that the naked longing set down in those pages didn't show her to be superior and chosen, but just like everyone else. That's the thing nobody ever mentions about being chosen and extraordinary and set apart from the common run of folk: everyone is the hero of their own story.

But even while I recoiled, I felt a sort of exasperated and embarrassed fondness for the embryonic me. She wasn't wrong, she was only ignorant and young, and her sins were those of the yearning and driven. Those were sins I found I could live with, so I took the elaborately ornate *"Book of Mist and Veils"* and put it in the bookcase under my altar.

Then I stuffed the t-shirts into an old battered backpack, hung the ancient leather jacket over a chair, and retired to sleep the sleep of the just. (The "just about to make a disastrous mistake", that is, not that I knew it at the time.)

*

Seattle is the place everyone thinks of when they marshal their clichés of Left Coast North. It has a gorgeous coastline, it has impressive mountains for a backdrop, and it is very clean. Its housing runs to impeccably restored Craftsman bungalows, glorious Mock Tudor faux hunting lodges, sweeping counterweighted mid-century modern, and Gothic Revival in brick.

None of that comes cheap.

The clean and beautiful people who live in the clean and beautiful houses tend to be very *very* well off. I wondered if Alexandria was very well off, and what she'd done to get that way.

The address she'd given me was in Federal Hill. It was a raw and rainy night, and by the time I got there, pitch dark.

It was Candlemas Eve.

It had taken me too long to remember that, and I was irritated with myself. The Goddess wouldn't care that I'd missed the festival, or had no one to share it with. She would just wait, patient as gravity, for me to come back to her again.

Or did Crone-hood mean I could engineer a final escape from Her if I wanted to? Was that why I was here, or hadn't remembered the significance of the date, or was arriving on the doorstep of fate wearing what I knew was a wholly inappropriate outfit?

No. (I told myself.)

I was here because I wanted to see those photos. I hadn't come here to see Alex, or Feral, or John. I'd come to see little

"KC" Hightower, age 23. To say hello, or goodbye, or something else entirely.

And so, when my Uber stopped in front of the house, I paid the fare and got out.

*

I'd known where I was going and Google Street View'd it, too, but the image hardly prepared me for the reality. It was an imposing Tudor manor house, lightly edited to titillate the sensibilities of the 1930s and the pocketbooks of the unwary. According to the Internet, the backyard contained two free-standing structures: an open sided gazebo and a "yoga studio". There was also a koi pond with a waterfall and an extensive terrace with a pergola. There was a three-car garage, a double and a single. The single was open, showing something small (ish), trendy, and expensive—a Tesla, I thought—parked most of the way inside. The double remained closed, and parked in front of it was a somewhat scruffier vehicle with out of state plates. Probably William's.

I reached the front door. It was "Olde Englishe" oak with black iron strapping, making this look like the place to be if you needed a swash buckled. Trying not to feel like an extra in something with music by Korngold, I rang the bell. Chimes bonged in the distance.

I heard an imperious shout of *"William!"* and then the pounding of running feet.

Saskia opened the door.

She wasn't the silver-gold fairy waif we'd all so helplessly adored. Not any more. Somehow she'd become... I don't know. More substantial? More *real?* Less? Physically, she wasn't much changed. Her hair was still long, still that improbable moon-silver shade (it might even have been natural, once upon a time), and her outfit—palazzo pants, kimono-sleeve duster, multilayered silk chiffon camisole, trailing scarf—was in the whites and pale greys she'd always preferred. She'd clearly had "a little work done" over the years, but her eyes were still faintly slanted and still the same shade of burning blue.

As for her expression, it was...

I wasn't sure. Wary? I watched her take in my appearance (jeans, boots, leather jacket) as her face went from nonplussed to satisfied to sympathetic and finally settled on welcoming.

"Kasey! Oh my god, I'd lost hope! You must be soaked! Come on in before you drown!'

I stepped inside. The entryway was essentially an extra-wide hallway with a staircase off to the left and a room to the right, decorated in Early Tasteful—hunt table, vast gilt-framed mirror, patterned rug over original hardwood floor. In the mirror, I could see myself clearly: unbarbered mop of greying hair, rimless glasses, cheap and timeworn leather jacket. Not my most becoming look, admittedly, but I didn't need to become, because I'd already been.

"William! For God's sake don't just stand there," Alex snapped. "Get Kasey a towel!'

William, aka Feral, stood at the end of the foyer with both hands jammed in his jacket pockets. I felt less a shock at the sight of him than a sense of relief. He looked as alien as someone should when you're seeing them for the first time in forty years. He still wore a beard, which had been an intermittent thing in our barhopping days, and his hair was still an unruly mop. Like mine, it was threaded in grey. Like me, he wore glasses. The studious horn rims added to the professorial look: jeans, white shirt, chukka boots, and tweed jacket, He held out his arms for a hug, and I walked into them, wet jacket and all.

"Feral," I said, and he chuckled.

"Housebroken and domesticated now," he said. "Have been for years. Let me look at you."

We pulled back, comrades from some ancient battlefield, reunited after a lapse of years. Feral—*William*—studied me meticulously. "You look well," he said decisively. "What are you up to these days? I—"

Saskia stepped between us, brandishing a towel of such whiteness and vastness and fluffiness that it would have been suitable for buffing the Holy Grail, should that turn up anywhere nearby. She wrapped it around me, making faint mother hen noises. "Really! I suppose I shouldn't be surprised at having to do everything around here all by myself. Artists! Where's your suitcase? It must still be in your car. William—"

Our eyes met. His laughed, inviting me to share the joke. I didn't know what it was, but I still had to stifle the urge to giggle.

"No, Sass, I didn't drive. I've got my stuff right here." I exhumed a hand from the coils of the towel and gestured vaguely at my backpack.

"Is that all you brought?" Alex sounded as horrified as if I'd traveled naked. "Oh, well, I'm sure we can find something around here to fit you. Come on, let me show you to your room. Have you eaten? Of course not. William, be a lamb—" I waited for her to laugh at what must surely be an intentional joke, but she didn't. "—and open the wine, will you? I'll give you a quick tour on the way up."

One thing hadn't changed. Saskia dominated every conversation around her.

Meekly, the towel and I followed Saskia into the bowels of designer consumerism.

The wall-to-wall carpet was ivory, the couches were another shade of ivory, the occasional tables sparkled gold and glass, the exposed wood was *au naturel* and pale. The bibelots were timeless, expensive, and pedigreed, and none of them possessed any utility other than to be stared at.

This was not a haunted house (trust me: I know). This was the absolute opposite of a haunted house. It was beautiful, but it wasn't was a place somebody lived. If Saskia decided to move to Fiji tomorrow, she could leave the house's entire contents behind without any sense of loss. Even the living couldn't make their mark here.

After we'd done a lap around two rooms full of "gathering spaces", we reached the kitchen. It was enormous and blindingly achromatic, with breakfast nooks, coffee stations, wine fridges, floating shelves, and other hallmarks of gracious living, all in white marble, white tile, white cabinets, and high-wattage task lighting, looking like an uneasy hybrid between a stage set and a place that might actually produce food.

We had apparently come to the kitchen to use the stairs, although there had been a perfectly suitable-looking flight of stairs off the foyer. We went up the stairs and then down an ivory-carpeted hall with tastefully beige-on-ecru wallpaper.

About the time I decided we were simply going to wander until we both died of exhaustion, she stopped in front of a door and opened it, gesturing me inside. "Don't do anything," she said. "I'll be right back."

I kept myself from asking what she expected me to do, and went to the closet to hang up my jacket. I dropped my backpack on the floor beneath it and turned my attention to my surroundings. Apparently color was permitted above the first floor, so long as there wasn't too much of it.

The bedroom held one queen bed with duvet in sage and eight coordinated throw pillows, two nightstands that matched the bed, a sage velvet bed bench, a comfy chair (in a tasteful grey-green chintz) with ancillary lamp and occasional table, and an imposing pier-glass in the corner. I had a terrifying moment of thinking I'd fallen into an *Anthropologie* catalogue, but everything was much too neat for that. The curtains (pinch-pleating, pale grey slubbed silk, lined) were closed, but I peeked through them for long enough to discover that my room overlooked the back garden. The promised koi pond was illuminated from the bottom and glowed eerily. I wondered how the fish felt about that.

In *lieu* of another iteration of stunningly expensive mass-market *baubleoisie,* the tasteful sage-green walls were decorated with gallery-matted black-and-white photos: Rainier with a crown of clouds; the Space Needle through mist and fog; the neon of Pike Place Market in the rain. For a fantastic moment of insanity, I thought they were Katie's, as if she'd lived to grow up and gone on making art.

But Katie had been murdered almost half a century ago.

"I don't know why I never throw anything out; the least I could do is return some of it, but oh, no. I'm pretty sure these will fit you—" Saskia returned, mid monologue, with her arms full of clothes. "And honestly, I would never have suggested—" What she would never have suggested was to remain unknown. "Kasey, honey, are you *all right?*" (It occurred to me in that moment that at no point so far had I shared with her the name I was currently using.)

Those last two words were inflected in the way that meant: *"Are you a starving homeless person in desperate need of money and probably currently on SNAP?"*

"These photographs are wonderful, Sass. Did you take them?" I asked. One of the best ways I have found to avoid answering questions is just to skip ahead several stanzas in the conversation.

"Oh, not me." There was the abrupt sour ring of honesty in her voice and I wondered why. "I've never been an artist. And you might as well call me Alex; everyone does these days. I run a small gallery downtown. I'm planning—well, let's not get ahead of ourselves." She tossed her armful of clothes onto the bed. 'See anything you like?"

"I really wasn't expecting to pack for more than a there and back again," I said. "You know, visiting old friends? That sort of thing?"

"Are we?" she asked, and then turned to the pile on the bed. "I guess. Try this. You look cold."

She picked up a grey pullover hoodie, rife with cabling down the front. It was more a sweater than a sweatshirt; the furry nimbus standing out from its surface proclaimed the presence of angora somewhere in its bloodline. I took it from her and pulled it on over my T-shirt. It actually fit pretty well; Alex had borrowed my clothes a lot back in the day. We were still pretty much the same size. And it *was* warm.

Of course, so was the stuffable puffer vest in my bag.

"There," she said. "Much better. Take a look."

I turned to the pier glass standing in the corner. The sweater didn't go as badly with my jeans as I'd anticipated. I pulled the hood up just to see how it would look.

"Oh, no, no, no, no," Alex said fussily, pulling it down again and arranging it pedantically upon my shoulders. "Come on. You must be starving."

She herded me out of the room like a Border Collie in desperate need of Ritalin. "Those are John's," she said. "He'll be here tomorrow."

It took me several seconds to realize she was answering the question I'd originally asked.

John (not Jon) had taken the photos.

*

We ate in the living room, sprawled out on couches, the enormous coffee table actually performing a useful function. After the unpromising start, the evening went rather well, fuelled by good food, a warm fire, and several bottles of wine. Alexandria Kaczka was a figure of note in the local art scene: conservator, tastemaker, yadda. I'd actually heard of Lapwing Gallery, but of course I hadn't made the connection.

She'd been married, once, a long time ago. I couldn't tell whether the marriage had ended by divorce or murder. No kids. She made a point of telling me that all her personal needs were met by her gardener and pond-boy. "Jesus, Kasey, you would not believe how much work those fucking fish are! And every single one of them a ten thousand dollar loss if it goes belly up. Some days I'm tempted to pour a bottle of bleach into the pond and be done with it."

In turn, she was appropriately delighted to hear about my line of work, and I was happy to tell her that one of the services The Baffled Spaniel offered was the rebinding of a cherished old book—or exhibition catalogue—in the fine materials of your choice. (I'd been tempted for years, but... no.)

And William Farrell né Feral (he was delighted to fire off the implicit pun at long last) was a wholesale buyer of vintage and antique everything, which he apparently collected by wandering all over the US and sometimes Canada, buying anything that wasn't nailed down. Up to and including, he said, entire carousels. He said he'd wanted to do something where he was always on the move, and there was too much competition for acting roles. "The part of handsome devil always seemed to have been cast just before I showed up."

He and Alex had both bid the Aquarian Frontier farewell by the end of their twenties, William driven out by Lodge politics, Alex because (she said) she got bored with it. William had married more times than both of us put together (five), and said he wouldn't mind going for six if he could find someone who didn't mind him being away from home eight months of the year.

(I noted, if only to myself, that depending on the health insurance he carried, that would not really be a difficult thing to find.)

HORSEMEN IN BABYLON

Both of them were suitably astonished and regretful to hear that The Snake had closed years ago (another indie bookstore casualty of Amazon and of the fact that the occult had mainstreamed for the brief period before the chain bookstore also vanished). For my own part, I said I'd been a Solitary for the past couple of decades, and we left it at that.

By then we were all merry-drunk, in that rollicking and expansive way the young find so unpleasant in the old. Out came all the olden stories of the olden days, to be told and retold for the only audience who could appreciate them... or who cared. Talk of The Snake led to tales of The Slaughter, and The Slaughter led to Left Rite, and William said he'd brought a couple of their bootleg CDs, and he slipped one into the player so we could listen.

It wasn't the same. *We* weren't the same. I remembered how it had felt to be there, wearing the music like a second skin, certain the Gods danced beside me. But now it was faintly embarrassing to listen to the yipping and howling of the audience and wonder if one of those voices had been mine.

I poured myself another glass of wine.

By unanimous, if silent, consent, Alex turned off the music. Now the only sounds were the crackling of the fire and some faint noises from outside.

"So, well, I guess you want to hear the story," she said, after a moment or two. She took silence for assent, which it was on my part; I assumed William had already heard the story. "Once I took on John as a client, after a few years—you know how it is—it gave me the idea of looking up everybody else, you know, curiosity. I found out that Jon, Jon Butler—I don't know if you ever knew his last name? –and George Kate—*Mistress* Kate, and ain't that a laugh—were both dead, but William was alive and kicking. I wondered if he'd given up magic, you know—measuring the compass, we used to call it. John was away doing whatever, some commercial assignment. When William told me about his business, I asked him to keep an eye out for some pieces for me—bits for the house and the gallery, that sort of thing. Nothing really special or particularly expensive, just... stuff. He and John kept missing each other—you know, if John makes it this weekend it will be the first time all four of us will actually be in the same place. So, long story short, John asked me to ask William to find him some old luggage—chests, foot-lockers, steamer trunks—I can't remember why he wanted them. And William called me and said—where had you been?"

"Nebraska, for my sins," William said, sounding piteous. He might have skipped out on the acting life, but he still had an actor's trained voice and timing.

"Nebraska," Alex agreed, satisfied. "Some kind of auction. It doesn't matter. He dropped them off—I've got them out in the studio right now; you can see them tomorrow—and asked me if I wanted him to break the locks, and I said I'd check with David—David's really the one who wanted the trunks for god knows what—and he said he'd be in the area a few days, and that was it."

"And Katie's body was in one of the trunks," I guessed pertly. Alex made a face.

"*Something* was," she said darkly. "And David didn't really care, so I got a crowbar and got the biggest one open—and I guess the Gods are still watching over me after all. I don't know how they got there—or to Nebraska, for chrissake, but—"

"You're leaving out the middle again, darling'," William said amiably. "The part where the trunk was full of all Katie's stuff."

"You have got to be kidding," I said flatly. "All her stuff was already gone from her apartment when we checked, remember?" I'd already fallen irresistibly back into the habit of the royal "we" to refer to The Lambs' activities. I remembered I hadn't gone to Katie's apartment, and William hadn't either. It was John or Jon, and... Alex? I thought so.

"It was," Alex said feelingly. "Becky was such a thieving whore—I told Katie all about her, but she moved in with her anyway, serves her right. And the place had been practically looted—her props, her clothes—her *stash*. Oh my god, it was like locusts, and Becky good-as had the room rented again the same day! But joke's on her: Katie's cameras and negatives weren't there. Of course they weren't. Why would they be?"

"Because she lived there?" I suggested. I was starting to feel somewhat giddy with all the names Alex had run through, and it was hard to keep the story straight. Who'd wanted the vintage trunks? John? Becky? David? Whose apartment had it originally been? And who the hell *was* David, anyway?

"But she didn't have a darkroom there," Alex said as if it were something I ought to have known. "She used the back room at the Snake."

"Of course she did," I said obligingly. "Why wouldn't she?"

It was possible, even probable. The notorious "back room" at The Serpent's Truth had been many things: stock room and lecture hall and temple. Anybody who'd come around to The Snake often enough to get onto Tris's less-mercurial good side was familiar with the infamous "secret chamber" that was reached by a not-very-secret door (which was also the way to the bathroom and the shop's miniscule back office). The secret chamber wasn't one room, but several, and all of the windows were painted black. Add the running water, and it could easily have been used for Katie's purposes, and Tris would rent it to anyone who had folding money. The only reason it hadn't ever been rented out as a meth lab was because Tris had always possessed a certain low cunning for not getting himself into actual trouble.

"And how come you knew that and I didn't?" I asked Alex. I glanced toward William. He shrugged one-shouldered. He hadn't known where Katie's darkroom was either.

"Oh, she probably told me some time," Alex said vaguely. "I don't even remember. It all makes sense. She knew Becky was a thief, so she kept all the important stuff locked up in her trunk."

"Which then teleported to Nebraska," I agreed solemnly. Alex emitted a surprised giggle and William grinned at me.

"Sure did," he said, eyes theatrically wide with the performance of innocence. "And fortunately for all of us, Miss Itchy Fingers here didn't open any of the cameras to see what was inside. She whistled up John Smith—"

"Really?" I asked, enchanted.

"Really," William said solemnly.

"—and he checked the cameras for film, and developed what was there, and salvaged as many of the negatives as he could. Apparently, spending forty years in a barn in Nebraska isn't the best way to take care of either film *or* cameras."

"The Tarot series?" I asked, hoping.

"The whole thing," William said joyfully. "Every single bloody Arcanum. There's a book in that, I guar-an-tee you. C'mon, Alex, you want to drag out some of the prints and give Kasey a look?"

*

Alex opened a drawer in the end table at her side, and pulled out a manila folder full of copier paper. She handed it to me. "This isn't everything. I haven't had a chance to go through all the negatives and do more than a rough inventory. Still, you should get the idea. You were in some of them, weren't you?"

"Weren't we all?" I asked, opening the folder.

The images had a grainy *cinema verité* quality, making them look like old newspaper photos from the days when print newspapers and their photos had been an actual thing. Katie'd taken several shots of nearly the same subject—every good photographer did, even these days, when everybody carried a high-end camera in the guise of a phone.

The first ones had been taken at The Slaughter—I remembered the evening, but I'd never seen the pictures. Katie hadn't been using a flash, so the images were very dark; a chiaroscuro pattern without mid-tones that took time to resolve for the viewing eye.

The Lambs were in the foreground, but Katie was clearly focusing on shooting Left Rite. John was there in his ragged trench coat, Jon in fedora and suspenders, Saskia in that white velvet cape she spent more time cleaning than wearing, looking like a faerie caught in car headlights, Feral in the hairy and ragged goatskin vest that Mistress Boom had made for him as a joke, the diva herself in full Elizabethan, starched ruff and all...

And me.

I was wearing an enormous wooly grey sweater I'd probably stolen from Feral. My hair was long then, down to the middle of my back, and I had on a necklace I'd made myself and strung with various sigils and charms. I was the only one who'd noticed we were in the shot; in the first several I was holding up my hand to block my face. Then the others noticed what Katie was doing, and Jon grabbed one of my hands and John grabbed the other. I looked startled, and very young, caught between laughter and dismay.

So young. So convinced I'd already rung all the changes that Life could expect of me.

"Those were the days," William said softly, looking over my shoulder. "Alex, darling, you look magnificent."

"She always said I was her favorite subject," Alex said proudly, peering over my shoulder at the pictures.

I paged through until I reached a different image. Someone had clearly wrestled the camera away from Katie for a moment—John, probably, since he'd been the only other of us interested in photography. Katie was raising her hands to cover her face—having just grabbed for her camera and failed, clearly—but he'd caught a shot beforehand, and her face was fully exposed in the image.

Heart-shaped face, ash-blonde hair. Enormous aviator frame glasses (a style that's gone out and come back in twice since the day the picture was taken). T-shirt. Photojournalist vest covered with slogan buttons—Blessed Be, My Other Car Is A Broom, Magic is Afoot—over a thermal undershirt.

"I wish I knew who killed her," I said softly. Alex handed me my wine glass again in silent sympathy.

The rest of the images were from the Tarot series. Jon-not-John as the Hanged Man, crucified upside down on a chain link fence somewhere in a New York that wasn't there anymore; Mistress Boom as The Empress, seated regally upon a discarded chair somewhere in the Bowery, with dumpsters and piles of trash everywhere. Saskia as The Star, standing in the fountain up by the Met, wearing nothing but a crown of flowers and a white shift the water had turned transparent. The Alex beside me sighed wistfully at the sight of the Saskia that was.

Feral as both The Emperor and The Hierophant—the doubling was intentional. Someone I didn't recognize as Death, on a pale hobbyhorse I'd made for Katie. The thing lingered for months after she didn't need it any longer and finally ended up in the Snake with a price tag on it. The Devil was Tris, looking appropriately pleased and Luciferian, standing in the doorway of The Serpent's Truth wearing a gauzy bat winged cape. Someone I didn't recognize swathed in Hecubean veils in front of the

Empire State Building was The Tower. I wondered if that was the much-maligned Becky, but I couldn't quite remember.

I was pictured twice, once as Strength (sitting on the back of either Patience or Fortitude, the New York Library lions, wearing a lion-tamer's top hat and brandishing a miniscule wooden chair), and once as the Charioteer.

For the Charioteer, we'd gone all the way out to Coney, where the carousel was. Katie'd tied glittery ribbons to two of the horses and I stood in one of the chariots, holding my make-shift reins and trying to keep my tiara from falling off. Everything fluttered, because the carousel was turning. I looked appropriately preoccupied, and even noble, because all around us people were yelling that Katie needed a permit, and that she couldn't do that here, that they were calling the cops and we should get out of here immediately.

I remember how we fled, laughing, up the Boardwalk as though the Furies were at our heels.

"She'd decided on final versions for most of them," William said, "and X'd out the others on the negatives. A couple, like the last one, the World, she didn't have time to pick through."

"Where are—?" I began, as Alex yawned theatrically and turned to smile at me. "'Come away, o'human child'," she quoted. "We can look at the rest in the morning. *Some* of us need our beauty sleep."

William snorted, I made a rude noise, and for a moment, we were Kings and Queens in Babylon again.

*

Alex helped me find my guest room again, and she and William went on down the hall, though to different rooms, I noted. I closed the door and forced myself to not simply fling all of Alex's loaner clothes and the multitude of brocade accent pillows from the bed to the floor. Instead, I moved the stuff to the bench at the foot of the bed and laid the angora hoodie carefully on top of the pile.

The internet had said there were seven bedrooms in Alex's house (including the master suite) and eight bathrooms. My en-suite was just as *Architectural Digest* as everything else: heated towel racks, heated floors, the culturally-ubiquitous double sinks, and a shower of such size that most New Yorkers would call it an apartment. All the elements of gracious living were pristine and present. They gave the bathroom the look of something in a five-star hotel. It seemed oddly off-putting in a non-Airbnb context.

Hedonism red in tooth and claw warred with the desire to sleep. Hedonism won. I took a lengthy and sybaritic hot shower, used every one of the high-end products, then wrapped myself up in the fluffy white bathrobe hanging on the back of the bathroom door. I found an outlet by the nightstand and plugged in my phone, then insinuated myself into bed and turned out the lights.

I had a vagrant thought that I had so much to think over that I'd never fall asleep, but I was asleep before I finished it.

*

I woke up abruptly, thinking my phone must have meeped, but no. Something else? I sat up, listening, but I didn't hear anything. My phone said it was 3:48, presumably a.m. as it was dark outside, and nobody had called, texted, or emailed me. I turned the phone off just to be sure no one could, and put it in the nightstand drawer. Then I lay down, snuggled back into what were surely 800-thread-count Egyptian cotton sheets, and prepared to go back to sleep.

She said she had to find all of us, but she already had.

I frowned, attempting to glare at whatever part of my brain it was that wanted to start a conversation at O-drunk-thirty. I already knew Alex had lied about how she'd found me, and tonight she'd piled more lies on top of that. Saskia had always had a fine free hand with the truth, sacrificing it instantly for the sake of a good story, but...

Once upon a time there had been seven Lambs. *'Leave them alone, and they'll come home, bringing their tails behind them.'* Two died of plague, and one was murdered. And then Alex, who had once been a faerie sprite named Saskia, phoned me, and...

What had she said? I cudgeled my brain, growing more awake by the moment.

"Can you come up this weekend? I found John and Will so much easier than you and they're coming."

Only she hadn't needed to find them, had she? John Smith, photographer, exhibited his work at Lapwing Gallery, owned by one Alexandria Kaczka.

Saskia.

"Once I took on John as a client, after a few years—you know how it is—it gave me the idea of looking up everybody else, you know, curiosity."

Maybe. And she'd found that Mistress Boom was dead and so was Jon-not-John, but William Farrell was alive...

And she hadn't bothered with me. Yes? No? Did even Alex remember by now?

William bought some locked trunks on a whim, or because John (or someone named David) asked him to, and Katie's photos and cameras and everything else was in one of them, because she'd done her developing in the back room of The Serpent's Truth and stored her equipment in the trunk. Which was locked. Which Tris had not opened, and which somehow had gone, still locked, to Nebraska.

It didn't matter at this late date. Or it did, but it was too late to do anything about it. Far country: wench: dead. Maybe I was just as superannuated, because tonight was Candlemas, and where was I? Not in a Circle, that much was clear.

I thought of the magic I'd once stepped into and out of as easily as a river, having been taught the knack of walking between the worlds. I was told by my teachers that the skill would never leave me.

But the problem was, those who'd taught me left instead, as did their friends, and my friends, and all the members of all the covens I'd joined and formed and dissolved and left, breaking apart in fractal disorder, leaving me alone and drifting, my lode-stars gone, wandering through the world that everyone said was the real world but that I knew to be only half...

Pay attention.

Between one heartbeat and the next I felt a chill rush of vertigo. My skin crawled and my scalp prickled as my hair stood on end. Something was here—something I'd tried to convince myself was a fluke of the trained imagination, a learned reflex. Something I hadn't felt in a long time and had never expected to feel again.

Not real.

Only it *was* real.

At least my sense of Her presence was.

She was here. Diana, Melusine, Lady Moon, The Goddess—*my* Goddess—was here with me, had come to me, as inarguably perceptible as She had been within the many Circles I had raised to Her. She was bitter and sweet, love and terror, nurture and destruction, just like the world She belonged in. And if I closed my eyes, I could see Her clearly, as objectively real as the furniture, or the sunrise to come.

Suddenly, I was drunk on something more potent than Chardonnay: the knowledge that I was Hers, and that I was never going to leave Her, and the thought that I would or could was simply as stupid (a trait many have said I am known for) as saying I was going to leave sunlight, or oxygen. I could ignore Her—I'd been doing that a lot lately—but I could not leave Her, nor would She leave me. She was a fact, like the existence of my fingers and toes was a fact.

'For She is Themis, Lady of Truth, and She is Ma'at, Goddess of the Balances, and She is Æquitas, Spirit of Fairness, and in Her measures She metes out fate.' I felt tears prickle at the back of my eyes, and in that moment I forgot Alex, Katie, Feral, and the puzzle of the trunk. I'd written those words in my "Book of Mist and Veils", a heartbroken demand for *fairness* in a cruel and arbitrary world.

The world is never fair and always cruel, but there is still joy. That was the lesson I'd known and pushed aside, as if, having learned it, I was too busy to live it.

But last loves are lasting, and She had been my first love and now my last. It was oddly comforting to know I could neither leave nor be left, no matter what came next.

Why here? Why now?

The only possible answer to that has always been: why not? It isn't really satisfying, but though They come to us, the Gods, like cats, rarely come precisely when They're called.

Slowly the sense of exaltation and numinousness faded, but this time I knew it was still there. That it would always be there any time I chose to take a half step away from the world and *look.*

I realized I wasn't going to get any more sleep tonight, and that I really didn't want to. I'd fallen in love again, but there was nobody to tell.

"If you weren't there, you'll never know."

"Behold, I will shew you a mystery."

I lay there in the darkness, staring at the ceiling, making happy plans and vowing vows I knew even in the moment I was never going to keep, and gradually coming to the annoyed realization that not only had I not gotten to the hangover part of the night's drinking yet, the part of my brain that was secular and worldly and unimpressed would not let go of that damned trunk.

'John and William and Alexandria (and the mysterious David) went to sea, in a beautiful sea-green trunk…'

Alex knew John as of old, and had tracked down William, but where did that leave little Kasey Hightower? By Alex's own story, her connection with William and John predated the (re) discovery of the Tarot. So why come looking for me at all? Why not just leave me out?

I have as much right to see Katie's pictures as they do!

The primal rage at being excluded is the earliest hatred we learn. To be shunned in the schoolyard, cast out, *left* out, leaves psychic scarring that never heals. The only saving grace is that adult society rarely stomps upon those primordial wounds, because if it did, we might find ourselves in somebody else's house in Seattle thinking of strangling our gracious hostesses. Every archaic instinct—not derived from Ancient Man, but from Kindergarten Me—screamed "trap" and "betrayal" and "evil plot", and for a brief instant I was utterly furious with Alex.

Then the moment passed, and while I was no less confused (it was a night for it), I was completely, extremely, and very wide awake. (And, as I was coming to know all-too-well, one's sixties are far less forgiving of an evening of wine and song followed by a night of no sleep than one's twenties were. Ah, well, coffee is a sacrament in almost every religion.) I went back to the beginning of what I knew in hopes that if I repeated it for long enough it would somehow manage to make sense. Alex had found Katie's Tarot, and that was why she'd tracked me down. It didn't matter that she'd already known William and John.

But she lied about it, didn't she?

Because *Saskia* had always ignored the truth in favor of a good story and *Alex* still did. *Pay attention*, The Goddess had said. But I didn't know what I should pay attention to. Not yet.

"Next year, goddammit, I am going to stay home and do Candlemas," I grumbled half-heartedly, throwing back the covers.

*

I got turned around coming out of my room, so I ended up at the top of the front staircase instead of the kitchen stairs. Now that everyone was asleep, Alex's house seemed even more like a stage set: eerily silent and lit only by the ambient light entering through exposed glass (and the judicious use of my phone). I was glad I'd grabbed Alex's sweater instead of my jacket when I'd gotten dressed, because the house was chilly and the back yard would be more so. I wondered if it had stopped raining yet, and I was pretty sure it hadn't.

William had banked the fire in the fireplace before we went up to bed, but its glowing embers gave a cheerful light, so I settled back down on the couch. The evening clutter was still here—Alex had said to leave everything for the morning—so I located my wineglass, half-full, and finished its contents. Possibly not the brightest and most adult thing I had ever done, but it was Candlemas. There was the fire, here was the wine.

That train of thought led directly to ritual, which led to libations. I picked up the nearest half-full wine bottle and got to my feet.

*

Prudent and provident owners of expensive and delightful houses have home security systems that are equally expensive and not particularly delightful, and Alex was no exception. I'd seen the discreet wires taped to the inside of every window when Alex gave me the tour, and the kitchen door had an alarm box that matched the one at the front door. If I opened the door without providing the proper propitiatory sacrifice, I was pretty sure the entire system would go off with a healthful barrage of lights and sirens and chatty calls to whoever was in its memory bank.

Fortunately for my plans, an (actual, physical) key to shut down the system was hanging from a hook beside the wall unit. I shut down the system, stuck the key in my pocket, and exited the house through the garden door.

The late winter rain hadn't stopped, and I shivered in the sudden chill. The beginnings of a poisonous hangover vanished as mind and body made wild protest: *Cold! No: Freezing! Also: Wet! Very Wet! Help!* I pulled the hood of the sweater up over my head to make what amends I could to my outraged mortal parts, but I was pleased to note that the rain hadn't weakened my resolve.

The stone terrace was inadequately covered by a redwood pergola that swept grandly northward along the back of the house. The terrace debouched directly into what I was positive was an exceedingly well-cared-for lawn in an exceedingly well-landscaped yard. Said yard had tactful security lighting scattered throughout. I looked around for a shrubbery or some ground suitable to my task.

Straight ahead was the gazebo, wreathed in gleaming fairy lights. To its right gurgled the koi pond, glowing from within, and behind that loomed the "yoga" studio. It was a more substantial structure than I'd imagined.

(Hadn't Alex said Katie's negatives were in the studio?)

I walked out onto the grass, turned to the east, made the appropriate libation accompanied by a silent recitation of one of the prettier parts of the Aradia, and was left with an empty wine bottle to dispose of.

(Diana Tregarde never has these problems.)

I walked slowly back toward the house, using my phone to make sure I didn't trip over something. As I skirted the koi pond, I wondered if I could catch a glimpse of the fish. Hadn't Alex said they cost ten thousand dollars apiece? It seemed odd for her to invest so much money in something she seemed to so dislike.

HORSEMEN IN BABYLON

I stopped at the edge of the pond to peer in. There was the most gossamer of nets—two layers—strung above the surface of the pond: coyotes, raccoons, and hawks prosper unexpectedly in urban environments like Seattle, and any of them would enjoy this high priced snack bar. The water was greenly murky, with the lily-pads on the surface illuminated to a dark true jade where they floated directly above the lights. Ghostly forms beneath the water came rising up to see what I was doing (and probably to see if I had food).

I was trying to remember the Pantone numbers for the colors I was seeing when something confusing and abrupt happened, and I found myself lying half in the pond, my legs still on dry(ish) land, and somebody's hand on the back of my neck keeping my head firmly underwater.

The netting pressed against my face and neck, and I thought about monofilament and blood and piranhas and sharks in a split-second absurdist thought-collage of disaster. My first thought was for my phone, which was now somewhere in the pond. My second was for my glasses, which might be anywhere. When I tried to move my hands and arms, I realized they were also tangled in the spider-web strands of the fish netting. When I opened my eyes, I saw fish making faces at me, but most of my attention was on *trying not to inhale.*

The need to breathe was becoming urgent, and, far worse, I felt a tickle in the back of my throat that told me I really needed to cough. Coughing, by the way, is one of those fence-sitting involuntary reflexes: sometimes you can suppress it, or you can consciously trigger it, but you can't really reliably control it.

It would be very bad if I started coughing underwater.

I thrashed as well as I could (which wasn't very), and was collecting myself to make one more lunge for freedom (and wondering if The Lady had visited me tonight because I would be joining Her before morning), when light flared behind me and the hand on my neck disappeared.

I reared backward, slamming the back of my head into Alex's face.

Seconds later, I lay on the grass coughing my lungs out and wishing I'd taken up smoking so I could vow to quit. Alex was patting me all over—it felt as if I was being assaulted by teddy bears—and begging me to tell her I was all right. I groped my face exploratively. No glasses.

I heard a door slam. William heaved me up to my feet, efficiently depositing me in the nearest lawn chair.

"What the actual hell just happened here?" he demanded.

I had reached the point where I was actually breathing, though I sounded like an asthmatic marathoner. "Pushed me in," I croaked.

"I did not!" Alex yelped righteously. I looked toward her, blinking futilely to bring her into focus. Clearly I'd hit her nose with force, because there was blood in her hair, blood down her chin, and blood all over the front of her vampire bride nightie. She kept trying to stanch the flow with her sleeve, which made her look as if she was starring in a low-budget spatter film. "When I got out here, he ran away."

"Who?" I wheezed.

"Never mind," William said. "Can you walk?"

I wondered just how bad I looked. "My phone's in the pond," I said.

"Come on," William said. "We need to get the two of you inside."

*

Alex followed us as William conducted me chivalrously, or at least determinedly, up the back stairs. Her entire sleeve was wadded against her face to keep from getting blood on the ivory carpet, reinforcing my random and incidental feeling that this was a house in which nothing ever happened. My teeth were chattering with the shock of my near-mortality by the time William marched me into my bathroom, sat me down on the teak bathing bench, and turned on the shower.

"*Hey!*" I said, plucking ineffectually at the grey hoodie and trying to duck out of the spray. Alex's sweater looked more or less done for, but still.

"Don't worry about that!" Alex called from the bedroom doorway. "Just throw it out! I'm going to go clean up."

"I've seen all you've got, remember?" William said. "You need to get warm fast. Stay under the shower until you're warm;

those clothes can't get any wetter. I'll be back."

He disappeared, and I regarded my boots unhappily before bending down to unlace them. My fingers were numb and they ached, and I didn't think it was just because of being chilled to the bone.

Somebody had tried to kill me. I could feel the ghost of that hand on the back of my neck, and shuddered. There'd been no doubt about the sincerity—for lack of a better word—of the assault, but what was the reason? It didn't feel like a random homicide, but I didn't have any enemies that cared that much, and nobody could have known I'd be in Alex's back yard in the middle of the night.

Yet here we all were.

I set my boots outside the shower. They weren't any wetter than a walk in the rain would've made them. My jeans went to the floor of the shower—it would save me from having to wash them. The grey sweater had developed clingy and elastic properties, and I had just managed to remove it when William returned with a steaming mug and my freshly washed bifocals.

"I got your phone out of the pond. I put it in a bag of rice, but I don't think it's in the phone business any more. Which one's that?" he asked, nodding toward my t-shirt.

"Left Right's *New York Is The World Tour*," I answered, taking the mug and seeing if its content was at a drinkable temperature. The return of my glasses gave me a feeling of being rearmored, no matter their inability to provide actual protection. "You should have left the phone in the pond. Maybe the fish want to call their lawyers."

"I had a couple of those," William said, fondly reminiscent, ignoring my insights into piscine sociology. "I don't suppose you want to sell it. Their merch is hot, in a quiet way."

He didn't end the sentence in the usual and vulgar (and obvious) way. He didn't have to. Before the Plague Years, when sex was simpler, we'd slept together a handful of times, and William was tactfully letting me know we could do that again.

Women who do not have extensive stock portfolios and second homes in the tropics rarely receive spontaneous propositions after the age of (let's be generous) fifty.

"Nah," I said. "Every time I wear it on the streets the

Youngs try to lecture me on imperialist colonialism."

"Couldn't give that up," William agreed solemnly. "Come down when you're ready. Alex is climbing the walls. I think she's worried you're going to sue her over this." He waggled his eyebrows at me, Groucho-style.

"Go," I said.

*

I finished the hot toddy William had brought, shampooed the pond-water out of my hair, hung up my jeans to drip, spread out my t-shirt to dry, and put my boots in the back of the closet. They'd be fine by the time I needed to catch the train for home. I deliberated upon the wisdom of wearing the Slaughter t-shirt, which was still clean and dry, but decided that warmth trumped sarcasm at this hour. Fortunately, Alex had left half her wardrobe here earlier. I liberated a duster-length cardigan, a random long sleeved t-shirt, an asymmetrical boat-neck tunic to keep it company, a "chunky knit" scarf/shawl that looked as if it'd been dragged backward through a disco, and a pair of velvet leggings (my only other choice being caftans, which would finish what my koi assailant had started). All of them were in what I was coming to think of as Alex's signature colors: ivory, cream, and off-white, with some random splashes of apricot. Everything that wasn't *moiré* was hand painted or tie-dyed.

As I turned to leave, I caught sight of myself in the pier glass. I looked like an exceptionally organic forest sprite from a Grey Panthers' production of the Condensed William Shakespeare. I vowed that when I got home I would find the brightest orange designer-label garment to be had and mail it to Alex. Thus armored and fortified (if barefoot), I ventured forth to wage knightly battle against anything available to wage knightly battle with.

*

In my absence, the breakfast nook had been led to prematurely execute its function, to the tune of a bright yellow folkloric tablecloth, three place settings, and a toast rack. It looked only slightly odd at this still vaguely predawn hour, but the dishwasher was chugging, the coffee was brewing, and William was scrambling eggs with an air of negligent confidence.

Alex, on the other hand, was fluttering about like an agitated moth. She'd clearly showered and changed, and her new ensemble consisted of a mostly transparent beaded robe with enormous batwing sleeves over a quilted vest and pants, making her look like a cross between Tinkerbell and a hockey goalie. She'd probably put on makeup, too, but it was difficult to tell through the large blue ice pack she was holding over her face.

At the sight of me, Alex burst into arias of sympathetic anguish. I would have taken them more seriously if I hadn't known her back in the day. Mistress Kate had once suggested Alex had missed her calling as a professional mourner.

"Are you okay? Kasey? You look terrible," she said flatteringly. "I feel so guilty! There's never been this kind of problem around here! I don't know what to do!"

"Breakfast is up," William said. "Ladies, take your seats."

*

It was a rather East Coast menu: scrambled eggs with salmon and cream cheese folded in. No bagels, but a tall stack of toast and a strawberry jam that was so refined and exclusive that the name of its maker appeared nowhere on the jar.

The coffee was pretty damned good, too.

Alex spent the meal holding the ice pack to her face and trying not to glare at me beseechingly. William, insouciantly oblivious, took back the scrambled eggs he'd served her when it became clear she wasn't going to touch it, and attacked the toast stockpiles with efficient ravenousness.

"So," William asked, once I was on my third cup of coffee. "Why *were* you out there in the middle of the night?"

"In the rain," Alex added in doleful and congested tones.

"It's Candlemas," I explained.

There was a long pause. "You still do that?" There was a stifled sort of incredulity in his tone indicating that while he thought I was crazy, it wouldn't be kind to say so.

"It seemed appropriate," I said. I glanced over at the empty wine bottle sitting accusingly on the white marble kitchen island. It beat providing the long-form explanation, even if I could have managed it in a tactful fashion at this hour.

"What about you?" William asked. This time, the question was directed to our gracious hostess.

"I don't *know!*" Alex said in her new foghorn voice. "He ran away when I put on the outside lights."

Alex seemed to have skipped ahead a few questions in the What Just Happened Playbook. "Who did?" I asked. It seemed to me that the assault had been oddly personal, if misguided, enough so that Alex might have ventured a guess whodunnit, or at least a shortlist of subjects.

"I didn't see him, Kasey!"

After a few more Abbot and Costello exchanges, the three of us established that there was a portable remote provided by the security company specifically to notify a client if any of the house's doors—including the garage and the outside studio—were opened, alarm on or not. Alex slept with it. And, having been awakened by it, she came downstairs to see what her unruly houseguests might be doing. When she opened the back door, she saw someone kneeling beside the koi pond, and turned on the security floodlights to see better. The bad guy fled, Alex succored yours truly, and William came along to see why all the lights were on at that hour of the morning.

"Listen, Kasey, we don't really have to bother anyone about this, right?" This was the third or fourth time Alex had asked me some variation of this, so apparently William's guess about police reports was correct. Anything involving the police would jack her homeowner's insurance to new and painful heights.

"She was *not* out there taking a close look at the fish, Alex!" William said forcefully.

"But you're okay, right? Nothing's really happened," Alex said to me beseechingly. "Right?"

"It's okay," I said to her. "I'm fine. No worries."

"You sure you don't want to file a report?" William asked, while Alex glared daggers at him.

"Much as I'd like to know who wanted to drown me, I don't want to get involved in some kind of investigation that would drag on forever and not change anything," I said, rather tartly. It was only after the words had left my mouth, I realized I could just as easily have been talking about Katie's long-ago murder.

"Thank you," Alex said in relief. "Besides, John's coming tomorrow. Today, really. You don't want to miss that."

By now, I wasn't sure whether I did or not. I tried to summon up an image of him, but all I could see in my mental eye was Katie's pictures of a very young man dreaming the same dreams we'd all had. He might have grown up to be anyone. All I knew of him now was that he took very good photographs.

Our original plans (meaning Alex's original plans) for Saturday had involved a tour of Lapwing Gallery to see the current show, followed by a visit to one of the choicer bistros for lunch, followed by a return to the house to welcome the last of our Lambs.

It had seemed to be a reasonable, if exhausting, program, but that was before my phone and I took a dive. I told Alex my day was going to be involved with figuring out how quickly I could get a replacement, and catching up on the sleep I'd missed.

She did not take it well.

"But I had this *all planned out!*" she said. Her voice rose in pitch and volume throughout her speech until I feared for the integrity of any wineglasses in the neighborhood. "You can't just *change your mind because you want to.* What would you do if John showed up early?"

I'd assumed that what I'd do would be to say something on the order of "Hello, John," and let him into the house, but Alex's question made me wonder if she knew something about John that I didn't. Such as, perhaps, his penchant for midnight walks in other peoples' back yards.

"Of course she can," William said. "And anything I might add to that would get me drummed out of the Simone de Beauvoir Marching and Chowder Society."

For that matter (if I was being unfairly fair and suspecting everyone), if William had been sound asleep, he'd certainly gotten dressed pretty damned fast. His bedroom was two doors down from mine, and therefore also faced the back: he could have looked out the window into the garden, saw me go out, come down to drown me, jogged around the house when Alex turned on the lights, come in through the front door and out the back with perfect timing to play the stalwart rescuer.

Of course, I couldn't think of a single reason either of them, John or William, or, for that matter, Alex, would want to kill me. Except maybe Alex, right now when I was spoiling her plans.

"Besides," I said. "You'd probably better see if your doctor wants to do anything about your nose. I hope I didn't break it," I added.

But while I *did* hope that, I was saying it more to divert her than because I meant it. In the preoccupied world of the young, her self-obsession had hardly been noticeable. In the somewhat older world we both now inhabited, her pseudo-solipsism was making her someone hard to warm up to.

"It will be fine," she said in forlorn tones resonating with the hope of being contradicted. "But I must look awful."

"It's really hard to tell when you're holding that thing over your face," William said helpfully.

"I should go look," Alex said seriously, and got to her feet.

And that left William and me alone. I raised a defiant eyebrow.

"Usually they shoot you," William said. "Or hit you over the head with a handy crowbar."

I was again struck by the *intimacy* of the attack. "He thought I was somebody," I said slowly, forgetting for the moment I was speaking to someone on my Assailant Shortlist.

William raised a doubtful eyebrow. "Someone who'd be wandering around Alex's back yard at four am? If you think someone's stalking Alex, I don't think that timing works. I think they were probably after the fish."

Irresistibly, I imagined someone scuttling down the street holding several large water-filled bags of illicitly acquired fish. But it neither explained nor absolved Alex's nighttime caller.

"I don't see why she doesn't just get rid of them," I said. "She doesn't seem to like them very much."

"Oh, they aren't hers," William began, and was interrupted by Alex's return to the kitchen.

She had changed clothes again, and was now dressed in what I imagined was probably one of her "work" wardrobe outfits. A very chunky knit sweater with an enormous cowl neck so long that, even artfully rolled, it obscured the lower half of her face; pants (in something approaching a color, assuming olive-grey counts) whose legs were ornamented with straps and wraps and buckles and cinches and all manner of interesting and expensively-retailed texture, and black ankle boots with enough presence to talk back to the pants. Her nose, while still reddish, looked as if I hadn't actually managed to break it.

"See?" she said brightly. "All fixed."

*

Alex wanted to show off her gallery to *someone,* and William was willing to let it be him (even though he must have seen it before, if they'd known each other for as long as Alex had implied). Since it was going to be "only him," she added a number of errands on to the front end of the expedition, moving the departure time back almost to 8:00 am for no particular reason. I was reminded that—in the world I had left and that Alex apparently still inhabited—female power lay in passive-aggressive victimhood. To win, one must become the victim in any situation—even one of triumph. After which, one extorted a number of meaningless concessions to consolidate their gains.

I did wonder why Alex was still playing the game when she was the boss. Just not enough to go digging.

*

As Alex prepared to leave with William, he gave me a number of eloquent looks which I was wholly unable to decipher, but which left me faintly worried. Meanwhile, I made great play of my feeble and exhausted state, and on inspiration added: "Alex, do you have a computer I can borrow? I'd like to get the whole replacing my phone thing started."

"Oh!" Alex said. "I keep the computer out in the studio, or I'd be on it all the time. But I have a tablet you can borrow."

Alex trotted off up the back stairs (we were all still in the kitchen—it's where the coffee was—and I realized that I didn't

172

think I'd ever seen Alex use the front staircase, which was another eternally-ignorable conundrum) and returned with an iPad Mini, which is basically a too-large phone you can't make calls on. I expressed my delight in it nevertheless, topped up my mug, and made my doddering way back to my room, replete with good food.

And with a head stuffed full to bursting.

*

Magickal folklore, if not magickal theory, holds that every magician dares the Abyss somewhere in their thirties, undergoing a test of nerve and will which must be passed if their magickal development is going to continue. Folklore expands to mention that a lot of junior *wunderkinder* who flare up and burn out IRL are also victims of the Abyss, because, as Nietzsche never said, "If you don't go to the Abyss, then the Abyss will come to you."

The Abyss is both a real metaphysical danger and a useful metaphor. Statistically, I was an outlier, for example. Wiccans generally came to the Craft somewhere in their twenties, hung on for a couple decades at most, and then drifted away. Only a few had the will, the stamina, and the stubbornness to juggle work and family and real life and the Craft as the years passed and the mundane obligations accumulated. I'm not sure I was statistically relevant, owing to my frequent timeouts and lack of a family and (some might say) a life, but the fact remained: I was (now and probably for the rest of my life) Wiccan, and I was sixty-five.

The moral of that story is: I was properly situated to sit in judgment on Alex.

Not that I thought sh'd done anything that was actually *bad*. And not that whatever verdict I reached would have any real-world consequences. In fact, it wasn't something I expected to *ever* have a conversation with Alex about. But I was familiar with the sort of oaths she would have sworn, back in the day, and the fact that she was here in this lovely hermetic little life of hers indicated exactly one thing: she'd dared the Abyss and she'd failed.

173

HORSEMEN IN BABYLON

You may not be familiar with this idea, so I'll explain. When crossing the Abyss, you meet and must conquer your Jungian Shadow Self. Conquest is rewarded with a perfect and true knowledge of one's own inner self, which is about as annoying as it sounds.

But to fail the Abyss...

Failure means spending the rest of your life trapped in a wilderness of mirrors, never getting what you want because you don't *know* what you want. Nothing in the world is real enough to penetrate the veils of illusion. The only one who could save you is you, and you've already blown your chance.

As Alex had. Maybe even before she'd become Saskia for us. I remembered how we'd all adored her, but that intensity of engagement is not something that survives maturity. I suspect that from her point of view, her worshippers just incomprehensibly faded away, and she'd never been able to get them back.

*

I took care of the digital housekeeping that goes with a bricked phone and arranged, via text, for a new phone to be sent to me c/o my place of employment. Maybe tomorrow I could return the current one to its maker for last rites.

(Maybe tomorrow I could go home.)

The longer I was here, the more I had the sense of something about to go really wrong, and I didn't know what it was. I did know that I did not want to be here when it happened. Furthermore, I would be happy to live out my days not even knowing what the nature of this Impending Doom was. That was one of the differences between me and Baby Me: I did not want to find things out *Just Because*.

But I *did* really want to see the rest of Katie's pictures. Since I was positive Alex intended to make me jump through a strenuous number of hoops for that privilege, I thought I'd wait until Alex and William were firmly entangled in Seattle's trendaliciousness, then go look for them.

And so, I prudently settled myself in the guest room's Comfy Chair with a book extolling the romance of growing lavender in Provence.

When I opened my eyes again, the clock on the computer tablet said it was noon.

*

The koi seemed disappointed that I didn't stop for them today. A flicker of light as I moved past their pond drew my attention to something I hadn't seen the night before. I'd heard the splashing of the fountain then, but I hadn't seen that the fountain included a mermaid up at the top of the pile of stones at the back of the fountain. She held up her mirror, but she didn't seem really happy at what she was seeing, since she held it away from herself. The mirror was a real mirror. That was why I'd noticed it this morning.

I reached the "yoga studio", put my hand on the knob, and stopped.

I'd smacked Alex in the nose trying to escape from a watery grave. We'd all seen the results. And I hit her because I was doing my best to get my head above water, which I did the moment my attacker let go.

Last night, I'd unlocked the back door, walked out, made libation to the Goddess, and returned by way of the koi pond, into which I had shortly thereafter been pushed. Say five minutes. Ten at the most. I was not held underwater long enough to drown or lose consciousness, so call that ninety seconds at best.

In that six to eleven minute time frame, Alex had to wake up, get up, come downstairs, check the back of the house, register the presence of a stranger, turn on the floodlights to give herself a solid alibi, and run to my side as my assailant fled, leaning over me at the exact second I reared back.

It wasn't that I thought Alex had tried to drown me.

It was that I thought she'd definitely seen who had.

*

The door to the studio had one of those state of the art keypad locks because it was tied in to the rest of the very expensive security system. I took a chance and put in the code to shut down the house system. It worked. I stepped inside.

The studio was divided into two rooms. An archway, covered with a dark red curtain, blocked the view into the inner one. Watery mid-afternoon light came from the windows on three sides.

The only items in the outer room were a long-handled peacock feather fan propped up against the wall and a number of empty ornamental baskets tumbled into a corner. These had pink gingham ribbons tied around their various necks and handles. The floor was wood, stained dark, with one of those very on-trend hand-painted sailcloth rugs covering most of it. The space had the air of being a kind of doll's house, wherein some very adult children would gather to drink notional tea from empty cups and tell each other the imagined details of their unreal lives.

It was the perfect conflation of twee and horror, and I wondered why, when I realized it was the colors.

The outside of the studio door had been painted the same red as the front door of the house. Its inside, and the interior window frames, were painted a vibrant organic pink. The room had painted paneling in a violet that seemed as if the organic pink had died of anoxia, and above the chair-rail there was a Victorian-adjacent pattern of stripes, lace, crocheted swags, and nosegays of pink rosebuds that somehow managed to look hostile. The rug was definitely Mary Engelbreit-influenced, if not a direct copy of one of her designs.

Who spent their time here? Who'd chosen these colors? If it had been Alex, what had she been *on?* If it *had* been Alex, which one of these two—home or studio—accurately reflected her tastes? (Maybe I'd ask her sometime. From a safe distance.)

And where was the computer—not to mention the chairs?

I went on through the curtain.

Bingo.

The inner room was set up more or less as an office, one belonging to a slightly older child, perhaps. Certainly one with better taste. The walls were papered in William Morris. The windows were curtained in the same pattern. The floor had a couple of nice antique "Oriental" rugs that managed to not clash with everything else. There was a Lawson chair, upholstered in cut velvet, beside a standing lamp with a stained glass shade in shades of green and yellow. Alex's computer sat on a small round table on top of a gigantic crocheted doily spread over a pink paisley glazed chintz tablecloth with ruching and gathers cascading down to the hem. The chair associated with the table, a vintage Bentwood side chair, would induce lumbago in any unwary person who tried to use it.

On the back wall, between the two windows artfully overgrown with ivy, was Katie's prop mirror. Like most of Katie's props, it had begun as sidewalk salvage: a round convex mirror about ten inches across, with sunrays of various lengths composing the frame. I could not imagine what it was doing here. Katie wouldn't have kept her props at The Snake—there wouldn't have been room. The only thing I could imagine was that Alex had looked high and low until she found a duplicate.

(That was the only possibility, right?)

(Oh, KC, why are you really here?)

(My name is Bast.)

By now I realized that wanting to see Katie's pictures wasn't a good enough reason to be here. I didn't know why I was here. I was here because I had to be, and that wasn't Here-and-Now Me, that was Other Me.

Witch Me.

I took a deep breath and forced myself to keep going.

Beside the computer was a state of the art large format printer-scanner which would set you back at least six grand retail. I wondered why Alex had it, until I saw the frames stacked along the baseboard. Clearly, she was printing out some of the art for her gallery. Maybe posters? I made a note to go through them if I had the chance before Alex and William returned. Alex struck me as the sort who lunched from 1pm to 3pm, which meant I should have enough time to take a good look at her computer.

I had only taken a few steps toward the computer when I saw the trunks.

Stacked beside the archway—and thus invisible to anyone who didn't actually enter the room—were three vintage-or-antique storage trunks of various sizes, all open, as if they were there as some kind of decorative accent. More of Katie's props hung from the lid of the biggest one. I recognized the top hat I'd worn for the Tarot project, a jester's cap and bells, a "magic" wand with a glittery star on the end. I approached the trunks as cautiously as if I expected to find Katie in one of them, but no.

Just a couple of Katie's cameras, and most of Katie's props.

Why were Katie's *props* here?

I put together everything I knew, and even with a generous amount of hand waving of the "and then a miracle occurred" sort, it made no sense.

Katie was murdered. Her photographs and negatives were safe because they'd been at the Snake, which (hand wave) passed the locked trunk on to a barn in Nebraska (hand wave, hand wave). Katie's props had been at her apartment, which she shared with Becky, whom Alex didn't like. Two or three days after the murder, Alex and John-or-Jon checked Katie's apartment. Everything was gone.

"Oh, *Alex*," I sighed. She'd probably stolen and squirreled this stuff away and made up a story to explain how it had all gone missing. Just like her, really. Then she'd brought it out again once the trunk was discovered, because she had a magpie streak a mile wide and wanted her entire treasure trove together.

I turned away from the trunks and sat down in front of the computer. It was password protected. I entered the security code for the house and it accepted it without hesitation. (This is why it's easy to steal from the rich.) Most of the files were irrelevant to my current investigation. I wasn't interested in correspondence, or bookkeeping, or the details of shows held at Lapwing, and—oddly enough—I wasn't here to spy.

I just wanted to see the rest of Katie's Tarot.

Lost along with all the rest of her work, and she hadn't finished even the Major Arcana, as far as any of us had known. Until last night, when Alex told me that the final Arcanum had been found inside one of Katie's salvaged cameras. Which had somehow made it from her body back to...

Where?

Thinking about that brought me to a stop again. The cameras would have been the most clearly valuable items she had with her. Why would some unknown mugger shoot Katie and not take her valuables? Did the police (at the time) say the photographic equipment was missing? Or did they just not say anything at all, because none of us was related to Katie?

If Time is a thief, then Memory is a playa. I couldn't remember which it had been—but I knew that if I tried to remember long enough and hard enough, I would absolutely believe whatever I decided was true.

I surrendered to intuition once more and abandoned the computer to investigate the frames stacked against the walls. As I'd thought, most of it was notices of upcoming shows. A few were art pieces like the ones in the guest bedroom.

When I found the second Arcanum (Justice), I started putting the framed Arcanum aside.

Alex's gotten an awful lot of work done on these, hasn't she? Good enough to hang for a show. Too bad the artist is dead and can't negotiate a contract.

Twenty-two 18 x 24 glass and metal picture frames is a lot of picture frames.

I started laying them out face up, from the back left corner of the room, leaving gaps in the sequence for the ones I hadn't found yet. Gradually, the rows of frames backed me into the opposite corner, until I was leaning against the big trunk with 'The World' in my hands.

There are twenty-two Major Arcana in a Tarot deck, numbered zero to twenty-one. (Magic: not about Earth Logic at the best of times.) Katie had done her shoots more or less in card order, but it was essentially a fluke that the last card she had to shoot was the last one in the Arcana.

Card XXI: The World.

It wasn't the final version; the finished cards included their names and numbers in the image. But even if this wasn't quite what Katie had intended *The World* to look like, it was all we were ever going to get. I gazed at it, thinking something was a little off, wondering if Alex had just taken a random "close enough" image and called it the last Arcanum. Or hired somebody to fake it for the sake of a good story.

But no. Anybody who wanted to fake Katie's work would have to have a time machine and a solid grounding in the metaphysical Tarot. Or at least deep pockets and a large warehouse full of vintage Americana. And this card had all the proper symbolism for it to be at least a test composition.

Something was off, though. I studied the picture more closely.

The image was composed of street signs and scavenged stuffed animals all grouped around Katie's favorite prop, the sun mirror. She'd managed to balance the mirror on the top of a bunch of crates, so that it was about eye-height. Behind it was a brick wall with the faded remains of some long ago painted advert; "The World" was the only part still legible.

Finally, I realized what was wrong.

Nothing was reflected in the mirror. Not even sky.

Someone had erased the reflection in the mirror before this image had been printed.

Why?

And *Who* and *When* as well, though I suspected I knew the answer to that. It was John (so I'd been told) who had salvaged the film in the cameras—although he couldn't have, because the cameras were with Katie when Katie was shot and so the shooter stole them. Only they hadn't been stolen, because they were here, in a trunk with all of Katie's finished work.

My head hurt.

Of course, I didn't know for sure the cameras I'd seen were Katie's cameras. But if they weren't, where had the last Arcanum come from? Katie had been shooting it the day she was murdered.

Cameras, trunk, negatives, and props. (All were going to St. Ives.) None of which had been anywhere near each other when Katie was shot, all of which were now here, and I didn't know how it had happened or what it meant.

By now, I'd backed myself into a corner (in all senses of the word). I'd have to move all the framed Arcana before I could move me and get to the computer to see if Mystery Photographer aka John aka Prime Suspect had saved the original of the last image before he'd altered it. I started stacking the nearest frames, making no effort to get them back into their original places. I figured I had a good ninety minutes before William and Alex got back, and then I could…

Well, honestly I didn't have the faintest idea what I'd do then.

I never got a chance to find out either.

The outside door opened, delivering a blast of damp Seattle air. I held very still. Alex's office was full of mirrors, and Katie's sunburst had been hung up in a straight line with the door. In its distorted reflection, I saw a man about my age standing in the doorway. A stranger. He wouldn't be able to see me without coming farther inside. Maybe he was looking for Alex. Maybe he'd go away.

I concentrated on breathing shallowly and evenly. For some reason, the possibility of a second murder attempt in less than twenty-four hours made me amazingly twitchy. I was willing to bet that I was looking at the lost Lamb. John Smith, photographer and man of mystery.

He looked good, in that "I'm too hip to notice I'm bleeding cool" sort of way. Chinos with suspenders, a collarless shirt, an old man cardigan with leather elbow patches, rubber soled duck boots, wire-rim glasses. He had a portfolio under his arm. As soon as he saw the computer was on, he closed the door and came in.

"Alex, I thought we'd agreed that you wouldn't—"

That was when he saw the rest of the Tarot laid out on the carpet. Another step brought him to the shoreline of the sea of frames and he saw me. We stared at each other for a moment, then he went over to the Tiffany-adjacent floor lamp and reached out over the framed pictures to turn it on. It had gotten darker in here while I'd been working.

"You must be, uh, Kacey?" he asked. "What are you doing in here?"

I didn't correct him about my name. I didn't want him—not any of them—to know my name, much less my *real* name. "Looking for proof you killed Katie," I answered. *And tried to kill me.*

I hadn't expected to say it. I hadn't intended to say it. But those who go on about "the patience of age" are idiots. Live enough decades and you'll be more than ready to cut to the chase.

John looked astonished. It was the expression of someone who was guilty of one thing but accused of something completely different. Either that or he was trying to remember who "Katie" was—although if he couldn't, that was hardly Alex's fault.

"Katie? Why would I want to kill *Katie*?" John demanded. "I loved her—didn't you?"

"I did," I said. "We all did." *Too much,* I thought now. *Too much to tell her when she was being reckless.*

But that wasn't right. It had been *Saskia* we'd all thoughtlessly adored. Hadn't it?

"But you tried to drown me in the fish pond," I said, just as if one murder implied another.

"Sorry," he said (and he did actually sound at least regretful). "Alex's always talking about poisoning my fish. You were wearing her clothes and waving around a wine bottle. I thought you were her. When the lights went on and I saw her on the steps, I realized I had, um, it wasn't her."

"Alex strikes me as someone who values her beauty sleep," I said. John's smile flickered briefly.

"Wait. How could she be...? *Your* fish?" I said. I wondered if he would have actually gone through with the murder if it really had been Alex. Or if he would have intended only to scare her, and accidentally held her down for too long. *No, just an accident. Sorry. These things happen.*

"I got burnt out—wildfire—a couple years ago. I managed to save my koi, but I had to keep them somewhere while I rebuilt. She had this crazy big house, and it already had a pond. She said I could keep my koi here until I could move them back home. It should have been perfect."

He set down his portfolio beside the Bentwood chair and began stacking the rest of the frames. Every time he had a stack of four, he passed them to me, and I stacked them all around the trunks. There I was in a top hat. There was Feral, *faux*-fierce. Jon, John, Mistress Kate. Other people I'd known once, names now irrevocably sundered from faces in my mental card catalogue.

And Saskia. Alex. A white gold flame, glowing with the delight of being adored.

"Why wasn't it perfect?" I asked quietly.

John picked up his portfolio and sat down on the Bentwood chair. He held the portfolio across his knees, drumming absently on it with his fingertips. "Alex figured she owned me now, and she had this dumbshit idea that one photographer's style is just like another's, and—"

There was a skirl of cold damp air. The outer door had opened again.

"It wasn't a dumbshit idea!"

I knew Alex hadn't been listening long, because she could never manage to keep from inserting herself into any conversation. Her appearance was the latest exhausting shock of the day: she was wearing my leather jacket and my The Slaughter t-shirt. Alex had always borrowed my clothes, but this time it was different. This time it wasn't something I'd freely handed over. She'd gone into my room. She'd taken from me. It was a clear message: *I rule, you submit.*

"You said yourself her style was like yours, and this would be your juvenilia, recently unearthed. Eighties New York is red-hot right now, this could be the show that puts you over the top!" Alex said.

John rose to his feet, weaving from side to side like a wounded bear.

"But it *isn't my work!*" he bellowed. "It's hers! You want to show it, do it under her name! You took everything else from her, Alex. Don't take that."

"She's dead, she doesn't need it," Alex snapped. "And I do. And she owes me! She does! She broke her promise!"

The sheer high school inanity of Alex's words made me look sharply at her. This wasn't some black joke that just hadn't landed. Alex was serious.

"She told me I was going to be the *World* card! Me! And then she said she'd changed her mind! You aren't allowed to change your mind! She wasn't even going to tell me! I went down to where she was working—I was sure I could make her see that I'd be better than whoever else she'd picked. But when I got there, she said she was done. I was so angry with her."

"Sure you were. Only to be expected." John sounded tired, his voice quiet and even. The only light in the room was from the floor lamp, a small golden puddle of civilization surrounded by shadows.

I got up from the floor. "I'm going to go see where William

is."

"Take this," John said, handing me his portfolio. "It's what you want."

I took the portfolio. For a moment our eyes locked. His looked resigned. I don't know what he saw when he looked at me. Maybe it wasn't me he saw.

*

There's a 4pm train to Portland, and I was on it. William drove me down to the station. He offered to drive me all the way home, but I turned him down. We exchanged business cards. It was all very civil and polite. He asked me to text him when I got there. I said, "yes, ma." He hugged me goodbye. I probably hugged him back.

I waited until the train pulled out of the station to open John's portfolio. Each image had its own sleeve; you could page through the photographs as if holding an exceptionally large book. The Arcanum were there—the same prints I'd seen framed in Alex's studio. The last three pages were all Arcanum XXI. The World.

The first image was the same as the framed one had been, except for the fact that the reflection in the mirror hadn't been edited. The next was a blow-up of just the mirror. The last was the same image, only it had been cleaned up—sharpened—digitally. Just as I'd thought, the mirror did hold a reflection.

Only it wasn't John. It wasn't William. It was Alex.

It was Saskia.

Why are your hands in your pockets, Sass? What do you have in there?

I don't think Katie could have seen her, but the mirror did. Alex, standing against a grimy brick wall, wearing that white velvet cape she'd spent so much time cleaning.

After Katie was murdered, Alex never wore her white velvet cape again.

I hear that blood is very difficult to get out of velvet.

*

Once upon a time there'd been seven Lambs to the Slaughter. We'd all been honest starving artists and magicians, except Alex. Alex never had any artistic talent—or artistic eye—at all. "*Oh, not me. I've never been an artist.*" And so, little Alex had to exist in the art of others. Like Katie.

Then Katie told Saskia she didn't want to use her for The World, the last card in the deck. Maybe Katie said she wanted to re-do The Star as well. Maybe Katie's camera saw more clearly than any of us had.

Saskia had gone to where Katie was working anyway. Maybe Saskia hoped she could change Katie's mind.

But Katie had said she didn't need her.

So Saskia shot her.

It doesn't seem like a big enough motive for murder, but ask any cop. People have killed over a candy bar. Murder is quick and so easy when the right tools are easy to hand. The impulse is there and gone like a flash of lightning, and the reason most people aren't murderers is luck. Theirs, and their potential victims.

Neither Saskia nor Katie was lucky that day.

*

The train went clickity onward through the night, an interstitial passageway between past and future. In a couple of hours, I'd be home and safe. I would light a candle to my Lady and She would enfold me with Her presence. For a little while, I would be able to set aside the burden of knowledge.

But I wasn't there yet. And there were still strands to unweave.

So Once Upon a Time, the Lamb who would grow up to be Alex shot Katie, and then took Katie's cameras and anything else she wanted—like the mirror—away with her. Then Alex went back to the Snake and carried off the trunk Katie kept stored there, because Alex knew as well as I did that Tris would open it the moment he heard Katie was dead.

Alex took Katie's trunk back to her own apartment. None of us had ever been there, and now I think it was because she was afraid to let us see where she was living—and see that she had no trouble affording Manhattan rents.

Next, Alex went up to the apartment Katie shared with Becky and grabbed everything else of Katie's she could find. She probably told Becky that Katie was moving in with her. Maybe Jon, or John, or Feral hadn't even gone inside with her when Alex went back later on her so-called "sanitizing" expedition. Maybe all of us had taken Alex's word for the condition of Katie's bedroom. That part hardly mattered.

Then Katie was dead, and Alex had Katie's photographs, and after a few years almost nobody remembered either Katie or her Tarot series. (Even us. Even me.)

And everyone lived happily ever after, or they didn't, but either way, many years passed. I was willing to bet that Alex never forgot about Katie, and the horrible injustice (she felt) Katie had done her. I don't know what the trigger was. Maybe it was William showing up again. Maybe John wanted to change galleries. "*I need this*," Alex had said, and I doubted I'd ever get the whole story. But I had enough.

Alex thought it would be simple to mount an exhibition of Katie's work and have John take credit for them. Alex had no idea that John's style could never be mistaken for Katie's. Alex was art-blind, the way some people are tone-deaf. What Alex probably intended was to stage the show while John was away and present him with a *fait accompli* when he got back.

But to resurface the items—since John would see them eventually—Alex needed to explain where they'd been, so she got the bright idea of asking William for a steamer trunk, and for plausible deniability's sake, claimed it was John's idea. (Or David's. Someone named David kept showing up in the narrative and by now I had no idea of whether he was real or not.)

I don't know whether the trunk was locked or not when Alex got it (or for that matter, if that part of the story was true at all), but it would have been easy enough to *re*-lock it after she'd put Katie's stuff inside. Now the negatives were deniably, so she thought, back in play.

John would have known that the undeveloped film in a camera couldn't survive forty years in a barn. William would have known whether a trunk he bought was full or empty, locked or unlocked. But neither of them pushed very hard. When they saw Katie's things, they might have assumed Alex was merely a thief. Theft would have fit most of the available details. And so, neither of them wanted to push matters—until John found out Alex intended to put his name on Katie's work.

Had he already developed the last Arcanum? He must have understood what he was seeing, or he wouldn't have scrubbed the image. But Alex had hostages, so he couldn't afford to anger her.

I think that unthinkable thing—the glib assumption that he would take credit for the work of another artist—was what caused John to finally take a good hard look at Alex, and he didn't like what he saw. When he saw me that night by the pond—and thought I was her—he'd had an impulse. I don't think it had ever occurred to Alex that John was a frequent and unheralded visitor to her garden. She recognized him when the security lighting came on, and then had to pretend she hadn't.

John realized he'd been attempting to murder the wrong person, and fled. William suspected *something* wasn't right, so he sacrificed himself to give me a clear shot at snooping. Alex, having discovered that John wanted her dead, decided to make sure William and I were on her side. It was why she'd reacted so badly when I innocently opted out of the mini-tour of Seattle this morning.

"*You aren't allowed to change your mind!*"

"*You can't just change your mind because you want to.*"

I was lucky I'd survived breakfast.

Why had I been there at all? I was supposed to be the useful idiot, the one who would confirm the salient details of Alex's story for some magazine interview I was sure she'd already set up. That was why she'd gotten in touch with me. The only reason. That was why her responses at the beginning of that first night rang so hollow. She was still getting into character and putting the last touches on the script.

And just what did I do now? I had circumstantial evidence in a forty-year-old murder. Even a first year law student could get Alex acquitted: all that had to be said was that Alex had left the area before the shooter arrived. Maybe Katie had developed a sense of self-preservation at the last. Maybe she'd taken Alex along that day. She could have.

I knew she hadn't.

*

It took me a few weeks to write down everything I knew and had guessed about the murder of Katie Larkham. By the time I finished I was racing against the clock—the rumors about a new plague had become facts, and nobody knew what to do to keep from catching it. I knew as little as anyone, but I knew I had to get my project done before anything happened to me.

I'd included all the names and addresses I could find. I included my theory. I even included a copy of the photograph that told me so much and wouldn't tell anyone else anything at all. I wrote it all down and packaged it all up. I'd had to think for a good long while before I'd figured out who to send it to. New York City has a very well organized Cold Case Squad, and after all, it was a Manhattan murder.

The Fed Ex envelope was on my altar, all addressed and ready to send off, but before I did, I intended to give it all the help I could.

So I cast the first Circle I'd cast in fourteen years.

*

"I call upon You in Your aspect as Themis, Lady of Truth. I call upon You as Ma'at, Goddess of the Balances. I summon Æquitas, Spirit of Fairness. In Her balances, She weighs out Justice. I call for justice to be done here. Justice for Katie Larkham, for Jon Armstrong Butler, for George Rodney Alvin Kate. Let there be justice for John Smith, for William Sebastian Farrell. Let there be justice for Alexandria Kaczka…"

I paused for a long time before I could bring myself to speak the last name.

"And let there be justice for Karen Celeste Hightower. In their names, I call for justice. Let these words be the voice of the one whose voice was taken. Let them bring truth to the one who reads them. By my will, it is done."

I felt the subtle rise and cresting of power as my words were heard and my spell was cast. I did not intend to ever again explain everything away as self hypnosis and wishful thinking. I had called for truth, and it was time to take up mine.

Light a candle for the past. It's the country of the dead. I know this because I have walked the dead lands.

My name is Bast, and I'm a Witch.

Author's Note: Some readers may recognize that the idea of a photographic New York City Tarot did not originate with me. I had been kicking around an idea for a story involving a group of old friends having a reunion and somehow in the course of the weekend it is discovered that one of them is the murderer in an old unsolved murder case. Eventually, I put that together with my copy of The (Real and Actual and Not Mine) New York Tarot (which I bought from Giani Siri back in the day), and a story was born. Of course, the cards as I describe them, and the people who are in them, are totally fictional, figments of my imagination, and NOT REAL.

The following description (better than anything I could write) is from an article in the blog Bedford and Bowery, April 19, 2008, by Hanna Frishberg: *"In 1987, bike messenger Giani Siri self-published The New York Tarot, a 93-card deck with photos of New Yorkers and city scenes used as art for the traditional major and minor arcana characters. Largely unknown and never widely available, the deck is both a time capsule and a love letter to New York in the 1970s and '80s."*

Yeah, that pretty much says it all. The Tarot images accompanying the article seem to be gone now, but you may be able to pull up some of the images on the web.

New York Times best-selling writer Rosemary Edghill (aka eluki bes shahar) has been telling tales for over 35 years, and is the author of *Bell, Book, and Murder: The Bast Mysteries*. She's written not just science fiction and fantasy novels, but also romance, mystery, steampunk, comic book tie-ins, young adult urban fantasies, and technothrillers. In addition to working as an editor, anthologist, book designer, illustrator, and reviewer, she's known for her collaborations with such notables as Marion Zimmer Bradley, Andre Norton (*Carolus Rex I* and *II*), and Mercedes Lackey (*The Bedlam Bard's Series* and *The Shadow Grail Series*).

Rosemary Edghill has won a KISS Award from Romantic Times for *Paladin* in *The Hellflower Trilogy*. She was also shortlisted for the Rhysling Award for *Frozen Hitler Found In Atlantean Love Nest*, which appeared in the anthology *Alien Pregnant Elvis*, edited by Esther Friesner.

She currently lives in Oregon, USA.

By Christopher Gorman

"MR. DRAYCE?"

"That's me," Jonas said as he roughly shoved all but one of his sketches into his beige canvas backpack. He'd had the backpack since his early teens, and had covered it in embroidered patches representing all the places in the world he would one day visit—the Great Pyramid of Giza, Machu Picchu, Stonehenge, among others. Over the years, he had lovingly stitched it back together in three places. As the only part of his wardrobe not unassuming or neutral, it was part of him.

He stood up, slinging the backpack over his right shoulder. Absent-mindedly, he scratched at the golden-brown stubble on his chin, straightened his black coat, and smoothed out the wrinkles on his black skinny jeans. Apprehension filled him for the eighth time since entering, and his green eyes flitted about the tiny space again. The banged up front door, the rickety metal reception desk that squealed in protest every time the receptionist ground her mechanical pencil into it, the irritating flicker of the fluorescent light above him, and the three burnt out letters in the sizzling neon sign all added to the tattoo parlour's appearance as nothing but a tiny hole in the wall on Yonge Street, just north of Wellesley.

He had been suspicious about the quality of the place from the moment he laid eyes on it, but several of his administrative assistant coworkers at the University of Toronto raved about the tattoo artists here. He swallowed and ran a hand through his finger-length tousled hair, the same golden-brown colour as his stubble. He focused on the sample artwork coating almost every surface of the lobby. Regardless of the state of the building, the artwork was among the most beautiful he'd ever seen.

The receptionist haphazardly waved her hand toward the short, rather dimly lit hallway to the left of the desk as she giggled into the phone. He peered down the hallway at the three closed and one open door. He tried to get the receptionist's attention again to ask which door, but she swivelled her chair away from him and ignored him, completely engaged in her conversation.

He walked past two of the closed doors and peered through the open doorway into a small, private room. A bright swivel spotlight hung from the ceiling, illuminating the black tattoo chair in a brilliant glow and casting a bright, cheery splash of light on the rich purple walls. Black, Gothic style mirrors and candleholders lined the walls, sharing the space with artwork even more intense and beautiful than that in the lobby. A woman in her early twenties sat on a black swivel stool. Her ink and tools lay organised on a sterilized tray in front of her. The purple highlights in her spiked platinum hair and her gold hoop nose ring drew his eyes, and he paused in the doorway.

She looked up at him with bright and cheerful eyes. Gesturing at the black tattoo chair next to her, she smiled. "Take a seat. Jonas, right?"

Jonas nodded. "In the flesh."

Her eyes perused him and seemed to sense his nervousness. "First tattoo?"

"Yes. I've wanted one for a few years now, but I never knew what I wanted." He glanced down at the sketch in his hand. "This feels right though."

Hesitantly, he passed her the paper and draped his black jacket on the rose-shaped metallic coat hook behind the tattoo chair. He slung his backpack to the floor where he could still see it. He sat, a mixture of apprehension and excitement filling him as he rolled up the right sleeve of his dark grey Zelda Triforce tee shirt and waited for her to study the design.

"He's beautiful," she said. Her eyes soaked in the intricate details that he hoped she could replicate. He couldn't help but be nervous that it wouldn't come out perfect, even though he had researched her work and knew her to be one of the best artists in the city. "It'll cost extra for the details on his face."

Jonas nodded. "Worth it."

"Putting him on your right arm then I take it?"

At his nod, she picked up the disposable razor blade from her tray and shaved from his shoulder to his elbow, an area just larger than the tattoo itself. She worked quickly and methodically, and when finished, she put him at ease by washing the area with antibacterial soap.

Then she picked up her black ink needle. The sound of an electric buzz filled Jonas' ears. Fear rushed through him. He felt himself tense and she smiled. "Try to relax. It doesn't hurt as much as you think it will."

"You sure about that?" Jonas' voice quavered.

She laughed and started on the first antler.

*

Jonas stood on the 506 Carlton streetcar trying not to scratch his arm. Jennifer, the tattoo artist, had told him it would likely be itchy, and she was right. The pain while she drew was tolerable, but an hour later and he was acutely aware of the tattoo under the bandage.

At the end of the workday, people bumped into him as standing space grew scarce. In another couple of stops, the streetcar would be far too bustling for his tastes. Being crammed into the same space as a hundred other commuters and their body odor held no interest for him, even if he did appreciate the convenience.

He hopped off the streetcar at River Street. From here, he could walk up through Riverdale Park and cut through the Rosedale Ravine to the place he rented north of Broadview

Station. The subway was quicker, but something about trains hurtling through underground tunnels made him uncomfortable. Plus, he needed the exercise.

The park was busy with a mixture of jocks playing soccer, couples walking their dogs, and stoners hanging out beneath the trees. He quickly passed by them all.

He crossed the bridge over Bayview Avenue and took the concrete stairs down to one of his favourite places, the Lower Don Trail, where for hours he could leave the hustle and bustle of the city behind to meander beside the Don River. As he descended the stairs, the sound of roaring cars and blaring horns gave way to the music of the river rushing over rocks and birds singing among the low hanging branches. He came here to meditate, to stroll, to find peace and be at one with nature.

His family could never understand how he could abandon their country village to live in a city as busy as Toronto, but places like the Don Trail system made it possible.

The trail took him north, the river flowing alongside him as he passed the small shrubs and tall grasses. The tranquility of the woods filled his soul and quieted his mind. The scent of freshly budded trees washed through him and filled him with an inner sense of peace.

Wrapped in the magic of the forest, Jonas almost missed the man standing at the edge of the woods. At about six foot two, an inch or so taller than Jonas himself, the man wore green camo shorts and a black, fitted V-neck shirt that camouflaged him almost perfectly into the bushes.

Mesmerized by the man's chiselled jaw line and the rough stubble around his sensual lips, Jonas' gaze dropped to the hint of chest hair escaping the man's shirt and to the abs he could see clearly through the thin fabric. His gaze dropped to the barely concealed bulge in his shorts. Jonas swallowed, hard. The man appeared to be in his early twenties, a year or two younger than Jonas.

The man smiled as Jonas passed, and despite himself, Jonas slowed, stopped, and turned around. Their eyes met. Time slowed and Jonas' heartbeat thudded in his ears. He could not turn away.

The man's grin grew, and he gestured toward the bushes

with a tilt of his chin.

No words were spoken as they entered the bushes and closed the distance between them. Their lips met and heat exploded between them both. The man pulled him closer and their bodies pressed tightly against each other. Raw, animal passion took over and his new tattoo burned in tune with the intense heat between them.

As the wild passion overrode his ability to think, movement in the bushes caught his eye and a tall, naked man with horns faded back into the trees.

Cernunnos, he thought, lust consuming him.

*

"You did *what*? You, Jonas Drayce, the most uptight gay man I know, had a frolic in the Rosedale Ravine? In full daylight?" Claire stared at him in shock from the other side of her plush burgundy sofa, where they both sat cross-legged facing each other. She had more chairs, but the sofa was the only one not piled high with clothes, books, and other random objects waiting to be put away.

He blushed. Claire was his go-to for advice when it came to dating men, and he had run straight to Claire's apartment after his ravine escapade.

Her brown eyes pierced him from a pale, freckled face, framed with shoulder length raven-black hair that had been dyed so many times that he didn't even know what her natural colour was.

She shook her head in disbelief. "If I give you a beer will you give me all the juicy details?"

He laughed. "Not a chance! But I'll still take that beer."

She scowled and crossed the dark, original oak floor to the kitchen of her one-bedroom apartment, pausing twice to straighten some of her framed paintings along the way. He heard her rifling through her fridge. A very liquid-sounding thump echoed out of the kitchen, followed by a curse before she reappeared at the entranceway. She tossed him a can and grimaced. "I'll be right there. Last night's leftovers just wound up on the floor."

"Need some help?"

"No, no. I've got it."

He chuckled, knowing that she wouldn't want him to see her kitchen. She tried hard to present an organized and controlled face to the world. A few months ago though, she had been swept up in downsizing at a chemical engineering firm and had downgraded from her two-bedroom loft to this much smaller one-bedroom apartment. She had more belongings than room, and couldn't bear to part with what she still had.

He glanced at the can of beer, as he cracked it open. A local stout. He cringed but took a swig anyway.

"It's good, eh?" Claire asked as she flopped back onto the couch, clutching a glass of red wine.

"Mmm," he answered with a little sarcasm.

She laughed. "Liar. What were you doing down there anyway? You don't usually work Tuesdays."

He smiled and as he brought the beer to his lips again, whispered, "Just getting a tattoo."

She almost choked on her beer. "I'm sorry. Random sex, tattoos, your hair a complete mess... who are you and what did you do with Jonas?"

Jonas laughed and shrugged.

In truth, he didn't know what had gotten into him. Lately, he felt alone and adrift. Even though he had plenty of friends only a quick text away, he seldom reached out. Claire was the only one he kept in contact with.

He had been changing. Part of it had to do with what the tattoo symbolized. Many of his friends were atheists and agnostics who would scoff at him if they discovered what he researched while holed up in his apartment.

Of course, those same friends never scoffed at Claire. He glanced over at the small side table by her window. A black silk cloth with a silver crescent moon in each corner covered the simple wooden table. Two taper candles—one black, one white—in her grandmother's brass candle holders, a silver goblet, a small hand-carved wooden wand, incense cones, and an athame rested on the cloth.

Wiccan born and raised, Claire cherished her practice with the same devotion that Jonas tried to avoid his.

"Some sort of midlife crisis?" he offered meekly.

"Please," she scoffed. "You're twenty-six."

"Okay, quarter-life crisis then," he said, his defences rising.

She smiled and leaned toward him, placing a hand lightly on his hand. "Can I see it?"

Jonas hesitated, and then slid off his jacket. The moment of truth. He held his breath and unwrapped the white gauze. Slowly, he removed the bandage and waited apprehensively for her reaction.

Claire leaned in close so she could see it better. She gasped and grabbed his hand in both of hers. She tore her gaze from his arm and stared deep into his eyes. "The Horned God! Jonas, He's stunning!"

She pulled his arm closer and peered into Cernunnos' eyes. "Look at that detail!" Her mouth fell open and her eyes focused back on his. "Does this mean you'll come to a Circle with me?"

He laughed. "Maybe." He tried to put genuine conviction in his voice even though he knew it would be unlikely. His growing admiration for the spiritual world was something that he still viewed as being very private.

Claire couldn't talk about her Craft without talking about the God and Goddess, and how they intertwine to create magic—to create life. His eyes flicked again to the black and white candles on her altar. So much of her practice was based on male and female fertility. Certainly, he agreed that the creation of life was full of magic, but he just couldn't relate to it personally. How Claire did, baffled him.

Jonas had been curious for years, however, and at long last he had found his calling. Cernunnos, the magic of lust, the magic of the forest, the touch of a man; that, he could relate to.

"*Please*," she pleaded. "There are some amazing people there, and trust me, hanging out with people who share your beliefs makes things much easier." Claire sighed and her demeanour grew muted as she reflected on her own uncomfortable memories. "Coming to university here was one of the hardest things I ever did. Nobody says anything about my being Wiccan, but sometimes I think it's the elephant in the room."

Jonas stared at her. "You always seem so confident and comfortable."

She nodded and gave him a ghost of a smile. "It is getting easier now that I found this Circle, but it started out as an act. I couldn't let people think that being an outsider bothered me. Honestly though, I could use a friend to talk to about it all."

"Well, when you put it that way... When's the next one?"

"Sunday!"

"Then yes, let's do it."

Claire's entire face lit up. "Thanks Jonas! You won't regret it! Now, Annie's on her way over, so you're going to have to hit the road."

Jonas grinned and tossed back the rest of his beer. "Is that the same Annie from two weeks ago?"

"Yep." Claire stood and walked toward her apartment door. "This is date number three, and I'm cooking, so I need some alone time to prepare."

*

Claire's apartment was one of five units in an old duplex near Chester Hill Lookout that had been converted to rentals years ago. Still riding high with excitement, Jonas skipped down the steps of her front stoop two at a time. When his feet touched the sidewalk, something moved in the bushes to his right, and he just about jumped out of his skin.

Was that a deer? For half a moment he thought a deer hid in the shrubs at the bottom of the stairs, but he found it hard to believe there'd be a deer this deep in the city. He peered closer as he parted the shrubs, revealing vaguely antler-shaped branches.

He shook his head and trotted across the road to his own apartment four doors up the street. His new tattoo had him seeing things, first in the bushes while in the throes of passion and now a deer in the middle of the city.

Once inside his junior one bedroom apartment, Jonas tossed his backpack on the wooden bench by the door, followed by his jacket. He kicked off his shoes and stared at the tattered black leather couch. The urge to nap called out. He glanced around his living room, taking in the ragged couch, the flat screen television and the gaming console tucked into the bottom shelf of his bookcase. His eyes settled on the barn-board-framed mirror leaning against the wall at the edge of the living room, tall enough that it reflected him in his entirety, short hair dishevelled and the bottom half of his Cernunnos tattoo peaking out of his t-shirt.

He thrust the urge to nap or game aside. The tattoo had been part of his personal initiation to the spiritual world. The next step was performing a ritual to Cernunnos. Already, familiar excuses that would justify not performing the ritual filled his mind. Chief among them was that since Cernunnos was a god of the forest, it would be more appropriate to do this ritual in the forest.

But he wasn't comfortable doing his personal rituals in public.

He sighed and forced himself to pick up his wand from where it sat in a place of honour on the centre shelf of his book-case. It was a rough-hewn branch of an apple tree that had found him in his grandparents' backyard last fall.

He still remembered that day like it was yesterday.

Jonas had been lying in a hammock under his grandparents' apple tree, texting with Claire about ley lines, when he fell asleep and found himself dreaming of walking along a ley. With every step along the dream path, the energy of the earth filled his soul. It led him through space and time back to his childhood. He found himself eight years old again, standing on the outskirts of the Arctic National Wildlife Refuge. A herd of wild caribou grazed in the distance.

While his parents took turns passing the binoculars back and forth, Jonas had sneaked behind one of the nearby rocks to get closer. He got the shock of his life when a mother caribou and her calf stepped out from behind a grove of trees and came face to face with him.

He gazed into her big round eyes, full of warmth, tender-ness, and protectiveness, and felt instant love and connection. He didn't panic. Somehow, he knew the caribou would not hurt him. She seemed the epitome of peace.

He reached his hand out in a gesture of friendship, and for a moment, he thought she would let him touch her. She had looked up with alarm before she and the calf ran back to the safety of the herd.

A burst of thunder had startled him awake, interrupting his dream, and he had rolled out of the hammock. When he had put his feet on the ground to stand up, the wind picked up, the leaves rustled, and a small branch about a foot long and the thickness of his thumb dropped to the ground between his feet. As the memory faded into his present-day apartment, he rolled the wand through his fingers, remembering that day last fall and how the branch had thrummed with life as his fingers had closed around it for the very first time. He hadn't recognized it then, but from his studies this past year he knew it to be the Nwyfre of the apple tree calling to him. The wand had been a gift from the apple tree, and it gave him the impetus he needed to start performing rituals instead of just researching.

Setting it down briefly on the coffee table that would soon become his altar, he collected the plants in his apartment and arranged them in a circle in the centre of his living room. He had eleven plants of various sizes. Together, they emulated the forest well enough.

In the centre of the circle, he repositioned his coffee table and set a tall beeswax pillar candle and the sketch of Cernunnos that he had tattooed to his arm in the centre of the table. Beside it, he placed a tumbler of mead and a small plate of carrot cake that he had brought as an offering.

Standing back from the make-shift altar, he removed his socks, his shirt, and his pants.

He stood naked at the western entrance to his circle, relaxing, centring himself. His awareness filled the space, reached down through the layers of concrete in the apartment to the foundation. He envisioned his toes digging into the earth, and calmness filled his soul. Slowly, he reached out and picked up his wand with his right hand, stretching out his arms above his head and extending his being up into the sky. He drew in the energy of the setting sun and let it charge him.

Then he stepped forward, wand outstretched to his left side, and began walking around the circle sunwise. With every step, he envisioned the circle being charged by his energy.

When he reached the north, he stopped and faced north. In his mind's eye, the wall before him became a deep forest clearing beneath a sky full of stars. "With the blessing of the great wolf of the forest, I call upon the powers of the north."

In the image of the deep forest clearing, a wolf stepped forth, its fur rippling with the muscle beneath, and released a howl. When the howl faded, he turned and continued along the circle to the east.

In the east, he imagined a sky, clear and blue for as far as he could see. The sun began to rise, and through the radiant beams, a hawk soared toward him. "With the blessing of the great hawk flying through the dawn, I call upon the powers of the east." From the east, the cry of the hawk pierced the air around him.

He continued along the circle to the south, envisioning a charged line of energy flowing behind him, weaving a thread of connection between the directions.

At the south, he stood with his arms outstretched. The hot midday sun warmed the lands before him. Smoke rose from a blacksmith's forge, and a mighty roan-coloured stallion stood before him, free and strong, ready to offer him his power. He paused, drinking in the heat and freedom. "With the blessing of the great stallion in the heat of the sprint, I call upon the powers of the south."

After several moments of stillness, Jonas continued to the west. Here, he envisioned the sun setting over a calm and peaceful ocean. The water rippled and an ever-tenacious salmon swam against the current. "With the blessing of the great salmon, I call upon the powers of the west."

He turned to the centre and with closed eyes envisioned ocean currents pulling the energy of the earth up into him and the energy of the sky down into him, melding earth, sea, and sky within himself.

After some time, he opened his eyes, and still facing the centre, stretched his arms out to either side, palms out. "This is sacred time. This is sacred space. I am fully present, here and now."

He knelt before his altar and lit the beeswax candle.

"Great Cernunnos," Jonas said as he gazed into the flickering flame and the umbrella tree behind it. "I thank you for coming into my life, for filling my soul with masculine energies." Around him, a low rumble grew, and he stopped speaking. His eyes flitted from plant to plant as their leaves trembled.

The rumble grew deeper, sounding almost like the subway. But the subway was too far away to be heard from his apartment. In the kitchen sink, dirty glasses rattled. Despite himself, Jonas laughed. First time in a month he tried to do a ritual and it got interrupted by his first ever earthquake. He heard his mobile phone chirp from the bedroom—probably Claire wondering if he felt it too.

The rattling glasses fell silent. The trembling plants fell still.

Still kneeling before the altar, the mead beckoned to him, and he swallowed most of it in one gulp.

He pondered for a moment. Something told him he should pause the ritual and peek out the windows.

Grasping the table with one hand, he stood.

A loud knock filled the air, like somebody pounding on the very air around him.

Suddenly, his apartment lurched. The glasses in the sink shattered. The tumbler of mead in his hands fell to the floor with a crash and exploded into myriads of glass shards.

Jonas staggered backward, his arms spinning in a vain attempt to regain balance. For a moment he thought he had it before, in shock, he noticed that the full-length mirror before him had transformed. Instead of reflecting his naked body amongst the ruins of his apartment, dark orange and red leaves churned within it. In the centre of the mirror, the mother caribou from his childhood stared out at him.

His world shifted again, and this time, he fell. His head bounced off the wood floor with a hollow thud and everything went black.

*

The incessant chirp of his cell phone ultimately dragged Jonas back from unconsciousness. He couldn't be sure if he was happy that it did. His head throbbed and warmth trickled down his arm. He touched his arm without opening his eyes: it was sticky, and he knew it would be red. He had fallen on the shattered tumbler. Thank the gods that it was his left arm. Cernunnos was safe.

His eyes cracked open. The apartment was dark and silent except for his cell phone. Only a faint trickle of moonlight came through the living room window. Somehow the candle had gone out. It was probably a blessing that it still stood upright.

With trembling hands, he lit a match. The candle cast shadows across the room. With trepidation, he glanced out of the corner of his eye at the mirror, nothing but his reflection staring back. His imagination had played tricks on him.

He pulled himself to his feet and inspected his arm in the candlelight. A piece of glass had lodged in his left forearm.

"Shit."

Gritting his teeth, he pulled the glass out with a yelp. Blood poured from the wound. He stumbled to the kitchen and grabbed a tea towel and wrapped it around his arm, tying it tight. Already blood soaked through, but it would do.

Jonas walked to the bedroom and scooped his phone up off the bed.

Twenty-eight text messages, all from Claire.

Annie couldn't come... Are you feeling this?... What the hell is happening?... You have to come outside... I'm outside your apartment. You have to come...

They went on and on like that.

Be right there, he typed. *Passed out.*

He tried to call his mom, but the recorded message told him the number was out of service. He tried his dad and got the same response.

How could both of their numbers be out of service?

Panic rose. He tried to reason his way out of the dread, but he could come up with no explanation for any of what had happened. He needed to reach them. Maybe he could hitchhike. Maybe Claire's parents could give him a ride.

He pulled on a fresh pair of dark blue jeans—the ones even skinnier than what he'd been wearing previously and torn on each thigh—his black and white Converse high top sneakers, focusing on lacing them to try to drive out the panic. He pulled a plain white t-shirt over his head and grabbed his backpack, because he never left home without it. He approached the door leading out of his apartment with a strange sense of trepidation, and slid open the deadbolt.

FINDING BALANCE

The door opened with a creak that echoed through his unit. He stepped out, looking down either end of the hallway. Complete darkness. He cocked his head. Except for the sound of sirens in the distance, silence filled the air.

Where the hell did everyone go?

He made it to the stairwell. His apartment was on the sixteenth floor, and while he knew where the stairs were, he had never taken them before. Ignoring the pain in his arm, he took the stairs two at a time. The fluorescent lights had exploded, leaving the stairwell with broken glass. Throbbing white emergency lights pierced the dark.

On the seventh floor, Jonas stopped. Taking deep, ragged breaths, his mother's perfume filled the stairwell. His breath stopped. His eyes widened. Her presence loomed large all around him.

"Mom?" he whispered. But she wasn't in the stairwell. She wasn't even in the city. He swallowed and started back down the stairwell.

Claire stood outside the lobby door when he got to the ground floor, but with the power out, the sliding glass doors wouldn't open. He tried pushing on them, but they didn't budge. He tried sliding them by force, but they didn't move.

Outside the apartment, Claire started trying to open the door, too. It took all of their combined strength, but finally the seal between the two doors cracked and they got the doors parted enough for Jonas to squeeze through.

The air outside clung to him like molasses, making it hard to breathe. A dense fog swirled around everything.

Claire ran up to him and hugged him like she hadn't seen him in months. "Did you see anyone else in your building?" she asked.

He shook his head, not trusting himself to speak yet.

"Me neither. I knocked on three of my neighbours' doors, but they're all either asleep or missing" She peered through the fog in vain. "What's strange though, is the air is only thick like this near your apartment. At my place there's just a hint of it."

She started to head to the street, but Jonas grabbed her arm and put up a hand to silence her for a moment. He took three slow, deep breaths, hoping that air this thick would give him enough oxygen. "I cut my arm open on glass when I got thrown to the ground," he rasped. "I smelled my mother in the stairway, and somehow my mirror had turned into a forest."

Claire glanced at him. "I don't know what you were smoking when your mirror turned into a forest, but I want some next time! Let me see your arm."

She gently touched the bloodstained towel and then untied it. Looking under the towel, she smiled. "You're going to live. The bleeding has almost stopped, so the wound must not be that deep."

"It sure looked deep when I pulled the chunk of glass out." He glanced around. "I need to get to my parents," he said with a shake of his head. "Do you want to come? They'll help us with whatever this is."

"They live three hours away, Jonas, and there's nobody around anymore to drive us." Her voice softened. "Let's go for a walk around the neighbourhood and see if we can learn anything."

She waited several moments for a response, but when none came, she started walking. Jonas groaned and started into the swirling fog after her.

Ten minutes later, he almost ran into her.

"Whoa! You can't stop that quick in fog like this!"

She didn't answer him in words, but held up her arm with a single, trembling finger extended ahead of her. He followed her finger and saw his apartment building, right where it had been.

"How could we have walked in a circle?" she asked.

Together, they stepped forward again, into the fog. Ten minutes later, the fog dissipated, and the apartment building was beside them once again. They moved closer to the apartment, and then started walking again, glancing to their left repeatedly. They walked for five minutes and his apartment building stayed right there with them.

Jonas swallowed hard as they come to a stop.

Claire absent-mindedly scratched an ear. "We should check it out."

"My building?"

She nodded. "Your apartment appears to be the epicentre of whatever's happening."

FINDING BALANCE

She stepped through the doors to his lobby. Jonas groaned at the thought of climbing back up the stairs.

*

It took Jonas and Claire almost half an hour to reach the sixteenth floor with several breaks to gasp for air. They didn't see anybody all the way up the stairs. Claire even popped into the hallway of several floors to knock on random doors, but they seemed to be the only two people left alive.

His apartment was a disaster. Broken glass was everywhere, and the candle had overflowed, running wax all over the floor. Two of the plants had somehow been knocked over. The only normal thing was the mirror. And—he swallowed, pointing at the floor.

Claire followed his gaze and gasped.

Muddy hoof prints crisscrossed this way and that through his apartment.

A wooziness swept over them, and a slight keening sound filled the air.

Before their eyes, the mirror swirled and became a dark forest. Irresistibly, they stepped closer. In the mirror, a mother caribou stepped forward. Jonas sensed that she was the same one from his dream and the one he saw when he regained consciousness earlier. Only this time she kept walking out of the forest and seemingly toward the surface of the mirror.

As the doe approached the mirror's surface, she grew taller, her face began to transform, becoming more feminine with every step, and her antlers lengthened. Soon, a beautiful woman with big brown eyes and a full set of gracefully curving antlers stood before them. Her red hair cascaded down her shoulders and over her bare breasts. Dawn was breaking in the land of the mirror, and her naked body glowed ethereal in the rising light of the sun.

Jonas gulped. The tattoo on his arm felt so hot it almost glowed.

The caribou woman stepped up to the mirror's surface and reached her arm out in welcome.

"Hello, Jonas. Hello, Claire," she said silkily from within the mirror.

Claire trembled. "Are you the Goddess?"

"I am a manifestation of an aspect of the Goddess," the woman in the mirror answered. Her big brown eyes turned to Jonas. "Many know me as Elen, and I have been watching you for a very long time, my child."

"Since I was a young boy hiding from my mom behind a rock," Jonas answered.

She inclined her head in acknowledgement. She turned and looked at Claire. "And I have been watching you for almost as long a time. The world is changing, my children. I know I don't have to tell you that. It exists in perfect balance and harmony between the masculine and feminine energies of the land. For quite some time now that balance has been upset and I need help restoring it."

Jonas' eyes widened. "What would the Goddess need our help with?"

"We are not all powerful. We rely on humans to hide our foibles. Gods and Goddesses are too much of one thing. We need humans to tone us down, to keep the earth in balance." She fell silent for a moment.

"Walk with me," she said finally. She stepped away from the surface of the mirror and parted the vegetation with her arm.

Mist drifted lazily across a lake in the distance. The haunting call of a loon filled the apartment, and a cool forest breeze drifted through the glass. It flowed over Claire and Jonas, offset by the warmth of the Goddess Elen standing before them.

Jonas turned to Claire. "I don't think we're dreaming."

Claire swallowed, staring at Elen, speechless for perhaps the first time in her life.

Jonas stepped forward, holding Claire's hand in his right hand and reaching out to the mirror with his left.

At his touch, the surface of the glass rippled, softened, parted. Elen's fingers entwined with his own—powerful, yet compassionate. He shivered as he passed through into the realm of the Goddess. Claire followed, her eyes wide.

Claire looked around. Her grip on Jonas's hand grew stronger. "Are we inside a mirror?"

He nodded. "Either that or we're both having the same

dream. Do you feel that?" He thought back to that day in his grandparents' backyard, to the energy flowing through the apple branch. That same energy flowed through him now. Nwyfre rushed from Elen's hand through his being, making him intimately aware of every hair on his body. He felt supercharged with life.

"Yes," Claire said. "I am... *strong.*"

"Your belief gives me power," Elen said smiled. "With that, I can help restore balance to the world."

"Is this a real place?" Jonas whispered.

She inclined her head. "I call many places home, but right now we are in the north of Scotland." Elen let go of his hand.

The flush of energy diminished, but did not disappear. They stood at the edge of a small clearing, a dense forest surrounding them. At their feet blossomed hundreds of tiny seedlings.

He knelt to the ground and cupped his hand around one of the infant plants. He envisioned sunlight filling the tiny plant with life and nutrients rushing up its roots.

With awe, he watched as the tiny seedling grew into a lush shrub before his eyes. He turned his gaze up to Claire and Elen. "Did I really do that?" Amazement spread across Claire's face and she looked down at her own hands. An odd sadness filled Elen's eyes as she nodded.

The shrub grew larger and more lush. Leaves unfurled, the fresh, light green of spring, and darkened as they matured. Before him, a fully formed shrub now stood where the tiny seedling had been but a moment before. He took his hands away and stood, a grin stretching from ear to ear.

The moment he stood, the deep green leaves began to wither. They dried, became crisp, and one by one fluttered to the ground.

In as much time as it took for him to breathe it full of life and energy, the shrub died before his eyes.

Elen stepped forward. She reached out a hand and touched one of the branches of the shrub. A tear rolled down her cheek. Then she turned to Jonas and Claire.

"You work energy the way of your God," she said, sadness in her voice. "You fill something full of life before its time and the delicate harmony of balance gets trampled. All things must be nurtured. To grow to their full potential, they must receive only that energy they are capable of sustaining on their own."

Her eyes swept the barren shrub. "You flooded that shrub with life, and it drank it in while you provided the energy conduit. But it didn't learn how to pull from the earth itself. Its delicate seedling roots did not have the opportunity to push their way through the obstacles in the rich soil to the underground stream that flows beneath us here. You gave the shrub instant life, but did not teach it to grow by itself."

Jonas swallowed, and the joy that had been in his soul felt marred. "Can you bring it back?"

The Goddess Elen turned her eyes upon him, and oceans of love and anger churned within them, threatening to wash him away with sadness.

Claire squeezed his hand, anchoring him.

"No," Elen said. "To restore life to something that is dead is an even graver disruption of the balance of life than giving it too much life to begin with." She reached out, and the tips of her fingers brushed against Cernunnos on his upper arm.

The energy of Cernunnos rushed through his body: his strength, his passion, his lust for life.

"Those feelings are completely unbalanced. They have not been tempered by patience, by joy, by vulnerability, by love. You are looking at the world with a child's eyes, lacking the understanding that passion which burns without love will fizzle, lust that consumes you without patience will fade, that strength that fills you without vulnerability will destroy you."

She reached down and cupped Jonas' chin, turning his gaze to meet hers once again. "Because you love men, you think there is no room inside you for the feminine. But you cannot truly live until you embrace both sides of your being Jonas. You must open yourself to the power of the Earth Mother to reach your full potential."

Claire swallowed. "Is that you?"

A musical laugh filled the clearing. "No, child. I am the Goddess of the Ways, of balance. I wander the pathways of time itself to ensure the balance is never upended. I serve the Earth Mother as the God Cernunnos serves Her, each in our own way.

"I work to maintain balance and harmony throughout the

world. If you choose to enter service to the Earth Mother, to stand against those who are working to destroy Her, I can help you reach your full potential. Your mother's prayers called me to you that day you saw me in my animal form. I have been watching you ever since, Jonas."

"My mother prayed to you?" he asked, incredulous. His mother was the least religious person he knew.

"When you were a child, she lit a candle every night and prayed to the spirits of the world that her son would grow to be a man full of compassion and love. She did not have an easy childhood, Jonas, but that is her story to tell should she choose."

He thought back to the stairwell of his apartment, to his mother's perfume, and sudden anxiety filled him.

Elen's hand reached out and squeezed his. "She is fine, child. Your mother has ever been close to the veil between worlds, and she sensed you were in trouble. She is doubtless on her way to visit your apartment as we speak."

Relief flooded through him, and he looked between Claire and Elen. "So, what do we do now?"

"We devote ourselves to the Earth Mother," Claire said. "If you're willing."

Elen's eyes stared into his soul. They were the eyes of a mother: full of compassion, of strength. They embodied all the qualities he longed to embody.

"I am," nodded Jonas.

Elen smiled. "Then it is time for you to return from whence you came."

Jonas and Claire looked behind them, but there was no mirror in the clearing.

Elen smiled. "That Way can only be opened from your world. You must return through the world of dreams." She stepped into the forest, holding the branches back for them to follow.

They followed Elen through the trees, and it seemed almost as if the forest itself reached out to caress them. They entered a clearing, where a large moss-covered boulder rested in the centre.

Elen stepped aside and extended a hand toward the boulder.

"Your way home."

They stepped toward the boulder, and then stopped in shock when the boulder cracked open and a massive, golden eye stared out. It focused on Jonas and Claire. A deep rumbling filled the clearing.

The ground beneath them shook, and slowly the boulder rose out of the ground. All around them, the clearing trembled and the ground broke apart and rose into the air.

Jonas managed to maintain his footing long enough to move closer to Claire, his body quaking as panic filled him. "Is that a dragon?" he called out over the din before the shaking earth knocked them both to their knees.

Claire nodded, clutching at his arm. "I think so," she shouted back.

The original moss-covered boulder now towered twenty feet in the air. The giant creature shuddered. Huge chunks of moss, soil and grass showered across the clearing.

They covered their eyes as dust and debris landed all around them. When silence filled the clearing, Jonas wiped the grime off his face and found himself staring up at the massive dragon with a strange mixture of awe and terror. It was at least thirty feet long from the tip of its tail to its snout, and its emerald green scales glittered in the rising sun.

The dragon stretched its wings, easily filling the fifty-foot clearing. It stretched out each of its legs in turn, and loud cracks echoed throughout the clearing. The dragon seemed to sigh with each crack, and Jonas wondered how long the dragon had been sleeping under the ground.

The golden eyes focused on him. "I was sleeping long enough that the ground almost swallowed me whole." The dragon's voice reverberated throughout the clearing and made the leaves on the trees dance.

The large green head swept gracefully down to the earth and turned one golden eye to focus directly on them. The slit pupil flitted from Jonas to Claire to Elen. It settled on Elen, and Jonas could see recognition flare to life. "Daughter Elen," the dragon said, not so much with reverence as with respect. "How many years has it been?"

Elen smiled and reached out a hand to caress one of the

emerald scales. "Not since the time of the Fae, Elder Brân." She turned to Jonas and Claire. "My children, meet Brân the Blessed in his true form. It has been almost three thousand years since he last walked the earth as a king so giant that his legends persist today. Brân, these ones have entered the dream world at my bidding, but it is time they return to restore balance to the realms."

The dragon nodded and his eye focused once more on Jonas and Claire. "You may stand. I shall take you where you need to go." With a shudder that caused the ground to shake, Brân settled his massive bulk to the ground. "Climb on and hold on tight."

Jonas and Claire glanced at each other and then gingerly climbed to their feet. As one, they turned to Elen, and she smiled once more, inclining her head in a wordless admonition that they should obey the dragon.

Swallowing, they stepped up to Brân's side. His scales were like rocks, and once they figured out how to find the appropriate footholds, climbing was easy. They straddled his neck, Jonas in front and Claire with her arms wrapped around Jonas.

Brân rumbled to his feet, and Jonas gripped his scales hard, terror and anxiety filling him as he suddenly remembered his fear of heights. But there was no time to react. The dragon's mighty wings beat down three times, lifting its mighty bulk up into the air above the forest, and then with a thrust that caused the long blades of grass beneath them to flatten, those wings propelled them through the sky.

Jonas looked over his shoulder at the clearing they had risen from to see Elen fading into the forest. In a strange way, he could still feel her presence within him.

They soared over the forests and Munros of Scotland and Wales, higher and higher into the sky. The mighty dragon's wings carried them across the channel, over Ireland, and out over the open ocean, heading for home.

On a whim, Jonas glanced down and saw a shimmering pathway. Without a doubt, he knew that these ancient ley lines were the paths the dragons of old used for flight, for he could feel them burning in his own soul.

And the power of the Goddess flowed through them once more.

Christopher Gorman has been a passionate reader and writer since he was a child. He is a member of the Canadian Authors Association and a co-host of the podcast *Words with Writers*. Spiritually, he follows the nature-based path of Druidry and is a member of the Order of Bards, Ovates and Druids while studying other magical paths. Christopher is the author of *Dawn of Magic: Rise of the Guardians*, in which he explores what he identifies as the trilogy of powers in this world—nature, faith, and science. Traveling throughout Canada and the world, he has participated in pagan rituals in the mountains and explored sites of ancient wisdom in England, Wales, and Ireland.

The Family Business

By Stephen B. Pearl

AMMUT LOOKS AT ME AND licks her lips in anticipation. The long tongue playing over that crocodilian mouth sends a shudder up my spine. The way the lion claws flex promise a gutting, and her sturdy Hippopotami hind quarters are fit to crush the life from a man.

Actually, a little too late for that job. I really had needed to get to the gym more often. Too late now. I hope someone shows up to look after Pakhetel, my cat. That is my biggest worry. Of course, at sixteen, my little love will probably be joining me soon anyway. I miss her, and I suspect that she misses me. I hope she's drawn to me on this side when the time comes. If I'm on this side for her to join me when her time comes, that is. My disposition is still up in the air.

The room around me is huge. The walls are done up in gold, silver and inlaid gems to form frescoes depicting Egypt when the Nile Valley housed one of mankind's greatest civilizations. A spectator balcony occupies one wall. I'm standing beside an elaborate set of scales as tall as I, which occupies the middle of the floor. The scale is inlaid with lapis lazuli.

As ornate as the room appears, it can't hold a candle to its occupants.

It takes an act of will to look at any of them—they are so beautiful. I suspect that they're down-playing their grandeur so that I don't lose what little is left of my mind. One can only take so much beauty. So much wonder.

"Stanley Frances Bartholomew Winterbottom."

Yes, my parents had a sick, sadistic sense of humour. Given my age at the time, I didn't get much say. Later, it was too much trouble to change it.

The voice comes from a splendidly built jackal-headed man standing beside the scale. He continues, "I have checked the balance, and the scales are ready. Do you surrender to the judgment of Ma'at?"

"Not much choice, all things considered." All the crappy things I'd done in life parade through my mind. I go pale. On the astral, everything is an allegory. I haven't been dead that long, so I'm still manifesting as if I had a body. I know at an intellectual level that everything around me is fields of energy, but to make sense of it, my still largely mortal mind is forcing order on it in keeping with my expectations. At least I've got a truly impressive show to see me off. Whether I'll remember it or not has yet to be seen.

Anubis's warm and gentle hand falls to my shoulder. I accepted the comfort he offers.

"Buck up. Worst case, your memories are blocked, then you'll be sent back to try again. Your personality will still come through. It's not that bad." How a jackal's smile can be reassuring, I'll never know, but Anubis manages it.

We've always got on well. I've always understood that he was not the cause of separation. He is the guide through the inevitable that eases the way. In a sense, like a garbage man. He doesn't make the garbage, but people look on him with apprehension because he hauls it away. People can be silly. I was glad to see our relationship hasn't changed. Especially considering that I was dead. It's always good to have friends in high places.

"Maybe not, but have you seen the mess they are making of

things back there?" I shook my head disparagingly."The shit is going to hit the fan in the next hundred years or so. I'd rather not be around for it in the flesh." I smile at the jackal-headed figure and make my voice light."A nice cottage on the Aaru fields would suit me fine, thank you."

Anubis snorts."I'll toss you a bone." I swear his grin grows wider. "You can choose a little house on Lake Huron if you want. It's not two thousand BCE anymore. We'll even omit the mosquitoes."

"Sounds as good a Scooby snack as any, if I can make the grade." There's a certain comfort in being able to share bad jokes with one's gods.

"Will you get on with it?" demanded the figure that sits on an ornate wooden throne with a gold and lapis inlay of falcon wings forming the armrests. The throne sits on a podium at the end of the hall. The figure has a green face and a body wrapped as a mummy holding a crook and flail. Plants grow around his throne.

The most stunning female I have ever seen sits on a twin throne beside him. Her luxuriant midnight-black hair falls to the middle of her shoulders. She is slim and graceful, and her skin has a golden hue. Her eyes are the colour of dark lapis lazuli, and in them, you can see the cosmos.

"Relax, my love, it's not as if this takes much of our attention, and it is rather a big day for our little brother." Isis squeezes her husband's arm.

"As you say, my love." Osiris smiles at his wife.

I can see the love between them and feel under that the power of life, the cycle of the seasons.

"I thought you were going to call her," Anubis spoke softly but with an edge to his voice to the slender, Ibis-headed god that stands to one side of the scale holding a computer tablet ready to record the result of my judgment. Do you really think Thoth god of science and mathematics is going to be behind the times?

"Don't get snarky with me, puppy breath! I sent the message," snaps Thoth. There is more of friendly banter than hostility in the words. Nice to know I matter so much in the cosmic scheme of things that the gods joke about the disposition of my immortal soul. Of course, it is nice to know I have never been in a position to really mess things up.

"Bird brain," Anubis rolls his eyes and flares his nostrils before he turns his attention to me, "Sorry about this, but we do need to move on. There's a back log, and too many delays result in hauntings. You know what a mess they can be to clean up. While it still matters, nice work on that place in Dundas. He was a nasty old bugger."

Anubis reaches into my chest and pulls out my heart. My ears fill with white noise, making it hard to focus on anything.

Ammut licks her lips, as her eyes glisten."Sssummy."

I realize she is probably vocalizing a crocodilian version of "Yummy."

Sighing, Anubis puts my heart, all my memories, all I've learned of science, literature, the paltry achievements of a lifetime weighed against a feather. Ma'at, clad in a robe made of stars against darkest black, looks down from a balcony. As lovely as Isis, but more distant, harder for my mind to grasp. I realize I still exist. My sense of justice, my kindness, my love, the core of me cannot go to Ammut. She eats only the tripping blocks of memory that could block growth. In a way, what is left of me is the feather that lays as a counterweight.

The heart sinks on the scale."Oh, crap!" I speak without thinking about the company I'm in. I resolve myself to the little death and my return to earth to begin again. Gods, I hate being a baby. Childhood isn't much better.

Ammut takes a step closer. A commotion erupts. The door opposite the thrones on the other end of the hall flies open, and a flood of furry bodies rushes in. They charge the scales, one jumps into my arms, brushing his cheeks against mine. A love I value more deeply than life reminds me there are no endings. The cat I hold left my mortal world less than a year before. Given my age, I'd thought it unfair to open my home to a kitten I would certainly leave behind, so he'd rested with the gods waiting for me. Now he is back with me in my hour of need. He leaps from my arms, catching the scale that holds the feather, dragging it down.

Three other cats stand in front of Ammut, backs arched and hissing in full threat display. The devourer of hearts takes a step back before the pure fury of the onslaught.

Blacky, Big Eyes, Guest, Hobo, Bessa, Bastel, Anew, QT, Sag, Tanya, Ming… to name all the cats, between strays I'd fed and beloved pets who were part of my family, would take an hour. A group of raccoons rushes in and joins them. I remember a spring where a Mamma 'coon and her five kits came to the back door. Bread crusts and old cat food were the order of the day, but all five kits and the mother lived.

Squirrels charge the scales; I'd always put out bread and nuts. I see one squirrel who'd I'd found crippled, dragging itself over a lawn, obviously hit by a car. I'd beheaded it with a hatchet I kept in my trunk to end its suffering. I always questioned my action. No more. It leapt to the tray and chitters. I'd returned it to the cycle of life, stilling its terror. I glance at Anubis, I'd done his work, and it had been a good thing.

The scales tip so that my heart is light.

A cough sounds at the door, and I glance over as a beautiful being struts into the room. She has a dancer's body with firm, high-set breasts and is clad in a linen kilt. Her head is that of the most beautiful grey cat I have ever seen.

"Bastet." The name lingers on my tongue like sweet wine. My heart lurches. Isis is beauty incarnate, and so is Bastet, but Bastet seems less aloof, closer to the human heart and spirit. I guess it's like the girl next door versus the supermodel or actress. I've always preferred MaryAnn, though Ginger had her advantages.

"Took you long enough!" remark Anubis.

"Oh, fiddle, you old dog. I do have other obligations," she teases, amusement bubbles out from her like water from a spring. It eases my scattered mind. She strides across the floor towards me. "Do you think it was easy to find all of these? Next time, you sniff them out. You have the nose for it, brother mine."

"Don't be catty. We're all short-staffed. If we don't start promoting from within, we're going to be in trouble," observes Anubis. "Thanks for helping out, sis."

Bastet smiles at Anubis, then waves to the podium. "Hi, Mum. Hi, Dad. Great-great-granddad says you should give this poor bugger a break. He did his best to kick Apep, that hissing SOB, whenever he got the chance. Oh, he also says that you should clean up the snakes. It's getting to be like pythons in the everglades out there. It was bad enough during the inquisition. This new wave of intolerance and negativity has them hanging off the trees. I personally blame social media."

"Not my fault. I only give humans the tools. What they do with them is up to them." Thoth sounds annoyed.

"Talk to the incarnates, dear. They're the ones who are feeding the snakes. If they could only get along," replies Isis with strained tolerance

"All the more reason to give this one a break. He at least tried to be a peacemaker." Bastet turned her gaze to me. "Didn't always succeed. You know you can be a bit of an ass sometimes, little brother."

"Yes, My Lady," I reply, dipping my head. What else are you going to say to a goddess that is in the process of pulling your ass out of the fire?

"We appreciate your input, Bastet, but this isn't your department," observed Osiris.

"Healer of the mind, Dad. And given how stressed out Stan here is, I think the lines are more than a little blurred." Bastet grins at Osiris with an, 'I'll get away with it because I'm cute!' expression that anyone familiar with cats would recognize.

Osiris shakes his head in defeat, as I've so often done with Bastet's mortal children. Isis laughs. The sound is like tinkling bells and a babbling stream and all the other good sounds that life can hold.

"What should I input?" Thoth glances up from his tablet. I see Spider Solitaire before he changes it to his logging program. I don't tell him he has a red eight of hearts open with a seven stack that would complete the suit. I figure kibitzing the God of Numbers would be bad form.

"Sorry, I didn't say hi earlier, Uncle Thoth. Can we have a minute?" Bastet's voice could melt steel as she bats her eyelashes.

Thoth blushes, don't ask me how an ibis can blush, but he does. I guessed some young goddesses can appreciate older gods. It happens. As above, so below. Lucky old fart!

Bastet grows serious and continues, "I really am short-staffed. Things are slipping through the cracks. If he's close to ready, I'd like to recruit him as an oversight agent."

The various animals continue to hang off the scale in an imposable configuration, pulling up my heart. It reminds me of the Barrel of Monkeys game.

Bastet turns to me. "It would seem that there are those who think more of you than you think of yourself, little brother." Bastet gestured to the hoard of animals who, with their point made, drop from the scales to wander around the room. In seconds, both Isis and Osiris have cats on their laps and are absently petting the fur balls. An American Blue from my childhood drapes himself over Isis's shoulders, purring loudly into her ear. The Goddess smiles. Other of my feline saviours climb the curtains by the podium. Both Anubis and Thoth reach down to pet furry bodies that are walking figure eights around their legs. A ginger tabby squats amongst the plants beside Osiris's throne, while Osiris diligently ignores it and rolls his eyes with a 'Cats, what you gonna do?' expression.

"And love is the greatest power." The words come from the part of me that isn't on the scales.

An even voice fills the room, sending a shudder up my spine. "This doesn't matter. The heart must balance. Not lighter, not heavier. No false virtue, no self-deluding lies. No denial." Ma'at stands on the balcony and eyes me with indifference.

"Perhaps we should allow an over-eager pursuit of mercy at this time. Mankind does so much ill to the other living creatures. Here is one who at least tried to live up to something," observes Bastet.

I find my voice, and through the fog having my heart on the scales casts over my mind, I remember a line from the book of *Coming into the Light*. "I am not a man perfected, but a man perfecting."

Bastet turns to me. I sense a smile on her feline lips.

"Some of my better work." Thoth cocks his ibis head to one side.

"Does sum it up nicely," agrees Anubis.

"All-Mother, Ma'at, can't a little lightness balance some of the heaviness. He doesn't think himself perfect, simply good. Who doesn't want to look at themselves that way? Even you sometimes err on the side of kindness. Have you forgotten who steered the raccoon and her children to this one's back door?" Bastet continues to make my case.

The raccoons had climbed up on Ma'at's balcony. A wrestling match breaks out between the raccoons who tumble around Ma'at's feet. The Goddess of the Cosmic order looks charmed. She sighs and waves her hand at the scale, which balances. "My distant daughter, stubborn and too cute by half. No wonder the incarnates clad you in the form of the feline."

Anubis takes my heart from the scale and pushes it back into my chest. I remember all my missteps and inadequacies. Times I was not kind, times I was arrogant, even a few when I was hypocritical.

"Hail to Stanly exalted among men," called Bastet.

"No." My voice is soft. "I am not!"

"Good," remarks Isis. "You have mastered the first lesson. There is a place for you in the Aaru."

"Take some time to settle in, and then we'll put you to work," says Bastet.

"Work?" I echo.

"You didn't think one being could administer an archetypal, spiritual, energy ray by themselves, did you? We all have staff. Just remember to put your mask on when incarnates might see you. Had a staffer forget to do that, and it started a whole new religion. Talk about inconvenient." Bastet lifts her wrist in front of her face. A Timex appears out of thin air... well energy... well... you know what I mean. "Sunrise in Kenna, I have to run. Some idiot is hunting a lion on an African game preserve and needs to be taught a lesson." She turns to Thoth and speaks flirtatiously, "I'll see you after work."

Thoth, god of wisdom, blushes and kicks his heels like an embarrassed schoolboy.

I nod. "Could I do one pick up from my old home before I settle in the Aaru?"

Bastet nods. "She'll be happy to see you."

"Sebastian," I call.

My most recently transited feline love runs to my side. I

notice that his form flips through several of the most special cats I'd had throughout my life. Tabbies, a Siamese, a tabby calico mix. All different, but all springing from the same source.

"Let's go get Pakhetel."

*

Months later, or perhaps seconds, time is different here. I sit in a cottage overlooking a crystal-clear lake and trace patterns of energy in the air. I'm accustoming myself to my new level of being. Streaks of light flow around me, sometimes manifesting as cats, or other animals, that settle on chairs or in front of a comfy fire I have in the hearth. It's all energy, all illusion, but more real than most things on the material plane. It also helps me focus while I get accustomed to this new, 'life'.

The boss calls. I no longer need the crutch of visualizing a phone. I simply know that Lady Bastet has a task for me and what that task is. I slip from my chair. A beloved cat is lost, and it is for me to guide it back to the child for who it is the world. A child that, with love, can grow into a source of light in the world. A beacon of kindness that others will be inspired by. I remind myself not to overstate my own importance as I don the appearance of my Lady.

It is still true, 'I am not a man perfected. I am a man perfecting,' and one kindness at a time is still how I forge a cosmos where I'd want to live in her Ladyship's name.

Ankh em Ma'at.

Stephen B. Pearl is an author of several novels, including *Nukekubi* and *Worlds' Apart*, and has numerous short stories published in anthologies, such as *Canadian Dreadful*. His works range from romance to dark urban fantasy to dystopian genres. He has been an author guest at a multitude of literary and media conventions. When he is not writing, he spends time with his wife and plays servant to his beloved cats. For more information on his works, www.stephenpearl.com

Bend In The Wind

By James Dick

ALL CONVERSATION STOPPED WHEN THE Russians walked into the pub.

Five of them, led by a handsome blond god who was six-foot-five if he was an inch, brought a chill wind that blew all the mirth out of *The Destrier*.

From a stool at the bar, Mantas Dambrauskas watched them out of the corner of his eye. His hands curled into fists atop the polished mahogany of the bar.

Then, all at once, the place stuttered to life again. The talking, flirting, and drinking recommenced, this time with an element of playacting.

"It's not good to be distracted when talking with a woman."

Mantas looked at the barmaid, Jadvyga, standing on the other side of the bar from him; she of the bronze hair and deep green eyes.

Mantas felt his heart race. "This from someone as distracting as you?"

Jadvyga chuckled as she refilled his wine glass with a pre-war Shiraz. "Anything to separate a man from his litai."

"For you, a man would part with anything."

The barmaid lifted the wine bottle by the neck and waggled it at him. "Now you're trying too hard, sweet thing."

Inexperience was understandable. In fact, Mantas could hardly be called a man at all. At barely eighteen years old, he had precious little tutelage in courtship. Bombs, mortars, and burning buildings tended to put all other concerns out of a boy's mind.

Mantas sensed the Russians approaching. They carried with them an aura of cold air and silence. Ignas, the proprietor of *The Destrier*, intercepted them and offered to take their orders. Four of the Russians engaged him, but the Blond God continued on towards Mantas and Jadvyga, his eyes the colour of water in a frozen lake.

"Pay no attention to him," Jadvyga whispered, taking both of Mantas' hands and leaning across the bar. "Look at me. Pay me compliments." A note of urgency in her voice couldn't be concealed.

Her touch sent blood rushing to Mantas' head. It wasn't hard to look at her. Her irises appeared wide in the candlelight, inviting him to take refuge within. In those huge, gleaming pupils there'd never been a war, never been hardship or starvation. And there were certainly no Russians.

A voice as airy and devastating as a blizzard spoke at Mantas' side. "I've often wondered if it was worth it to trade home for a new country." The Blond God settled on the stool to Mantas' left. "Now, I see that it was."

Jadvyga's eyes flicked over to the Blond God. She unfurled a new smile that was both wider and falser than the one she'd given Mantas.

A hand landed on Mantas' shoulder. "You, my friend," the Blond God said, "you must tell me what experience you have with this particular vintage." He nodded at Jadvyga. "I feel I have a lot to learn."

Mantas' blood boiled.

Jadvyga squeezed his hands tighter and smiled at the Blond God. "Some vintages are simply priceless."

The Blond God chuckled. "Then it's a good thing I have very deep pockets." He patted Mantas' shoulder again. "Come, tell me what tickles this beauty," he nodded at Jadvyga. "Share a drink with me. Tell me what this beauty laugh."

Mantas' jaw clenched. He felt Jadvyga's grip on his hands tighten, as if she could hold the reins of his anger. She couldn't. No one could.

Bad enough he had to share the air with these Russians. He couldn't stomach the thought of sharing a drink with them, too.

"I'll tell you what makes her *frown*," said Mantas. Jadvyga tried one last time to keep a hold of his hands, but he slipped free and rose from his stool.

The Blond God rose as well. He was a head taller than Mantas and twice as muscled.

The Destrier went silent.

The big Russian raised an eyebrow. "And what's that?" His smile turned bloodthirsty.

"It's Moskvich pigs like you," said Mantas, picking up his wine, "who can't take a fucking hint." He emptied the glass all over the Blond God's chest, staining his crisp white shirt and grey jacket crimson.

The Russian's friends surged forward, but the Blond God froze them with a raised hand. "Well," he said, eyes twinkling, "thank you, *tovarisch*. Now I am as red on the outside as I am on the inside!" He broke into laughter, as did the rest of *The Destrier*. The tension evaporated in an instant.

It could've ended right there. Mantas could simply have turned back to the bar, kept on drinking. He could've taken his glass to a booth in the back, out of sight and mind. He could've left *The Destrier* entirely. He could've done any number of things other than the thing he ended up doing, and he did it because of Jadvyga, because she looked at him with *pity*.

That was more than the young man could bear.

He punched the Blond God right in the nose. There was a snap. Jadvyga stifled a yelp, and once more all activity ceased in *The Destrier*. For good, this time.

The Blond God stumbled back a step, blood streaming from his nose. He touched a finger to it and looked at the red, utterly surprised. He placed his index fingers on either side of his nose and gave a sharp tug. A second snap echoed in the bar, and this time *everyone* stifled a yelp. The Blond God's face was intact once more. Aside from the blood, he remained the image of male perfection.

Even bloody, Mantas thought dimly, *any woman in here would want to bed him. Maybe even more so* because *of the blood.*

"All right," the Blond God said. "If you insist."

He came at Mantas.

The young man knew instantly that he was outmatched. The Blond God had been trained to fight. Mantas had not. He had speed and strength. Mantas had neither. The Blond God could plan an assault, execute it, and parry any response Mantas gave. Mantas could do none of those things. Mantas threw his fists out blindly, connecting with muscle and bone but doing no real damage, whereas the Blond God effortlessly tenderized Mantas as a butcher would a side of beef. A jab here and Mantas couldn't breathe. A hook there and Mantas saw stars. At one point, Mantas made the mistake of lowering his guard to protect his beleaguered ribs and the Blond God attacked his face. Left-right, left-right. Over and over. Unrelenting.

Mantas started seeing double. A pair of fists appeared in his vision, growing larger, coming together, fusing into a single wall of meat that connected with his face and sent him wind-milling to the floor.

The world swam. He couldn't catch his breath. Couldn't even *think*.

The Blond God said something to his friends, and the Russians hoisted Mantas up by the arms, nearly wrenching them out of their sockets in the process. They dragged him along the floor to the staircase that led up to the street. As they ascended, one of Mantas' shoes slipped off, then the other. His bare heels thumped painfully all the way up the steps.

Then he was outside. The cold air embraced him. He wasn't sure which of the stars in the sky were real and which was a result of his abuse.

"Baltyskoye der mo," said one of the Russians. They threw him into the gutter and went back inside the bar.

Mantas lay on the cobblestones, surrounded by bombed-out buildings. He was a ruin within a ruin, too weak to move. Darkness came for him and he sank into a dreamless sleep.

*

When Mantas woke it was still night, but the eastern sky purpled. His feet felt warm. Someone had put his shoes on. Jadvyga had probably returned them to him when she slipped outside to throw out the rubbish. Part of him wished she'd stayed with him, tried to help him, but he understood why she didn't. If she had, it would've incited the Russians to abuse him further. Mantas knew exactly how it would've happened: the Blond God's minions would've toyed with Mantas while the God himself tried to charm Jadvyga at the bar.

In fact, that's probably what the Blond God did after Mantas got thrown out. *Did she resist his advances, or are they in bed together right now?* The thought sickened him. Jadvyga had sworn she'd never lie with a Russian, not after what they'd done to her sister during the First Occupation, but the Russians could exert pressure in many ways to get what they wanted, including threatening to close down *The Destrier* if Jadvyga didn't willingly consent.

Mantas hated feeling helpless, especially where Jadvyga was concerned.

He rolled onto his side and spat out a tooth, chasing it with a mouthful of blood. When he'd regained some measure of strength, he got to his feet, buttoned his jacket against the cold, and began the long march home.

*

Weekends were useful for recovering one's wits after a fight. Alone in his apartment, that's exactly what Mantas did.

He had a ten-year-old bottle of wine secreted away, something he'd found during the clean-up of a bombed-out restaurant. Such finds were usually to be kicked up to the foreman of the clean-up crew, who then decided how best to distribute them, but every once in a while, Mantas withheld his finds for times like these. He got down on all-fours and reached into the treasure trove beneath his bed. The bottle was entombed in sketches of nude women and graphic love letters from a levelled post-office.

At the centre of his trove sat a lacquered box, but he didn't touch that. *Not yet.*

He uncorked the bottle, sat on the bed, and faced the dresser. The images of his family stared back at him from wooden picture frames.

First, he drank to his mother, who died in childbirth during the first Russian occupation: "To you, Mama, who gave me life. I'm so very glad you didn't live to see such shameful times."

Next, he drank to his father, who died resisting the Third Reich: "To you, Papa. The bastards got me good, but I'll pay them back soon enough."

Finally, he drank to his sister, Gudaitis, who died of malnutrition at the beginning of the second Russian occupation: "To you, sweet one. I'm likewise glad you didn't live long in this new world, but selfishly... I miss you."

Mantas drank and continued to drink until he'd worked up the nerve to bring the lacquered box out into the light.

The box was a small, two-hinged oak chest, five inches wide and three inches tall. He lifted the hasp, opened the lid, revealing a Tokarev TT-30 pistol.

Small-arms were fairly easy to find in the ruins of Vilnius. The Wehrmacht and the Red Army had left their hardware lying around like driftwood on the banks of a river. Finding them wasn't hard, but the Soviets mandated they be turned in to Red Army officials immediately upon their discovery. Possessing one was forbidden.

Mantas cradled the weapon. He'd found it in the ruins of a pub on Žalgirio, a place known as a watering hole for soldiers on both sides of the war. He hid it under his coat and took it home. Every now and then he practiced ejecting the magazine, emptying the chamber, reloading and cocking it again. He'd never fired it. The magazine held only eight rounds, and he'd found no more in all his time with the clean-up crews. The day he used this gun, he'd have to make every shot count.

And he *would* use it.

He stood in front of the wardrobe mirror, stock-straight like a proper soldier. He put the gun inside his coat, and then whipped it out lightning quick. "*Life does not matter if the Fatherland is once again enslaved by its enemies,*" he said. Those were the words his father had taught him. They would be the words Mantas cried on the day he shed blood.

He replaced the gun under his coat and pictured the face of the Blond God, with his strong jaw and self-assured smile, as if he were standing in front of Mantas. "I'm going to kill you."

In one swift motion, Mantas reached for his gun, wrapped his fingers around it, and pulled it out. But in his drunken state, he'd neglected to restore the safety after removing and reloading the magazine. When he took aim at his reflection and squeezed the trigger, the gun fired and he shot his reflection, shattering the mirror into a thousand pieces.

Mantas dropped the gun and covered his ears. The pistol landed on the floor and bounced under the wardrobe.

He froze.

Footsteps thundered up the stairwell outside his apartment.

Moving quickly, he got down and retrieved the pistol, making sure to flip the safety back on, and put it back in its lacquered box.

The footsteps grew louder and would be at the door in seconds.

Mantas slid the box under his bed as far as it would go and fetched the bottle of wine. He mussed his hair a little bit and made sure his shirt was untucked.

The footsteps stopped outside his door. Someone pounded on it. "Dambrauskas!" a voice bellowed.

Mantas stumbled to the door and eased it open.

The landlord, a bespectacled, balding little man by the name of Mr. Balchunus, stood on the threshold. "What the hell is going on up here? I heard a gunshot."

"No, no," Mantas said, making sure to give Balchunus a face full of his alcoholised breath. "It was the wardrobe." He opened the door wide enough for Balchunus to see the shattered mirror. "Bumped into it and smashed the mirror."

Balchunus' nostrils flared. He stared hard at Mantas. "Mr. Dambrauskas, it is four-o-clock in the morning and some of us have to be at work in three hours."

"What? It's Saturday!"

"No, it is now *Monday*," Balchunus enunciated. "And if you can't keep the noise to a minimum, I'll happily find another tenant who can. And where's last month's rent?"

"I'll get it, I'll get it!" Mantas said hastily.

"My patience with you is reaching its limit, sir." Balchunus looked at the wine bottle in Mantas' hand, scornfully shook his head, and walked away.

Mantas closed the door and blew out a long sigh. He finished off the bottle and lurched back to bed, his thoughts turning once more to the gun. He fell asleep with pleasant fantasies of violence circling in his brain.

*

Work that day involved cleaning up the wreckage of an apartment complex in the Old Town. As a rich district of Vilnius, the whole crew was alert for anything of value. Of course, taking things from wealthier neighbourhoods was a tricky proposition. Rich people were more likely to have relatives and friends who were as eager to pick the bones of the dead as the clean-up crews. The trick for men like Mantas was figuring out what pieces of property wouldn't be missed.

No one said anything about Mantas' bruises.

Mantas stood on top of a mound of rubble, king of his own little wasteland, and shuttled brick and wood from the top to the bottom. The rubble was then carted off in wheelbarrows by a separate team for disposal. Sometimes Mantas found a body in the rubble, sometimes many bodies. Today, it was the latter.

When air raids occurred during the war, many couldn't make it to bomb shelters, so they hid under the tables in their homes. For all the good it did them they may as well have stood out in the street.

Whenever Mantas found a body, he signalled his foreman, Volter, to oversee the extraction of the poor soul. Among the dead today were ten men, twelve women, six children and two infants.

Around midday, just as it was getting on lunch time, Mantas looked up from the rubble and saw the Blond God crossing the street, flagging Volter down as he approached the work site. His retinue were in tow, all dressed in fine suits and ties, strutting like peacocks.

The golden-haired Russian dwarfed Volter. Mantas could see the two men's lips moving but couldn't hear what they said. Volter's shoulders sank further and further as the conversation progressed. Twice the Blond God pointed at Mantas, and twice Volter regarded Mantas with pain and regret.

Finally—inevitably—Volter turned away from the Russian and started climbing the rubble.

Mantas felt a sting in his palms and realized he was clenching his fists so hard his nails dug into his skin.

Volter reached Mantas but said nothing. There was nothing to say.

"Did you fight for me, at least?" asked Mantas.

A muscle twitched in Volter's brow. He looked down.

This is what it has come to: not the end of the fight, but the end of the will to fight. Hate and shame filled Mantas' heart in equal measure. He stepped past Volter, climbing down the rubble heap. The other workers halted their digging and turned to watch him go. With each step he took, Mantas felt smaller, all the while, the Blond God loomed larger. The big Russian smiled at Mantas as if they were lifelong friends.

Mantas imagined picking up a brick and smashing that smile into a red pulp. The only thing that stopped him was the knowledge that the Blond God was quicker and stronger. Mantas wanted the Blond God dead, nothing less.

So, instead, he passed the Russians by and headed off to *The Destrier* for a drink.

*

Mantas could've found his way to *The Destrier* blindfolded; he'd walked the route so many times. He arrived at the pub just as it opened for the day. No one else was inside except Ignas, cleaning a pint glass behind the bar with a damp rag. *Where's Jadvyga?*

"Glass of red, please, Ignas," Mantas said, taking out a few litai. *This is probably the last cash I'll have for a while, but I need a drink.*

Ignas set the mug down and wiped his hands on his apron. He slowly approached Mantas, passing the wine rack.

A cold feeling settled in Mantas' belly.

"I think you'd better go," Ignas said firmly.

Mantas held up the litai. "My money's as good as anyone's."

"We were lucky the Russians didn't close us down." Anger bled through into Ignas' voice. He stared hard at Mantas.

"Where's Jadvyga?" Mantas asked, looking over Ignas' shoulder.

"Go home."

Mantas leaned around Ignas and called to the back of *The Destrier.* "Jadvyga!"

"Go. *Home.*" Ignas' nostrils flared. "Don't make me call the police."

Numb, Mantas collected his cash and pushed himself off the stool. He climbed the stairs with leaden legs.

Half a block down the street, he heard someone call his name. "Mantas!"

He turned. Jadvyga ran towards him as fast as her heels allowed. She had a bottle of Shiraz Cabernet in her hand.

"I managed to sneak it out," she said, holding it out to him.

Mantas started to reach inside his coat for his money. "I'll pay—"

"No." Jadvyga grabbed his hand and pressed the bottle into it.

Mantas turned his black eye away from her. "You shouldn't see me like this."

Jadvyga shook her head. "I've seen you in worse states." She reached up and put her warm hand on his cheek. "This pain is going to kill you. You have to let it go."

Mantas' chest tightened. "I can't."

"Sweetie, it doesn't matter who you fight, or how hard you hit."

The young man's eyes stung.

"None of it will bring them back."

Ignas appeared at the door of *The Destrier.* "Jadvyga!"

"I should go." Mantas moved away from the barmaid.

Jadvyga took a step towards him. "Wait, Mantas—"

"I don't want to get you in trouble. Thank you for the wine." Mantas turned his back on her and marched down the street.

He sat on his bed and drank the day away.

We lose everything, he thought. *We lose always. We are destined to be raped forever.*

The rage within him burned like a forest fire, begging to be quenched.

On hand and knee, he pulled the lacquered box out from under the bed. The pistol lay inside like an undressed lover, enticing him. Mantas lifted it out and lovingly caressed the metal. This would be the instrument of his release. Seven bullets remained.

Let's see if the Blond God's still smiling when his brains hit the sidewalk.

*

Mantas took to the streets. The late afternoon sun set the faces of the Old Town buildings ablaze with golden light. He walked with his coat buttoned up, acutely aware of the weight of the gun hidden within.

Maybe there'd be witnesses, so much the better. If the people saw one man stand up to their enemies, publicly, without fear, they might be emboldened to similar acts of rebellion. What Mantas did tonight might echo throughout history. Knowing this, he felt tremendous responsibility. *I mustn't fail.*

Work had ended for most of Vilnius. Mantas went to the Destrier. He stayed near the front door so as not to be seen and peered inside—no sign of the Blond God or his retinue among the patrons. Mantas moved on to the next bar, and the next one, and the next. Nothing, nothing, and nothing.

He shambled through the city, tracing a rough spiral ever outward, letting the flame of his rage warm him against the cold. He tried cafes, restaurants, and gentlemen's clubs. Half the time he didn't find the Russians, the other half he wasn't even admitted because he failed to meet the dress code. As night fell, he abandoned the search and simply wandered, a ghost that couldn't find the afterlife.

In his drunken state, he'd lost track of the hours. He

thought it near midnight, but he couldn't be sure.

The buildings around him shrank in size and age, becoming smaller and newer. He moved forward through time, his path charting the story of a city that had existed under occupation for longer than it had ever been free. The banks became apartments, the apartments became houses, and the houses became trees as the city gave way to virgin forest.

Mantas realized he was lost.

He was on a dirt road surrounded by tall pines. The lights at his back told him he was on the outskirts of Vilnius. Ahead, dark woodland grew.

His gut clenched. He leaned against a tree and vomited all over its trunk, his stomach fluids a deep crimson from the wine. After coughing up the last of the bile, he hung limply from a low branch.

A million stars shone down upon him from a cloudless, moonless night. Mantas' laboured breathing filled the silence.

In the distance, Mantas heard laughter.

He stumbled toward it, following it into the woods. As he walked further, the laughter was joined by the sound of gregarious Russian conversation.

The pistol bounced against Mantas' chest as he picked his way through the underbrush. A light shone ahead: orange, flickering light, from a campfire. He picked up the pace, rounded a tree trunk, and crouched behind a bush.

In a clearing near a promontory of sand at the bend of a river up ahead, five Russians, including the Blond God, sat on logs around a campfire, passing a bottle of wine around like a cheap whore.

The Blond God took a long pull from the bottle and rose from the log he'd been sitting on. He unbuttoned his pants, took out his cock in full view of his comrades, and pissed into the fire.

Mantas reached inside his coat, drew his pistol, and cocked it. He charged from the bush.

He forgot about his father's words. All he managed to utter was an incoherent cry. The Russians all turned and stared wide-eyed at him as he aimed at the Blond God's heart and pulled the trigger.

The gun jammed.

Mantas stood across the fire from the Blond God, whose cock still dangled from his pants, gun aimed but unfired. When he realized what had happened, he pulled the trigger again. Nothing.

The Blond God cracked a smile, tucked his manhood back into his pants, and started to laugh, as did his fellows.

Mantas' rage turned to fear. He'd gone from feeling mighty to feeling cornered.

The Russians nearest tackled him, wrenching the gun from his hand and beating him with it. Fire exploded all over Mantas' face.

Mantas tried to flee. Strong hands arrested him.

One by one, the Russians punched, kicked, and head-butted Mantas, laughing like children, jabbering in their disgusting language.

Eventually, it was the Blond God's turn.

The huge man rolled Mantas onto his back, straddling him like a lover. He made Mantas look him in the eyes as he delivered every single savage blow. As the young man looked up at the huge Russian, a strange thought came into his mind. *I wonder if they all had the Blond God's face—all the others who've raped and bloodied Lithuania. Maybe there was only ever one face, down through all the ages, worn first by a Viking, then by a Christian knight, then a German soldier, and now by this Russian.*

One of the other men handed the Blond God the empty wine bottle, and he swung it at Mantas' face. The last thing Mantas heard before his world vanished was the deafening pop of his skull splitting open.

*

The sky hung overcast with soft grey clouds, and birdsong drifted down from the treetops. The river silently glided past. For a moment he couldn't remember how he came to be there.

Then, it all came back: the campfire, the click of the malfunctioning gun, and the sound of his temple cracking under the wine bottle. *Shouldn't I be dead?*

He was also wrapped in a quilted blanket.

"Back in the land of the living?"

Mantas lifted his head, a little stiff but free of pain. He lay on the beach at the bend of the river where he'd ambushed the Russians. Three women shared the space with him, seated on logs around the dead fire.

One wore a flowing green dress, her belly swollen in pregnancy. She worked a needle and thread as she stitched together a doll with long black hair and an eyeless face. Another woman, a brunette in drab olive trousers, chopped deadfall with a hatchet. She passed the split wood to the third and youngest woman, a redhead in the most vibrant, fiery dress Mantas had ever seen. The redhead knelt over the ruins of the fire, labouring to rebuild it with the chopped deadfall.

She smiled at Mantas. "We feared your flame had been snuffed."

"Would've been a chore to bury you," the woodcutter grumbled.

Mantas tried pushing himself into a seated position.

"Don't you dare," said the pregnant woman, rising from her stump.

"Madam, please," said Mantas, face burning, "don't get up."

"Take your own advice," said the pregnant woman. "Lie back down."

A wave of fatigue washed over Mantas and he came to rest on his elbows again.

The pregnant woman fetched a bucket and dipped it into the river, then knelt beside Mantas. She used a ladle to bring the water to Mantas' lips. Thirst overwhelmed him, and he drank long and deep.

"You were in quite a state when we found you," the pregnant woman said as she gave Mantas another ladleful. "Body broken, bleeding inside and out. It's a wonder I ever managed to put you back together."

Mantas finished off the second ladle in one draught. "I'm most grateful to you for helping me."

"It was very tempting to leave your sorry hide for the wolves," the brunette said, pausing to wipe sweat from her brow.

The pregnant woman rounded on the brunette, her gentle

countenance suddenly turning stony. "Žvėrinė," she growled.

The brunette's expression soured further and she hacked at the deadfall with a vengeance.

The pregnant woman turned her attention back to Mantas, her face once more becoming a vision of warmth. "Please forgive her. She's spent so long in the woods she's forgotten her manners."

"That's all right," said Mantas. "I take no offence."

"However," the mother continued, "she does have a point in that it was quite foolish to take on five powerful men the way you did."

Mantas swallowed. "You saw?"

"We did," the redhead said with a bemused smile. "It was quite a sight."

"Stupid," the brunette—Žvėrinė—muttered.

"We were in the trees," said the pregnant woman. "We waited until the men left to come to your aid. You're extremely lucky; not just that you survived, but also that your gun jammed."

Mantas stared at her. "How am I lucky that I was left defenceless?"

"If you fired that gun, you would be a murderer." The pregnant woman stood. "You would've had to run, leaving behind all you knew and all who cared about you. What kind of life would that be?" She turned away from him, resumed her seat by the still-unlit fire, and continued knitting the little doll in her hands.

"It would be better than the one I have now." Mantas threw off the quilted blanket and started to get to his feet.

"What did she just tell you, idiot?" Žvėrinė hissed.

"I would like to try standing," Mantas said. Rolling onto his side, he used arms and legs to push to his feet.

Žvėrinė paused, snorted, and hawked a fearsome gobbet of sputum onto the ground beside her, drawing frowns from the other two women. "I won't pick you up if you fall."

Mantas carefully rose, placing both feet flat on the ground before lifting himself upright. A chorus of pops rippled down his spine. A wave of dizziness washed over him, but he could walk a straight line, and his shiner had disappeared so he was no longer half blind. He approached the women. "May I know the names of my saviours?" He looked at the brunette. "I know you are Žvėrinė."

Žvėrinė grunted.

Mantas looked to the pregnant woman.

"I am Žemyna," said the mother.

"And I am Gabija," said the redhead, giving Mantas another of those bemused smiles from beneath her flaming locks.

"Mantas Dambrauskas," said Mantas. "At your service."

Gabija giggled.

"Well met," said Žemyna. "Now, tell me something. Why were you so determined to become a murderer?"

"They were Russians," said Mantas. "It is my duty to kill them."

Žemyna exchanged a sceptical look with the other women. "And who instilled this particular duty in you?"

"My father. He taught me to resist our oppressors with all of my might."

Žvėrinė gave a snorting laugh. "But not with all of your *wits*, if a jammed gun is the best you could bring to the table."

Mantas' jaw clenched. "That won't happen next time."

All three women regarded him with astonishment.

"*Next time?*" Žemyna said, horrified. "You're going to try *again?*"

"Oh, enough, Žemyna," Žvėrinė said. "If he's so intent on getting himself killed, let him. One less fool in the world."

"My family died because of invaders like them," said Mantas.

The women fell still.

"First my mother," he continued, "in childbirth, because she was so weak from malnutrition—the Soviets had taken all our food. Then my father was killed resisting the Germans, when they came. Then my sister died of starvation." His hands curled into fists.

None of the women said or did anything for a very long time. Finally, Žemyna put down the doll she was making and approached Mantas, tears in her eyes.

She threw her arms around him and pulled him into a hug, so tightly and so suddenly he gasped. He couldn't remember the last time another human being had held him like this. It had been so long ago that, when Mantas returned Žemyna's embrace, his arms moved haltingly, as if it were an effort to recall that simple gesture of comfort.

"I'm so sorry," said Žemyna, her tears falling on Mantas' shoulder.

Mantas felt something nudge his stomach.

Žemyna felt it too and chuckled. She peeled herself off him, wiping the tears from her eyes. "Sorry about *that*, too." She put a hand to her belly.

Despite himself, Mantas started to smile. A bashful laugh bubbled out of him. "It's all right."

"Would you like to feel?"

Mantas nodded.

Žemyna took his hand and placed it over her navel. It only took a moment for him to feel a small kick against his palm.

"She's more impetuous than *you* are," Žemyna said.

"You hope it's a girl?" Mantas asked.

"I *know* it's a girl." Another, stronger kick made Žemyna smile and wince. "Ooh... better sit down." She turned away from him and settled back onto her stump.

The world grew blurry, and Mantas realized it was because he had tears in his own eyes. He wiped them away and was surprised to feel no tenderness in his face at all. It wasn't that his black eye was gone...*all* his injuries were gone. *How is that possible?*

"Are you a... nurse?" Mantas asked Žemyna.

She shook her head. "I just know some home remedies."

"Including some for broken skulls?"

"Well, *that* took a little extra." Žemyna exchanged a knowing look with the others. "You won't need to go to a doctor, if that's what you're asking."

Definitely impossible. "I don't think I could afford it even if I was at death's door."

"Which you were," said Gabija.

The kindling in the dead fire pit caught, though Mantas never heard Gabija strike a match, use a lighter, or scrape flint and tinder together. A small flame burst to life and burned steadily. Gabija blew on it. The tongues greedily licked the surrounding twigs.

"Are you all sisters?" Mantas asked.

"Ha!" Žvėrinė barked.

Gabija grinned and shook her head. "Oh no." She giggled. "Sisters! Could you imagine?"

Mantas' ears grew hot. "Do you live around here?"

"In the forest," said Žemyna.

"Ah." Mantas nodded slowly. "I suppose you have less trouble with the Russians that way."

"No less than you." Žvėrinė stretched before taking a seat by the newborn fire. "We simply know how to survive."

Mantas took a half step toward the fire, paused, and at Žvėrinė's invitation, proceeded forward and took a seat beside her. She smelled heavily of pine sap. "And how is that?"

Žvėrinė gave Mantas a wolfish grin. "Well, we don't pick fights we can't win for a start."

Mantas groaned. "I would've won if my gun hadn't jammed."

"But it did, and here you are."

Some of Mantas' prior frustration returned. "If no one resists, we will be second-class citizens in our own country forever."

"No," said Žemyna, "not forever. Death comes to everyone, including those who've done you wrong."

"I'm just to forget my pain and do nothing? Tell that big blond bastard he can have my country?"

Žemyna held up her hands in a gesture of calm. "You see the golden-haired man, Mantas, but you fail to see the man behind him, or the one behind *him*; a line of men stretching all the way back to their frozen city."

"Then I will kill them all."

"That," said Gabija, "would be like throwing gasoline on this campfire." She gestured to the little blaze around which the four of them sat. "With each man who fell, the next would visit greater and greater retribution upon everyone you care for. As you killed those men, so too would you kill your homeland."

Mantas thought of Volter, of Balchunus, of Ignas… and of Jadvyga. He thought of Jadvyga being bloodied the way he'd been last night… being abused the way her sister had once been. His stomach curdled. "I… I'm fighting to *protect* my homeland."

"If you continue to fight *this* enemy in *this* way, you'll be responsible for the death of Lithuania just as surely as if you'd killed every one of its people with your own two hands."

"But…" Mantas looked into the fire, tried to collect his thoughts. "But we could still win if enough of us fought. Revolution is like this fire, too: it spreads, catching from person to person. All it takes is a spark."

Gabija considered this. "Sometimes, yes, that is true." She looked at Mantas. "But answer this: can you picture any of your cohorts wanting to take part in your revolution, of being ready to die?"

Volter hadn't even been ready to fight to keep Mantas employed. Ignas banned Mantas from the Destrier for fear the Russians would close the pub if he didn't. And Jadvyga and Balchunus…well, *they* were both merely interested in making a living.

Mantas slowly shook his head. "No."

"So, then what would be the point?"

Mantas turned to Žvėrinė, who regarded him with wary eyes. "In the woods," he said to her, "doesn't one need to fight every single second to survive? Isn't that struggle what keeps you strong?"

Žvėrinė was silent for a while. "Yes, that's true—"

Mantas threw up his hands victoriously.

"—but survival never just takes one form." Žvėrinė turned her head and looked across the river. She pointed to a tree whose branches were all bent backwards so that they faced in one direction. On the opposite side, the trunk was bare. "See that?"

Mantas nodded.

"That tree has been shaped by the wind. It has learned how to bend in the wind, how to let the wind mold it, and its roots have grown strong because of that. That single misshapen tree could probably withstand gales that would lay waste to any other tree in these woods, all because it learned to bend in the wind and strengthen its roots." Žvėrinė looked back at Mantas. "*That* is survival. Maybe the truest expression of it. The Rus are a cold wind—you can't stop the wind—so Lithuania must be like a tree to survive them. It must remember its roots, and learn to bend."

Mantas shook his head. "We have no roots. We have nothing that was not imposed upon us by someone else."

Žemyna frowned. "Are you so quick to forget us?" She set her needle and thread down on the ground and stood up, holding the doll she'd been working on with both hands. "We've always been here, and always will be." She circled the fire towards Mantas.

"And just who are you?" he asked her, his chest tightening.

Žemyna took his hand and pressed the doll into it. Straw crunched beneath its fabric skin. "We are your roots."

Mantas looked down at the doll, then back at Žemyna, and when he did, his heart fluttered.

Žemyna's skin was covered in vines, twining and criss-crossing like veins. Her hair flowed with leaves and flowers of every kind blossomed there.

Mantas turned and looked at Žvėrinė.

Not much had changed about the forester, but her eyes had taken on a silver sheen, like the eyes of a wolf when they catch the light of a full moon. She flashed a pair of sharp canines at him.

Finally, he looked at Gabija.

The redhead was engulfed in flames—flames which burned and gave warmth but did not scald or consume anything they touched, constant and unquenchable.

Mantas looked back at the doll in his hand. No, not a doll... an effigy. He knew then whose company he was in, though his mind could scarcely believe the evidence of his eyes.

"Burn Morana, Mantas," said Gabija.

"Burn her and put an end to winter," said Žvėrinė.

"Burn her," said Žemyna, "and remember your roots."

Mantas didn't know when it happened, but the campfire had transformed into a massive blaze, so wide and tall that his skin should've been blistering. Instead, he felt only a soothing warmth that reached all the way to his soul. Moving with dreamlike grace, he cast the effigy of Morana, the death goddess of old, into the flames, and she turned to ash in the space of a single breath.

Then the towering blaze shrank back down to a small camp-fire. Golden light bathed the beach. He looked up.

The sun had come out.

The goddesses of his ancestors had disappeared.

*

Mantas didn't return to Vilnius.

He walked through the forest, found the dirt road he'd travelled, and followed it north. A day's journey from the city, he reached a beet farm owned by a man with too many years on his back and too few men to work the fields. He took Mantas on instantly.

By day, Mantas toiled in the fields, and by night, he learned about the old gods; first Žemyna, Žvėrinė, and Gabija, then Dievas, Perkūnas, Giltinė, and then others as he learned their names. His teachers were few and far between. Nominally, Lithuania had been Christian for over six centuries, but here, in the rural communities, Romuva—the old ways—lived on, practiced by a handful of people in the shadows. Romuviai had been gathering at so called "folk festivals" for forty years. The Russians had banned these since the beginning of the second occupation, but the practitioners could still be found, if one was persistent.

Mantas Dambrauskas was nothing if not persistent.

He found them and prayed with them, studied the ritual calendars, and recited the ancient stories. The anger he'd lived with most of his life dimmed, and then vanished altogether. He didn't stand idly by for injustice, but he didn't seek out violence or think of it when he lay down to sleep.

There was still one tie with his life in Vilnius he was eager to keep alive. Perhaps it was an act of vanity, a need for another human being to see how far he'd come, but he believed it was something sincere.

One day, when he was finally ready, he invited Jadvyga to visit him on the farm.

*

Jadvyga met Mantas at the wooden fence that ran the perimeter of his employer's beet field. He stood on the inside, she on the outside. She reached into her handbag and took out the photos of Mantas' family.

"Thank you for rescuing them," Mantas said, taking the photos from her. The pictures appeared to be in good shape, the frames undamaged.

"I'm surprised your landlord even kept them," said Jadvyga. "From what you told me, you two weren't on good terms."

"I'm glad he did." Mantas smiled. "I don't want to forget about my roots."

Jadvyga smiled back. "Something's changed in you. It's like an inferno has finally been extinguished."

"Fire can be good or bad, but in my case, it was the latter."

They walked along the fence. A grey mist hung over the beet field and gathered into dew on the lush green beet shoots. The summer rains had come early and often this year. All the farmhands told Mantas that the coming harvest would be plentiful. Mantas looked forward to it. It would be a joy to reap a bounty of life instead of death.

"I hope things haven't been too bad for you," said Mantas.

Jadvyga shrugged. "No more or less than usual. City repairs are going well. Vilnius is healing."

"I'm glad to hear it." And, truly, he was. "It's a fine city. It deserves a chance to live."

Jadvyga gave him a curious look from beneath the brim of her sun hat. "I have some news for you, about your blond friend."

"The Russian?"

"Yes."

"Huh." Mantas' brow furrowed. "You know, I actually haven't thought of him in a long time."

"His name was Nikolaj Kuznetsov. He was an economist hired by the Russian government to assess the natural resources of Lithuania. Based on what I've learned about him, he had a remarkable amount of power."

Nikolaj Kuznetsov. So strange to finally put a name to that face.

Then Mantas realized Jadvyga had been speaking about the

Russian in the past tense. He paused in his tracks. "How'd you find out all this?"

"I read it in his obituary."

Manta's heart skipped a beat. "What happened?"

"He burned to death in a fire. His whole apartment went up. Apparently, a party he was having with his friends got out of control."

A fire... "Of course."

Jadvyga cocked her head. "What?"

"The night I left Vilnius... the night I planned to kill him... when I found him, he was pissing on a fire."

Jadvyga shrugged. "So?"

"It's disrespectful," said Mantas. "If you piss on a fire, you piss on the Goddess Gabija and risk incurring Her wrath." *But you'd never guess She could be wrathful at all when She has such a warm smile.*

"Did you become a mythologist as well as a farmer?" Jadvyga asked.

"I've joined Romuva."

Jadvyga's eyebrows rose a little. "Now that's something I *never* would've guessed."

"Neither would I," Mantas laughed, "but learning where we've come from... how much hardship our people have overcome... it's helped me."

Jadvyga looked into the tall trees. "I've always been more concerned with where we're going than where we've been."

Mantas shrugged. "A tree can't bear fruit if it doesn't have roots."

Jadvyga chuckled. "Are you a horticulturalist, too?"

Mantas smiled. "I am a Lithuanian."

)O( )O( )O(

James Dick is an actor, author, screenwriter, and director living in Toronto, Ontario. He is a student at Ryerson University's Creative School, working toward a degree in Media Production. James's media and acting studies inform every aspect of his writing process, from ideation to finished story. His work has appeared in Improbable Press, Ghost Orchid Press, and Blank

BEND IN THE WIND

Spaces Magazine. You can follow him on Instagram @james.patrick.dick, and find more of his written work and collaborations at www.storystation.net

Earth Mother

By Glynn Owen Barrass

TAMARA YAWNED, STRETCHED HER ARMS from beneath the bedcover over her head. A quick check of her wristwatch informed her it was a quarter to nine. She had set the alarm for nine. *Go figure*, Tamara thought, rubbing the sleep from her eyes. She had forgotten to close the beige curtains last night, and the small, green walled room stood illuminated from the sunlight outside. *What a night!* The village of Medea, their place of lodging while they investigated Ireland's Boho Highlands, had been totally deserted. This desolate place had no internet or mobile phone coverage either. When they arrived at the guesthouse, a place Tamara had pre-booked by phone two weeks earlier, the landline telephone had proven dead.

Completely cut off from the outside world. That's what it felt like. The four of them had decided to make themselves at home in the guesthouse despite it being empty. Fresh linen had awaited them in rooms probably prepared for their arrival.

Tamara stretched again and tucked her arms beneath the blankets. Could she snatch a brief fifteen minutes before the alarm on her phone chirped to life? Chances appeared low. Still, she turned onto her side, closed her eyes. A few seconds later, a tap on her door made her scowl. The door stood slightly ajar, so the voice came clear to her ears.

"Miss Lake, are you up?" Azer, her graduate student said, his voice quiet and apologetic. He had been so enthusiastic during the journey. Last night's desolation had nipped that in the bud.

"Just…uh," she cleared her throat. "Are the others up?"

"Up and decent," he replied.

She smiled. "Gimme five minutes. I'll meet everyone down-stairs. Kitchen, yeah?"

"We'll be there," Azer replied. "Still no sign of anyone."

As if she hadn't guessed that already. Tamara took a few more luxurious moments of rest, and then reluctantly pulled the covers from her body.

Her clothes lay in an undignified heap on the floor. This being a research trip, they were casual, just jeans, hiking boots and a faded green Queen's University of Belfast hoodie for her.

She stood up, and while dressing wondered if there would be time for a shower before they got started. *Started, that was a good one!* Nothing had gone to plan since arriving last evening, so what might today bring? Possibly, a return to Queen's University, with a stop on the way to report their findings to the authorities. Tamara sat down on her bed and fastened her boots. When she stood again, she stretched the kinks from her neck and headed towards the window.

What do I expect to see? Some sign of life perhaps? That would be nice, and would calm the fear and confusion that had hovered over her since last night. *Looks quiet out,* she mused, *but it is early.*

Beyond a small, well-groomed garden lay the B81, the road they had travelled three times looking for the villagers. Beyond that, past a rising grass verge, stood three houses, well, cottages really. Their whitewashed walls, the red-tiled gabled roofs, looked immaculate in the morning light. The curtains hung closed, the same as last night. Similar houses stood beyond the three, but not many. Medea boasted a population of less than a hundred and twenty.

To the right of the cottages, an upwardly sloping field held a few dozen lazily grazing cows. Tamara's other graduate student, Shellie, had commented that Medea probably boasted more cows than people.

"Lot's more," Tamara said, turning from the window to head towards the door. *And if we leave now, the cows will have the village to themselves.*

The doorway led to a narrow, pink carpeted landing with a staircase to the right. Three doors lined the floral papered walls, all ajar. From the voices filtering up from downstairs, her companions were up and about. She sent the far door, which led to the bathroom and shower, a wistful look as she descended the stairs. Halfway down, Tamara caught the scents of fresh coffee and toast. This brought a smile to her face and a rumble to her stomach. When she reached the foot of the stairs, she turned left, following her nose towards the guesthouse's kitchen.

The door stood wide open, the smells hitting her strongly as she entered the small, brightly lit kitchen. Wooden cabinets lined the whitewashed walls, the table at the centre covered in a white and red chequered cloth. Her colleague, Tim, a fellow tutor from the Biomedical Science School, sat at the table, his long grey hair in a ponytail. Beside him sat Shellie, another graduate student. Small and petite, she had tanned skin, her brown hair cut short.

Tamara had caught them mid conversation. Rather than interrupt, she examined the table's contents. Two plates stood piled with toast, accompanied by jars of jam and a square of butter. Her companions had obviously helped themselves to the contents of the guesthouse's pantry. Also, she noted a steaming coffee pot. *Precious coffee!*

"It goes back centuries," Shellie continued. "The whole area inhabited by Druids, high ranking healers, leading figures to the Celts and— Oh hey, Tamara!"

The pair looked at her, smiled as she took a chair and sat down.

"We were just discussing the Druids," Tim said. He pushed the coffee jug and an empty mug towards her.

"Yeah, their use of local soils to treat infections and toothaches, diseases. I think there should be further study, not just here, but globally," said Shellie.

EARTH MOTHER

Tamara poured herself some coffee, the delicious smell making her nostrils tingle. Shellie seemed so enthusiastic about this old myth turned true: soil with healing properties. Theirs was the second team to investigate the Boho Highlands, and the girl had begged for inclusion.

Tamara raised the mug and took a sip.

Shellie eagerly stared at her, awaiting a response.

"A fantastic discovery, yes," Tamara said after a large swig of coffee. The liquid felt a little too hot, just how she liked it. "But it could have been a wild goose chase. Many of these things are." She swallowed more coffee and added, "Folk remedies generally prove to be no more than old wives tales."

"Yeah I guess, though still..." Shellie leant across the table and sighed, retrieving a piece of toast.

Tamara hadn't wanted to curb her enthusiasm, but she considered the Boho Highlands an unusual case. The soil the original team found had proved potentially effective against four out of the six superbugs, including MRSA. And, the area had been inhabited for over four thousand years, providing plenty of historical records concerning the soil's healing properties.

Shellie, having a Masters in Celtic Studies, didn't look at things from a totally scientific viewpoint. This trip Shellie had hoped to interview some of the older villagers, learn some history not included in the records. That certainly wasn't going to plan.

From Tamara's viewpoint, the find felt exciting in a different way. Scientists were just discovering the broad spectrum of treatments the bacteria could be utilized for, hence the trip to acquire more samples.

"Just popped next door, door unlocked, tried their telephone and nothing," a voice said from her right.

Azer scowled as he leant in the doorway. His black hair, usually immaculate, looked ruffled, his spectacles drawn up above his forehead. Originally from Pakistan, he had emigrated and lived in Ireland most of his life, but hadn't developed an Irish accent.

Azer loped forward, took the seat opposite Tamara. She drained the rest of her coffee and began refilling her mug, intending to pass Azer the pot after.

Now they had to consider the real issue: the desertion of the town and the dead zone of isolation from the outside world.

*

Some discussion, coffee and toast later, led to a show of hands. Three to one, with Tamara the loser, saw them continuing what they had come for, deserted village be damned.

Tamara had had a bad feeling about the village soon after they arrived. After coming all this way, she now begrudgingly admitted that remaining was the right thing to do.

*

So, Tamara told herself, sitting in the car beside Tim. As he drove, Medea's streets, sparse of buildings in the first place, grew sparser as they left the village. He followed the B81, the same road that had brought them there the night before. His GPS, like everything else requiring a satellite signal, remained out of commission. However, Tim said he knew the way from the first visit.

Hedges flanked the road to the right, bare grass to the left. Beyond, on either side, hilly areas led to a horizon grey with clouds, warning of bad weather to come.

The graduate students talked quietly in the back. They passed a lone whitewashed cottage on Tim's side, and for a brief instant Tamara thought she saw someone in the garden. A moment later they passed it. A quick look in that direction showed nothing but tall flowers and a tree.

Tim glanced at her. "Gets a little bumpy soon," then to the others, "Hey guys, it gets bumpy." The road had begun rising. Tim slowed the Land Rover, pressed his direction indicator before following the right turn of a junction. Moments later, embankments and thick rugged trees surrounded them. This scenery continued for a while, and then the trees thinned out a little to the right, giving a view of the village below. From the height and distance, Medea resembled a child's play set, its few score buildings placed haphazardly between open fields. A left turn changed the view, and the road levelled out. They drove high above Enniskillen now, the road ahead a dark, leafy aisle. As Tim promised, it got bumpy, and Tamara's coffee-filled stomach lurched.

She pressed herself into her seat, hoping the nausea would pass.

A wide lane appeared to the left, leading to the sheds and silos of a farm. A little further along, a cow poked its head from the bushes, the bovine following their passage with sad brown eyes.

Tamara made a mental note to visit the farm on the return trip; see if that was deserted too.

Desertion. No wonder everyone appeared so subdued. Azer, usually full of conversation, was silent. The pair behind her had ceased talking some time earlier. Tamara noticed the silence, it felt like an unbreakable tension, something she dare not pierce with insignificant words. The village. The mystery of where everyone had gone. She wondered whether her companions felt a similar dead weight to the one she had in her gut.

The road dipped, and then rose again at a steep angle. The trees had grown thicker, their trunks smothered in parasitic ivy. The road soon narrowed significantly to one uneven, bumpy lane. The primeval forest made Tamara uneasy. A branch tapped her window and she flinched.

"It's a very diverse area, geologically speaking, many different habitats," Azer said, breaking the silence. Perhaps he had noticed her uneasiness. "The soil has an interesting chemistry wherever you look, or so I've read. Mr. James?"

Tim nodded, cleared his throat. "Yes. The Boho area is very alkaline, optimal for bacterial growth. We should be there soon enough."

Silence returned. Tim changed gears as the path took a significant rise. Dark clouds loomed lower as the car continued its ascent.

Then they reached level ground again. Tamara experienced a feeling of inertia from the altitude, but at least her stomach had calmed.

To the left, for miles around, tree stumps covered the landscape. Stacked logs, skinned of bark, lined the narrow road on that side. To the right, the forest primeval continued.

"Ah!" Tim said, "We're almost there now."

A short time later the road split into two, adding a left turn that led towards the forest. Tim followed the turn, the road becoming an asphalt path almost too narrow for the Land Rover. Ahead, the grey horizon had dark, jagged points of forest flanking it.

The path took them along a right turn, and a few minutes later the ground dipped to their right. Beyond it, a green land-scape stretched off for miles.

"Oh wow," Shellie said, the first time she had spoken in a while.

The view *was* quite breath-taking.

"Here," Tim said, "We're near the spot from last time."

Tamara saw uneven green hillocks beyond the dip. Rocky outcroppings gaped from the hill like the bones of the earth.

The road took another left turn, disappearing into an avenue of trees. Tim ignored that and sent the car forward, lurching it onto the untamed, grass-smothered earth.

He slowed the car to a bumpy halt and switched off the engine. He pulled the parking brake before twisting round to face his passengers.

"End of the line folks!" he said. Turning back, he nodded to Tamara and removed his seatbelt. He sounded so eager. Like every trip held a mystery like Medea.

Tamara shrugged, undid her seatbelt and opened her door. The cold air hit her as she stepped onto the ground, the grass and weeds spongy beneath her feet.

This area. It felt so… desolate; silent too, apart from a sudden, leafy whisper from the trees a few dozen metres away. She shivered, and then cringed as Shellie opened her door and jumped down. The girl sounded so loud. Not fit and proper in a place like this.

"Beautiful! It's so beautiful!" Shellie said. Her enthusiasm might be contagious, at another time.

Tamara stared at the trees. Her gaze locked on the shadows between the gently swaying boughs.

We're being watched, she told herself. Shrugging the paranoid thought off, Tamara closed her door and went to join the others at the Land Rover's rear.

Azer grinned as she approached. *Am I the only one feeling uneasy now?*

Tim began speaking as she arrived. "First things first, we should probably start cordoning the area off. Good job we have you guys for the grunt work, eh?" Tim referred to the graduates. Shellie sniggered. Azer frowned.

Tamara squeezed between her companions and examined the contents stored in the Land Rover's boot. Three aluminium cases stood beside two hiking rucksacks. She leant forward and retrieved a rucksack, the contents rattling metallically as she placed it on the edge of the boot. She tore back the lid and revealed ranging poles, white and red painted tubular steel with spikes on their ends.

"Come on, dig in!" she said with faked eagerness before turning to Azer and Shellie. "I'll supervise while Tim sorts the sampling cases."

She watched her graduates remove ranging poles, Azer tucking some under his arm.

With that rucksack emptied, she retrieved the other one. This rattled, too. It contained more poles, rope and other tools.

"Follow me," she said, pulling the rucksack over her shoulder. Stepping forward, she passed Azer and Shellie.

A map was tucked in the rucksack's front pocket, showing the areas they needed to cordon off. She had it memorized well enough though. Tamara headed left past the Land Rover, taking in the scenery as she did.

The landscape looked beautiful, just as Shellie had said.

They were near the edge of a hill, the immediate area heavy with bushes. Smaller undulating hillocks formed the hill's descent, the fields below stretching off towards a hazy horizon. The wide shape of Lough Erne, a system of two connected lakes, bisected the fields and shone metallic blue in the daylight.

Tamara walked forward, pausing around five metres from the edge. Sometimes prone to vertigo, she needed to brace herself with a deep breath. She removed the rucksack from her shoulders, turned to the graduates trailing her. "Hey guys."

"Yes. Coming," Azer replied. The pair came forward, knelt and dumped their ranging poles to the ground. Tamara went to her knees and opened the rucksack. The ripping sounds the Velcro straps made stung the air.

She rooted around a little, found two measuring sticks and handed them to her graduates. She next removed a coil of rope and passed it to Azer. Tamara smelled mint on someone's breath. Her face flushed at the proximity. She had difficulty locating any sign of the measuring tapes.

Screw it, she thought, abandoning the search. She pulled a ranging pole from the bundle and standing, left the rucksack on the ground.

"We'll start…"

The pair stood, backed off as she walked between them. Tamara thought for a moment, and chose a spot to put the pole. There should have been mallets in one of the rucksacks, she realized in disdain.

She examined the ranging pole, considered the tip sharp and pointed enough, and pressed it into the grass. A little resistance followed, and then the earth accepted the spike. It was a satisfactory feeling, shoving that pole in. Tamara smiled and turned to watch Azer and Shellie retrieve their poles.

Their preparedness made her smile again. Tamara realised she had briefly forgotten her troubles. So really, concentrating on work was the key.

A grunt made her look round. Tim approached, looking a little red-faced, an aluminium case in each hand and another wedged under his arm.

"Gosh, Tim!" she exclaimed and rushed forward to assist him with the cases. He stopped, grunted again, and twisted his left arm and shoulder forward so she could retrieve the precariously held case.

"Hey, let's sit a little." Tamara put the case on the ground and sat on it cross-legged. Tim deposited one of his cases and followed suit.

They faced the area the graduates worked on, Shellie efficiently placing the markers with Azer attaching the rope.

Slow, methodical work followed. The silence between her and Tim continued for a while, until:

"You're worried about the village right?" Tim asked.

Tamara looked to Tim, found him gazing into the distance.

"I think we should've turned tail and fled as soon as we noticed something amiss. Hell, it's a mess." She reached into her jacket, removed her phone and unlocked it with her thumb. The service bar remained empty. *Damn it.*

"I think if anything dangerous lurked back there we would have seen signs. You know, gas leak or something." Tim retrieved his other case and placed it on his lap.

"Gas leak. Yeah…"

They sat quietly for a while, watching Shellie place poles. Azer had disappeared downhill with the rope.

Tim put his hand out. "Thought I felt rain. We should get started ourselves."

He unclipped the latches on the case, opened it to reveal objects packed in black foam. The case held testing hardware, reagents, sample bags and containers, everything they needed to get their tasks done.

The case Tamara sat on held the same.

"Yeah, let's get this finished with and leave aysap. We've not left anything back at the village right?"

Tim closed the case, placed his elbows on it and hummed for a few moments before saying, "Toothbrushes, a few bits and bobs. But I think you're overreacting a little."

"I…" A commotion on the hill interrupted her.

Shellie gesticulated with a nervous wave of her arms. "Guys, hey guys," she shouted.

Tamara felt a chill run down her spine.

Tim shifted his case to the ground, stood.

"Shellie, what's up?" he asked, curiosity in his voice as he walked forward.

Tamara stood and followed.

As they neared, she noted Shellie appeared quite distraught. *Oh no.* The chill returned.

"Azer's gone," Shellie said. "He was just below me and now…"

"What?" Tim laughed, probably assuming a prank.

Tamara rushed forward, grabbed her graduate student by the shoulders. "Where?" she demanded.

Shellie turned, pointed downwards. Tamara prepared herself for the vertigo, and scrutinized the area below. She saw a hillock with a rocky outcropping; a white length of rope trailing down to an abandoned coil. Familiar objects surrounded it: ranging poles scattered across the uneven terrain.

Did he fall? Her heart in her mouth, Tamara made her way towards the rope.

"Tamara," Tim said behind her. She ignored him as she descended, half stumbling down the hill.

She heard Shellie talking quickly and nervously, this followed by a sob. Tamara tried to focus on not tripping. The hill was hardly steep enough to cause damage. A fall would merely lead to a lower hillock, unless she hit a rock.

It's what she expected to see as she descended, Azer, his limbs twisted, his head bloody because it had cracked like an egg against—

Stop this! she told herself, then slid down a little to land on the hillock. Tamara made pains not to look down, and leant against the slope. Some of the ranging poles lay right at her feet.

A noise above indicated someone else descending. A glance up showed her Tim.

Tamara returned her attention to the immediate area. She stood on the edge of a small grassy mesa, with an almost vertical rock outcropping ahead and to her left. She scanned it, and gasped. What she discovered appeared odd, completely unexpected.

Tim came down behind her, followed by Shellie. She felt a hand tap her shoulder, and she sent Tim an acknowledging glance before stepping forward.

The nearby grass lay mostly untrodden, with some evidence of Azer's footsteps. Further along however, forming an uneven path, the grass had been tamped into the earth, like scores of feet had traversed it from the bottom of the hill.

She took a breath then looked down to see a trodden path twisting down the hill before it disappeared in the distance.

People must have climbed here, on hands and knees when necessary.

"Oh wow," Tim said.

Tamara nodded at his words. But where could Azer be? It didn't appear he had fallen.

She edged forward, examined the rocky outcropping, the greyish-white stone pitted by the elements.

Then she saw it, a cave entrance. Framed completely by rock, it led deep into the hill. The footprints led there, too.

"You think... you think he went in?" Shellie sounded as anxious as she felt.

Tamara crept closer, put her left hand on the rock. It felt cold to the touch. She leant in, using the rock for support, and stared into the darkness.

A smell hung about the entrance, a gamy miasma that reminded her of animal cages in the zoo.

Bears? Don't be stupid, there are no bears in Ireland.

She fought the urge to cough, and stooped to enter the darkness.

Tim hissed. "What are you doing?"

Tamara paused, reached into her pocket to remove her mobile phone. A sharp shake of her wrist turned the torch function on.

"We have to find him, right?" she said. "Looks like the villagers went down here, too."

Shellie laughed nervously. "Why? Why would they do that? I'm not going in there, no way José."

Tamara sent her a look. Shellie stood arms folded, a stubborn expression on her face.

"We need to reconsider this." Tim stepped to her right, and despite his last words, produced a Maglite from his jacket.

"Azer?" he shouted into the darkness. Distant echoes followed.

Her foot nudged something, and looking down, Tamara saw a ranging pole. She knelt to retrieve it, stood and entered the cave.

Beyond the entrance, she encountered a sudden, steep descent. Tamara lurched backwards to save herself from stumbling.

"Watch out here," she said. "There's a steep slope."

"Azer," she called. Her voice repeated, like a dozen invisible doppelgangers lurked below.

Claustrophobia hit her as she descended between the pale, rocky walls. Echoes abounded, her footsteps, the sounds of small stones skittering away.

The floor turned level, the ceiling high enough for her to

stand fully.

Tim appeared to her right, stooping because of his height. He needed to press close to her in the tunnel's narrow confines.

"Still no sign of him," she said unnecessarily.

A beam of illumination appeared as Tim switched on his torch. Motes of dust danced inside the beam.

Footsteps turned both their heads. She saw Shellie coming down the decline. She reached them and said, "Couldn't handle it. Too spooky alone up there."

Tamara gave Tim a concerned glance, and then headed forward.

She had been spelunking in the past. Then, the air had been chill. This place however, felt warm and musty, like some deep underground womb. A sudden regret followed the analogy, for where there was a womb, a birth awaited.

A lump formed in her throat, and as she walked forward, Tamara held the ranging pole pointed forward one handed, like a spear.

The tunnel expanded, becoming a wide, pale-walled cave littered with debris.

Ahead lay a darkness her torchlight refused to fully dispel, with no termination to speak of. Stalagmites and stalactites lurked in clusters against the walls, their colour a dark shade of orange. The light created quivering shadows, lurching shapes that put her on edge. But apart from the odd large rock, their path forward lay mostly clear.

The trio stepped softly through this humid, stygian realm. The only signs of life were their own as echoes mocked their movements.

She moved her light across the left-hand wall, and her gaze locked on the impossible: a woman's naked form. *Oh my God.* Impaled in her nether regions by stalagmites, the woman hung suspended halfway to the ceiling. One stalagmite protruded from a bare breast, another jutted from her mouth. The latter joined a stalactite above. The victim appeared frail, drained of life, as if the very cave fed on her vitality. Her throat pulsed with a shallow breathing; her sunken eyelids fluttered.

Tamara's gorge rose, more so when she realized the stalactites and stalagmites throbbed as if they themselves breathed.

"Oh no," Shellie said.

Tamara stepped with trepidation towards the wall.

Tim's torchlight joined that of her phone's, the extra illumination making the sight much worse.

No, it's not possible, she thought. Tamara moved her light along the wall and discovered more living corpses, impaled and in various stages of dissolution.

"So this is what happened to the villagers," she said quietly.

Tim gasped. "This whole place is alive, with, with..."

She looked at him. He struggled to complete his sentence.

Tamara backed away from the wall.

"We need to—" Shellie paused mid speech.

"Azer?" Shellie continued.

Tamara turned, aimed her light beyond Shellie, and gasped.

Azer stood between them and the exit. His eyes closed tight, his expression betrayed physical pain.

"Azer?" Shellie repeated.

He came forward, halting before Shellie. His lips parted, and something wriggled in his mouth obscenely.

Shellie groaned then collapsed in a dead faint.

Azer croaked something unintelligible, and lurched forward.

With a sudden reflex action, Tamara jabbed the ranging pole into his chest. Azer stumbled back, his eyes opening to reveal two glowing opaque orbs. A sound escaped his throat: nothing human, but rather the squeal a lobster makes when dropped in boiling water.

A cacophony of screeches joined the squeal. Tim screamed in terror. A cracking noise followed, the nearby bodies breaking loose from their monstrous bonds. Then, the entire cave started to shake.

"They're all around us!" Tim cried, managing to make himself heard above the din. He appeared beside Tamara as she tried lifting Shellie to her feet. She didn't need his warning, for dark shapes loomed from all sides.

Shellie's eyes fluttered open. She blinked when Tamara gave her a harsh shake.

Tim's torchlight wavered around them as she pulled Shellie to her feet. The girl remained standing but looked weak, unsteady.

Their exit was visible ahead, but at least half a dozen stumbling shapes blocked their escape. Then she saw Azer. He had fallen to his knees, the pole still protruding from his chest. The object growing from his mouth had gained length. A tentacle now, it quivered with insidious life.

Movements appeared in the corners of Tamara's eyes, fleshy shapes closing in in the darkness.

Within the cacophony of sound, the very quaking of the earth, Tamara closed her eyes, tightly hugging Shellie. She found comfort in the embrace, even as a multitude of pawing arms started dragging them down.

*

How long ago had that happened? Tamara didn't know. Hours, she guessed, though focusing clearly took quite an effort. Her body hung suspended, her arms constrained, but her legs and feet dangled free.

She felt weak, but felt no pain.

A voice mumbled to her left, but apart from that, the cave stood silent. She knew she hadn't left it, for a humid atmosphere touched her skin and she smelled decay on the air. Tamara tried opening her eyes but found them crusted shut, a second try and she succeeded. Darkness concealed her surroundings. A mercy, probably. Someone's torch lay at her feet, sending a weak beam towards the source of the mumbling.

Her curiosity urged her to check that, but first, and for this she needed to brace herself, Tamara looked down.

What should have been a scream escaped her throat as a feeble hiss. Dark, ropy orange tendrils wrapped her arms, holding her crucified. Another tendril had pierced her chest from behind, its tip poking out above her navel. Her jacket had been removed, but her green hoodie remained. How could she not feel the pain of that violation?

Horrified, Tamara gagged, drooled onto the floor.

"It all makes sense now. All the legends."

The mumbling had ceased, replaced by clear words.

The voice belonged to Shellie. Turning her head, Tamara

looked left.

No. My god no.

She saw Tim, tendrils wrapped around his waist and neck. The ropy, rootlike growths veritably cocooned him. Beyond him hung Shellie, swathed in too many shadows to tell just what violations she suffered.

A glance around the space around her showed no sign of Azer.

"Shellie," Tamara asked, "What makes sense?"

The girl blinked then shivered from head to toe.

"The Druids here... they worshipped Cliodhna, you know. The Dark Goddess, Earth Mother of fertility and life, the hooved beasts of the forest. They worshipped her and drew spiritual and physical nourishment from the earth she stepped on. The soil."

The following laugh sounded maniacal. It sent ice water down Tamara's spine.

"The Druids used portals to the Otherworld, so they say." Shellie continued. "The journey there came with trials, physical transformations... Only the worthy gained the presence of the Earth Goddess."

Tamara licked her lips, tasted salt. She felt so confused and frightened.

"Tell me, Shellie," she asked, "Why are *we* here?"

Shellie laughed, a ratchet cackle that spoke of lost sanity.

"*She* awoke, and the descendants came. We're just in it for the ride. Or perhaps... Perhaps *we* are worthy too? I hope I am."

Shellie's head darted left. The sudden movement made Tamara flinch.

"Goddess?" Shellie asked, and an unwholesome, slithering noise answered. A clatter followed that sounded, and echoed, like horses' hooves.

"Here she comes," Shellie continued. "The Earth Goddess. Here to transform us. Are you ready for her gifts?"

Two phosphorescent orbs appeared in the darkness. *Lights? Torchlight?* Tamara's hopes dissipated. They weren't lights, she realized, but bulbous, blinking eyes.

Tim's abandoned torch flickered and died.

Glynn Owen Barrass

Glynn Owen Barrass lives in the North East of England and has been writing since late 2006. He has written over two hundred short stories, novellas, and role-playing game supplements, the majority of which have been published in France, Germany, Japan, Poland, the UK, and the USA.

About the Editor

Karen Dales is an award winning, best selling author of *The Chosen Chronicles*, and is the Managing Editor for Dark Dragon Publishing. Her short fiction has been published in several anthologies. She has been an author guest at Fan Expo, Ad Astra, Polaris, and many other literary conventions.

She lives in Toronto, Ontario, Canada with her husband and son as human servants to five cats.

You can find her works at www.karendales.com or www.darkdragonpublishing.com

If you have enjoyed this anthology, please remember that reader reviews are beneficial to authors and editors. Please consider posting a review. A few kind words goes a long way.

About the Artist

Currently living in Torrance, California, Mary Ancilla Martinez enjoys painting mystical, wild, free, ethereal places where unseen greets seen. Deeply inspired by nature, by the secret whispers of desert winds, the language of trees, the dynamism of the elements, and the infinity of the stars and cosmos, she appreciates the exploration of dreams, mythology, archetypes, alchemy and metaphysics.

Martinez' work is primarily figurative and narrative, created mainly in oils. Her current focus examines personal sovereignty inspired by Greek, Celtic, Spanish, French, African and Indigenous mythology. Martinez strives for meaning and intention in each piece, simultaneously enjoying the engagement found in pure process. She seeks a feeling of transcendence in her paintings, and desires for her work to touch the viewer with a sense of the divine.

Martinez has been working as a professional artist for 25 years. She started her art career as a licensed educator teaching K-12 art classes. She then worked as a scenic artist in the commercial world of set painting for television and theatre, followed by 15 years of graphic illustration. She has always painted personal work for pleasure. Martinez has recently left the commercial world to begin her career as a full time artist immersed in creating her own visions.

Presently, she is producing a body of work that highlights the different energetic states of a variety of sovereign goddesses found in mythology. Martinez' work can be found in many private collections and galleries throughout the United States, Canada, Europe and Australia, as well as in publications such as Spectrum, Infected by Art and ImagineFX. Martinez was an ARC finalist in 2021 for the Art Renewal Center's International art competition

You can discover more of Mary's art here: www.maryancilla.com

CANADIAN DREADFUL

An Anthology

Edited by David Tocher

Available in paperback and ebook.

"CANADIAN DREADFUL showcases some of Canada's best voices in horror fiction. This anthology is a harrowing tour of the northern landscape that will leave you both dazzled and terrified."
~*David Morrell, New York Times Best-Selling Author*

In the pages of this anthology, you will not find the Canada you are accustomed to, nor a Canada that the world has grown to know and love. Between the covers, you will discover a dark landscape that will challenge your perspective. From sea to shining sea, stories of a darker Canada will arise, and within them all a kernel of truth. Stories of sacrifice, cannibalism, ghosts, and mystical forests, the authors will plunge you into the country that is Canadian Dreadful

www.amazon.com/Canadian-Dreadful-Anthology-David-Tocher/dp/1928104150/

THE CHOSEN CHRONICLES:

Changeling
Angel of Death
Shadow of Death
Thanatos

By
Karen Dales
www.karendales.com

"Dark… compelling… that will keep readers turning the pages well past bedtime."
Kelley Armstrong,
New York Times Best Selling Author

"A dark and gripping tale by a true mistress of supernatural fiction. Karen Dales brings fresh blood to the vampire genre."
Michelle Rowen,
National Best Selling Author.

"For readers who adore textured layers in their literary tapestries, rich in colourful emotions, Karen Dales is one writer of vampire fiction they'll want to read."
Nancy Kilpatrick,
Author: Power of the Blood
Editor: Evolve: Vampire Stories of the New Undead

"A fresh and intriguing new look at the vampire mythos."
Violet Malan
The Novels of Dhulyn and Parno

Available in paperback and ebook everywhere where books are sold.

www.amazon.com/Karen-Dales/e/B004TG6U1Y

Abandoned and left to die, alone in the forest, the Angel's life is transformed, evoking demons that demand more than he can give.

The Vampires of London are being murdered and only the Angel of Death can save them. Plagued by demons from his past, the Angel walks a fine line. Can he discover the culprits without the discovery of what he truly is and the destruction of one he loves.

Haunted by nightmares of his past misdeeds and failings, the Angel wants nothing more than to be left alone. It is across the Atlantic, in a foreign country, that he takes up the mantle once more as a protector in a land where those who would see him dead have flourished.

The Angel embarks upon a journey to the past to discover the truth about himself and his connection with the white faced demons. Through the quest, the Angel discovers a threat that endangers to topple his beliefs about himself and change the Chosen forever.

BOOKS

To see a full list of our amazing books,

please check our website:

www. darkdragonpublishing.com/books.html

All Books Available At The Following Retailers:

Amazon.ca
Amazon.com
Amazon.co.uk
Amazon.com.au
Barnes and Noble
Books A Million
Book Depository
Smashwords
Powell's Books

Manufactured by Amazon.ca
Bolton, ON

22344093R00155